RA~~T~~

RATS twists from the shadows ~~...~~ ~~...g past to~~ front-page headlines hiding Washington secrets behind corporate incompetence when two warriors face off. Both skilled at violence. And deception. Both accustomed to winning.

Praise for RATS

"In Klingler's debut thriller, a female sniper tracks down a bomber who targets U.S. military interests. The theme of children suffering the worst during wartime—and long after—propels...the plot into suitably daring territory. A nuanced techno-thriller with both brains and brawn."

—Kirkus Reviews

"The military operations, too—especially the various scenes where characters ride motorcycles and other vehicles—are dramatic, vivid, evocative, and perfectly detailed."

—San Francisco Book Review (4 of 5 stars)

"One quality of the book that stands out is the juxtaposition of the Alaskan wilderness and the jungles of Vietnam. This gives the book a well-rounded feel as the intensity ratchets up."

—Clarion Foreword Reviews (4 of 5 stars****)

"RATS is a masterpiece of entertainment. Klingler is an incredibly skilled author...the story is gripping, thrilling, and addictive."

—R.L. Drembic (Book Adventure Blog)

"[RATS]...makes you sit back and examine your values. Klingler's stories are original...his characters are memorable. If you like fiction that touches on human relationships with technology and relation to nature, [Klingler] is the one to read. Not once does it lose any of that kinetic energy so artfully harnessed in the first chapter."

—Literature Typeface

ALSO BY JOE KLINGLER

Mash Up
Missing Mona

For previews of upcoming books by Joe Klingler and more
information about the author, please visit his website at
www.joeklingler.com.

J O E
KLINGLER

RATS

A NOVEL

Published by
CARTOSI LLC

ISBN 978-1-941156-02-5

Cover design by Ansel Niner
Cover Image Copyright J. Helgason, 2013 Used under license from Shutterstock.com.

www.joeklingler.com

dedicated to
Ruth Marie Sabin
ten was a good number

Acknowledgements

I would like to thank my friends Amy Brekeller and Jim Elliott who graciously read early versions of this work and provided invaluable commentary and much appreciated encouragement. My editor Robyn Russell contributed her keen eye, and insight into the mysterious inner workings of novels, for which I am very grateful. I would also like to recognize two non-fiction books that assisted me in my research: *Wired for War* by P.W. Singer and *The History of Landmines* by Mike Croll.

Lastly, my heartfelt thanks go out to Rhonda who read, edited, proofread, encouraged and cajoled through countless revisions to ensure this novel saw the light of day. Thank you, lover girl.

Chapter 1

HE WOKE WITHOUT A SOUND, his bones knowing it was time. Both eyes scraped open, followed a crack across gray ceiling, seeing a lonely road through wilderness. His bare back registered a rumpled sheet below the left shoulder blade. Gold light glowed behind a green curtain; darkness was finally arriving in Alaska.

He had been awake less than ten seconds when his mind began projecting images of roadway slipping under a motorcycle wheel. Like an athlete visualizing ideal form he saw gravel for eight kilometers, asphalt for the next fifteen, mud for three…on and on south to the river. The road held many ways to fail.

He rolled and stood. Walked barefoot to the window anticipating what blogs would call Black Monday. He pushed the curtain aside with two fingers. Dusk lolled opposite the streaked pane. Clear air, black sapphire sky, road disappearing into land pockmarked with hundreds of small lakes as if a typhoon had followed a B-52 bombing run. Not frozen in July. Nothing moved. He heard only his own breathing.

He turned, passing his eyes swiftly over oil lamp, bed, clumps of mud. They came to rest on a large motorcycle standing in the room, its curvaceous blackness shimmering in the fading light of the Alaskan summer. A huge piston protruded from each side. He liked it near him in the one-room cabin, and away from prying eyes that might want to know what was in the bags.

He wished for more darkness.

He crossed the room to the bike, scanning for the unusual: a spider in hiding, a rat chewed hose. He knelt. Pressure in the big-knobbed race tires was correct. He flipped up the side case lids and counted the payload: two rows of ten on each side. The parts had arrived on schedule through seven separate channels. He had worried about the CH-4B, a controlled substance that might be traced. But a seal fisherman with an ocean kayak and an old woman on a bicycle had traversed the last crucial miles at modest cost.

He touched an upturned rod. Its yellow LED gleamed. He tapped thirty-nine more, covered and locked the right case.

His chronometer chirped. Colored crystal showed 12:07 am—sunset at 70 degrees North latitude. He imagined the Arctic Circle running beneath his bare toes. Poetic license, he was too far north, wouldn't cross the Circle for hours.

He stepped past the bathroom door to stand over rust-streaked porcelain. His eyes roamed the tiny room for links to the name he had registered: Arthur Tresuniak. He turned to the sink, leaned forward and tossed icy water from the faucet onto his face. As he rose, a mirror that had been punched into a hundred fragments reflected nothing recognizable. He searched for his deep gray eyes—*like your father's* his mother had said. In the reflected chaos her features mixed with his despite a three-day growth on wind-buffed skin. He thought of the scientist who suggested the Mona Lisa was a Da Vinci self-portrait: Leonardo in drag.

He studied the reflected expression. Oddly quiet, as if she knew there was work that needed to be done, but wished he wouldn't do it. He reached across his body and outlined a tattoo with two fingers.

"Don't delay," he said to no one.

He reached for the cell phone lying beside a used bar of tan soap. When his fingers touched the anodized case his body tensed. He squeezed his eyes shut as his mind saw a bright white flash, felt her soft hand releasing his as they were thrown sideways. Weight on his back like a bag of sand. Falling sleet crackling to the ground. Time passing as he breathed hot air that smelled of earth.

He forced his eyes open and saw her in the mirror. He lowered his face. His hands were gripping the sides of the small pink sink, knuckles ice white, phone on the floor. With effort he unclenched his fingers, bent over, picked up the phone and touched the screen.

It rang once.

"It's okay, Mom. I'm prepared," he said.

He listened, watching his lips in the silvered glass. He shifted a tiny jagged piece of mirror with a fingertip.

"Has to be now," he said.

He took a deep breath.

"The last? Yes, I'll think about it."

He pressed the phone off and returned to the bedroom. He twisted the iron handle on an armoire carved with figures of bear hunts and seal killings, bones inlaid gracefully into dark wood. The smell of leather wafted at him. With one hand he lifted a dark black suit padded with government-approved armor from a brass hook and slipped the phone into the pocket.

He stepped naked into soft lining and pulled the jacket-pants combo closed with the front zipper. He bent forward for stiff boots: leather, carbon, titanium. Zipped them shut and closed the sides with the crunch of Velcro.

He moved to the bike. Touched the screen at the center of the handlebars. Blue and orange lights flickered as the machine self-checked its brain, then displayed a big zero for speed beside coordinates of its current location: 70° 12' N 148° 31' W. Global Positioning Satellites made his life easier. He was glad the U.S. government had put them up. He almost wanted to thank them.

He shoved a black nylon bag under a web of bungee between the all-important side cases. A heave on the bars tripped the bike off its stand with a swish of hydraulic shocks onto the worn carpet and through the doorway. His shadow flickered from the neon Caribou Motel sign overhead. He returned to the room, took a long slow look around and flipped his room key onto the unmade bed.

Outside, straddling the stationary motorcycle in cool gathering darkness, he felt exposed from all sides. Motion was preferable.

He inserted earplugs, slipped into a black helmet, and activated the heads-up display. A frozen image floated twenty meters down the road and three meters above the dirt. He laced the strap of the helmet through the double-D ring buckle and pulled it tight.

He felt protected in a helmet. As if he were more alone.

Key, kill switch, starter. The big engine leapt to life, barely whispering through the custom exhaust on its left side that did for it what a silencer does for a handgun.

He closed his eyes and focused on relaxed breathing while sliding into armored gloves. His left hand squeezed the clutch. He studied the GPS computer:

Delivery distance: 302 mi

Next target: 23.6 mi

Time Remaining: 3 hrs 15 min

Average speed: 92.9 mph

He thought about moving 90 mph in darkness on a surface of asphalt, loose gravel, meatball rocks and wet dirt. He would have to be very fast on the good sections to stay on schedule. Few would believe it possible. As intended.

3

His wrist urged the bike south out of Deadhorse, permanent population zero. Ahead lay Pump Station #2 and hundreds of miles of the famous North Slope Haul Road that served the Trans-Alaska Pipeline System. Aka Alaska Route 11: The James W. Dalton Highway.

The pipeline.

Billions of dollars slurping along at eight miles-per-hour.

Twin driving lights cut swaths of whiteness through the air as his speedometer climbed to triple digits. The bike slithered and hammered, filling him with the adrenaline of the starting gun—months of planning converted to action.

Speed transformed the road surface to a study in blurred browns. His left thumb touched a button and a full-color image of roadway came alive in the display. Now he had two roads: the one he was riding, and a GPS referenced recording made when he had ridden the same road in the sunshine as a tourist. Four times.

Tonight was the fifth. There would be no sixth.

He guided the whispering bike toward the side of the road and back to center. The two roads in his vision aligned like a snake in front of a mirror. Better data—improved probability of success.

Earlier, the weather girl on the satellite feed couldn't make up her mind: maybe rain, maybe fog, maybe not. But she had been clear on one thing, water would freeze at the higher elevations. He checked the setting of his electric suit—brain function required warmth.

Even at 100 mph his biggest concern wasn't the road, but the unpredictable: falling rock, migrating caribou, a slow bird. He flicked the switch beside his left knee. A dull green edged the road video as sensors scanned for radiating heat on the permafrost. Engine vibration mixed with the anticipation in his body as he glanced to the rear.

Alone.

The computer told him he was now twenty-two miles from the Caribou Motel. Handgrips told him he was moving fast on gravel smaller than the skipping stones he had tossed as a kid on a beach six thousand miles away. The sway of the bike indicated a developing crosswind. Dakar desert racers could ride a motorcycle fast in such conditions for fifteen days in a row.

He only needed three hours.

He had been running south at 102 mph for fourteen minutes, the flat road cutting straight through open space in all directions, when the synthetic woman in the GPS awakened inside his helmet.

"Target arrival in thirty seconds."

He slowed to 80, stretched back with his left arm, wrapped his fist around the front outermost handle, and lifted. The device came up feeling like a small dumbbell. He held it low to his side and flicked his eyes between the road and the heads-up display of the road. Small blue spots on the video pointed to the right. Beside them numerals indicated the horizontal distance in meters from his bike seat to the drop point.

Her voice counted like a shuttle launch.

"Release in ten seconds...five seconds...four..."

He focused on the leverage needed for sixteen meters, his right hand steady on the throttle. As she spoke the "z" in zero he swung his arm up in a wide arc, knowing the GPS computer had compensated for the bike's speed. Practice runs had shown he could obtain acceptable results 92% of the time in winds below 25 mph.

He wanted to hear it land on the hard dirt and come to life, but he was moving too fast.

She said, "Target number one receding."

"Thank you, Angel," he said, and sang *Thirty-nine bottles of beer on the wall, thirty-nine bottles...*the words lost to the rushing wind.

He returned his empty left hand to the bars and rolled on power to 120 mph.

"Six minutes to target number two," she said.

The bike floated on the magic black wings of Metzeler rubber, stabilized by the physics of frame geometry, gyroscopes and speed. He watched the road, waiting for the pipeline to arrive from the darkening night.

Nine tosses later he slowed to sixty to pass five buildings and the single runway at Sagwon airport. The first row had been delivered. Not linearly, but in clusters near pumping stations, and places where the pipeline poked above ground like a giant worm.

The highway rose into the Philip Smith Mountains of the Brooks Range that formed the Continental Divide in Alaska. Here, oddly, the divide ran east to west, shedding water north to the Arctic Ocean or south to the Bering Sea, directly across his line of travel.

Only one road through it: Atigun Pass, highest pass in the range.

Elevation rise induced fog. Fog diffracted his Flamethrower driving lights into a wall of gray, as if he were slowly losing his eyesight.

The road surface firmed to sno-cone slush.

He slowed to 80, the knobbed tires holding firm.

By the time he reached the pass he had delivered nineteen of the twenty units in the left case. He tossed the last sixty seconds later, slowed to a stop in the middle of the road, kicked the side-stand down and swung off the bike in one practiced motion.

Luminescent green numerals continued to count up along the top row of his GPS.

02:03:15

Two of three hours gone.

Only half done.

Chapter 2

THE AIR THUMPED WITH THE WAIL of a massive sea creature trapped in a fisherman's net.

Claire was running.

Her breathing accelerated with each footfall against the mud trail as it climbed and climbed toward tree line. The rain-coated weapon in her hands slipped as it leached warmth from bare fingers. Her shoulders ached from the weight. She ducked, felt a slap. A low branch tore her cheek as she spun behind the trunk, eyes darting across the night, searching for the black body.

The thumping was low.

She lifted her rifle. Breathed in.

The giant puppet machine hung in the sky.

Her weapon spit twice.

The machine's white eyes turned slowly to face her.

She twisted to run. Her foot slipped and slipped and sli—

Corporal Claire Ferreti cracked one eye open. She was panting. Her damp body lay entangled in a cotton blanket with blue stripes.

She really should drink less. In alcohol-fueled dreams, she always missed.

The television was on, flickering satellite pictures of the morning weather. She didn't have a television in her bedroom. Her brain fog lifted slightly. She saw hot, humid, scroll past. For a fleeting moment she thought about being a meteorologist. Then she could miss and still keep her job. No one liked a sniper who missed.

She sighed, wishing for a better word: sharpshooter, marksman, rifleman, rifle-person.

Uck.

The fog lifted more. She realized this wasn't her apartment. She was at Billy's place.

No sound. He must have muted it for her. She liked that about her General, whose Cornell lecture on the future of national security had inspired her to drop out of college to enlist. And specialize. One of only two men under thirty-five with a star, he wouldn't rest until he had two—though she teased that he only had one of something else, and that was plenty.

But could he be out jogging after a party? Too fanatic.

With effort she rotated her open eye. Blurry blue numbers glowed 6:28. Her lid dropped shut. She shifted. Her stomach gurgled. An ache blossomed in her shoulder from the last weapons test.

Fun party. Well, not at first. Billy had departed with a serious-looking going-bald guy from the President's office. That left her unguarded, subject to attack by a pudgy man wearing thick glasses and an expensive gray suit with a hint of herringbone camouflaged into the fabric. His pickup line was unique: *Was that General Williams you came in with? I represent an Israeli armor manufacturer. There's a rumor the General has procurement needs. Would you introduce us?*

She told Mr. Procurement the General was looking at suppliers for next generation tanks. She figured someone was always working on a new tank. She hadn't introduced them though, messing in Billy's affairs was a relationship no-no.

After Billy returned they shared good food and close dancing, and she drank triple her limit: six smooth Kamikaze specials, whose secret ingredient the bartender refused to reveal. Then Billy had driven home with one hand on the wheel, the other under her dress.

She smiled and rolled onto her back, dragging the arm that had been dangling to the floor up until it covered her bare breasts. She took a deep breath, longing to return to the land of deep slumber, but fluid was demanding an exit.

She opened both eyes. The room wobbled before coming to rest.

In slow motion she pushed back the thin blanket that protected her from District of Columbia air conditioning, rotated, and aimed both feet at the floor until achieving a seated position on the edge of the king bed. With one finger she tapped the remote lying beside the blue numbers. The television told her about a new green car.

"I prefer red," she said.

Automobiles flying across desert sand attracted her eyes. She took another deep breath and raised herself to a standing position. Barefoot and pink-pantied she moved her left foot toward the bathroom.

Chapter 3

THE MAN REGISTERED AS ARTHUR Tresuniak gazed out at slabs of dark gray rock under starlight. For a moment he thought of photographs by Ansel Adams. He lowered his eyes and stomped the heel of his boot into black gravel.

Surface ice.

He chewed an energy bar, rotated the cap from a water bottle, swallowed, crushed the empty and returned it to his pack. As he relieved himself, his eyes roamed the jagged ridgeline on either side of the pass, beauty in every direction, untouched by human hands.

Except for the pipeline.

It crawled across the land like a scar from a knife fight Alaska lost.

Moving swiftly, he opened the right case and relocated all twenty units to the left side. He unhooked the spider cord holding his gear and stuffed fifty-two liters of food and survival equipment into the now empty right case.

He remounted and accelerated south towards Wiseman, Population 30, seventy-five miles north of the Arctic Circle. Seven minutes later he twisted his body to reach into the left case for number 21. He tossed it as he crossed the Continental Divide, followed by nine more. Fourteen miles north of Wiseman, while holding unit 31 and listening to the countdown descend from nine seconds, Angel's voice changed.

"Infrared alert, infrared alert," she repeated, like a needle skipping on a vinyl record.

He glanced at the green overlay. An oblong object grew large.

He dropped 31 to the ground and braked. The rear of the bike hopped. He eased his fingers to find friction. The green object on the display became a brown wall in the road. He opened the throttle to force a power slide to the left.

The bike slithered, shot forward, and he wrestled it to a stop. Breathing hard, he looked back. His heart thumped at the sheer size of the beast staring at him. He blinked. The animal's 30-inch antlers were low, moving toward his taillight and about to end the mission.

His right hand twisted. The rear tire dug a trench. His mirror showed a brown blur approaching as the speedometer touched 40 mph. The sound of hooves pounding frosted gravel reached his ears over the rising whine of the silenced exhaust. He squeezed the gas tank with both knees and realized he was holding his breath. He exhaled, counted to three, and looked over his shoulder. The animal was standing upright in the road, motionless.

It watched him for two full minutes before strolling away, crushing mountain scrub with each step.

He waited for a hundred-yard gap to form between them before riding carefully back to look for number 31. He found it lying in a four-toe hoof print in the mud.

Elapsed time of 2:47:20 pulsed red on his display.

Now his computer was betting against him.

Chapter 4

BILLY NORTON WANTED TO BE a teenager like the Mutant Ninja Turtles, but his mom said to be patient, he was growing up fast enough; and yes, he had to stay in his room. This time since noon, and the wings on his Batman clock said it was now way past midnight. She had let him come down to take the garbage out, and have supper, and help with the dishes, and even watch an hour of TV. And he didn't mind being in his room, but he needed to get out of his private bat cave and roam the world to look for evil to fight.

And it wasn't his fault. Anyone who thought it was cool to have a little sister poke at you while you were reading Dynamic Duo comics was stupid in his bat book. He'd like to hang Hattie upside down from those boots Batman used, and tickle-torture her.

Mom would ground him for that.

He swung his feet to the floor, slid into his Batmobile slippers, and shuffled to the window. Dark. He didn't get to play outside in the dark much this time of year. His teacher said Alaska was close to the North Pole so it got a lot of light in July because the Earth was tilted. Billy didn't understand how the Earth could be tilted, but he didn't understand lots of what Miss Griffin said. He just wished there was more spooky darkness in the summer. Bats like him needed darkness, even if he did live north of Nolan.

He could see the outline of the trees that were supposed to hide the big pipe. They looked more like tall weeds to him, and they didn't hide much. The huge tube slithered across the icy ground like an alien snake looking for houses to eat. But it never moved so it wasn't much fun. Except to climb on. For that it was a mini Denali. He started unbuttoning his black pajamas with one hand and dragged his secret duffel of bat clothes from under the bed with the other.

Carefully he turned the rotating latch that locked the top wooden storm window. If he turned it super slow, it wouldn't caw and wake Mom. That was the easy part. Then he lifted. He had to push four tabs to remove the outer screen before he could lower himself from the windowsill onto the little roof over the front door.

His sneakers loosened gravel from the shingles sending tiny grains tumbling in a miniature rockslide that tick ticked into the gutter. He froze. It was hard getting down from the roof without a ladder, but he had worked out a system back in the third grade. Lying on his belly he swung both feet toward the front of the house until he could feel the curve of the downspout with his toe. From there he must place his right hand on the roof, left hand to the gutter, right hand to the spout, and he could shinny toward the ground. He dropped the last few feet to soft dirt in a spot his Mom couldn't see from her bedroom.

The pipeline pulled him like a magnet as he ran easily across the frozen grasses of the tundra. Soon he was climbing the giant brace that held it above the earth, scrambling toward his favorite lookout spot. Standing atop the big curve of pipe, bigger in diameter than his outstretched arms, he became the world Defender of Right, like his hero Batman. He puffed the cool night air and wondered why the moon was just a tiny curve. Miss Griffin had explained that too, but he didn't believe her.

He saw something move—something shiny in the grass between him and what the adults called a highway, even though it was just a big dirt path covered with stones.

It moved again.

He squatted on the cold steel of the pipe with his arms around his knees and kept very still. He wanted to see it up close, maybe even catch it. It dashed through the grass and stopped. Then shot forward, glistening. Maybe it was a snake. He watched it move. With each burst of motion it got closer and closer to the pipe.

He made himself stay still, like a bat hanging upside down.

It emerged from the grass directly under him then disappeared in a flash. He scuffed his jean-clad bottom along the pipe, flattened himself onto his belly, and slid down the curved surface feet first. He knew if he held his breath and counted to three the scary part where he felt like he was falling would pass and his feet would land on the big brace.

His left toe thudded against steel. He let out a long breath.

He took two steps along the brace and looked under the belly of the pipe. It was dark and grassy near the stanchion. He pretended his eyes were Batman's infrared goggles and scanned the ground. There.

His mouth opened wide. It was a machine.

Get ready. One…two…on three he jumped like a paratrooper, landed and rolled up to the thing, grabbing it with both hands. It whirred and its tail blinked red and yellow as he squeezed it tight with both hands.

He strapped it to his back with his belt and his pants almost fell down climbing up the downspout, but now he sat in his room staring at it. It wasn't much heavier than his Louisville Slugger bat, the wood one like Mickey Mantle used back in the old days before his Mom was even born. But it was lots smaller, about the size of his remote-control Batmobile. It had a metal tail that glowed red in the back, and a head shaped like a can of soup turned sideways. But the best part was the rubber tread around the ends of the can, like tracks on an Army tank. He'd bet they made that whirring sound when it moved.

But it was quiet now. It had only whirred a couple of times and must have somehow realized it was caught. He put it carefully in bed while he took off his dirty clothes, and hid them in the green duffle he kept buried under toys in the corner of his closet where Mom wouldn't find them and ask where he'd been. Then he buttoned his pajamas, turned out the light, put one arm around his new metallic friend and drifted into a dreamland of fighting machines and heroes in black masks.

Chapter 5

"WHO AM I?"

"Arthur," he reminded himself, slowing to 35 mph to pass through Wiseman, just a tourist traveling by night. He delivered three units before reaching Coldfoot twenty miles later, a place named for miners who turned back when faced with Alaska's climate, gold or no gold, and stopped at the first place serving alcohol. The town was crowded with traffic by Alaskan standards—a single dusty red pickup heading north.

South of Coldfoot he hurried to beat sunrise, concerned an early bird might remember a fast motorcycle. So he made an executive decision and threw 37 and 38 together, and 39 and 40. This doubled his insurance at two locations, but placed nothing near the river.

Improvise.

He slowed to fifty as he passed a roadside carving of a blue Earth circumscribed with a white line at latitude 66°—the Arctic Circle. The fuel gauge showed three gallons in the oversized Iron-Butt tank, used by thousands of riders who rode even farther than he did. He descended into a valley on road narrower than the Dalton, snaking and twisting to hug the curves of the Yukon River like Lycra on a supermodel.

The finish line.

He stopped, dismounted and repeated the Continental Divide exercise, moving water and survival equipment into the empty left side case. Only a tent remained strapped on the rear fender. He took a deep breath, 363 successful miles, and no longer carrying anything illegal.

But still far from home.

He turned away from the bridge that crossed the Yukon to follow the bank of the river east toward Stevens Village where 61% of the population lived below the poverty line. Now he wanted to be seen, a crazy biker tourist making the most of the brief Alaskan summer—*moving away from his ultimate destination.*

Seventeen miles later he entered the village. A brown historic-site sign read: Founded by Athabascan Indian brothers 1902, Post Office and Air Service 1939. He headed for the waterfront, passing shacks of unpainted aging wood, streaked dark from high winds.

Idling up a street main in function if not name, he saw a wide hull resting on the un-rippled waters of the Yukon, as if frozen on a picture postcard. He brought the bike to a stop under hand-painted red letters for Juke Joint Johnny's Saloon.

The silence of pre-dawn felt like weight on his shoulders after floating so long in the wind. He saw no one, though Johnny's and a building on the corner were lit inside. To his left the ferry's black steel hull supported a white structure that created a tunnel with room for bumper-to-bumper autos. Above it a long cabin for customers was capped by the pilot's house.

He removed his helmet and fished for aviator glasses, even though the sun had yet to rise. He ran his hand across his head, smoothing out what he knew would be unruly curls of helmet hair as he walked the length of the boat. Layers of meaty green at the waterline swam on the dark surface of the river. His eyes traveled up past a black NZ 4152 AK, and over red crust where rust had burrowed through white paint below the passenger windows. They stopped at rectangular smudges in the wheelhouse. Salty gray hair moved behind them.

He stepped close and tapped the steel hull with the titanium toe of his boot, sounding like a fork trying to empty a huge tuna can. Eyes and a stubby index finger appeared behind the glass. He couldn't wait long; it was almost sunrise. And the RATS were ready.

The pilot's window screeched open.

"That be you a-bangin?"

"Are you the Captain of this fine vessel?" he asked cheerfully.

The gray-bearded face shook with wheezing laughter. "Captain Plano at your service. And who might you be, my friend?"

He ceased being Arthur Tresuniak, the man who had registered at the Caribou motel. People remembered names.

"Jonathon Katow," he said, knowing the ferry was scheduled to depart shortly, and when it would arrive in Galena hundreds of miles downriver. "Need passage west."

"You've come to the right place, Jonathon. Me and the lady are sailing in…fourteen minutes."

Katow lifted his thumb. "Should I load my ride?"

A shiny head stuck out the window and rotated toward the stern. "That mud pile of a motor-sicle yours?"

"Every pound."

"We need us a ramp. Darn monster truck bent my good one." He pointed, "The stern."

"Thanks, Captain." He smiled, understanding now why there were no cars on board, and masking concern that the ramp he had intended to use wasn't available. "Save me a seat."

More wheezing accompanied the screech of the closing window.

In minutes a pair of ten-inch planks skirted the opening between the shore and the steel deck, hovering a dozen feet above the edge of the river. He walked to the middle and bobbed slowly up and down. They would never hold.

"Let's get her aboard, sonny," the Captain said.

He looked into the water and thought about forty waiting RATS. He needed to be on this ferry.

"Try them on edge?" he suggested.

He heard the voice of Yoda: *Do or do not, there is no try.*

"Suit yourself, Jonathon. Suit yourself."

He retrieved rubber straps from his bike and lashed the planks tightly together, rotated them 90 degrees, beat a trench in the shore with his boot, and stomped the planks in. He walked the length like an Olympic gymnast warming up on the balance beam.

Rock solid. No flex. Four inches wide.

The Captain stepped away. Jonathon strapped on his helmet. He couldn't see his face, but he was sure the guy would have a wheezing fit if the bike ended up in the Yukon. He rode thirty yards up the road and spun around, pointing straight back at the ferry. *Just don't move,* he petitioned the planks.

He rolled. As the front wheel shot onto the makeshift bridge he accelerated, eyes straight ahead. He landed on the grey deck moving fast, braked and hop-skidded across steel damp with dew, stopping halfway inside the tunnel.

He heard the Captain's laugh approach from behind.

"Nice riding young fella. Haven't had so much fun since the rodeo in Wyoming. Leaving in six minutes, get your ticket, get your ticket."

"From you, Captain?"

A stubby thumb jerked toward the saloon. "See Johnny."

At precisely 5:00 am, one minute after official sunrise, Captain Plano and his little ship threw off dock lines. Rays of first light touched the river. The truck rumble of a diesel reached through the oil-resistant soles of his riding boots as the boat slid smoothly across a slimy green pool table. He rocked the bike, decided it was stable, grabbed the GPS computer from the bar mount, and made his way up spiral stairs to the passenger cabin.

He would refuel downriver.

The water looked black thirty feet below as he leaned against a rusty railing. He placed a silver cylinder into his left ear canal while thumbing the control of the GPS unit to activate its satellite phone.

His call was answered after the third ring, as expected.

"Hello, Maxx," he said.

Audio identification software took two seconds to do its job.

A calm voice replied, "Greetings, Firesnake."

"Please make those calls we discussed over dinner at the yacht club."

"Call sequence beginning now. More?"

"Change in market valuation?"

"Less than 0.1% movement in after hours trading on portfolio."

"Thanks, Maxx. Call on ignition."

"Affirmative. Goodbye."

"Nice phone," a male voice said from behind him as he slipped the flat device into the napoleon pocket of his riding suit.

He turned to see an elderly man with a striking long white beard draped over all black clothing. He looked like a preacher. Or a hit man. How long had he been standing there?

"I had me a phone that would work out here. But didn't really have anyone to call so I got rid of it. It was a whole lot bigger than yours though."

The man's eyes dropped to Katow's jacket pocket.

"Sure looked like a nice phone."

Calculation. Show the phone and hope he forgets it. Or don't show the phone and hope he forgets the man who wouldn't show him a phone.

"Would you like to see it?"

The guy smiled. "Sure, I've been away from hi-tech for years, make my living consulting now. Funny how it's called consulting when all you do is tell people what they want to hear."

"What sort of business?" he asked, unzipping his pocket.

"Timber. There's good money to be made once folks figure out how to move the stuff cheaper. Alaska is big, you know. I've done a little oil too, but there's not much work. Once the pipeline went in, folks just watch her pump. There's more to be had up north, though, much more."

Katow flicked the device on in GPS mode. "Timber and oil. Strange bedfellows don't you think?"

"Both hide in the wilderness waiting to be taken by the right kind of men."

"What kind might that be?"

"The kind who aren't afraid of change…and risk. That's a right pretty machine you have there. Looks awfully complicated for a phone."

He held the device flat and rotated it until the internal digital compass showed north as up, pointing across the dark river toward a sky still losing its midnight blackness.

"It's also a GPS unit. Determines its location by talking to satellites. Take a look, that little dot on the map is this ferry."

"Nice to know where you are out here in the wilderness, ain't it?" His eyes followed the north arrow across the water up to the horizon. The old man squinted like he was trying to read a paper without his glasses. He stared for a long time.

"That's odd," he finally said.

Katow's eyes followed the man's gaze. He knew what to look for, and it was there: blood-golden color along the horizon.

"Are you sure that thing is pointing north?"

He looked down at the device knowing full well the indicated north was correct. He tapped it on the side with one finger as if to loosen a stuck needle. "Maybe not, I haven't calibrated it in a long time. That's an Alaska sunrise, eh?"

The man continued squinting. "Well, if that's a sunrise, it's the damned strangest one I've ever seen. But we'll know when the big ball shows up. Either way, it's telling me high time for breakfast. Do they have a kitchen on this tub?"

With that apparently rhetorical question the black clad figure turned and stomped down the steel steps one clang at a time.

Katow leaned on the rail and watched a sliver of orange below a dark formation, like a heavy cloud along a mountain ridge carrying rain. There would be no ball rising from the icy horizon in that direction.

The GPS blinked to 5:12 am, a little after nine in New York City.

The ferry chugged west through the still of the Yukon creating a breeze against his cheek. He felt the calm of the dark water, its peacefulness in stark contrast to what he knew was happening along the Dalton Highway: black oil and metal RATS.

The GPS vibrated. He pressed a button, listened.

"Yes, Virginia O'Hanlon, there is a Santa Claus," he said.

A map of the Dalton arrived with glowing digits: 1 through 19 in red: Detonated. The others were green: Ready. Except for number 31—it was yellow.

He was aware 39 represented 97.5% success.

He frowned. And 2.5% failure.

He slid his thumb along the side until number 31 selected. It was intact, but waiting.

20. 21. 22. Now red.

The GPS vibrated again, the screen indicating the caller.

"Hello, Maxx."

He took slow breaths and listened carefully, his eyes focused on a black cloud rising chimney straight. Not much wind now.

"Initiate phase two, all websites and blogs," Katow said, "before the New York Exchange opens at 9:30 Eastern."

He glanced down.

"You have fourteen minutes."

He sniffed the air, trying to smell the fire. It was too far away.

"Trade at will," he added.

Chapter 6

SOMETHING SCRATCHY PRESSED against Claire's cheek. She opened an eye to blurry beige. Was she on the floor? She shivered, rolled onto her back and hugged herself with both arms. Her head felt squeezed by an iron tourniquet. How could six of anything cause such pressure? The TV chattered. Satellite images of the eastern seaboard shifted. A flush of *déjà vu* swept through her—she had been getting out of bed. She had turned on the sound. Was this the same report?

The time?

She reached up to massage the tourniquet and found a lump over her right temple. She pressed softly. The tourniquet grew tighter.

She took a slow breath.

Her eyes tracked a ticker across the bottom of the TV. She rolled to her knees and crawled closer. *Fire...Alaska...largest since BP offshore* registered through mental fog. She waited, the ticker repeated.

A talking head appeared. An Asian woman with straight hair and a yellow dress described a fire in the Prudhoe Bay area extending toward the interior of the 49th state. Coverage switched to the stock market: tech, gold up, oil and gas down, the Dow itself inching up in early trading.

Early? She twisted her neck. 9:37 AM.

She stood slowly and moved to the spare bedroom, and her laptop. A DuckDuckGo search showed three pages of references: Fire in Alaska, More Spilled Oil, Wilderness at Risk. She scanned:

23 min ago: Apparent explosion. Pipeline compromised.

15 min ago: Largest spill since Valdez. Repeat of 2006 Prudhoe spill?

She tried another search. The 'ooo's in Gooooogle extended to seven pages. She read fast.

3 min ago: Unknown cause. No injuries.

She went directly to CNN.com and found the ticker from the TV as a caption below a satellite view of Alaska: a lot of white but no fire. She searched for Alaska Fire and skipped past three ads for fireplaces and Alaska Airlines before reaching the newest article, which was three days old.

She returned to Google seeking a professional sounding blog, and picked www.disastercenter.com/alaska because (a) they might know what they were doing and (b) they might be a government agency, possibly nullifying (a). As she hoped, the lead article was about a fire.

A report (05:33 am AKDT) called in by our Fairbanks correspondent, Tom Sailey, indicates something unusual has happened up north. Hundreds of 9-1-1 calls have been received in the past thirty minutes reporting explosions, fire, and lightning strikes. The locations border the Dalton Highway from Prudhoe Bay south to fifty miles northwest of Fairbanks. This is, of course, the path of the Trans-Alaska Pipeline completed in 1977 at a cost of over $8 billion.

She DuckDucked again. Twenty-three pages. Things were changing fast. The Associated Press wire service had a story. Sites were copying it in an effort to steal advertising traffic. Redundancy was rampant. She saw sites in France and Japan and some ending in .au and .nz picking up the news. Were they even awake down under?

She opened a site called wewatchuplay.com thinking it sounded vaguely pornographic even as she did so.

While you were out playing, this reporter has been finding news. Big things are brewing in Alaska, that biggest of the big states, and I do mean brewing. Fires folks, lots of them. And guess what, they're kissing the pipeline. Maybe the weirdest lightning strikes the world has known since hundreds of forest fires scorched California in 2008; no one hurt. But even with no supporting data, nada, evidence incognito, that this reporter could locate, guess what? Do you know who owns the pipeline? Let me tell you. The Alyeska Pipeline Service Company. But who owns them? Little guys like BP, remember the gulf spill, and Exxon Mobil, owners of the Valdez way back in 1989. How about Phillips? You see their logo at your local station?

True to our name, we're watching your money for you while you play. And what do we see? Prices. Dropping like stones tossed in Prudhoe Bay in the summertime. If not Black Monday, at least a crude one for certain. Yes, as of this writing, it's 9:35 am in New York, New York, that city that isn't sleeping and neither is your reporter, and BP down $3.54, XOM down $4.13, and our Phillips friends fell $5.12. And the Exchange has been open for less than ten minutes.

What does this tell us, my friends? Well, investors somewhere think that the little old pipeline in Alaska is in trouble, what kind we know not, but they are betting that it means huge costs for the owners and are dumping said stocks as we speak. Is this any way to respond to a natural disaster? Do you think these traders are spineless wusses who shouldn't be so squeamish even after BP lost a third of its value in the Louisiana spill? Well, then bet your money folks, and *we'll watch it while you go play.*

Claire sat up in her office chair. A good chunk of Alaska burning next to a big pipe full of crude oil was scaring people.

She zoomed in on the CNN satellite image of Prudhoe Bay. Something long and thin was showing up hot to sensors in the satellite. What could stretch out a fire like that except the pipeline? But how does pipe burn?

She heard the lock on the front door, and considered a dash for the bathroom. Before she could move Billy stood at her door in black running shoes, black shorts and a sweaty black muscle shirt that made his biceps look even bigger than their XL size.

"Surfing naked, Claire?"

"I'm not naked, look." She pointed at tiny panties.

He waved a hand. "What the hell is going on?"

She crunched her forehead. Billy wasn't one for bad moods. July heat? Hangover?

"Checking the news. Breaking story about a fire."

His eyes covered her body like he was considering a down payment before he crossed the room to peer over a bare shoulder.

"Alaska?" He grabbed the smartphone strapped to his arm. "I was on the trail when this secure message came in." His eyes moved to the small screen. "Seven minutes ago. 'Meeting at ten-thirty. POTUS. Call Spin.' That's it, no context. I came straight here."

"Is that why you're so cheery?"

He studied her display. "Why would the President want me on short notice?"

She sensed the tension in his body.

"Because you excel at combat," she tapped his shoulder, "thus the star. He has a problem. And..." her voice trailed off.

He stopped reading and turned.

"Because you're good with secrets. Refer to item one," she said.

He nodded and smiled. "You win. What do you know about this thing?"

"The networks have nothing, mountains of speculation everywhere else. Take a look at this."

She displayed the satellite photo of the orange line of heat.

"And compare it to this," she said.

He looked at the map, then back to the first picture, then back to the map.

"A long thin fire? That's nearly impossible." He pointed. "What's that?"

"The location of the Trans-Alaska Pipeline."

His face snapped around to meet her eyes, completely ignoring the fact that she was wearing less than a Victoria's Secret model. Her look convinced him.

"Holy shit." He spun on his heel and headed for the shower. "I've got to reach Spin."

"Wait, wait, I have to pee," she called, jumping from the swivel chair and dashing across the carpet.

Chapter 7

GENERAL BILLY WILLIAMS' DARK blond hair was still damp when he arrived at a mahogany door with a brass 3 screwed in the center. Spin had given him directions to it, and no other information. He paused, wondering if this meeting never happened: no calendar entry, minutes, recordings, nothing for an eager reporter to slip to WikiLeaks. And, most important, no classified documents that would someday be declassified when Congress passed another lame law trying to get reelected.

He opened the door. The room was small.

One other person had arrived: Bertrand Spin, the President's pudgy, balding, Public Relations Advisor. Billy was amused every time he thought about a PR guy named Spin. He had once thought it was fake—but Bert's sensitivity to name jokes had convinced him otherwise.

The wall clock bearing the official seal of the President of the United States of America ticked eighteen minutes and twenty-three seconds after ten A.M. Billy took a seat at the near end of the conference table along the left so he could see both doors to the room. It gave him the creeps to have his back to a door, since that first time, even if this wasn't combat.

Bert looked up from the far end of the polished wood slab and made eye contact. Billy nodded. Neither spoke. Bert returned to his skinny computer. Billy stared at the wall clock, watching the second hand jump, speculating on how his job watching domestic terrorists intersected with fire in Alaska. He thought of the jogging message, and digital breadcrumbs.

He frowned.

With twenty seconds remaining until ten-thirty the door at the front of the room opened and a Secret Service man stepped three feet inside and stopped. He wore the telltale black dot in his ear indicating a radio microphone. He said nothing, painted the room with laser eyes, then stepped aside.

Billy stood as President Mallor walked briskly past the agent, waved a hand at the two men in the room and sat down at the head of the conference table. He motioned Billy towards him.

The agent left and pulled the door tightly shut.

Billy felt the shock of the first hit of a cold shower as he realized what was happening. He wasn't attending a meeting with the President—he was the meeting. Spin was only the PR angle. Billy moved quickly to sit near the President.

He had been in the room for thirteen minutes—not a word had been spoken.

The President looked at Spin, who rotated his computer and pushed it across the table. The President spoke as his eyes scanned the screen.

"General Williams, you are the expert. How can two hundred and forty miles of oil pipeline," the President looked up," built on permafrost, for Christ's sake, *accidentally* catch fire?"

He silently thanked Claire for standing outside the shower stall and briefing him with the results of her Internet search.

"It can't, Mr. President."

"So, this isn't Mother Nature screwing with my reelection campaign for November?"

There it was. This meeting was surely off the record.

"We do not have confirmation that the pipeline is involved, Mr. President. Only that recent satellite imagery indicates heat along its length. However, much of the pipe is above the permafrost surface, as you said, where it's at risk."

The President stared like he thought Billy was bluffing in poker.

"You're splitting hairs, General."

"Sorry, Mr. President. I meant that we haven't received confirmation from the oil companies that operate TAPS, the Trans-Alaska Pipeline System, that the pipeline itself has been affected." He paused before adding, "There have been no reports of injuries."

The President looked back at the pad.

"Bert, what are we telling the media?"

Bert replied instantly. "Nothing yet, Mr. President. We're letting the press and the bloggers guess. Locals have posted pictures of burning fields, possibly flooded with oil, and some nasty holes in the ground that look like Howitzer craters. But no major news service has a camera crew on site." He paused. "Yet."

"Has Plake called?"

"Yes and no, Mr. President. Governor Plake has contacted your office, but has not officially requested federal assistance. It seems inevitable though, federal land is involved."

Mallor sighed. "He'll make this an election issue even if it was an act of God."

"We can move to limit his press exposure," Spin said.

Mallor nodded. He turned to Billy. The tension in his face faded. He spoke quietly.

"General Williams, find out what. Find out who. Our first priority is to protect the country from whatever this is."

Mallor's eyes drifted to the clock.

No one spoke.

Mallor was still staring at the clock when he added, "Stop them." He turned to Billy. "Stop them now. This can't happen twice to the United States of America."

"Yes, Mr. President. I'll leave within the hour."

More silence.

Billy's body wanted to shift in the chair, but he forced himself to remain still.

"Bert, we'll need to issue a statement the moment General Williams gets us something."

The President stood and walked toward the door. The Secret Service man who had screened the room opened it from the other side. The door clicked shut behind Mallor.

An air conditioning fan kicked on.

Billy was uneasy around PR specialists. Their job was to tell people things. His was to do things, and never tell anyone. Natural enemies. But he decided this was a special case.

"Bert, do you have anything on this?"

Spin leaned against the high back of the conference chair.

"We've been on it since minute one. A ranger thought she saw a forest fire, sent a report. Where were you, playing with your toy soldier?"

Billy detected the hint of a smile, so he ignored the reference to Claire.

"Working out. Try it sometime, good for your love life," he said, grinning. "Mind if I get a copy?"

Bert hefted his briefcase to the table, extracted a chip the size of an American dollar coin, plugged it into his pad, copied, and ejected. He pulled out a handkerchief and polished both sides of the tiny device. Holding it up with the cloth like a lit match he looked Billy straight in the eye.

"Whatever happens, this meeting never occurred, I wasn't here, you didn't get this from me, and for God's sake, destroy the damn thing after

26

you read it."

Chapter 8

CLAIRE SAT IN FRONT of the laptop she had used to search for news about the fire. Its screen was black as she flipped through snail mail from her post office box: a great way to end worries of an overflowing mailbox attracting helpful neighbors when she stayed with Billy. She paged through a lingerie catalog, dog-eared page 17, then bills for water, electricity, two credit cards. She sighed. An envelope from Halo Trust had *Thank You* stamped in red ink. A financial company maybe...why thank her? She opened it:

Dear Ms. Ferreti:

Thank you for helping us remove over 1.4 million land mines around the world. Your donation is greatly appreciated...

She flipped the page over, no mention of an amount. The envelope had her address. Weird. Must be a mistake. She tossed the letter at the square trashcan to the left of the desk and heard the front door unlock. Seconds later Billy went flying past.

"Who's chasing you?"

He called over his shoulder while moving toward the bedroom.

"The President made me a fireman."

"He wh—? Alaska? Why you?" She jumped out of her chair.

Billy dragged a plain black briefcase and olive-green duffel out of the closet.

"You know what I do for living, right?"

She stopped in the doorway, leaned against the jamb.

"Yeah, you—" She blinked. Studied his face. "He thinks this is terrorists?"

He pulled a drawer open and transferred shirts to the duffel. A glance in her direction served as an answer.

"But in everything I found nothing so much as hints at terrorists. No one claiming responsibility. No residue. No sightings of planes. I think Exxon cut back on maintenance and something went kablooey."

He stopped packing and gave her a slight smile.

"I see why you're not President. Not paranoid enough."

In one motion she grabbed a pillow from the bed, spun, and heaved it at him.

He slapped it away.

"And far too quick to use force," he said, laughing.

"Okay, let's go to Fairbanks."

His hand went up traffic-cop style.

"Whoa. Who mentioned you? Don't you have a job to do?"

He returned to stuffing his duffel.

She stopped herself from sucking her lower lip. Did he really not want to take her to the heart of the action? Didn't want her underfoot? Trying to protect her?

"The competition doesn't start until Thursday, I can make it to Ohio by then, especially if you let me use Army transport." She grinned. "I'm sure there's a place to shoot in Alaska, they hunt wolves and seals and stuff. Who will notice my little target rifle?" She paused before adding softly. "I promise to stay out of the way." She smiled sweetly and unbuttoned her jeans to flash a splash of aqua panties. "You'll like having me around, I've been boning up on Alaska."

He glanced up. "You're not authorized." He pushed boots into the duffel.

Security clearance? Now she wanted to go even more.

"Sure I am. I'm authorized to practice all week. No one said *where* I had to practice. And it's only Monday."

He stopped packing.

She held her smile and stood absolutely still. Then she inched her jeans down.

He stared at her for ten seconds.

"Okay. You're our data collector on all information related to the fire. Everything to me personally."

She squealed with joy, ran across the bed and jumped into his arms, depending on his strength and her 5 foot 5 inch, 129-pound stature to keep them upright.

As she hugged him hard he said, "You'll have to be ready in ten minutes. Told the man I'd be in the air within the hour."

She dashed for the bathroom where she brushed teeth and fluffed chin-length brown locks hanging straight from her shower. She grabbed the always-packed kit and twisted the doorknob. As she pulled the door open she saw him slip something small into his briefcase before snapping it closed.

"Hurry up, I wasn't kidding about that departure time."

She ran out of the bathroom and rummaged for clothes, guessing Alaska was cold even in summer. She stuffed her own duffel, then pulled a wooden case out of the closet and laid it gently on the bed.

He eyed the box.

She felt a problem forming.

"Don't worry," she patted it. "My boy is ready to travel. Besides, on a military aircraft, all you guys will be packing."

He nodded, hefted the duffel across his shoulder, grabbed his briefcase, and exited the room like the bed was on fire.

Chapter 9

THE FLIGHT TO ALASKA took less than six hours from wheels up to the moment Claire awoke with a stiff neck. The throbbing near her temple had ceased. Through sleepy eyes and the multi-layer acrylic of the modified Boeing she saw black smoky strokes on the horizon. She rolled her head away from the window. The General sat across the aisle staring at a laptop no thicker than a slice of bread. She couldn't make out details, but there was a picture. She guessed a recent satellite photo of Northern Alaska.

She shifted her weight to get more comfortable.

He looked her way and smiled. "Sleeping beauty awakens."

She returned the smile and stretched her neck left and right. She hated sleeping on airplanes, but liked it better than being awake. Planes were confining, and the miles of empty space between her butt and the ground…she shuddered and forced herself to stop thinking about altitude.

She watched Billy retrieve his briefcase from the floor, close the laptop, pull something from its side and slip it into the same small pocket he had used in the bedroom. He placed the laptop in the case and closed it. His thumbs rotated the rings of a wide combination lock beneath the handle.

A screech of rubber broke her concentration. She glanced at the Breil chronometer she had won in the Pan-Euro games with five well-placed rounds. Thin pain jumped from her right ear to her shoulder.

She subtracted four hours from 17:31 and carefully unbuckled the soft leather band before futzing with the tiny knobs to bring her watch to 13:31 Alaska Daylight Time. She leaned forward to stare out the window. Bright sunlight shocked her awake.

The plane lurched to a stop.

She lifted the backpack containing her rifle, grabbed her duffel, and headed for the hissing door. She stopped short. It didn't open. Through the small porthole she saw a two-story drop to the tarmac.

"In a hurry?" Billy called from the cabin.

She swept her arm forward, "After you."

While waiting she pulled out her phone and connected to the airport's wireless network. Her RSS counter glowed 255 in red. She scanned quickly.

The media was calling the disaster Firesnake, a term credited to an Alaskan blogger but picked up by the major news outlets. Finance articles predicting adverse effects on Wall Street had *Black Monday* in their titles.

Billy arrived and looked over her shoulder. "What's the punditocracy have to say?" He bent and peered through the porthole.

She read a headline. "Icy white lights of UFO sighted flying at 200 mph through Atigun Pass."

He shot a cool glance over his shoulder.

"OK, OK, I'm just the messenger," she said.

She scanned. Uh-oh.

"Petry has a YouTube video posted. Two hours ago. Has 135,288 views. Loads of comments. The first three think President Mallor isn't responding quickly enough. One mentions hurricane Katrina."

"Stairs are crawling this way. Go ahead and watch it," Billy said.

"Uh...can't we get one of those big tubes that suck people out of the plane like cattle?"

"Twenty minute wait for a gate. This is faster."

She swallowed hard thinking about falling from a second story window, then leaned against the bulkhead and played the video on her phone.

"It's six minutes and four seconds long." She waited for a canned ad promoting Petry to finish. "He's at a podium with four microphones, and a wall of fire behind him billowing black smoke. Can't say if it's live, or being faked with stock footage."

She watched and listened.

"First talking point. The oil industry is again being irresponsible, remember the BP well explosion in the gulf."

She waited, listening for substance.

"Second. If elected, he will, quote, 'drastically reduce military spending by ending policies of armed aggression.'"

She watched the video carefully.

"Wait. The picture behind him changed. Now it's a black-winged plane on the deck of an aircraft carrier. 'Unmanned fighting robots cost billions.' And get this, 'Will make us puppets of computer software.' He wants these machines banned through international treaties."

Billy watched out the window. "Does he say what he's going to replace them with?"

She waited while Petry continued hand-waving. "No, he's talking deficit reduction, and hints at reduced taxes."

"So we become sheep," Billy said. "Awaiting the slaughter."

Claire felt the plane shake.

A uniformed man emerged from the cockpit and opened the outside door.

It had been stifling hot at Dulles, now Alaskan wind gusted 50-degree air through her light jacket, making it feel like 40. Shivering, she stepped onto a metal platform.

She squinted at the horizon to steady her inner ear and noticed two vehicles. From the west a green Humvee twisted between painted white lines on the runway. From the opposite direction a dark sedan blasted across the pavement in a beeline for their plane.

She looked at the silver stairs and forced an image of standing safely at the bottom into her head. Then she walked down quickly, counting the steps to focus her attention, until her boots hit tarmac and memories of a childhood trip along walls of rock near the Salmon Fork River faded.

Rubber squealed. She turned. The doors of the sedan, which she now realized was midnight blue, carried the emblem of the Fairbanks Police Department with the slogan *The Golden Heart City* painted beneath. She wondered if a gold rush founded the place, or a friendly prostitute.

A man not much taller than Claire exited the passenger side. He walked briskly in a suit that matched the car, rummaging inside his jacket. Her thoughts flashed to a revolver. Too many Hollywood movies, she told herself, and paranoia from sleeping with a man who carried deadly weapons in his pockets like spare change.

"I'm Detective Qigiq," the man said as he flipped open a black case to show a shiny badge. "Who are you people?"

Key-jee? The name sounded like a manga character. His face was slightly square and deep surfer tan, with a short mustache. Black hair seemed to reflect the blue of his suit. She'd guess Asian.

She heard Billy's shoes scuff metal behind her.

Billy said nothing, so she glanced at the badge and caught *Detective* and *Fairbanks Police.*

"Hello, Detective Ka-jee." She stumbled over the name. "Thank you for welcoming us to Fairbanks. You have an unusual name. If you don't mind my asking, where is it from?"

He blinked and visibly softened.

"Um, Yupik, one of the native Alaskan tribes. It means: *White hawk that flies in the sky.*"

"Really? How do you spell it?" She reached inside her jacket for a notebook.

"Q-I-G-I-Q. A palindrome pronounced ki-JEEK."

Indeed it was, and he was getting friendlier.

"How unusual," she murmured. She said with a big smile, "You were asking who we are?"

"Yes. I'm busy with a sensitive investigation, but was ordered to the airport by the Chief. He didn't tell me more than that."

"Then that's all you need to know," interrupted the General.

Her shoulders tensed. Here they were, beginning to bond, and Billy had to swing his rank around like a fire axe.

Qigiq looked unfazed. "I don't believe we've been introduced."

She jumped in. "Detective, this is General Williams and I'm Corporal Ferreti. We're visiting Alaska to—"

"Look at your forests," interrupted the General. "Nice trees."

There was a moment of icy silence.

Then, to her surprise, Qigiq sputtered like he had just heard a terrific punch line. He reached inside his coat, this time withdrawing a pack of cigarettes whose round Lucky Strike logo she recognized instantly.

"Trees? You arrive inside a giant green whale to look at trees? Sir, you are a terrible liar," he said as he launched a cigarette from the pack to his lips.

Here it comes, she thought.

Billy looked the shorter man up and down and stepped off the stairway onto the runway. His lips cracked into a smile, and he started laughing too.

So she laughed, though she couldn't have explained why.

The Humvee that had been twisting its way between the lines pulled nose to nose with the police car. Two men inside stared in their direction. The driver exited the vehicle and approached.

"We're looking for General Williams."

Billy recovered quickly. "You've found him."

"You requested helicopter transport from the Forest Service?"

"Yes."

"We've been instructed to take you to the aircraft, General. It's ready to depart."

Billy hefted his duffel and headed toward the Humvee.

"Let's go, Corporal."

She fell in behind him.

"Wait," Qigiq called out. "I'm in charge of this investigation. What is it you plan to do?"

The General stopped and turned. "I told you, we're going to look at trees."

"Might those trees be near a pipeline?" Qigiq asked.

"Might," Billy said, and smiled.

She took a step back.

Qigiq exhaled smoke. "Well, I can't have you interfering with our investigation of this incident, General Williams."

The General looked at him the way he might observe a fly at a picnic. He headed toward the Humvee as he spoke.

"Why would we interfere? We have a need to know in Washington; we're here to collect information."

Qigiq took long strides to keep up. Claire and the driver followed.

"That would mean two separate inquiries," noted Qigiq.

"At least two, Detective. The media has probably launched ten or twenty, and the oil companies surely have a few of their own. We had better know more than they do." Billy tossed his luggage into the back of the waiting Humvee.

Claire figured the gloomy look on Qigiq's face meant he had already heard from the press.

"Do you have room in your chopper?" Qigiq asked. "I tried to procure one, but they're busy with traffic. The Dalton is impassable, and hundreds of trucks are stranded."

She watched Billy's face, knowing he would consider how to use the detective to his advantage.

"Gentlemen," he called into the back of the Humvee. "What kind of equipment do we have?"

"One blender, three seats in back," the driver replied.

The General faced Qigiq. "Okay, Detective. Wheels up in ten minutes."

Qigiq spun on his heels, jogged back to the dark police car and jerked the door open. As he ducked his head she overheard staccato speech, but couldn't make out the words.

Claire stuffed her duffel into the Humvee and walked around to slip into the back seat. She held the backpack containing her rifle on her lap. As they accelerated away she glanced over her shoulder.

The blue sedan was right behind them.

Chapter 10

THE DOOR SLAMMED, locking Claire into the passenger compartment with the General to her right, Qigiq to her left, and directly below an 1,800 hp jet engine. A rumble became a roar as she felt herself lifted like the first seconds on a roller coaster. She reached forward for headgear. As she slipped it on, crushing hair pre-flattened by her airplane nap, the cancellation circuits quieted the engine noise and she heard a voice in mid-sentence.

"...tain Verook, Sir. Where to first?"

"Wherever I can get a look at this thing," she heard Billy say.

The Detective's voice entered her headset.

"I have GPS for every call. The closest is here," he leaned forward and held a yellow piece of paper in an outstretched arm.

The Captain said, "On our way."

She felt the craft accelerate against her back and forced herself to swallow.

"Detective, what have we got so far?" Billy asked.

She glanced at Qigiq and wondered if she looked as funny in her headset. He pulled a flat phone from his jacket and tapped it with his middle finger, stared at it, tapped it again. Shook it. Tapped a third time.

"The first report of a fire was called in from Deadhorse about an hour after sunrise this morning." He looked at Claire. "Deadhorse is above the Arctic Circle, sunrise is around 4:00 am that far north." He turned back to his phone. "Two hundred and eighty-three other calls followed—all originating within ten miles of the pipeline, but spread over several hundred miles. Our preliminary hypothesis is that something has gone seriously wrong with the pipe."

"What do the owners say?" Billy asked.

"Their website reads, 'For pipeline emergencies only, call Alyeska collect at (907) 835-4709.' That number has been busy all day. The site claims TAPS was constructed to the highest safety standards to move crude oil from the North Slope to Valdez and admits, again I quote, 'However, emergencies may still occur.'" He paused. "Quite an understatement. The particulars of the pipe are listed. Would you care to hear them?"

"I've probably seen them, but go ahead," Billy said.

Qigiq continued, "TAPS consists of 800 miles of forty-eight inch Oil Pipeline, 148 miles of ten inch Fuel Gas Pipeline from Pump Station 1 to Pump Station 4, the Valdez Marine Terminal, and related facilities."

She heard Billy whistle. "Long sucker. No press release from the owners?"

The aircraft bumped through turbulence. Claire grabbed the edge of her seat and concentrated, thinking Billy had made a good choice bringing Qigiq.

"Nothing public yet. They might not know what happened. We've encountered work crews during traffic control, but if anyone knows what caused this, they aren't talking about it."

Qigiq tapped his phone again.

"One other thing. We were lucky. A satellite on a polar pass got a few pictures after sunrise. Whatever happened, it reached across 250 miles—like a giant string of firecrackers."

Claire wondered if the pipeline had failed in a freakish way. Strange things happen: Three Mile Island, the Challenger Space Shuttle, the Titanic. Technology was risky. Even traffic accidents killed as many Americans each year as the Vietnam War had in ten. She flashed to thoughts of her father, his tragic stories about pushing through jungle and crawling in tunnels. Yet he supported her desire to become a marksman.

Her insides floated as the chopper descended.

"Coordinates in twenty seconds," the Captain said in her headset.

As the pilot turned north she saw gray smoke to the left, drifting towards them. She craned her neck before realizing there was a flat screen in front of her seat.

"Interesting," Billy mumbled as he thumbed a control, scanning a camera up and down the highway.

All she saw was a brushfire fifty meters west of the road. And black smoke she guessed was burning crude oil, although she wasn't sure. Qigiq had also mentioned fuel gas.

Billy leaned away from the monitor, interlaced his fingers and stretched his palms outward to crack his knuckles.

"Notice anything?" he asked.

She noticed a lot of things: smoke, flames, chunks of torn metal strewn along the road like Mardi Gras beads after a Fat Tuesday parade. A clear blue sky that didn't seem bothered by the chaos.

"Explosion."

"Right. Fragments formerly known as the Trans-Alaska Pipeline are everywhere."

"Why would the pipe fail at specific locations?" Qigiq asked.

"Good question," Billy said slowly, as if considering something.

They flew in silence for nearly a minute, watching video from the chopper's belly.

"The debris surrounds the support infrastructure," Qigiq said.

"Yeah," answered Billy. "Like someone did a demolition job."

At the word *demolition* an image that had been haunting Claire's subconscious popped into view.

"Whoever did it blows the support structure where the pipeline runs above ground. The pipe is under pressure to make the crude move, right? So when it drops to the ground it acts like a huge tube of toothpaste oozing fuel from its innards to feed the fires."

"Innards?" echoed Billy, laughing.

Claire grinned. Okay, strange word. But lying on the ground hundreds of feet below her feet, that pipe seemed more like a fire-breathing animal than a ring of steel.

"Unless there's a reason the supports failed, and we're witnessing coincidence not causality," Billy said. "What about the sections where the pipe is underground? The innards can't ooze there." He chuckled.

"Sure they can," she said. "Only instead of adding to the fire, they leak underground and create an environmental disaster that will need that bacteria stuff to clean it up."

Qigiq looked her way. Nodded.

Billy remained quiet.

Claire realized that if she were right, someone had gone to great trouble to attack the pipeline. And Alaska. And maybe the United States.

"How could anyone do this without being caught?" she asked.

"Alaska is a big place," Qigiq said. "Over a half a million square miles, twice the size of Texas. A difficult geography to police correctly."

She heard him sigh. Then she heard tribal drumming midst the chopper noise. Instinctively, she wagged her head to locate the sound. Qigiq was digging in his coat. He came up with a small purple box, pushed off one earpiece and held it to his ear.

"Qigiq," she heard through the intercom. "What? Where? Did you send a squad? How long? Let me call you back." The box disappeared into his jacket.

She wondered how many phones he owned.

He pulled the earpiece back on.

"We got a call," Qigiq said. "Woman says her little boy found a small machine that looks expensive. She called the police hoping for a reward. The operator routed the call to Fairbanks."

"Holy Toledo, we can dismantle it," Claire said, "figure out what's going on." She turned to Billy.

Qigiq added, "The Chief is sending a bomb squad, but it'll take them hours with the traffic jams."

"Where's she located?" Billy shouted.

"The call was logged just north of Coldfoot."

"Copy that," said the pilot. "Head up there, General?"

"Affirmative."

She felt the aircraft rotate and heard the pilot call in a revised flight plan. Two hundred miles per hour sounded fast when announcers talked about Formula-1 racecars, but now she felt like part of a missile. A horizontal waterfall of tree and rock rushed past the window. The display showed a highway twisting on and off the screen, sometimes with gridlocked cars, sometimes completely empty.

In minutes she heard the pilot say, "Approaching Coldfoot. Where to?"

"I have a street address," Qigiq said.

"That'll do."

She peeked at the instruments as the pilot brought up an image of the Earth positioned over Alaska. He entered the address as Qigiq read it off. As if he felt her watching he said, "Google Earth technology. Like having a video game of the planet."

The chopper lowered toward scrub grass. Pine tree carpet under blue sky stretched in all directions. A gray hump on the horizon indicated a mountain whose height Claire couldn't begin to estimate. A few hundred yards to her right the pipeline ran undisturbed across the land: curved, cold, hard. But to the north puffs of black marked the sky like sprayed graffiti.

Through the rising dust she saw a small wooden house, painted white years ago, standing back from a dirt road. A shed with a rusting roof sat fifty feet behind the house. A boy ran onto the porch, stopped, shaded his eyes with a flat hand, and looked up.

The chopper dropped to the center of the road midst swirling dirt. Claire watched the little boy run toward them and stop abruptly. A woman in a green dress emerged from the tilted front door, mouth moving, her voice lost to the whine of the jet.

He was wearing a big pair of bright blue basketball shoes with protruding tongues, drooping blue jeans and a too large sweatshirt that had paid a royalty to Batman. He held something the size of a grapefruit—if grapefruits had handles. It was shiny dark in the eerie way polished metal almost glows. Her heart thumped as he lifted it to his chest like a lost teddy bear.

She spun to her right to see Billy stepping out of the aircraft.

"He's holding the bomb," she yelled.

He looked up, shook his head. "No kidding, let's go take it away from him." He walked away.

Leaping out of the chopper she bent low beneath the spinning blades, even though it wasn't necessary. By the time they reached the boy, the woman had also arrived.

"Wow!" the boy said. "Is that ever cool! How fast is it?"

"A hundred and seventy knots," Billy said. "Would you like to sit in it?"

"Oh yeah," the boy replied and started running toward the aircraft, clutching the metal grapefruit to his chest.

"Halt right there, soldier."

The boy stopped and turned around.

"What's that you're carrying? Is it safe to take on an armed aircraft?"

Armed aircraft? Claire thought. That chopper was Forest Service. The only armament it carried was water to drop on a forest fire.

"Uh, I don't know, Sir."

"Let's take a look at it."

The boy's feet inched his body back to the group.

Billy knelt on one camo-clad knee so his gaze was about level with the boy's light blue eyes.

"Hello, soldier, I'm General William Williams, but my friends call me Billy."

The little boy's eyes widened like he was seeing a ghost. Claire figured he must be impressed meeting a General, even a one-star like Billy.

"My name's Billy, too," he blurted out. "It's nice to meet you. Are you really a General?" He let go with one arm and extended his right hand to the General.

Big Billy shook little Billy's hand. "Yes, I'm really a General, Billy."

Claire saw the woman's mouth twitch towards a smile.

"And I'm here investigating the fire."

"Yeah, it's huge ain't it? I never seen one so close to the house before."

"Yes, it's huge," said the General. "And we're trying to find out how it got started. Do you have any ideas?"

Claire wondered why the hell the General was wasting time like this kid was his playground pal. They needed to determine if that device could have caused the fire. She'd put money on it, but the President wasn't interested in her intuition.

"Oh yeah, I do. See this?" Little Billy held out the device with two hands wrapped around a bar. "I bet it can blow up, and I betcha there were a whole bunch of 'em made the fire. I found it over by the big pipe, that way," he said, pointing to the east. "But mine didn't go off. Isn't it cool?"

The woman smiled and said, "My boy has a very active imagination."

The General's eyes took interest in the device.

"Yes, it's very cool, may I hold it?" he asked.

Little Billy nodded.

Claire froze.

The General reached for the machine and rolled the shaft in his hand so he could examine the bulbous top piece. Certainly the General handling it was no worse than the kid waving it around, but the folly of standing in a circle admiring what they suspected was a bomb struck her like a piano falling from the third floor.

"General, do you think this might be a job for the bomb squad?" she asked.

Claire heard the boy's mother gasp.

"Over an hour away," Qigiq said.

From his position on one knee the General cast a sideways glance at Claire.

"A fine idea, Corporal." He turned the device over. "Billy, can we take this back to headquarters and look it over?"

"No, it's mine. I just found it this morning, I don't wanna lose it."

"Now Billy, if they need it to help with the fire," his Mom said.

"Then I wanna go with them. Can I?" He turned to his mother to plead with his eyes. "Can I fly in the chopper like Batman does?"

Before she could answer the General said to her son, "What do you think, soldier? Do you think we should take this, maybe it can explode, maybe not, but do you think we should take it on the chopper and endanger a multi-million dollar aircraft and the lives of everyone on board? Does that sound smart to you?"

Billy thought for a moment, his young forehead furled. "Well, no. We don't want no one to get hurt."

"General," popped in Qigiq, "may I have a word with you?"

The General looked up at the Detective and stood slowly, holding the device in one hand.

"I'll be right back, soldier."

"But my—" Billy began before his mother shushed him.

The General and the Detective strolled toward the chopper. Whatever they were saying was lost to Claire in the thump-thumping of the idling engine.

"Have you lived here long?" Claire asked the woman.

"Almost eight years. Ever since his daddy left."

Her eyes looked sad. Maybe weary more than sad. Claire wondered what had happened.

"Can I ask you something?" the woman said.

"Sure. What's on your mind?"

"What's a young girl like you doing wearing a military uniform? You should be...well, what are you doing?"

"Making a living, Ma'am. I'm a very good shot with a rifle, and the Army has jobs for people like that."

"A rifle?" the woman said, bringing one had to her chest.

"My Father served in Vietnam, taught me to shoot when I was in elementary school. We use to have our own competitions. Sometimes I would win."

"Well, I'll be damned," she said.

"Mom," Billy said, causing her to turn to face him. "You shouldn't say words like that."

"Sorry, Billy. I'll be more careful."

She turned back to Claire. "Who would of thought a pretty thing like you could shoot a rifle? I figured you were the General's secretary or something."

Or something, Claire thought, and smiled. "I'm the data collection specialist on this mission."

Her answer disappeared into the roar of chopper blades. She spun around to see their aircraft warming up as the General and Qigiq returned.

"The pilot is calling for clearance. He'll go get the, uh...squad and bring them here," the General said. He turned to Qigiq and held up the device.

42

"Any experience with...?"

Qigiq shrugged. "The usual for a local boy. Dynamite for mine work, big fireworks on Alaska Day." He nodded toward the rod in the General's hand. "No high tech stuff encased in steel."

"I've seen a few bits in the Army, so I guess I volunteer." He squatted. "Okay to take pictures of your prize, son?"

Little Billy eyed him with suspicion. "Pictures?"

"Yep. We'd like to know who built it. If we get enough pictures, maybe we'll be able to track down where it came from."

Claire's eyes drifted to the device. The end of the handle was alternating dull red and yellow. Her shoulders tensed. Had something gone wrong inside? A bomb was bad, but a failed bomb?

"Uh, General Williams?" She gestured toward the lights with one finger.

"Can I watch?" the boy asked.

"Sure." The General glanced down at his hand. "But it would be safer if you watched from the house. There's no reason for all of us to take chances."

The General pulled a flat black box from his belt. "I'll turn on video from my cell phone and transmit to Corporal Ferreti so you can see exactly what I'm doing. And I'll take high-resolution photos for us to look at later. What'd you think?"

The boy's eyes scrunched as he worked on a decision. "Where you going to take pictures?"

Well, wasn't he the practical one? Claire thought. He wanted to know where the General was taking his new toy.

"Too many shadows in direct sunlight. How about if I use that shack over there?" He pointed to the failing wood structure. "And you take everyone else inside the house to watch."

"OK," Billy said, making an instant decision to trust an adult he had just met.

"Good man," said the General. "Let's get to work solving this mystery."

The General took the fat end of the device into his left palm and wrapped his long fingers around it like he was about to pitch in the big game. He opened his cell phone with his other hand and pressed buttons.

Claire took this as a cue and extracted her phone from the thigh pocket of her cargo pants. In a few seconds she had a live video stream from the General's camera. She bent over to show it to Billy.

"Keep everyone safe, soldier," the General said as he started walking slowly and smoothly across the yard with the camera pointed in his direction of travel.

In the kitchen Claire sipped hot cocoa beside Billy at a table topped with red Formica. Qigiq joined them in staring at her cell phone propped against a bowl of artificial fruit. Billy's Mom sat across the table entertaining her little daughter Hattie with a doll wearing a long pink dress.

Claire noticed the rumble of the idling chopper and wondered when it would lift off.

The little screen showed that the General had propped the wooden door to the shack open with a shovel from a stash of yard tools in a corner. The rest of the shack was empty. Billy's find was now on the plank floor in the center of the shed illuminated by indirect light from the open door. The General paced a circle around it while narrating into his phone.

"This is General Williams. The device is constructed of hardened metal whose general sheen indicates titanium content. The handle contains an illuminated indicator that has been alternating red and yellow since our arrival. The head end is cylindrical with two rubberized rings, like the treads on a tank, at either end. Thus far, these have not moved but visual inspection suggests that they spin to provide locomotion to the device under some, currently undefined, conditions."

Claire knew titanium came from ore, and made metal light and strong. But how could a machine containing explosives get into Alaska? It would have been detected on commercial aircraft. A ship? Private plane? No one could have looked at such a thing and passed it through customs.

The General's narration continued through the tiny speaker. "I'm taking close-ups of each section from orthogonal positions."

She watched as he stood the device on its head with the tail bar upright and the lights pulsing directly at the ceiling. He circled, shooting with every step. She tried to imagine what a 3D computer model of those pictures might reveal.

The General made his way around the device until he was between it and a pair of rusty rakes in the back corner. She heard a whir. The treads on the head spun and smoked against the wood floor, propelling the little machine directly toward the door.

Qigiq jumped from his chair, sending it flying across tan tiles.

"Catch it," screamed little Billy, racing for the front door as fast as his blue sneakers would carry him.

"Billy, stop!" his mother called in a vain attempt to keep him away from the machine.

No! Claire screamed inside her head as she saw the throbbing red light in the tail turn to flashing yellow as the machine disappeared over the edge of the doorsill, leaping two feet into the scraggly grass of the yard.

She ran from the kitchen through the small living room, clearing a square coffee table in a single leap, before slamming her shoulder into the screen door closing behind Billy. The door flexed wildly and smashed against the house. She saw the boy racing across the front yard on a collision course with the General who had exited the shed and was chasing the silver machine.

Even a physics dropout could see that the machine was putting distance on its pursuers. She stopped at the edge of the porch and scanned for a vehicle: bicycle, car, anything. But the yard was barren except for rock, wild grass and a woodpile.

She leapt from the porch in one motion and ran fast toward the helicopter, whose pilot turned to stare. She yelled, "Go go go go," while rotating her arm above her head like a crazed hockey fan spinning a cheering towel. His hands moved to the controls.

She ducked under the rotating blades still yelling, "Go go, up up up." The pilot pointed at Qigiq emerging from the house. She jumped through the open door, jammed her arm straight up, and yelled, "Now!"

As the craft lifted and spun she gestured toward the runaway bomb then dove into the back seat headfirst. With one hand she grabbed field glasses, the thumping of the blade loud in her ears. She saw the General sprinting, leaping rocks and bushes. Little Billy was trying his best, but was already twenty yards behind. She scanned in the direction they were running until she saw the silver fleck moving across the rough ground like a tiny tank, maneuvering around large obstacles.

"Holy cow," she whispered, "it has robot eyes."

It hit a rut and flipped upside down, causing it to suddenly go in the wrong direction. But the tail jumped over the top and one tread stopped spinning, causing the whole machine to rotate in place. Fast. It was back on course in a matter of seconds.

She guessed it was moving almost 30 mph—the General had no hope of catching it. She tapped the Captain on his arm and drew a pattern: forward, left and down. She calculated carefully—how far did they have to land in front to give the pilot time to land, and her to jump out and intercept?

"There," she called out, waving her left arm. She grabbed her seat and held on as the chopper dropped from the sky.

Chapter 11

HUNDREDS OF MILES WEST of the descending chopper, the tires of Jonathon Katow's motorcycle splashed along a shallow stream. He had floated on the ferry as far as Galena, and was now riding north through the roadless Koyukuk National Wildlife refuge, what many considered America's last great wilderness. A round light blinked inside the tachometer dial.

He frowned and slowed, not expecting contact. As he flicked a switch to activate the satellite phone he dropped from standing into the custom saddle that helped him ride 500-mile days in relative comfort.

"Hello, Maxx."

"Greetings, Firesnake."

"Go ahead."

"Rat thirty-one requesting assistance. Human proximity delayed mission objective. Currently one kilometer from original target."

He was glad it hadn't malfunctioned, especially the subsystem that recognized bipeds. But who had been close to his Rat?

"Status?"

"Clear one hundred meter perimeter. Pending decision: seek target, or go now?"

Thirty-nine out of forty was sufficient. Better safe than...

"Go now," he said.

"Please confirm: seek target, or go now?"

"Go now," he said.

"Affirmative."

The line went quiet. He stood on the foot pegs and opened the throttle. There was no reason to hurry; he had plenty of Alaska's famous summer daylight.

But he liked riding fast.

Chapter 12

CLAIRE LEAPT FROM THE CHOPPER before it touched the ground. Her left foot slipped on the asphalt-hard permafrost. She rolled, and popped up running on a collision course with the escaped machine. As she dodged waist-high scrub, she kept her head up and both eyes glued to the silver dot growing slowly larger, visualizing her fingers closing around its shiny neck.

The earth turned as a shock wave tossed her body backwards with the sound of a thousand thunderbolts. She saw a pillar of fire, yellow fingers high in the blue sky like the hand of the Devil. Her eyes filled with glorious colors...

Claire touched her fingertips together. She moved to touch her elbows and felt pain shoot into her shoulders.

She realized her eyes were closed.

She moved her head left, then right.

She was on a pillow.

She eased both lids open.

A hotel room greeted her. The air smelled of dust. She could hear tapping on a keyboard. She moved her eyes. General Billy.

"Is the little guy okay?" she asked. She licked her lips, and swallowed away dryness.

"Told you before your nap. You were closest to the blast at maybe a hundred meters. Then me. Then him. He was barely scratched. They have him at the hospital for observation." More tapping. "I think he's just really pissed we ruined his new toy."

She rolled over and watched Billy's hands on the keyboard.

"You've been at that for hours," she said, trying not to see the blast in her mind. Trying not to think about how close they had come to being a part of it.

"Work to do," he said.

She eased her body off the bed and walked over to stand behind him. He had succeeded in constructing a 3D model of the device, and a hypothetical breakdown of its internal components. She watched the screen as the machine disassembled before her eyes, then slowly, one piece at a time, reassembled itself.

"How the hell do you know what's inside?" she asked. "All you had were pictures."

He stopped typing, stretched his arms overhead and arched his back like a man who had been sitting on a hardback hotel chair for far too long.

"Right you are. But," he reached out and pulled her across his lap, turning her body until she faced the computer. "But, we also know a hell of a lot about what it can do. For example, we know it can explode. So we estimate that it had to carry a load of demolition material, like C49 plastic or something similar. I think that was inside the handle. And we know it was mobile. So we can guess an electric motor, and some kind of power supply, probably in the cylinder at the top where the tire treads rotated. When I lifted it, the head was heavy. Batteries."

She looked at the image assembling on the screen, then back at Billy.

"Pretty friggin' amazing for an Army dweeb," she said softly.

He stared at the screen but slowly massaged her back with the flat of his hand.

"Want to hear something really amazing? Hold on to your panties. How do you think they communicate? I say 'they' because there had to be fifty or a hundred of these to damage the pipe."

"Um…"

"Right. Cellular telephone. Maybe direct to satellite, but a tower would do. And how do I know that, you ask? Good question my sweet-smelling comrade. I know that because I had a search done on cell phone calls in the hour prior to 5:15 am ADT, our current estimate of the first explosion. Then I sorted by estimated GPS position. You knew cell phone companies could provide position, didn't you? Well, not always. But in this case—"

He stopped and reached around her with both arms, trapping her on his lap.

"Look at this map. One hundred and eighteen cell phone calls placed to within a mile of the pipeline. My bet is that some, maybe most, were to these devices. Only I can't prove it because they were all to different cell phone numbers. And a bit weirdly, they were all *from* different cell phone numbers. Still, I think this device carries a cell module, and if you look at the graphic," he pointed, "I put it right at the base of the handle, which I think not only held the explosive, but also acted as a powerful antenna." He paused, staring at the screen. "What'd you think?"

She looked at the diagram rotating slowly in front of her eyes like a silver helium birthday balloon.

"You reverse engineered it from pictures? Impressive."

"Not me. Mallor put experts on this with college degrees I can't even pronounce. And we didn't engineer so much as guess how it was constructed. Could be way off. But it's the best we've got."

"What now Mr. Magician?"

He turned his head to gaze out the window, as if there were something he needed to see.

"It's going to be a long night preparing to present this. Let's have dinner while the experts determine where our bomber sourced his parts? We know one thing for sure."

"And that is?" she asked, watching his eyes.

"It wasn't an accident, although it sure resembles a big industrial mistake." He sighed. "The environmentalists will have a field day. They already want Mallor to limit drilling. This fuels their protect-the-wilderness agenda. Won't help in November."

She stood and spun on bare feet. A wave of dizziness hit her. She took two deep breaths before saying, "You're not going to tell anyone?"

His eyes studied her face.

"Not in our best interest. For now, this device is classified."

"*Our* best interest?"

"The objective is to protect American citizens, and reelect the man I work for, not solve this particular little fire. Who knows, maybe the Exxon boys wanted to collect insurance on an aging pipeline, so they made lightning strike."

"You're crazy, Billy. They wouldn't do that." As she spoke part of her knew full well that, yes in fact they might do that. "But what about Billy Norton and his Mom, and even Hattie? And Qigiq? Won't they talk?"

"Qigiq won't, he's on the case as a government employee. The kids and their mother have been taken care of."

She said slowly, "By which you mean?"

"I mean their government has formally requested they keep their mouths shut...for a nice stipend. You didn't hear that from me, it's classified for the next twenty-five years." He pointed at her green panties. "They won't let you in the restaurant without shoes, Claire."

She scowled. The corner of her eye caught movement on the screen; the computer was downloading from those experts in Washington. She wanted to know what—she didn't like being in the dark unless she was in bed.

Chapter 13

CLAIRE STOOD IN THE HOTEL shower with both hands pressed against green faux marble, hot water pummeling soreness from her rag-doll tossed onto permafrost body. The calming effects of last evening's ice wine had evaporated, but the intense sweetness of grapes frozen on the vine lingered. She twisted her back gently. It was early to be out of bed, sunbeams and thin curtains had conspired with Billy's rush to get back to Washington, so she was left to fly commercial to Cleveland.

She poked her head from the steamy stall: 5:41, barely an hour till flight time. She closed her eyes wishing for more sleep...a pencil sketch of the bomb glowed on a giant display, revolving, as if her subconscious were studying it for a clue. The General sat next to her, staring. "Find the owner," he said, and walked away. She heard footsteps tap hardwood flooring, a bomb ticking. They stopped, the picture exploded into the Devil's hand, fire burst through the glass, reached directly for her face, wrapping fingers around her throat—

She shook her head to clear the recurring image. Pain erupted in her shoulder. She reminded herself to move slowly. As she stepped from the shower to reach for a towel she thought about those experts in Washington. What had they found from all the guessing and estimating with Billy's pictures? She had hinted so hard Billy reminded her that she had no need to know.

Half a day later, on the truck ride to the competition site in Port Clinton, Ohio, she was still trying to formulate a hypothesis. The device was clearly a bomb. Probably dozens of them had destroyed the pipeline. But how did they get there? The machines seemed too small to have much range. There was no record of a plane, no one had seen or heard a chopper, and it seemed much too far to drive. Nothing could move fast on that crazy road of rocks and ice cubes she had seen from the air anyway. If a militant or religious group had delivered them, why not take credit? And where were these people hiding? No suspicious activity had been reported. Except for the UFO.

She sighed for the hundredth time.

And why? Why would anyone destroy an oil pipeline that had been in use for decades? Green protest? No, the explosion had done more damage to the environment than the pipeline ever could.

She couldn't make one and one become two.

The truck pulled to a stop in a cloud of dust. She leapt out and dragged the backpack containing the tool of her trade after her.

"Thanks for meeting me at the airport, Kevin," she called to the driver.

"Anytime, Corporal Claire. Be the bullet."

She walked toward the range, feeling better than in the shower even though sleep on the flight east had been restless—the fiery dream looping whenever it wanted to. To focus she counted footsteps in the dirt. At 347 she passed through the fence separating the parking area from the firing range: empty except for two guys at the end. She heard the *pfft*, *pfft* of rifle rounds. She walked past station after station until she stood beside the guy firing. His peripheral vision eventually registered her presence.

"What the hell?" He swung to his left. "What are you doing sneaking up on a guy like that?"

"Missed, huh? Better learn to concentrate…" she searched his shirt for a name, "Putnam."

She watched brown eyes dance over her. His dark hair drooped over one eye from leaning over the weapon.

"And who the hell are you?" he insisted, not bothering to read her uniform.

She pointed to herself and smiled. "Moi? I'm the shooter who's going to kick your ass this weekend, Putnam."

"You?" He grinned a wide, expensive orthodontia smile and stared her in the eye. "I thought only blondes had dumb dreams."

She leaned forward to look around him to the curly blond guy at the next station. He had been ignoring them while reloading his weapon.

"What do you think? Will this hunk of useless meat beat me this weekend?"

His eyes moved from her to Putnam. She wondered if they were friends. All she knew was they happened to be out on the range at the same time.

"I wouldn't know. But for sure you'll be fighting over second place," he said, adding his grin to the festivities.

Putnam was big, maybe a solid 205 pounds, but his hands were smaller than hers.

"You boys are awfully confident considering you've never seen me shoot."

"We don't need to see you shoot, girlie," said Putnam, "you're what we call self-explanatory."

"Hold on, Putnam, she might really know how to handle a rod." They both laughed, apparently fans of middle-school humor.

She assembled her rifle slowly, loaded five round, lifted the slender weapon to her shoulder and breathed. She checked the limp windsock with one eye, rotated a small dial on the rifle sight and sent the first round away with a *Whap!* A second Whap. Then three, four and five.

She was standing in slot 17 so her new friends looked to the huge target with a 17 over it in the distance. A red flag waived indicating no hits. Both burst out laughing, Putnam verging on tears. She reached into his station and grabbed a two-way radio.

"Target 18, show us what you have please?"

Putnam stopped short, looked at her, then down at the number 18 on the ground in front of his toes. The target operator indicated a bull's-eye old school style, by holding a white disk in front of the location of bullet entry. Entries two, three, four and finally five were all within a circle the size of a DVD. The three stood in silence.

"No worries, Putnam, I'll be careful not to cross-fire into your lane this weekend."

Chapter 14

JONATHON KATOW KICKED small rocks toward the perimeter as he paced circles around his motorcycle listening to the satellite phone dial. Comfortable he wasn't being watched except by moose because of thick overhead foliage, he thought about 31. He hated failure—it was dangerous.

The satphone connected.

He had been riding creek beds toward Cape Deceit and the ship he needed. Not fast, but steady and safe.

He counted to five, and said, "Hello, Maxx. History on thirty-one."

"Greetings, Firesnake. Unit thirty-one report. Microphones on threshold activation. Play recording?"

"Yes."

"Playing from start."

He heard a rustle of grass and the voice of a young boy. "I got you. Wow, this is so cool." The sound of shoes shuffling mixed with the whir of the Rat's wheels. He could hear the boy starting to pant, as if running.

"Is there more?"

"Fourteen minutes later," Maxx said.

A sleepy voice whispered, "You stay here with me, okay? Mom can't see you or she'll make me take you back. Just stay right here."

"Anything else, Maxx?" he asked.

"Yes."

Katow looked at the sky, marveling at how much daylight he had seen in the past forty-eight hours, and listened.

He heard a name, Key Jig. Sounded native. Maybe they had hired a local guide.

"This is General Williams…"

Why not FBI? Did they think the fire was an act of war? Or were they guessing terrorists, an easy catchall when they didn't know what was really happening, and wanted latitude to act under anti-terrorism laws.

"I'm taking close-ups of each section…"

Pictures. How damaging? They might be used to gain public sympathy. He laughed; the sound disappeared into the trees. He didn't need sympathy to be effective.

What else could they be used for?

"Catch it," he heard someone yell, someone distant from the Rat. A woman's voice. He listened closely. "Go go go." Yes, definitely a woman.

The recording stopped.

"Thanks, Maxx. Do you have more?"

"Negative. Rat thirty-one activated forty-three seconds after the last recording."

"Check back in twelve hours."

"Twelve hours confirmed." The wireless connection turned silent.

He switched his phone off and sat cross-legged on the bike's seat to meditate. In the entire recording only one word worried him: pictures. How many, how close, from what angles? He examined his eyes in the left rearview mirror. Alert. Not stressed. The existence of pictures made him paranoid. But he knew paranoid, had lived with it as a close and welcome friend since he was six. He spoke to his reflection. "Remember Mom, only the paranoid survive. Andrew Grove, 1996."

Chapter 15

A SWEATING WHITE MALE lay on a low twin bed. The jleep-jleep of an electronic alarm sliced through the tropical Chinese air. He listened to the pattern of the alarm: three, four, two, five. He sprang upright. His head swam while his blood pressure adjusted. He stumbled toward the closet and pulled open flimsy folding doors, leaned on a computer printer with both hands to steady himself and took deep breaths.

The machine wanted a pass-code. He shook his head to inspire it to wake up. Waited. Entered nine digits. Waited. Phase one approved; a sheet spewed out.

Origin: Grease Gun. Target: Typhoon.

Yes, it was for him. He shuffled across the rough wood floor to locate pants hanging over a straight backed chair, reached into a zippered pocket on the thigh and withdrew a rectangular medallion that resembled an ancient brass coin. Holding it to his mouth he said, "Typhoon" and spoke the same nine digits he had entered into the printer.

It replied, "Ready."

Back at the printer he read a 48-digit number from the single page into the medallion and waited. It replied with its own 48-digit number that he dutifully typed into the printer.

Sheets of paper, an archaic form of storage, but portable and easy to destroy, began exiting the printer slot. He crossed the room and this time put the pants on, noticed the battery clock glowing 5:13 am, wished he could go back to sleep, knew he couldn't until after he read the message, and wondered what he could scrounge up for breakfast. He watched the printer spit pages.

"This is going to be a doozy."

Shirtless, he made his way to the coffee maker standing on a small table stained dark red. The tabletop was hand carved, hundreds of human eyes staring up at him. He leaned forward to check the outside thermometer, but it was too dark. He reached into a thin drawer bolted to the table and withdrew a pocket flashlight. 35 degrees C.

He groaned. He hated humid jungle heat. Maybe he should move after this job.

The printer stopped.

He collected the pages and sat on the edge of the bed. The document was requesting identification of an electronics supplier presumed to be located in China. This supplier had produced parts for what looked like an overgrown throw toy for dogs. Most were commonplace computer chips available anywhere, or cylindrical shapes capable of being made from lengths of pipe. There were very few specifications on the electronics: clock, cell phone, electric motor, battery…maybe an antenna.

"From this mash-up of crap they expect me to pinpoint a supplier?" he mumbled.

He sipped coffee and studied the pictures. He opened a drawer and found a pencil with blue lead. On the diagram showing the presumed internals of the device he drew an arrow to the motor and made a note to himself: *at least 100 suppliers. Not helpful.*

He drew a second arrow to the rubber rings on the head—check tread pattern. Might be traceable to a specific mold.

Beside a structure that could be a handle he wrote check dimension and wall thickness, could be unique.

He scratched an oval around the small area of the circular handle where Grease had put the cell phone. He wrote *cell module could be anywhere, why does he think it's here?*

He stopped. Sat up straight. Stared at the diagram.

Cell phone. He reached into his pants pocket, found nothing. He crossed the cottage to his nightstand, pulled a tiny drawer open. Inside he found a cigarette lighter. He picked it up, flicked it, and stared at the open yellow flame. Then he twisted the bottom and pulled its insides out, exposing a row of numbers from zero to nine. He slid it back up into the case. Flicked the lighter again, stared at the flame. Snapped it off.

He took it back to the table and studied the dimensions on the drawing. Slipping the lighter into his pocket he went to a narrow closet and withdrew a light blue shirt and leather boots with steel toes. As he buttoned the shirt he stared at a worn brown leather jacket thinking of 35 degrees of heat, over 95 Fahrenheit back home. He hated the stinky little motorbikes all of Asia seemed to love. And he wasn't a great rider. If he crashed…he reached up and pulled the jacket off its hanger. He stuffed the document into the inside pocket, bent low and reached to the back of the closet. There, he located a sealed yellow envelope, and added it to the jacket.

Outside he threw his leg over a 250cc motorbike of Chinese manufacture, kicked it once, adjusted the choke for the single carburetor, kicked it again and wiggled his right wrist. Swore at the machine, the heat, the jungle and Grease for waking him up. He kicked it again, and it kept running.

For the next forty minutes the rocky shore and calm green waters of the Yong River became his intermittent friend as it twisted away, only to rejoin the road miles later. Between river sightings he bumped over dirt paths through bamboo growth where stalks reached fifty feet high. A Chinese man who pulled a handcart for a living had told him bamboo could grow three feet in a day, and only flowered once every thirty years. Thirty years? Made his jungle-isolated intermittent-trips-to-Nanning love life seem promiscuous.

The vegetation gave way to gray industrial sprawl as the bike sputtered into Nanning, a hundred miles east of the border between China and Vietnam. He pulled onto paved road and crossed the river, watched a complex of three white towers standing beside a tennis court go by, then curved onto a second bridge. To his right, workboats along the shore, their bows pointing directly at the heart of the city, competed for too few docks. He saw an isolated yacht mid-river and wondered which executive was in town, and why he sailed at dawn. After he rolled off the bridge, he counted seventeen yellow stone-block warehouses: all alike. He found the alley adjacent to the eighteenth.

He stopped the bike between large cans of rotting garbage with a squeak of poorly maintained brake, shut it off and listened. Hearing silence, he walked to a dented steel door painted red in the feng shui fashion. He knocked twice, spacing them by more than a second. The door creaked outward and a bent elderly woman looked into his eyes.

Barely above a whisper he said, "Typhoon."

She bowed once slowly and bid him to wait by holding up a finger.

He stood in his leather jacket in spite of heat pressing toward 40 degrees C, stared at the red door, and reminded himself of how well Grease Gun paid for good information.

The door opened.

Two Chinese men he'd bet hadn't yet seen their twentieth birthdays led him down a corridor filled with nothingness—no pictures, no paint, no carpet, just raw materials of sheet rock and flooring— until they arrived at a door. Dragon eyes carved into rich polished cherry wood met his. The dragon's tail slithered the length of the door beside the hinges. The two men departed without a word.

He knocked three times: a single measure from a waltz.

A male voice speaking Mandarin invited the guest to enter.

He opened the door and stepped into an office that could have been located in an executive tower in New York City. His boots made no sound as he crossed plush carpet toward a Chinese man sitting at a wide desk wearing a white suit suitable for summer heat, though the office was cooled to a comfortable 23 degrees Centigrade. Two ancient paintings of a single-oared sampan gliding through river mist adorned the walls. They were not reproductions.

"Hello, my friend," the Chinese man said in English. "How may I be of service today?"

"I must find a supplier," Typhoon said as he withdrew the cigarette lighter from his pocket and placed it on the desk. He inserted his left hand into the inside of his jacket and withdrew the yellow envelope. This he placed beside the lighter.

"You enjoy smoking, my friend?" the Chinese man asked with a raised eyebrow.

"Not smoking," Typhoon replied with the hint of a smile, "talking." He touched the lighter and without picking it up, twisted the base and slid out the round cell phone.

"You would like to buy cell phones?"

"I would like to know who manufactures this particular cylindrical phone." He pointed to the device with a thin index finger. "And who has placed a small quantity order in the past six months."

"This may be difficult. But of course I will try," the man said as he reached across his desk and picked up the envelope. "What is small quantity?"

"Perhaps less than a hundred. Certainly less than five hundred."

"Barely prototype units for a cell phone, wouldn't you agree?"

"Yes," said Typhoon, "I do. That's why I hope you can locate the supplier."

"And let us say that I find this supplier of small quantity, and perhaps even find the buyer of small quantity, my friend. What then?"

Typhoon smiled fully this time and pointed at the man's chest. "Another envelope for the supplier," he raised his hand and fanned it out like a jazz dancer, "and five more for the buyer."

The man withdrew a small white handkerchief from his jacket and patted it across his forehead, which was perspiring despite the cool temperature.

"My friend, if he exists, I will find this buyer."

Chapter 16

THE PRESIDENT PACED an oval path at the rear of conference room #3, pausing occasionally to stare at rotating pictures on the ten-foot screen at the front of the room. His mouth moved silently as if he were chewing tobacco and needed to spit.

General Williams stood beside projected images of Billy Norton's big find feeling the chill of air-conditioning melt through his green shirt. He had told the President everything about the Alaska trip, explained his assumptions regarding the construction of the device, and described the active mission to find suppliers. He was waiting for feedback.

Hushed fan motors blended with the muffled whoosh of President Mallor's shiny black shoes scrubbing the carpet. In the dim room, colored light from the screen washed the angular features of the President's face into a cadaver-at-a-disco glow.

Bert Spin sat at the table, observing.

The President stopped walking and spoke to the right wall.

"Do I understand correctly that there is at this moment a person operating under our direction inside China, a country with whom we have friendly economic relations, trying to find the supplier of the parts for what you are suggesting is a mobile IED?"

Billy didn't move.

"How autonomous is this thing? Are we looking at swarm capability in an unmanned ground vehicle? Damn it, I'm trying to fund development of unmanned weapons, for which Petry beats me up daily, and one shows up on our doorstep."

The President paused, chewing. "What the hell are we going to do once you find the supplier?"

Billy forced himself to wait.

"You know we can't be screwing around with the Chinese less than four months before an election, General. That's not even an eye-blink of time in international affairs. If this gets fouled up..." His voice trailed off as he turned and found Billy's gaze.

Billy felt the laser intensity in the President's brown eyes he had seen on television so often. He spoke slowly.

"Mr. President, I understand the risk to your image and the election. However, the incident in Alaska may be a far more challenging problem than an isolated attack. I am attempting to address it with minimum visibility."

The President sighed. "Alaska. Why the hell does someone have to attack Alaska, of all the God-forsaken places, on my watch? There isn't enough oil up there to run the lights in Vegas." He paused and pressed his lips together hard. "What do you mean not isolated?" He pulled a chair from beneath the polished conference table and sat. "What aren't you telling me, Billy?"

Billy spoke quickly, as if reading from a teleprompter, so the President wouldn't lose interest.

"Mr. President, no one has claimed credit for the action in Alaska. Yet, based on the retrieval of this device," he gestured to the screen, "we know it was not an accident. We are faced with a sudden, technically sophisticated attack against the assets of a U.S. corporation. We have no motive, no one making demands, and no leads."

"Keep going, Billy, you're cheering me up."

"But we have an MO. There are two cases on record. Two years ago, a ship docked in the San Francisco harbor sank before it could be unloaded. It contained a large number of custom electronic devices to be delivered to the Army. While not happy, the Army could wait for a second shipment. But the loss sent MiloMicro, a company that had been designing such devices for decades, into Chapter 11 before a settlement could be reached. The insurance company insisted there had been a failure to properly maintain the ship, and went to court rather than pay the claim. No reason for the hull failure was ever found."

"A company bites the dust, so what? It happens all the time, especially to those whackos in California," said the President.

"Eleven months ago, with no warning and no one taking credit, a story was leaked to the press about the failure of security at a Boeing facility that constructs heavy fighter aircraft, notably the new F-555. South Korea had been set to place an order for $6 billion of equipment to be delivered over two years. According to the story, a specialized, custom, essentially irreplaceable machine required for constructing the blades in the plane's engines was destroyed. Details were never disclosed, but the Korean order has still not been placed, and no one knows if Boeing is able to build the 555 or not."

"And this has exactly what to do with Alaska, national security, and my election?"

Billy watched the President's eyes in the flickering light, trying desperately to read what was behind them.

"I believe we are seeing the shadow of a systematic attack on companies that support our military, Mr. President."

The President placed both elbows on the table, folded his hands together in front of his face, and frowned. He remained in silent thought for thirty seconds.

"Three events, General. A machine fails, a boat sinks, idiots bomb the pipeline. Could be green fanatics whose plan backfired for all we know. And you come up with a conspiracy theory about military suppliers. Now I know why I have you watching the terrorists—you don't have a box to think outside of. So, besides the fact that I think you're crazy, what exactly would we do about this systematic attack?"

"I know who it is"

The President stared and began the chewing motion again.

Billy tapped his laptop to replace the picture of the bomb.

"Him," he said.

The President stared at a screen containing rows of numbers, statistical analysis, and one small colored graph. No pictures, just data.

"Who is he?"

"We don't know. Our intelligence hints at someone calling himself The Daemon, sometimes spelled D-A-E, sometimes just D-E. The word refers to a kind of supernatural being between gods and humans. He's been active for at least the past three years. We think he hides in China."

"Why him?" asked the President.

"The activity on the network that we think is him correlates highly with each of the three actions. It begins about forty-five days before the event, peaks a week to two weeks after, then disappears."

The President leaned back in his chair to stretch. He stared at the numbers.

"Activity?"

"I'm speculating, Mr. President. But we've data-mined tens of millions of Internet actions: phone calls, bank accounts, stock market transactions, anything the Patriot Act lets us see," he paused, "and a few other items. There is a correlation between these catastrophic events and segments of the stock market."

Bert Spin, sitting orthogonal to the President, sat motionless, as if the cold air in the room had turned him to ice.

The President bolted upright and blinked repeatedly.

"The stock market? That fool thing correlates with everything, and nothing. All three of the events you described, the pipeline, fighter, ship," the President ticked them off on the fingers of his right hand, "any of those could adversely effect a stock price. Hell, if you're right, and this person is attacking American businesses, the stock price would be the first to go. So what?"

"I want to go after him, Mr. President."

The President drew a deep breath, blew it out as a low whistle.

"You want to go after him based on statistics? On Chinese territory? Have you gone insane? I wouldn't try that even without the election staring me in the face. You remember what happened to Jimmy Carter when he sent helicopters across the desert? And he was trying to free hostages. A military action is out of the question."

Billy spoke carefully. "Mr. President, if this is the third event in a series, there will be a fourth."

The second hand on the clock could be heard ticking.

The President rocked back and forth slowly, his chair squeaking.

"You're right, there can't be. Not now." He paused, studied the screen. "You know I need plausible deniability." He took a deep breath. "Don't get caught. No Nixon audiotapes to be analyzed. No Clinton DNA on a dress. No Hollywood movies about outed CIA agents."

The President stopped rocking.

"And no aftermath publicity making celebrities of elite military units. Disney trademarks *Seal Team 6*. How are we supposed to run a government with so much transparency?" He put both elbows on the table and stared at Billy over clasped hands. "I don't know anything about this. That is, after you show me your plan. When can you have it ready?"

"As soon as I hear from my operative in South China, should be by the end of the week," Billy replied.

"Good, we have a non-meeting next week then. Thank you, General." He turned his head to Spin, and nodded. "Bert." The President stood and exited the room.

Billy started to sigh, but caught Spin watching. He willed himself not to smile.

Chapter 17

JONNY MUNCH SAT ON A WORN leather couch in his one bedroom apartment on the outskirts of Fairbanks. He had picture-in-a-picture on his TV, and a satellite dish that let him watch one channel big, and the other in a little box in the corner. Both were tuned to news channels. Both news channels were showing the fire that had Alaska buzzing. He reached for a handful of Lay's potato chips, the baked kind because they were healthier, and he never tried to eat just one.

His eyes drifted past the TV to the newly dusted empty spot on a pinewood bookshelf. That was where he would put his Pulitzer someday. The day he found the right story, and got the right break. Jonny didn't know what a Pulitzer looked like, or if it would fit in that spot. But all the books said to visualize what you want, and it will help you get there. He was only 24-years old and working freelance for whatever newspaper would publish his stories. The rest he put on his blog *Jonny On The Spot*. He had time.

He turned back to the TV. This could be it: a huge unexplained disaster involving one of the world's largest pipelines. And right at his doorstep.

But how? How could he get the story?

He watched aerial footage of rising black smoke, twisted pipe, and not far away, cars creeping forward like big metal zombies marching on the Capitol. How could he get a closer look at this thing?

He reached for more chips.

Who would have information?

He tapped the chip bag with two fingers, listening to the rhythmic crinkle, and tried to think outside the box. The TV channels switched back to talking heads, almost simultaneously, as if they had both been showing the same live feed. A guy in a suit with a too bright red tie was on one channel and a pretty girl in a suit with too much ruffle was on the other. They sure wouldn't know. They were in a studio someplace while images got beamed behind them from a helicopter.

Jonny stopped chewing.

Of course. No one was closer to the action than chopper pilots. And if they were like those guys in Top Gun, they were macho types that loved to brag.

He reached around the chip bag for his Android tablet and started tapping. The news had said the Forest Service was providing choppers to aid with the effort. So where did they fly out of? Probably all over, but for sure some had to fly from the big Fairbanks International Airport. And the pilots needed a bar to hang out in. Jonny frowned. There was usually an exotic dance club near an airport. But he doubted a pilot looking at women would be able to concentrate. He needed to find something simple, with decent food, and not too far away because pilots worked all kind of odd hours and shifts and stuff.

He started with a ten-mile radius on Google Maps and asked for restaurants. Damn, there were a lot of places to eat. It'd take him a week to visit them all. And what if he showed up, but the pilots were in the air?

He'd go after dark.

He read the names. Nothing sounded like a place he'd want to eat.

He reached for more chips. Rattled the bag. Got a handful of crumbs.

Jetstream. That sounded like a flying place. He kept reading. A dozen entries later he saw Prop Chop. Was that a propeller thing? Like Prop wash, turbulence, that kind of stuff? Then he saw Club Rotor.

He looked up *helicopter* on Wikipedia. Sure enough, the rotor was the big overhead blade. He shut off the TV, crunched the bag, shot for the wastebasket, hit the rim. The bag spun onto the floor, spewing tiny chip crumbs onto his gray carpet.

Later.

He found his black Converse high-tops and tried to decide which jacket would make a flyer want to talk to him. Not a coat and tie, he'd look like a skinny just out of college wannabe journalist, which was too close to what he actually was. Leather? They might think he was pretending to be one of them. He decided on his brownish-olive cross-country ski jacket. It was synthetic, cut short at the waist, and had a stripe across the shoulders like the NASCAR guys wore. He stuffed a narrow notepad into the inside pocket, double-checked that he had a pen, and ran to his old black Jeep.

It started on the first try. He followed the Android's directions to Airport Way, then along it for another five miles. Club Rotor was a wooden structure painted dark green with a huge rotor attached to the roof, as if the building could lift off at a moment's notice. The parking lot was half full: 4WD pickups, a couple of SUV's and one Miata sports car.

He parked next to the Miata.

It looked tiny, and too low for potholed roads. But it was sleek.

He entered through the front door and was glad to see a chalkboard menu behind the bar. The potato chips were wearing off, and he could do a better job of eavesdropping if he could sit quietly and eat. With luck, he'd hear something. With double luck, someone would actually talk to him.

Two blue-felt pool tables were in use just beyond a bar with stool seating for six. Dining tables to his right were occupied. A waitress carrying a platter of beer mugs breezed by and said, "Sit anywhere." He noticed a propeller missing a blade bolted to the wall, an empty table under it. His sneakers stuck to the floor as he crossed the room, hoping he would be within eavesdropping distance of the pool players.

First things first. He studied the chalkboard. Debated burger or pastrami. Figured he could nurse one· of those· big beers for quite awhile. He brought out his notepad and placed it on the table, then flipped pages pretending to look for something. On a blank one he took notes about the place so he'd be able to describe it. He'd much rather take pictures, but a move like that could make his stay short.

He glanced to the left. The wall behind him was a propeller museum, or maybe they were all rotors. The broken one, then shiny silver, and a dark silver, and black, left to right along the long side of the building. He had expected all men, but nearly half of the 31 patrons, counting him, were female. Pretty much everyone wore jeans and a variety of warm shirts. No one was in any kind of flight suit, although he saw a number of cool jackets he'd like to have in dark greens and blacks with patches on them.

"Hi, what can I get ya?"

The waitress stood beside him. She was also wearing jeans, and a dark blue T-shirt with *Going up?* across the front in orange letters.

"Pastrami or burger. Which do you recommend?"

She touched the end of her ballpoint to her lips and paused. "I think the burger today. We got a delivery from the butcher and he was raving about this Kobe stuff."

He nodded. "Burger it is. And a light ale."

"Gotcha," she said, scribbling and walking away at the same time.

He realized he hadn't been listening to the crowd, so while writing a description of the rotor wall, he tuned in.

"Yes, she was hot. Army. And hot." A male voice from the far pool table.

"What is an Army babe doing in Fairbanks?" Different voice.

"Yeah. And talking to you, Sammy?" Third voice.

"She was riding in my aircraft because of my obviously superior stick handling," Sammy said.

Jonny wrote: *Army girl*. Not understanding why that might matter.

The second voice. "Stick handling. I heard you almost crashed the thing when the lady tried to escape."

Laughter...and the crack of an opening break.

"She wasn't trying to escape," Sammy said. "She was yelling down, down."

"So you went down," the third voice said. "No wonder you almost crashed."

More laughter. The clack of balls.

The going-up waitress returned with his beer and a nice smile. Jonny nodded while scratching notes about yelling down.

"You guys are missing it. I'm telling you, this girl was beautiful, and she was here with brass from Washington. A General or something," Sammy said.

"Or something."

Jonny couldn't make out the speaker. He wrote General and felt his Pulitzer meter nudge up. Brass in Alaska? Sure, the pipeline, but why?

"I'll tell you this," Sammy said. A pause. The crack of a cue stick. "Whatever exploded scared the bejesus out of me. I'm holding low, the screaming Army bitch jumps out and seconds later whammo, blinding light and noise. Took me back to Nam."

"You put Army babes down in Nam?" the second voice said.

"You ever think of anything else, Chuck?" Sammy replied. "I mean, you know, like once a month just to prove you can still do it?"

"Chuck doesn't waste his brain like that. Doesn't have much to spare," the third voice said.

Jonny was staring at the word explosion on his pad when the waitress lowered a plate with a sizzling burger, thick potato wedges and lettuce and tomato off to the side.

"Need anything?"

He shook his head, not really thinking about food. He reached for the beer and took a slow sip, trying to put a picture together of what Sammy was talking about.

The rumble of voices from the room to his left continued, but the pool players had fallen silent except for the click of balls. Jonny was halfway through his burger, which he thought was a hell of a lot better than the ones he made with ground beef from Walmart, before the guys started talking.

"So, Sammy." He thought it might be Chuck's voice. "How did you end up with an Army bitch trying to get you killed when you're supposed to be helping us fight fires?"

Click-click. "I figure this babe must have called and requested me." A chuckle. Another click. "My boss got a call from the Governor to ferry VIPs from the airport. I caught it because I happened to be refueling and was due out in thirty minutes. They put the hurry up on the ground crew and sent me over in fifteen."

"Ooh...VIP Army babe requests Sammy's stick," Chuck said. "Did you tweet that?"

"Hah," Sammy said.

"Where to?" the unnamed voice said.

Jonny stopped chewing so he could hear better.

"Get this. The VIPs want to see the pipeline. But then some local cop hands me an address, and suddenly I'm a taxi service to a shack outside Nolan."

Balls clicked once.

"You lose," Chuck said. "Pay the lady for the beer."

Jonny finished his burger staring at his scribbled Nolan, which he knew was to the north, but he didn't know how far. Or what he was really looking for, though his meter nudged up another notch.

Chapter 18

CLAIRE INSERTED A KEY into the oak door of Billy's fourth floor condo. As she pushed it open and dragged luggage through the doorway she heard a TV announcer promise she could lose twenty pounds in only six weeks. She glanced at the time.

"Damn, it's already after eight," she called toward the den. "Fucking traffic."

"Did I hear someone refer to fertility rituals?" a distant voice replied.

She smiled, dropped the bags and danced around the corner. As she entered Billy was closing the briefcase he had taken to Alaska. He looked up as he snapped it shut, spinning the combination wheels in an automatic move to lock it.

"How was the match?" he asked.

"I finished third out of two hundred and fifty. But I beat a loudmouthed, misogynistic creep named Putnam."

"Sergeant Cam Putnam of Special Forces? I've heard he's good."

She grinned wide. "Maybe at badminton. I stomped him."

"Good for you. Dinner?" he asked.

"You bet."

"Want to change first?"

"Are you kidding, I'm starved. Let's get out of here."

Ten minutes later they were parking the General's gray sedan in front of her favorite sushi bar: The Raw Meet. Five minutes after that they had ordered Asahi Super Dry for him, Sapporo for her, and an assortment of raw fish draped over rice.

"What have you found out?" she asked.

"About what, dear?"

"On Monday I'm chasing a crazed robot with a chopper, and on Sunday you say, 'About what, dear?'"

He gestured toward the flat TV on the wall, silent, but with closed captions jerking along the bottom.

"Haven't you been watching the news? Exxon and friends proclaimed it a freak accident. A structural flaw in support welding coupled with weird vibration from a failed pump set off a chain reaction. You know, like dominoes." He poked at her shoulder, "Push one and click click, they all fall down."

She looked asquint at him as he drank. "Fell down and just happened to catch fire? In the middle of the night?"

"Once one of them caught fire..." he shrugged.

She studied his face. "You don't believe a word of it."

She swigged Sapporo from the bottle and turned to watch the sushi chef's knives flash on the other side of the partition. She glanced at the TV. Weather maps shifted across the screen. Billy said nothing so she rotated toward him, put one leg on the footrest of his stool, and rubbed it against him.

He finally said, "I didn't say I believed it. I just asked if you had seen the news."

"So, tell me. What's really going on?" she whispered.

"You know I can't."

"You can't? Me? Girl Corporal. Keeps you warm at night. Why?"

He waved a hand. "Not exactly a secure area."

Claire saw the weather pattern on the TV become a talking head of an Afro-American woman wearing round glasses.

"To quote the Beatles, 'Yeah, yeah, yeah.' At least tell me what you found out about that silver thing. It looked amazing before the kaboom." She laughed and aligned chopsticks in her left hand to attack the Suzuki.

"In Alaska you saw the reconstruction of, uh, the toy. We've been working backwards to find suppliers."

"And?" she mumbled through a mouth full of rice and sea bass with double wasabi.

"And," he mumbled back at her, laughing. "We might have a supplier for a certain component."

She finished chewing and swallowed. "So?" she said clearly.

"That tells us where it was manufactured."

"No kidding?" She stopped her beer in mid swing. "Where?"

"China."

She brought her chopstick hand to her mouth in mock surprise.

"Oh, wow! That narrows it down to nine million square kilometers. You've got it pinpointed there, General."

She sipped.

"I'm glad you're amused. This is not easy, you know."

"That's right, we're trained professionals, don't try this at home." She burst out laughing, spewing bits of rice at his pants and attracting the attention of an Asian woman in a black skirt sitting in front of a bowl of miso soup. Claire put her hand over her mouth, struggling to be quiet.

"See if I tell you anything else. Like where in China. Or who in China. No more secret information for you."

She pouted, pushing out her lower lip. "Are you going to be mean?"

He huffed.

"Hey, speaking of his toy, how's the little guy doing?" she asked.

"Classified."

She scowled at him and tapped her chopsticks repeatedly against the sushi plate because she knew it irked him.

"Okay, stop the torture" he said. "We know the location of the factory that built a particular component. We found only one plant that manufactures it, so we're quite confident." He paused and took a long swallow of beer. He placed his glass on the counter. "Situation is unchanged on our little friend, but he's back home now."

That meant the little guy still wasn't talking. Not right for a kid.

"Does he have a good doctor?"

Billy nodded. "Army people are up there now. He's getting plenty of attention." He turned to face her. "And yes, they are keeping an eye on him."

"Do you think he's scared?"

"You met him."

She shook her head. "No, he wouldn't get scared. He'd step up and try to help his Uncle Sam."

They ate in silence, the woman on the TV still talking.

She leaned over and whispered, "So how does this manufacturer help us?"

"It doesn't."

"It doesn't?" The sea bass slipped from her chopsticks and splashed in the soy sauce.

"It's like knowing that the lug nut from the right rear wheel of a Honda Civic was made at a particular plant in China along with millions of similar lug nuts. How would that help you?"

"I thought the Honda was built in Ohio?" she said, smiling.

"I'm ignoring you."

She thought hard. "The People's Republic of China is behind this?" she whispered.

He ignored her.

"No, probably not. They export lots of stuff to us."

"And buy our treasury bonds," he said.

She sipped her beer and bounced ideas around inside her head. So parts for that machine had been made in China. In fact, in a specific place in China. Why didn't that help with the *Who done it?*

The woman was replaced by another talking head, one she recognized. She elbowed Billy.

"Petry is back. How many press conferences does this guy do in a day?"

She and Billy tilted their faces to the screen.

"Lack of oversight on the pipeline. Cleanup equals new taxes. Global warming melts permafrost. What doesn't he talk about?" she asked.

"He's taking the opportunity to get noticed without paying for television time. Watch, he'll pitch himself shortly."

"What's that?" she asked, as images of a strange aircraft with a downturned tail and a propeller at the back replaced Petry. She read softly. "The unmanned Predator is combat equipped with Hellfire missiles, and strikes targets by following programmed coordinates. This is what your tax dollars build—machines to kill. I believe we are on an unsafe and expensive road. The disaster in Alaska is not the first warning event. If elected I promise to reduce—"

"Told you so," Billy said.

She watched the plane fly, thought about its range. Wondered if there would be a job for a sniper in the new hi-tech Army. Then she thought about the location of the part.

"Maybe he lives close to the plant?" she suggested.

"Or maybe he lives across the street from The Raw Meet, and is at this very moment wishing he had air conditioning to escape this crummy heat. China exports a trillion dollars worth of goods every year, Claire. He could be anywhere."

"Damn," she said. "It feels like we're so close."

"We are." He picked up her bottle, and tipped it to refill his empty glass.

Chapter 19

TYPHOON LAY SHIRTLESS listening to the ping of summer rain on the metal roof. Grease was anxious this time, pushing for results in unrealistic time frames. Typhoon had quick success in tracing the cellular device only because he had been lucky. Cylindrical cell phones were rare, but he happened to have one. And it led directly to the manufacturer.

But that's not who he needed to find.

He rolled onto his back and lit another cigarette, his third in under an hour.

He knew where the pieces had been manufactured in Southern China. Grease thought they had ended up in Alaska. There must be a way to connect them.

The phone bleeped.

"Yes?"

"Hello, my friend, I have some good news for you."

He recognized the voice of the white-suited man he had sought out earlier that day.

"Any news is welcome."

"You mentioned a region of North America that interests you. Perhaps you are considering a vacation there?"

"Yes," he agreed. "If the climate is right for fishing."

"The climate is very good. My colleague tells me of forty species, near a town far to the North."

"And where might that be?" he asked.

"Did you know that China itself has sub-arctic regions? We have a very large country indeed."

"I see." He hated the way Chinese circled the point. "Will it cost a great deal?"

"Sadly. Are you interested in such a fine vacation? It will be well worth it."

He used the code name for the first time.

"Mr. Renminbi, whatever is needed to locate these fishes, I will provide for you."

"Excellent, my friend. I will deliver details when we meet. But I wish to tell you this. Forty fishes each swam a separate way, but all arrived on a horse that could no longer be ridden."

"Thank you, I will visit soon."

He hung up, uncovered his computer and activated a satellite link. He asked for a list of major cities in Alaska. None contained the word "horse."

He searched for Horse, Alaska. Got a hit for Tanadgusix Corporation, in Wikipedia of all places.

"Enough chimpanzees," he muttered.

Tanadgusix was a shareholder-owned Aleut Village Corporation over a quarter century old on Saint Paul Island. He scanned the copy and found that they operated a natural gas power plant on the North Slope in a place called Deadhorse.

Google told him Dead Horse was a thrash metal band from Texas, and a tiny industrial camp on the North Slope. The description sounded like a form of hell: no alcohol, no entertainment, no mall, no food store, near the Arctic Ocean. But there was a Post Office: Deadhorse AK 99734.

"Forty naked cell-phone modules shipped one at a time by multiple couriers to Deadhorse."

He tapped keys lightly, creating rhythm in the silence, wondering how much he could charge this time.

Chapter 20

FROM INSIDE THE TENT he heard three rising tones. Fumbling the screen's zipper, he reached the bike on the fifth repetition. He opened the case next to the satellite antenna and plugged the bud into his ear.

"Hello, Maxx."

"Greetings, Firesnake. Project Honeypot update. The fish have been delivered to the fryer."

"Acknowledged. Portfolio?"

"Down 5.6% over the past forty-eight hours, maximum 13.4%, minimum 0.8%. Five day moving average: down 8.1%. Trading moderate across holdings. Heaviest on XOM. Sufficient to cover."

He glanced up at a sky that had finally become night. Brilliant stars peered back, tiny white eyes watching his every move. How long should he wait? He counted stars and picked a number. Eight felt right.

"Proceeds?" he asked.

"53.26 million U.S. at current exchange rate."

"Shares pending?"

"13.51 million, average unrealized gain of $11.32 per share," Maxx replied.

"Slow cover to eighty percent."

"Confirm alteration to cover at eighty percent. Time to completion, forty-four days."

"Thanks, Maxx. Anything else?"

"No other activity."

He removed the bud from his ear and watched the tiny screen report the series of phone numbers that had been used to make the connection, turn them red and erase each one so it wouldn't be used again.

He was tired, but not weary, nothing four or five hours of sleep wouldn't cure. The crisp Alaskan air satisfied his lungs. He gazed down the pass he and his bike had climbed up from the Yukon. On the road less than a week, the travel rugged and slow, some experts would claim impossible, on a 500-pound two-wheeled machine. The challenge relaxed him as he dealt with this latest complication.

He crawled into an expedition tent more capable than he hoped would be needed, and zipped the mosquito screen behind him. He dug deep in his pack for the map of Russia and spread it on the ground. He sat cross-legged and meditated calmly, inhaling breath consciously and chanting softly with each exhalation. His eyes roamed to absorb details of roads, elevation changes, rivers—and the names: Anadyr, Kamenskoye, Evensk.

Tomorrow he would find the Russian fisherman.

Chapter 21

TYPHOON STOOD BESIDE his black motorbike outside his shack, smoking one last cigarette. Darkness had descended, but he was awaiting the arrival of the deep, silent part of night when most were asleep and the few out roaming more concerned about being discovered than discovering. He dropped the cigarette on the dirt and pressed it out. He pulled on a black helmet and flipped a yellow shield over his eyes. Damn insects.

The 76-degree air felt cool as he motored northeast toward Nanning and a certain manufacturer of electronic communication equipment. He favored the unpaved ox paths, where hooves would obscure tire tracks within twenty-four hours.

After two hours of buzzy travel he saw a bulge of light pollution on the horizon. After three he was climbing the last hill between him and the target, his arms sore and butt numb from so long on a small machine. When he crowned the hill he silenced the engine, doused the narrow slit of headlight and began a downward glide. Two kilometers later he dismounted and quietly pushed the bike off the trail.

He knelt beside the machine and withdrew a yellow paper from his pocket. He oriented the pencil sketch to align with the building before him, made gray by a sliver of moon. What he sought was on the second floor. He looked up. The yard behind the building was smeared with light from three windows to his left and one on the second floor, to his right. Refolding the paper he moved to the fence.

He slithered up the fence and over the razor wire, the jacket and gloves protecting him. He dropped silently to the dirt, and moved along the fence in shadow until reaching a gray steel door. With his back to it, and scanning the surrounding hill for movement, he withdrew a box from his pocket and placed it an inch above the lock. He took a step sideways and listened to the sizzling sound of a burger on a too hot grill. When it stopped he turned and pulled the handle with both hands. The lock provided no resistance.

Inside, his rubber soles moved swiftly across polished linoleum. With the map in his mind's eye he glided down a hallway, turned left, took twenty steps and moved into a stairwell. Open steel stairs carried him upward. He stopped at the top, listened, pulled the door open and moved into the corridor. No sound. Thirty-two paces to his right he reached a wood door. He inserted a key. It failed. He inserted the next on his ring. It too failed. Eighteen keys later the knob turned.

He eased the door closed behind him and heard his breathing inside the helmet. The quiet, steady hum of computers surrounded him. He flipped up the face shield and sat down at the first machine. Forty-eight attempts using names favored by network administrators yielded nothing. The forty-ninth, Gninnan, password gninnan, opened a user account. A text search revealed nothing related to the names he was seeking.

He froze.

Footsteps and male Chinese voices approached. They spoke of parties, comparing the qualities and attendees of each. One mentioned an upcoming gathering hosted by a customer who appreciated excellent service. They spoke of a female coworker and their desire to use her body. Footfalls passed the door, shadows flashed along the doorjamb. He sat boneyard still, aiming a silenced Glock at the entrance. One man thanked the other for helping on a weekend so he could keep his job under the overbearing prick he worked for. They laughed.

Footfalls receded. Typhoon guessed they wouldn't use the shipping entrance. Renminbi had assured him the building would be empty this weekend.

He searched desk drawers and folders. He found a note attached to the underside of the lowest drawer in the corner desk. It held six passwords; there were six machines in the room. Sloppy security, the very reason he had decided to visit.

All six machines opened. Searches for the names provided by Renminbi revealed billing documents, shipping notifications, e-mails, account balances. Everything seemed proper for a manufacturing business. Except each of the forty had only ever ordered a single part from the company—a cell module to be delivered to addresses in Alaska.

He retrieved each document, focused his eyes on its center, and pressed a small button on the side of his helmet. His wrist chronograph vibrated indicating he had only a few minutes remaining in his allotted schedule. He logged off each machine in succession, replacing chairs and keyboards, knowing if someone looked they would find breadcrumbs. Best they weren't motivated.

As he reached the sixth his search returned another document. He sat down. *You are invited to the celebration of our great success in North America.* There were GPS coordinates. And a signature: *Deacon Wong.*

A customer, or supplier? What did *our success* mean? The recipient was one of his forty. He snapped its picture.

He checked the time: two and a half minutes overdue. He repeated the search for the second of the names and was rewarded with an identical invitation. He searched for the content of the invitation and found exactly forty records, one for each name on his list.

He shut the machine down and hustled to the door, now over six minutes behind schedule. Thirty quick steps placed him at the top of the stairwell. He raced down, pausing to listen before opening the door to the corridor. A few yards later he made the final right turn toward the shipping entrance and froze.

Twenty yards in front of him two men spoke in hushed tones, gesturing at the melted lock. He retraced his steps until he could press himself against the wall.

"What could have melted steel?"

"Someone wanted inside badly."

"Break into this old building?"

"They will think we did it."

"Why? We have a key to the front."

"They'll think we wanted to steal something large."

"They'll know we were here."

"Not if we leave quickly."

"But we've been working."

"Monday very early, we work then. Tell no one about today."

"We must not be here if police arrive."

He moved backward to an office door, fumbled keys until it unlocked and stepped inside. With the door open slightly he aimed carefully, and fired one round.

A light bulb covered by wire mesh exploded deep in the recesses of the building. He pulled the door closed. The voices stopped. He heard the two men run past the office he occupied. He counted to five to give them time— wanting no stories of a tall stranger.

Silence.

He watched the luminescent hand of his watch tick ten seconds.

He opened the door. With smooth silent strides he moved to and through the shipping door. He ran across the dirt lot, climbed the fence effortlessly and dropped low into the brush, crawling the remaining distance to his bike.

He looked back. The building sat dark, silent, like an oil painting. Exactly as he had found it, light streaming from four windows. No sign of the workers. He kicked the bike alive and started up the hill, keeping his speed low. At the top he took a long last look back.

Chapter 22

SNIPE—OFF TO BACKGROUND briefing for big-A fire. See you for dinner if you can get back in time.—B.

So Billy was at a Monday meeting and she had slept late instead of practicing, her insides overwound from the tournament and wanting time away from bullets. She pulled open the freezer, felt cold soak through her robe, and grabbed the Peet's. She loaded the coffee maker and was about to shower when the obvious hit her. Billy was at a briefing, which meant his organization was pursuing it. Therefore, someone higher up agreed it wasn't an accident. She thought about the briefcase.

What was inside? Should she try to find out? Would he tell her?

She didn't like secrets—made her feel like she was living with a spy. And he was just protecting the information, not hiding it from her.

She twirled on the balls of her feet and headed for the den. Of course, he would have taken it to the briefing, so she wouldn't find anything anyway.

She stopped in the doorway.

It was lying at an angle on the left side of the desk.

Closed.

She walked slowly through the room, which wasn't off limits to her, exactly, though he seemed to know if she so much as disturbed the dust. She sat in his leather chair and jumped at the big squeak as it rocked. She laughed. She hadn't even done anything. She was just sitting in a chair.

Just sitting in a chair staring at a briefcase wondering how to get inside. Three simple latches, but if she touched it her fingerprints would be on them. She slipped her hands into the oversized pockets of her robe, but stopped six inches from the case when she realized the fibers in the cloth could be traced.

This wasn't as easy as it looked in the movies.

She stood and surveyed the office for something to cover her hands. She caught sight of herself in a mirrored bookcase. Her reflection asked if she really wanted to crack open her boyfriend's briefcase to find out what was happening with a classified situation.

Yes. And what the government planned to do about it.

She shuffled across the carpet and opened the folding doors to the closet. Three pairs of gloves were stacked on a shelf to the right. She slipped into Billy's driving gloves. Back at the desk she pried at the snaps.

Locked.

She looked up with a start. Just after noon. What time would he be home? She inhaled slowly through her nostrils and blew out through pursed lips.

The case had numbered dials like her bicycle lock in middle school. Only there were nine of them. She dropped into the soft leather chair and laid her head back. Nine digits? That was a big number. But she thought about it. Free associate. Pretend you're Billy. Nine digits was almost a phone number.

She sat up and tried the first nine digits of the number for Billy's apartment. She tried the last nine digits. She tried reverse order. She tried her cell phone number. His cell phone number. First nine, last nine, forward, backward.

Nothing.

She leaned back again and closed her eyes. It had to be something he could remember. Nine digits. What the hell was nine-digits long? Three groups of three, he would like the symmetry of that.

She chuckled.

36-24-36. *That* he could remember.

She sat up sharply.

She ran to the bedroom and dragged out her laptop. Those numbers converted to 914-610-914 in millimeters. Back to the den.

Locked.

She stared at the little dials peeking from the side of the black case.

He wouldn't.

She converted 34, then 23, and finally 35, numbers he had acquired one night when they had been playing with a tape measure. She worked the tiny gold dials with the large leather gloves. 864...584...889. She held her breath.

Click. Click. Click.

Love him or hate him?

She tilted the case open. His portable computer lay atop a handful of papers. The chip was there. She held the case with her right hand, and lifted it from the pocket with the left. She carried the chip in the palm of her gloved left hand and walked gingerly to the bedroom. She desperately wanted to know what was on it, but if she put it into a computer a messy trail of bits would be created. Alternatives did not present themselves. She frowned, stared at the chip, and kicked herself for not thinking ahead.

Her body made a suggestion.

She placed her left hand on the bed and slipped the glove off. She was still peeing when a loud knock surprised her. Leaning forward, she could see the glove on the bed like a disconnected robot hand.

But Billy wouldn't knock. Unless he forgot his key.

She placed the left glove into the top drawer of her dresser. Racing to the den she smoothly closed the lid of the briefcase with her gloved right hand. A few steps later she was at the front door hiding the glove in the pocket of her robe.

"Who is it?" she asked, holding her breath.

"Post Office. Need a signature."

Her body relaxed. She opened the door and accepted a Priority Mail box from the courier, dutifully signing her name where indicated.

"Thank you," she said.

He touched his blue cap and walked away.

Addressed to her and postmarked Port Clinton. Later, she decided. She carried the package to her dresser and placed it in the same drawer as the chip. She tried to imagine what she would find on the chip and what her options were after she found out whatever it was she was going to find out.

She slipped her left hand into the glove to retrieve the chip. She crossed the floor, the rug scratchy under her bare feet, and sat on the bed to focus. She needed a computer that could be wiped clean inside and out, no bits lying about to be retrieved by experts.

She thought about Billy's laptop. It had already seen this data. But her access might be noted and he would know someone had used the machine. She looked at her laptop on the bed displaying the last inch to millimeter conversion. If they confiscated the machine and put forensic people on it they would surely find something she didn't know how to hide.

She poked at the chip until it flipped over. Her eyes drifted around the room, landing on the case in the corner.

Maybe.

She dragged the box onto the bed and assembled the rifle with one hand. She verified the chamber was clear and studied the slot used to save settings for the onboard target computer that compensated for wind, humidity, and other stuff that could affect the trajectory of a bullet. Hoping she wouldn't damage it she aligned the chip with the slot. Holding her breath, she pressed gently. It disappeared into her weapon.

With two fingers of her right hand crossed for luck she raised the rifle to her left eye and pressed the button to tell the computer to load data. Instantly the sight filled with text. She brought her right knee up to hold the weapon and read as fast as possible.

Communication component traced to manufacturing facility in SOUTHERN CHINA.

Identity of buyer UNVERIFIABLE. Forty parts ordered by forty different, unrelated, individuals.

Delivery to Prudhoe Bay, Alaska via separate shipments over TWO-WEEK period.

Method of operation resembles two PREVIOUS ACTIONS against American multinational corporations (both unsolved).

Method of operation consistent with activities of unnamed individual believed to use the CODE NAME Daemon (alternate spellings: daimon, demon).

NO picture, address, alias, or identification records available.

She continued scanning: estimates to repair the pipe of $4 billion and almost two years. Simulation of explosions along the pipeline in a chain reaction—sequenced to spread crude. She found a graph of the stock price of the ten major oil producers in the world. All were down.

She lowered the rifle.

They were chasing a shadow.

But Billy was after someone specific. Not someone he could define, but a person, not an organization or foreign country. She thought about how to go about exploding two hundred miles of pipeline without being seen, lifted the rifle and continued speed-reading.

Project DEMON DROP.

Infiltration behind Great Wall.

No identification.

Absolute Zero tolerance on public exposure.

Elimination.

She swallowed. A mission inside China to assassinate a person they couldn't name. She ejected the chip into her glove. It felt oddly heavy and dangerous. She slipped it back into the case, and reset the dials.

She stared at the closed briefcase, her chest feeling like it was being pressed between angry sumo wrestlers. This was far different from winning rifle matches. A hot sensation spread across her chest and down the back of her legs.

She returned to the bedroom and was about to remove her robe when the open drawer caught her eye. The postman. She retrieved the package and pulled the string to reveal a gift-wrapped package and card.

Slipping the card from its envelope she was greeted by an exploded view of an SX-16M rifle in 3D. It looked like the CAD data for the weapon, but with subtle color and soft lines to give it a hand drawn look. She flipped it open:

Hello Hot Shot— Five of five is impressive. Truly. Sorry for playing the macho asshole on the Ohio range, but you must admit beautiful women who can shoot like you are few. Please accept the enclosed peace offering and consider having dinner with me at the next match.

Bang,

Cam P.

P.S. You finished third, so don't let your pretty head swell.

She slit the wrapping paper to reveal a chocolate rifle surrounded by twenty rounds of white chocolate bullets, and a tiny trophy wrapped in gold foil.

Chapter 23

MORNING LIGHT STREAMED through the screen. Typhoon sat in white boxer shorts sweating, his back stiff from riding. He had found the expected. Except for the invitations. They might represent new opportunity. If so, time was short.

He hesitated, nervous about initiating contact. He connected the phone in his lighter to a cable. It was attached to an antenna on the shack's roof he had personally concealed in an iron weather vane the shape of a Chinese junk. With it he could reach a satellite, which could relay to another secure satellite, which would reach another, without ever passing through Chinese censorship computers.

He entered security codes.

The tiny display on the phone scrolled as it tracked the progress of his call.

Seconds passed before the transmission found a reliable path through the satellites and the image stabilized. Streetlights flitted past in the background, but only a dark silhouette of a head was visible. No eyes. No face. Nothing recognizable. Like always.

"I apologize for interrupting," Typhoon said.

"You risk a great deal," replied the man he knew only as Grease Gun. "You have reasons?"

"Timing. I reached the target. Forty orders were present, but they were the only ones. Have the names led anywhere?"

"Yes," replied Gun. "Middle class Americans, a French couple vacationing on the Mediterranean, a retired Japanese man in an apartment in Tokyo. Not one has ever heard of Deadhorse."

"Not involved?" he asked, annoyed that his information wasn't useful. Concerned he might not be paid.

"There are many explanations," Gun said. "The obvious: identities were stolen and used for Firesnake."

Typhoon remained silent for a moment. "Why invitations if these people aren't involved? You've seen the images?"

"Why an invitation at all? Does Mr. Wong just love a party?"

"Are forty people secretly being reached, each monitoring a stolen identity?" asked Typhoon.

"You're the communication expert."

Typhoon nodded. "I think yes. Orders, invoices, this crazy invitation. Nothing else refers to the forty names."

"Then we have a party to attend."

"I will arrange for invitations using my photographs. How many?" asked Typhoon.

"Only one. For a woman."

"Done. Do you want me there?"

"You're our best chance for identification."

"Next Saturday. Barely over a week."

"Enough time depends on our strategy. Where?" Gun asked.

"In the jungle near nothing. Closest city is Kontum."

"South Vietnam? Why?"

He wished he could see Gun's eyes. But he knew the question was rhetorical.

"The invitation provides GPS coordinates. I've checked topology. No easy way in on pavement, and landing an aircraft would be a magic trick."

"I'll check up my sleeve," said Gun. "How does he expect guests to arrive?"

"The invitation suggests SUV or all-terrain vehicle. It includes the comment: *Free valet.*" Typhoon laughed, imagining dozens of SUV's parked in a tropical forest.

"Have your suit pressed."

"I'll be ready," Typhoon said, thinking about how much he could bill for his additional involvement.

Chapter 24

"*BILLY, I HOPE YOU'RE HERE* to tell me something creative about Alaska," President Mallor said. "We're only having this insanely early breakfast because I'm losing two points a day since that pipe puked on Forest Service land. I need to take action. Another catastrophe will be the end of my campaign—"

He met Billy's eyes across a dining table holding salmon, fresh fruit, scrambled eggs and a tall stack of pancakes.

"And your gravy train."

Billy hadn't slept. He had been given a gift from the gods of war and had spent all night devising a strategy to take advantage of it. He poured iced apple juice down his throat to punch up his energy, and dove in.

"Mr. President. I have solid intel that will put the gentleman we discussed at a specific time and place. This unusual opportunity is imminent. We should send a welcoming committee."

President Mallor held Billy's eyes. "Will this committee be able to convince our friend to cooperate?"

"Armed drones. Attack helicopters. There is solid precedent from prior administrations for dealing with external threats. I'm certain we could be quite convincing."

The President stuck a fork through chunks of pancakes and rolled them in 100% Vermont maple syrup. He chewed. The corner of his eyes hardened.

"But can you be invisible?"

"Completely, Mr. President."

Mallor picked up a cup of black coffee and washed down the pancakes.

"Impossible," he said.

Billy gritted his teeth. Civilians were bad. Civilians with political power the worst.

"Correct, Mr. President. We would, however, take all possible precautions: small team, obtuse orders, no named geography. Time within borders is less than twenty-four hours. Possibly as low as twelve."

The President twirled his half-empty coffee cup on the table.

"You'll leave a trail. A hyper-energetic Post reporter lusting for a Pulitzer will find it."

"This will be classified for at least twenty-five years. What records exist won't reveal anything." He paused, wanting to add, needing to add, finally adding, "If you let me run it my way."

The President returned to soaking up Vermont's finest, his fork moving slowly.

"I've been losing sleep over that device. Small, mobile, remotely activated, capable of inflicting serious damage—a damn landmine on steroids. You're a student of history, Billy, remember World War II?"

The President paused; Billy assumed he wanted an answer.

"Armored war. Million of mines buried by both sides. Dozens of complex designs. Took years to demine, mostly by German POWs."

The President nodded. "What you showed me promises to be worse." He sipped coffee, glanced at a clock. "We need to be leading the race to robotic weapons...not following." His fork stopped moving. "Fifty countries are developing machines. Machines that empower small groups to do big things." He took a slow breath. "We stay ahead with proper investment, or our security situation deteriorates. But to do any of this, I must win. Petry will kill it all."

The President lifted his pancakes.

"Nothing, absolutely nothing can happen."

He stared at Billy without moving for long seconds; syrup dripped from his fork onto the edge of the plate.

"We make nothing happen. And we guarantee this friend makes nothing happen."

The President shifted in his chair, lowered his fork without eating.

"Like I said before, no tapes, no DNA." He paused. "I know that's a tall order."

"We have an opportunity that will not be repeated, Mr. President."

Chapter 25

JONATHON KATOW CHEWED seasoned potatoes between sips of Ikon vodka on the middle deck of a steel ship ferrying across the Bering Straight. Striped with rust streaks, it shook with a constant vibration only a nymphomaniac could love.

He smelled soot as he watched low buildings on a dirt street grow nearer: Uelen, population 500, the closest Russian city to the United States. He thought about bored guards, loading ramps designed for cars, foreigners asking questions—small things causing large delays. He now had a deadline; the boy had caused a disturbance in his universe.

The ship banged the pier. Then nothing happened. No gangplank, no one disembarked and no friends arrived to meet the ship. All was quiet, as if they had docked on a deserted island.

He clanged down stairs to the vehicle deck and made his way between muddy trucks to his bike. The restraints were still tight, all the way from the western shore of Alaska. He mounted, leaned against the pack across the rear fender, and stretched his legs over the handlebars—knowing he was on bureaucracy time.

A truck engine echoing in the steel cavern woke him. The soft light of dusk glowed through portholes in the steel infrastructure. He tapped the multi-function GPS on the handlebars with his boot, and fired up the bike. He released straps, dropped into gear and weaved between parked vehicles until stopping behind a blue Ford pickup with a bent rear bumper. Looking straight through its cab, he could see a man in green overalls waving flashlights with orange heads.

He followed the truck to the bow of the MT-22 cargo ship to a ramp slanted down to a concrete road. He glanced at scattered gray clouds then at damp steel. Dragging his boots he crept along behind the Ford until he was safely on concrete and stopped in a line of cars waiting to clear customs.

He wished for sunshine. A man in a uniform with a red patch wearing a clear overcoat walked along the row of cars talking to each driver. When he reached the bike he shook his head.

"You must be American," the customs man said.

He nodded.

"Papers for the machine?" He waved the capped end of a ballpoint at the bike.

He removed a Gortex pouch from his jacket, cleared his mind of Jonathon Katow and prepared to enter Russia as Richard Tonver. He unzipped the pouch and showed the bike's Minnesota registration, a passport for Tonver, and a visitor's visa through a clear plastic window.

The uniformed man took the whole pouch. Richard pushed up his helmet so his face could be matched to the passport Wan Tong had made for him.

The man leaned over to examine the bike.

"How far you ride this?"

"About 2000 kilometers so far," he answered. "But this is the first rain." He smiled, trying to appreciate the fine Russian weather.

"Where you go?"

"London, England."

The official's eyes widened. "Very far," he said, the tone of his voice communicating that anyone who would ride a motorbike such a distance must be unbalanced. "Why you go?"

An image flashed behind his eyes. Green waving rice, dirt road, warmth of a hand, the sun, noise in his ears, falling, falling...

He blinked hard.

"Business...to take pictures." He tapped his side case. "And pleasure, I like to ride."

"What's your business in Russia?"

"I am following the path of Ewan and Charley."

The man frowned.

"Ewan McGregor the actor. You know, Obi-wan from Star Wars. And his friend Charley Boorman."

"Ah, Star Wars, yes Mr. Kanobi. My son likes him," the man said, nodding.

"He rode through here years ago. Called the trip *The Long Way Round*. I'm following the same roads, only in the opposite direction."

The man smiled. Respect? Incredulity? Hard to tell. But he handed the pouch back.

"Good luck on your ride, Mr. Tonver. You take nice pictures of Mother Russia. Show the world our beauty."

"Thank you, I'll do my best."

He gave a broad smile before lowering his helmet, wishing he really were taking pictures so he could honor the man's patriotism.

The official stepped back and held up one hand to stop traffic from behind. Then he pointed at Richard with his pen cap and waved him out of line and toward the front to the guard station.

He rode carefully past the line of muddy cars and trucks, knowing that each driver was secretly wishing dark things upon him, wondering why the man in the raincoat had singled him out. He stopped at the gate. An official in a wide-brimmed hat stepped out into the rain and walked to the bike. A whistle pierced the air and the man turned to look along the line of waiting cars. Rain dribbled from his hat brim onto the pavement.

Richard watched through the water droplets on his rearview mirror and saw the first official waving his pen frantically. The man next to him disappeared into the guardhouse and the gate swung up. Richard stood over the bike, turned around and made a two-handed Obi-wan light-saber slashing motion toward the official in the raincoat.

The man held his ballpoint in both hands and slashed back at him.

Chapter 26

CLAIRE'S FINGER TIGHTENED to squeeze off her ninth round. Mott the Hoople screamed: *It's good for your body, it's good for your soul.*

The rifle fired. Missed.

The Golden Age of Rock and Roll.

She flipped up her lapel pocket and grabbed her cell to silence the ringtone her Dad had given her.

"You ruined my shot," she said into the mouthpiece.

"Hello, to you too," Billy said. "Got an invitation. When can we talk?"

"Another officers' party. Oh boy."

"Nothing like that."

"What then?"

"Are you running today?"

"About an hour," she said. "I was planning Country Club hills."

"Ugh. Why do you like hills? I'll meet you there."

"Thanks for messing up my shot."

"It's practice, Claire. Could you be taking this too seriously?"

"I finished third," she said, and hung up.

* * *

Running downhill to complete her first two-mile lap through the irrigated green meadows around the golf course her heart and feet pounded to a hip-hop beat in 104-degree heat. Wiping sweat from her eyes with her forearm she saw Billy exit the clubhouse and start down the trail away from her. In less than a minute she pulled up beside him.

"Hey."

"You know heart attack is one of the leading causes of death among women?" he said, without looking at her. "You could pick a cooler day."

"This is cool, barely over a hundred."

He turned, his expression blank. She couldn't tell if he was annoyed, or teasing. He remained stoic so she prodded.

"You mentioned an invitation?"

He panted as his body accustomed itself to her pace.

"There's a little party coming up. I'm thinking of attending."

She slowed slightly, their feet beating the path into puffs of dust.

"In the land of ice and snow?"

"No, the East. Far in the East."

They curved left and the path began to rise.

"What kind of party?"

"One attended by a pipeline specialist. I think we want to make him an offer."

The hill, heat and lack of sleep were affecting to him, so she slowed. If this kept up she'd have to do extra laps.

"He invited the Army?"

He shook his head. "Friends from industry. We got a peek at the invitation."

Ah, a time and place. "Is this at a nice resort where we can dine and dance?"

"More of an incognito visit."

She tramped along into the wooded area of the trail. It was cooler in the shade, maybe not more than ninety. Why go to a party incognito? Who would they pretend to be?

"Will our representative be staying long?" she asked.

He was mouth breathing, but holding steady.

"A quick in and out would be best. The terrain is challenging."

East. Challenging terrain.

"Population center?"

"Beyond isolated. Impossible approach. And..."

She glanced over her shoulder. His cheeks were red, but he hadn't stopped talking for lack of air.

"I'll bite. And...what?"

"The location presents delicate political issues."

She laughed through her exhale. "When was the last time there weren't delicate political issues when you're involved?"

He grinned. "Yeah, I just love politics."

They ran in silence for minutes, winding past grass Billy usually said was manicured better than a French whore. He made no comment.

Claire broke the silence. "So what do we go in with?"

He faced her, caught her eyes.

"There is no mission objective yet. There is also no strategy." He looked up the road and pressed the pace slightly. She accelerated easily to stay with him. "And there's certainly no we."

Her jaw tightened. Was he really saying she couldn't be part of the mission?

"No room on the team for a sharpshooter, huh?" she asked as calmly as she could muster while running a seven minute mile.

No answer. They covered half a mile.

"I said there was no strategy. How could I know if there's a sharpshooter slot?" he said out of nowhere.

Had he really been thinking about it that long?

"Sorry. It's just that this Alaska thing is so strange. It's gotten inside of me. Maybe because of the kid."

She braced herself for his lecture about not getting emotionally involved in projects. She was just there to do a job, it would cloud her judgment, she would make a mistake.

But he only said, "Cute kid. I still wonder why he's not dead."

She imagined the little blond-haired body charred in the flash of fire she had seen when the machine exploded. What if that had happened in his bedroom? She blinked hard to make the image go away, wishing for someone she could shoot at.

"I know I keep asking. But how is Master Norton doing?"

"Doc Klemson sent an update yesterday. He's still at home, but they're thinking of taking him to a rehab center so he'll be around kids his own age."

"He thinks that'll help?"

"She. Joanne Klemson, some kind of children's specialist on Uncle Sam's payroll. Yeah. They haven't found anything physically wrong, so they're guessing trauma."

She thought about a little kid seeing a big explosion, then being told not to talk about it.

"Think it'd be okay if I sent him a gift?"

He shrugged. "Let me check with Klemson. I think we shouldn't confuse the kid."

They plodded along until the woods gave way to sunshine. Thinking about little Billy had changed her mood. Now she thought it was too damn hot to run.

Eventually she asked, "So what's next? Can I help?"

"You're familiar with the situation and have clearance, you'd be a good consultant."

She beamed inside.

"But it's complicated," he said.

Chapter 27

THE MAN WHO STARTED Monday as Arthur Tresuniack, became Jonathon Katow, and was now Richard Tonver, rode for fourteen hours straight, wanting to put distance between the Russian coast and his taillight. He watched curved cracks in asphalt slide under his front wheel, knowing bones buried beneath the pavement belonged to the political prisoners who built it. Which pissed him off. He tried to center himself by focusing on the present. He was thinking about sleep and gas when a building appeared.

He maneuvered through broken rubble to a single fuel pump with a hand-lettered sign: forty rubles per liter. He parked the bike at the pump and wandered into a wooden hut whose World War II paint was almost gone. Empty. He placed two twenty dollar bills he hadn't needed in Alaska on a flat wood desk, reached under its front edge, and pressed the only button there. The clankety reset of the mechanical pump reached him through the door.

The pump slowly wheezed fuel into his bike. The surrounding fields were bare of anything but short rough grass losing the battle to grow so far away from the equator, leaving gray dirt to merge with a gray-clouded sky. Inside his helmet the air froze his nostrils. He inched the dial of his electric suit up.

Petrol stations had personality. This one didn't have the color TV, free Wi-Fi, wouldn't you like a hot dog of a typical U.S. station. But it had the necessity—fuel—and a sense of calm that most everything in the U.S. lacked.

Thirty-six pumped liters later he was still alone. He replaced the handle and stared into the cracked dusty glass covering the spinning mechanical digits. A leather-clad alien behind a tinted face shield stared back. He was glad he couldn't see its eyes. He felt cut-off, isolated. And liked the feeling just fine.

He plugged in his suit, stood on the pegs and bounced the bike out of the station via frozen mud ruts, then up twenty centimeters of hard-edged asphalt. His GPS told him fifty kilometers to Axelburg.

When he spoke, his voice echoed softly against the foam of the helmet. "Twenty-two hundred kilometers, and we'll see Quan again."

Chapter 28

THE DOOR CLUNKED CLOSED behind Billy's exit, filling Claire with the momentary terror of being locked into a prison cell. The windows along the far wall were covered with slate-gray vertical blinds, rotated closed, holding the room in the dimness of an after-hours jazz club. She crossed carpet to the large rectangle occupying the center of the room, expecting a conference table, but found two by four meters of smooth dark glass. Looking through the glass she saw a flickering image of terrain, as if viewing old aerial footage of mountains. She squinted and could make out roads of gravel twisting through hills. A structure toward the upper right might be a large residence, or small warehouse.

She walked to the far end of the table, surprised to see that the flickering image now showed the back of the building. A row of four garage doors convinced her it was a residence—of someone who could afford to put vehicles in those garages. She wondered where it was located.

The door opened and Billy slid through with two cups of Peet's and a bag of something that smelled like calories.

"Snack before lunch," he announced. "How do you like my magic table?"

"It flickers," she said.

"Because you don't have Wizard Eyes," he replied, standing a cup on the edge of the table and giving her the bag.

He knelt on one knee, opened a door and handed up a pair of sunglasses.

"You steal these from the Men In Black?"

"Wait till you see what they do."

Colored objects grew out of the table like the miniature architectural models businessmen use when trying to sell new condominiums. Rolling hills with furry trees, blue water flowing through streams. She reached out her hand and saw it change color as it passed through the hills.

"This is a three-dimensional projection of multi-sensor satellite topography data. It's accurate to five centimeters on the surface, but the foliage is only approximate."

"What is it?"

"The location of the party."

"Where?"

"Let's just say it doesn't snow there."

The world shrank before her eyes like a deflating balloon. A blue arrow beside the word *North* floated above the trees.

"Hmm." Two rivers converged. The building was now the size of a sugar cube.

"We're looking down from 10,000 feet. Here's the first problem."

She saw yellow lines appear between the hills, across streams and roads, dividing the area into jigsaw-puzzle chunks. Words she guessed named villages appeared. A curved word along a border sent optimism on vacation: China.

So this was the Daemon guy's hang out. She checked herself. *Did they know it was a man?* Smart location. It would take a powerful reason for the U.S. to enter China. She leaned closer. The word on the opposite side of the border loomed: Vietnam.

Her father had served there.

She thought of being a kid beside him on the shooting range. "Pull," he'd call, then pop the clay disk high in the air. Her turn. At eleven she could get half of them. *What did you do in the war, Daddy?* "Sorry honey, classified."

She blinked.

"First problem," she said, "Chinese soil makes this more politically sensitive than Monica's lips."

"Such a way with words. But you're right. We don't get a vote, though, it's his party."

"Do we know the target is male?"

Billy shook his head.

Blue curves drew, flowing up and dropping.

"These are the approved flights in the area. And here," giant cylinders of transparent orange grew upward from the ground, "are the no-fly zones."

She stared at the projection and moved around the table. The terrain adapted perspective to where she was standing, as if she were in a helicopter.

"The first problem says no feet on Chinese soil," she said. "But that doesn't matter because the second problem says there's no way to get through the airspace. You sure pick easy ones."

"You have cut to the essence of the challenge. So?"

"I suggest a beach in the Bahamas, a nice seafood dinner followed by Mai Tai's, and we let someone else handle Alaska," she replied.

He was silent.

"The President wants you to solve this?"

"It's my job," he said. "Let's talk constraints. Then lunch, and maybe work in a Mai Tai if you don't have to be on the range."

"Hey, if Bode Miller can ski drunk, I can shoot. It's just a matter of practice."

She wondered what his eyes were doing behind the glasses.

"Bode had won the overall title the day before, first American in twenty-two years," he said. "When you shoot as well as he skis, go ahead and shoot drunk. Just make sure I'm in the next county."

She grinned. "First problem. Getting in." She pointed with an outstretched arm, "Can we put a plane along the border here?"

"We could, but it would be on radar every step of the way. And there would be questions. What kind of plane? What is it doing? Who owns it? Questions we don't want to answer."

"Can we walk in?"

"Based on current intel, we have until Saturday night. Six days."

"Can this thing show distance?"

His gray-shadow hand rubbed a control surface that could have been for a Game-Boy.

"What distance?" he asked.

She pushed her finger into a glowing hill. "From here on the border, to there." Her finger touched the sugar cube.

A ruler connected the two points and showed 172 kilometers.

"Estimated from satellite data," he said.

"How the hell are the guests getting there?"

The image rotated and zoomed toward the house. "It's better if you're coming from China. There's a hard pack road that will handle a four wheel drive if it doesn't rain."

"And if it does?"

"I suspect a lightly attended party."

"You're not making this easy, General."

"I'll order sunshine from the Pentagon."

She stared at the house and traced her exit path. Her father had taught her to only enter a business arrangement if she had a good exit strategy. She found his advice useful in any endeavor, especially ones involving guns.

"I'm in the house, illegally on Chinese territory, and you can't get me out with a chopper."

"Who said anything about you?" Billy asked.

The biggest thing that had ever happened in her life, and he wasn't going to let her go. She should have let it be his idea.

"Let's say, hypothetically, for the purpose of this discussion," she said.

He was quiet for seventeen seconds. She counted.

"Okay, hypothetically."

"I exit the house here and circle around to lower elevation. Do you have topo info?"

He thumbed. Rings coated the hillside.

"See, I come around here and there's a trail, maybe even a road leading west. I follow that to this creek. After that, I run the streambed. How deep is it this time of year?"

His gray shadow shrugged. "We don't have that data. Estimates show it ranges from dry to two feet during August. But if it rains—"

"You had to say that. All right, so I have…"

"A hundred and seventy-two klicks. Call it a hundred and seven miles."

"…to get back to Vietnam where you pick me up." She turned to look at him, but the weird glasses blocked eye contact—making her feel like they were talking in a very dark room. "If I can do twenty miles-per-hour with a Hummer, I'm out in five hours. Ten mph, I can be out in under eleven. Not bad unless there's something else going on in that area I have to worry about."

"You mean like the Chinese Army?"

She decided he was serious. "Is that river wide enough for a Hummer?"

"Maybe," he said. "Where are you going to get a Hummer?"

"You'll air drop one."

"Where am I going to get a transport plane that's invisible to radar? See," he pointed to the large orange cylinders growing out of the ground, "we have an air space problem. You recall that the Communists are touchy about our planes ever since that U-2 they shot down in 1960."

"That was Russia," she said.

"Do you think the Chinese are more lenient?"

She stared at the projection. What a great way to plan a mission. Only it made the constraints so apparent she was getting depressed.

A lousy hundred miles. Ultra-distance runners could do that in a day. She was in shape, but had never even thought about doing four marathons back to back.

"Go in on foot. Hike the 107, do the job, hike out. One soldier on foot wouldn't attract much attention."

"One soldier on foot wouldn't have a high probability of success."

"What's this line?" She pointed at an arc that ran parallel to the North-South border between China and Vietnam.

"What about it?"

"It's in a good place. Fly in along that line and jump out here," she pointed with a dark finger halfway through the arc. "I'm in Vietnam, not China, and a hundred and seven miles from the target."

Billy's thumbs moved on the controller. "Flight QT54: Vietnam Airways. It's a commercial flight, Claire. You going to ask the stewardess to open the door?"

He laughed. She could see the shadow of his body shaking.

"The Chinese expect to see it on their radar," she said with as much huff as she could muster.

"Hmm," Billy said. "So you want to fly in the radar shadow. It would be tough to be close enough and not scare the commercial operators."

"What choice do we have? If we take a plane up there, the radar is going to bleep like a stuck sheep," she said, wondering why she had thought of sheep getting poked.

"True. What about that Humvee you suggested?"

"They need roads. Where do I start? How many government checkpoints would I have to pass through? What about the border? How do I cross that?"

She stepped back and sagged into a leather chair along the wall, her mood falling with each failed suggestion. She couldn't fly in, she couldn't walk in, and if she tried to drive in she would attract so much attention she'd spend her life in a Chinese prison.

The room was quiet except for the sound of a boot scuffing Berber carpet as she swung her foot forward and back.

She froze as an idea blossomed.

"Hey, do you think you can cancel QT54?"

"Sure, I play golf on Tuesdays with the CEO of Vietnam Airways. I'll give him a call. Why?"

"I'm serious." She removed her glasses and looked at him.

He stared, got the idea, and took off his glasses.

The room was dim, but she could see his eyes now: blue and tired.

"Quietly cancel QT54 and put our plane on its flight plan, something with about the same airspeed and radar profile, but that I can jump out of.

And drop a Hummer for me while you're at it."

He studied her with keen interest, the way he did when she was getting undressed.

"Substitution," he said.

"Yeah. Let them think it's the standard commercial flight. Does it fly often enough that we could do it twice?"

He tapped on his Game-Boy. "Four times a day. You can't jump twice Super Girl. And there's no airfield to stop and pick you up."

"I meant substitute twice. Use a chopper to get us out that's also flying close to QT54's plan. Hide in plain sight, right where the radar expects to find flight 54."

He slipped his glasses back on and turned towards the table.

She did likewise.

All meta-information dropped away except the single blue line. Wind vectors lit up. Billy pointed. "If you jump here, you might be able to drift across the border and land in China directly, skipping the pleasant conversation with border guards. You could be seen, but at night...what's the damn moon doing over there in six days?" He punched around for a long bit on his controller and the scene shifted to night with a sliver of a moon in the sky.

"A bit of luck," she said.

"Okay, you're in. On the way out you cross the border unassisted, or we pick you up in China. We could use a plane *and* a chopper. Gain altitude in the chopper until it's close enough to the QT54 decoy to look like one blip on long-range radar. The radar..." he tapped, "is five hundred miles away. Satellite might be a problem, if one is watching." He paused. "Timing will be critical."

"So what do you think?" she asked, fighting to contain her excitement.

"I think it's fraught with risk."

"Well, sure. But what's the worst that could happen?"

"You go in, miss the target, get grabbed by the Chinese military, end up on international television. Become the Internet poster girl for clandestine U.S. operations while rotting doing hard labor in a Chinese correctional facility. Maybe not the absolute worst, but close."

She said softly, "You're so cheery."

"Not my job. Save that for the PR dweebs." He began pacing circles around the table. "Questions. First, since you're not going under any circumstances, who does? And is one man enough?"

"I know you're saying *man* to irritate me so I'm ignoring you. A two-man team isn't the right answer. The biggest risk is capture by Chinese authorities. Two men can be grabbed as easily as one if they're together. If you send two, it has to be two missions as completely separate as possible."

"Two missions? If you're going to do that, why not three?" he shot back.

"Good idea. Three independent missions: a man, a woman and a Chinese speaker. Maximum success profile."

He stopped pacing.

"Three? You're serious?"

She studied the projection wondering if she could find three paths through the mountains. "My Dad says three is the magic number for success: balanced instability." She smiled.

He watched her sip coffee. "Where did you learn to plan missions?"

"Simulators. You know I don't use my rifle just to shoot paper targets." She paused for his smart-ass comment on her talent. When it didn't come, she said, "It depends on what needs to happen at the house. Three might not be enough."

"Just one objective."

"I was hoping for a laundry list."

"Prevent this Daemon character from ever making the news again."

The dim room was quiet; the magic table didn't seem to make noise. She stared at the flashy electronic mock-up of an assassination, knowing such things were done. But she had never been this close before.

"Still three," she said. "Insert and extract independently. Assume one won't make it in, and one will be stopped at the target. That leaves the third to get the job done."

He traced his finger down the blue line of the flight path. "You want me to put three men, uh, operatives, in a plane with three Hummers that drive back across this border, unseen and unheard."

She imagined her Hummer sunk in mud as a hundred Chinese soldiers closed in. Operatives? She bolted upright.

"Relinquish ID?" She drained the last of her coffee. "We, or I should say they, are on their own after the jump?"

"How else could it be?"

"You're sure we can't just take a chopper over China? Land close, do the job, lift everyone out. Worked in Pakistan. Bush and Obama both set precedent about crossing borders to take out threats. It'd be a lot easier."

"How could radar miss a chopper flying a hundred miles into Chinese air space?" he said. "I could barely get a drone in there undetected. And if I could, I'd have to blow the whole house."

"He has the Chinese government protecting him, elevation protecting him, isolation protecting him. And that's not counting security measures on the property. We might be up against cameras, mines, motion detectors, armed guards, dogs and the Chinese Mafia," she said, trying to keep pessimism out of her voice.

He laid his glasses on the table and brought up the lights. He popped open one end of a long plastic tube and pulled out a roll of paper, which he stretched out on top of the electronic table.

"Let's look at this the old way. Here's the same region on paper without the pretty electronic data. Only thing on here is topo, like a hiker would use," he said.

"Or a racer," she added.

"What?"

"Dirt biker. Remember those guys who raced a thousand miles through the Baja desert in that movie *Dust to Glory?* They used maps on a roll to stay on course."

Their eyes met.

She said, "It could work."

His mouth twisted. "Light. Fast. Good on narrow trails. Can be equipped for deep water. Will fit in a chopper. Who do you know that rides well?"

She pressed her lips together in thought. "Twenty-five percent of Army personnel ride motorcycles. We'll be able to find the right team."

She moved her jaw left and right.

"I rode a Honda in middle school." She paused. "And I learn fast."

He held her gaze.

As she was preparing for him to refuse he said, "There's an off-road school in New Hampshire we've used before. Spend a few days with them. If Ben and Max give the okay, you can be *considered* for the team."

Chapter 29

WHEN THE LIGHTS OF EVANSK began to glow on the horizon Richard Tonver realized his body ached. He rode slowly into a town with white and gray clapboard buildings on both sides of the street, up close, as if they wanted to touch the asphalt. Hand-painted signs indicated a General Store, Best Vodka in Town, and Black the Smith. William Gibson had been right when he said, *The future is already here, it just isn't evenly distributed.* It wouldn't find Evansk for decades.

"Where going?" the slouched man behind the ticket counter asked after realizing the rider in front of him didn't speak Russian.

"London, eventually," he replied.

The man squinted. "Train truck to Irkutsk."

He held up a finger. "One ticket to Irkutsh, and transport for my motorcycle." He pointed through a window splattered with mud.

The old head swung sideways to look. Deep creases visited his brow.

"How much weigh?"

"Two hundred and fifty kilos," Tonver said.

The frown deepened. "Very difficult." He moved a hand. "Load, unload."

The man's greasy gray hair wiggled as he spun the crank on a mechanical machine that reminded Richard of drawings of Pascal's Difference engine. It rattled and emitted a ticket. He fiddled with it, cranked, and it emitted another ticket. After six such excursions six printed cardboard pieces were placed on the counter before him. The man rattled off what must have been the names of cities, but Tonver only caught the last: Irkutsk.

His cranking hand came up and waved towards the left. "Load. that way."

Once loaded into a plain boxcar, he pulled his sleeping bag from the bike to use as a chair. Leaning against the wall he recalled the railroad map from the old man's wall. He turned on his GPS and double-checked the coordinates for Irkutsk, set an alarm for two hours hence and closed his eyes.

* * *

Darkness hadn't arrived when the kathump of steel wheels against rails woke him. The GPS said he had traveled only 100 km from Kamenskoye. He saw endless fields of gold and green glide past the picture window of the open door. The mission was on track, except for the boy.

After verifying scramble mode, he placed a call.

"Hi, Maxx. Firesnake."

"Everything is fine?" Maxx asked.

"Affirmative. Honey Pot status?"

"Forty invitations out, forty RSVPs in. All accepted."

"How many more?"

"Estimate five with 95% confidence. Standard deviation is 2.8."

"Wide," he said, mostly for his own benefit.

"An intact Rat has created a new situation."

He shook his head. Maxx was brilliant at stating the obvious.

"Thanks, Maxx. Switch to tracking."

He held a button on the GPS to lower the encryption level and send synthetic voice, for the benefit of those who eavesdrop on telephone conversations.

"I've purchased six tickets to take me through to Irkutsk. Am on schedule."

A woman's voice replied, "That's wonderful Richard, I'll meet you at the station. Call when you know what time your train will arrive."

He released the button.

"Thanks Maxx, we're a go."

"Affirmative."

He stared at the gravel racing past below his feet. He set the GPS to compute mode and reviewed everything he knew about the train: current speed, height of the car's floor, width of the door, estimated traction of the ground. The computer displayed options. The biggest challenge remained the speed of the train.

He accessed topology maps for the region outside of Kamenskoye, looking for an uphill grade that would slow the train. His first opportunity would be the climb to Gizhiga: only six percent, but enough to help. He had a two-hour wait.

He sat down with a piece of jerky to play his version of what-if, like the oil boys were probably playing. If he were an oil boy, how would he try to find the perp of the pipeline?

He imagined a trusted group around a huge conference table at the top of a skyscraper, drinking coffee, and nibbling on cookies to feed bloated waistlines:

"We've been lucky with the cell phone, the perp doesn't know we found the supplier."

"So he got one part from China."

"If he's in China, we can't search without the help of the Chinese government."

"We can't tell them who we're looking for."

"Or why."

"For all we know, the Chinese government is helping him."

In the distance a series of bangs sounded like a twenty-car pile-up on the Los Angeles freeway. As he looked up he was slammed onto his right shoulder. He grabbed the GPS with both hands and spun on his hip. The bike was upright, but the handlebars were shaking.

Why were they stopping? Could authorities have tracked him to this point? Impossible. But if so...

He latched the GPS to the bars, yanked his helmet into place and released the bike. It disturbed him that he had no explanation, but he decided the glass was half full: a slow train meant he could exit now.

He warmed up the bike while securing the cases and making certain he was leaving nothing behind, except the straps supplied by the railroad. After a moment's thought, he took those too, so this car would look like all the others.

The train continued to slow.

He positioned himself in the far corner opposite the open door. One try, no net. Car-coupler clangs were coming his way; the engines were pulling.

He released the clutch and opened the throttle as much as he could without lifting the front wheel. He crushed the gas tank between his knees and as his front tire passed through the door he twisted the throttle hard.

Chapter 30

THE TURBO-PROP'S VIBRATIONS reached through the fuselage and the metal bench up through Claire's coccyx. They couldn't use a jet; its stall speed was too high for the required maneuver. She was leaning back with eyes closed, visualizing the magic table where the team had worked tirelessly, saturating themselves with details of the mission. She knew where she was, and where she needed to get to, but the part in between was sketchy. Maps and satellite imagery weren't the same as feet on the ground.

Friday evening. Her chrono showed six minutes past ten in the internal blackness maintained for security, less than an hour to the drop point. The other team members sat opposite in the CF-152 transport, the military plane whose radar profile came closest to the ATR 72-500's used by Vietnam Airways. It was short, too small for Humvees. And couldn't lift them anyway.

Three lightweight motorbikes sat tire to tire down the middle of the aircraft. She could see Cam's shadow through the frame of the second. He had ridden motocross, and tutored her over two intensive days at the Max BMW school in New Hampshire. She dropped the bike a hundred times searching for traction on gooey surfaces, but had eventually received high marks from the instructor.

The third member was Wu Ching, a Chinese speaker and bronze metal winner of the International Six Days Enduro race. He was the best rider; she was the best shot. He had been easy to find, a Boolean search for off-road motorcyclist and marksman popped his name out of a military database. He had volunteered immediately.

Good men, and she was glad to be with them, even though once she jumped they would be invisible until it was all over. It had been unanimous. Once in, each soldier was alone. Even Billy had agreed.

Billy.

Forget that she was well qualified and had personally suggested the strategy; he had tried to stop her. It had taken days of fierce persistence to wear him down.

She leaned left to check her pack for the seventh time. The top contained survival gear: food, clothing for the climate changes induced by elevation, medical supplies. She expected to be awake for most of the next twenty-four hours, but there was a blanket and her backup parachute. The bottom held a bladder of spare fuel for the machine, and integrated above it, a second one of electrolyte fluid for her.

A red light came on overhead. She maneuvered straps around her body and tightened them until she and the pack were one. The captain's voice came through the headset in her helmet.

"First drop in fourteen minutes. Ambient wind speed: twelve knots, southwest."

She crawled to the first bike in the row. The experts had insisted that the best way to find the bike in the dark in the hills of Vietnam was to jump with it. But the thought of drifting toward unknown terrain on a 250-pound machine conjured images of X-Games riders with broken bones—despite the practice jumps.

"Six minutes."

She stood in the cargo area, threw her leg over the bike, and secured her waist and thighs to the machine.

"Claire," said Cam's voice. "A rematch, and date for my victory dinner."

"You'll have to win first."

"See you tomorrow, Corporal," Wu said.

"Ready to open?" the captain asked.

She checked both gloves. "Ready to open, affirmative."

The rear of the plane cracked horizontally and the floor swung down to become a ramp to nowhere. Wind roared inside the cargo area like the Devil had been awakened from a nap.

"Sixty seconds."

She squeezed the front brake and kicked the latch to release the wheel. Her heart raced as adrenal glands punched in.

"Thirty seconds."

She kicked the back latch to release the rear wheel. It didn't move. She kicked it again, and rocked the bike side to side.

"Fifteen seconds," she heard blood pulsing in her ears.

It dropped free. The bike inched forward. She tried not to think about 10,000 feet of air between her and the ground.

"Wind speed, eleven knots. Go at will."

She eased the brake, rolled down the ramp, forced her eyes to stay open—and dropped into space.

* * *

The engine roar ceased. Not quiet, she was falling at over a hundred mph, but a new oceanic hiss. She tucked her elbows, amazed at how the bike stayed under her like she was riding Main Street, and watched the orange glow of the altimeter. At two thousand feet a small black chute popped. The bike slowed, pressing up against her. Then the darkness of main chute curved above her, blocking the sliver of moon. The bike seemed to stop, supported by invisible hands. She grabbed the control lines and looked down.

She saw a sea of banyan branches reaching skyward for the light of life. She steered in an arc to look for something better. Breaking her leg in a tree would end the mission, or worse. She visualized a meadow of soft grass.

It was too dark.

"Night vision," she said and the world turned the lime-gray of Hollywood swamp movies. She caught a glimpse of trail, a narrow single track probably trodden by human feet. It disappeared beneath jungle canopy, but returned two hundred yards later, curving to the right.

More trees. She floated in the direction of the last chunk of path she had seen. A small hole appeared in the canopy, a path under it. More trees. She hoped the path didn't turn. She slowed her descent. To the left the trail emerged again. She swung in its direction, letting herself drop through the hole as fast as she dared. She pulled hard on the chute's brakes and stood tall on the foot pegs.

The bike hit the dirt.

Her butt hit the seat.

They rebounded and the chute jerked at her harness. The bike landed hard but stayed upright. She skidded to a stop.

She gathered the chute fast and stuffed it into an expandable pack behind her seat. She would do a better job once clear of the insertion point. She heard Billy: *Leave only footprints, and not many of those.*

She pressed with her thumb. The engine whirred but didn't catch. She took a breath to relax. It fired the second time and purred through stealth mufflers. The GPS, pre-loaded with her destination, pointed ninety degrees to the right, directly into the forest. She clicked the bike into gear and shot forward on the trail, using the night goggles: a headlight in the darkness being an invitation to her funeral.

The smooth trail slipped under her front wheel for a full mile before she could turn in the direction the GPS arrow wanted her to go. It estimated

113 miles and a maximum travel time of seven hours to arrive before sunrise at 5:29 AM. It also showed she must average 16 mph through jungle, including stops for food, fluids and falls, to avoid daylight.

She was pleased she hadn't broken the bike. She thought about Cam and his bravado. She wished Wu safe riding. She imagined them miles apart, converging on the jungle house, no radio contact, alone in hostile territory...each to deliver a bullet.

Chapter 31

CLAIRE LAY PRONE IN LONG curved grass three hundreds yards from the southeast corner of the house she had first seen on the magic table. The ride and three falls had taken six hours and two minutes, followed by a sweltering day of hiding in jungle shadows while trying to rest.

She turned her head until she could see the sky with her peripheral vision. The clouds were growing fatter, had been for three hours.

Her watch showed 5:14 PM above 17:14. She wished she could know if Cam and Wu were in position. She peered through the scope and examined the second floor room on the near corner. It matched Billy's intel: cherry wood desk, black computer, a pair of telephones, shelves of books, and windows on two walls allowing multiple lines of fire. Her eye stopped on a picture of a woman with white skin and brown curls. American, or British. She was holding a child's hand and wearing a blue and white print dress that touched the top of army boots. The boy by her side wore only white underwear.

Claire lifted her head and scanned the area around the building for movement. She thought about Cam and his chocolate gun that she hadn't mentioned to anyone. She enjoyed Billy, but she was young. Maybe she'd let Cam have a consolation dinner the next time she beat him.

A black Land Rover bouncing up the road startled her. 5:24. The first guest. She watched a blond white male get out who looked like he spent time on a surfboard. Maybe mid-twenties. She wondered vaguely if he was their man.

Lightning flared inside gray clouds to the west like it was trying to get out. She petitioned the rain gods and rolled onto her back. Her motorcycle was barely visible at the bottom of a long hill beneath a camouflage of branches. She shifted back into position and adjusted her black suit—treated leather for water, ventilation, ultraviolet reflection and impact protection. Another flash in the sky made no sound.

She watched the entrance. A shiny gold Jaguar sedan with the all-wheel-drive option according to the trunk lid crawled up the trail. A Chinese couple exited, the woman stepping from the driver's side. A valet pulled the car away leaving them to walk up a path of flat, irregularly shaped stones. He wore a business suit in dark gray, she a knee length skirt in black.

5:36.

Claire studied the second floor. Vehicles meandered up the dirt road. A young Chinese man with spiked hair passed in a low-slung Volkswagen. The sky flashed. She focused. She would deal with rain and mud after doing her job.

A Caucasian male stepped out of a silver Audi as it lowered itself toward the ground: dirty blond hair, maybe six feet, soccer-player body. Pressed off-white suit over a pale blue no-collar shirt. Two Americans so far. She corrected herself. Perhaps not, could be European, or even Australian. But they weren't Chinese businessmen.

For some reason, she had visualized the target as a Chinese male. But anyone could call himself a daemon devil. The definitions had surprised her: *inner spirit or inspiring force*—along with one from computers, something about working in the background and going dormant.

She gazed through the scope at the driver of the Jaguar making her way toward the house, stepping carefully from stone to stone in slender heels. Would a small Chinese woman in her gun sight make it harder to pull the trigger?

The valet took the Audi away, but its driver loitered outside, glanced down the road, looked around at the countryside. She felt him make eye contact through the rifle's scope and it jittered her heart, even though she knew she was invisible at this distance. Human eyes had limitations.

5:48.

She waited without moving, a monk in meditation.

5:52.

She thumbed the safety off and focused on her room. No one had gone in or out. She visualized the mission unfolding: a person enters the room to answer the phone. Where would he stand? If he walked behind the desk she had a clearer shot. If he sat, the window sash would block his body. She would go for the head.

Her chrono, rotated to the inside of her right wrist so she could read it without moving, showed 6:00 PM. She consciously relaxed her left hand to prevent tension from building in her trigger finger.

6:01. A 4-wheel-drive van arrived with three guests: all Asian women under thirty wearing short skirts.

6:02. The sky flashed a single brilliant white sheet.

6:03. Three cars crept up the road in a dusty caravan: red, blue, tan.

6:03:30. She placed the crosshairs on the nearest phone.

6:03:45. She started counting.

She hadn't gotten far when a shadow flashed on the floor. The door was moving. She stopped counting. If someone answered the telephone, the call was early.

A stoop-shouldered Asian woman shuffled across the floor to a bookshelf and slowly ran a finger along the spines. She had touched perhaps a dozen books when she turned, walked to the desk, and lifted the phone, holding it like a delicate teacup between her index finger and thumb. Claire saw her mouth move. The woman placed the phone gently on the desk. As her face passed, the deep black eyes seemed like holes. Many folds of red cloth waved as she glided back toward the door.

Claire's heart beat her chest as she watched the shadow. She swiveled her sight left and it passed behind a drawn curtain of woven bamboo. She twisted more, tracking movement in each window. The woman emerged from a curved stairway onto the first floor, turned to her right and walked up to a man at the bar. He shifted slightly to face her, but Claire could only see his back.

She watched seconds tick with the peripheral vision of her right eye hoping for a peek at the man on the other side of that conversation. At eight seconds the woman turned 180 degrees. She crossed the front of the house behind shades, a glimpse of her in the hallway, more shadows in the room beneath the telephone. She was talking to someone tall. Based on height, one of the Caucasians she had seen drive up.

Claire calmed her left hand.

A shadow shifted. She focused on the stairwell, saw him flash past, walking fast. She returned her scope to the telephone handset and took smooth even breaths. She saw shadows dance across the floor followed by a torso. He was scratching the back of his head with his right arm and his elbow blocked her view of his face.

6:04:41. Nineteen seconds.

He didn't walk around the desk, but picked up the phone with his left hand. The handset disappeared behind his right elbow.

Her heart rate accelerated. This man was on the phone in the correct room at the precise time.

He dropped his right hand to the desk. What she could see of his expression said he was asking a question.

He turned and pressed his left hip against the desk, facing her.

She positioned the crosshairs.

Time ticked in slow motion 6:04:55…56…

The man's mouth opened wide. Surprised…or shouting?

6:05:00.

Her R-21 rifle, handmade in China, spit into the darkness. She felt the thump against her left shoulder. The curtain beside the open window shuddered.

She blinked.

The man fell away from the desk, the phone swinging in the air like a film noir effect. She shifted her sight to find him: on the floor, spasms jerking his body.

She rolled until her back was to the house. She took three seconds to orient before flipping the crystal closed on her chrono, creating a handsome Gucci watch that Gucci had never seen. She crawled, reached the bike in twenty-three seconds, disassembled and secured the individual parts of the weapon against the sides of the fuel tank and closed the panels. She pulled away branches, slipped her helmet on and heaved with both legs to roll the machine into a gulley. Near the bottom, she engaged the clutch to ignite the engine. The muffler whispered. She saw no traffic that might notice her, so she climbed the gulley's side through weeds that crackled under her tires.

When she reached the road, she flicked on the headlight, and accelerated.

Chapter 32

APPROACHING THE HOUSE AT 40 mph with a cloud of dust chasing her, Claire locked the rear wheel and skidded to a stop in front of the valet. He stared into her face shield stone-faced, like he was seeing a naked woman for the first time.

She flicked the kill switch with her thumb, peeled off her left glove and handed it to him. He took it without blinking. She followed with the right and her helmet, freeing a cascade of brown curls she had created while hiding in the jungle. She flipped the side stand down and swung her right leg forward over the tank.

"The keys are in it."

She spun on her toes and walked briskly toward the front door, digging inside her black suit for the invitation and shaking out her hair at the same time. When she reached the door, a Chinese man with a thick neck in a pale suit blocked her way.

"Hi," she said, handing him a cream-colored card with a shadow of gold along its edge.

"Uh," he took the card. "Uh." He examined the card. "Welcome Ms. Hoong. Please, please…this way." He stepped toward his left. "Kim Su will take your, uh…" he stared at the dust on her riding clothes.

She smiled. "Ladies room?"

"This way please." He led her down a corridor paneled with slender bamboo, past three men clinking iced cocktails near a bar with a thick brass foot rail, beyond the stairway she had seen through her gunsight, and around beneath it. "Please let me know if you need anything." He departed, still holding her invitation.

She turned a smooth knob to enter a ten-by-ten-foot bathroom with gold fixtures, pushed the door closed, and slid the latch. Listened. Lute music and voices reached her rather than screams of panicked guests. Maybe the acoustic model of the terrain was correct, and the shots had been dismissed as thunder.

She yanked off boots, unzipped her suit and stepped out wearing a simple black bra and panties. Opening a zipper in the back of the suit she removed a tiny pouch, two flat sandals with faux diamonds, and a long cylinder. The cylinder yielded heels that screwed into the sandals, adding three inches to her height. The pouch produced a folded piece of black fabric. One shake and she wiggled it over her head into a portable version of the little black dress pop stars preferred. The same pouch provided circular gold earrings, blush to brighten her face, and Candy Apple lipstick. In sixty-seven seconds, she was party ready.

She rolled the riding suit around the boots and carried the bundle to Kim Su the coat girl whose coal black hair shot out from her head arrow straight. Kim smiled and wrote a number on a little card, as if someone else might mistakenly take the gear. While watching her write, Claire realized the girl didn't have a left hand. Her insides tensed and she forced her eyes up to Kim Su's face.

Claire smiled. "Thank you, please keep it close, I have another appointment. The bar?"

Kim pointed to a diagram on the wall, and said something in Vietnamese that apparently meant, "Down hall, turn right, then left. Go straight. Bar is there."

Claire thanked her with a practiced, "Bachiani."

The couple from the Jaguar stood between Claire and the bar on a stone floor of gray rock with black veins. Maneuvering around them, she stopped before a panoramic painting of mountains in morning mist. Thoughts of the body on the second floor urged her to hurry. She slowed her breathing. Reflected in the painting's glass she saw the man from the Audi gazing at the mountains. She shifted to the bar. The Asian gentleman behind it looked her way. She pointed at a wine bottle, lowered her eyes and studied the black wood. Judah tree was local, she remembered from a briefing.

The Audi man waved to the bartender, who brought a fresh bottle from below the bar. Now, on top of doing her job, she was going to have to deflect advances from an American yuppie wannabe playboy doing business in China. She smiled in his direction.

"An unusual carriage for a Princess," he said in English as the bartender placed two full glasses on shining wood. The man picked them up and held one out.

She accepted the glass with a nod. "I'm an unusual Princess." His eyes showed something she read as enthusiasm.

"I enjoy two wheels myself."

Claire recognized rule number one from *Picking Up Women for Dummies*:

seek common ground.

"The roads aren't much to speak of," she said, watching his face. Dark straight hair hung down to his eyebrows above a mustache out of a Charlie Chaplin movie.

"With your long suspension and custom exhaust, I suspect our roads are...entertaining."

She categorized him: bike fanatic hoping to get laid. Could tell her the size of the throttle bodies on her engine, but forget the color of her hair.

"A bit," she said. "What an unusual location for a party."

"We won't wake the neighbors." He lifted his wine glass to her then sipped. "My name is Alex."

She extended her hand American-business style. "Kara. Do you know who owns it?"

"A guy who gives parties for business associates, as I understand it. You must know him if you have an invitation."

"I'm covering for a colleague. What's the rest of this place like?"

"Wood, paint, stone. The key is craftsmanship." He lifted his glass. "Shall we explore?"

She sipped while thinking about how to dump him, do the verification and get back on the trail in the allotted ten minutes.

They strolled to a front room that her memory placed directly below the den. Her eyes followed the jagged stones of the fireplace upward to scan the ceiling for seeping liquid. Thirty people spoke languages she didn't understand. Most were Asian. Most were male. All were drinking. A woman in a dark green gown with golden embroidery twisting down its left side made eye contact and smiled. Claire returned the smile, wondering if she had heard the gunshot.

"Noisy here," he said. "Would you like to see the second floor?"

Not with him. But she nodded.

They headed back and turned up the curved stairway. She admired the woven carpet in the center of each step: thick, deep gray, with a blood-red pattern that made her think of the scales of a dragon. Metal sculptures resided under lights every ten feet. The first looked like a chrome coke can. The second, a large ring etched with tiny stripes. The owner liked geometry. At the top of the stairs she caressed a sculpture with the back of her fingers that looked like a racecar mirror chiseled from a block of gold.

"Lovely metal."

Alex watched her hand. "Craftsmanship."

Her eyes followed the second floor hall to the left where a mahogany door stood between her and the body. She turned in a circle, taking in the forum created by the curved staircase. The ceiling was painted puffy white clouds, making this floor seem larger than the one below. She walked backward down the hall in small steps, an art connoisseur who couldn't peel her eyes from a masterpiece. She stopped in front of another panorama, this time of a forest hiding a small stone building. More mist. She finished her wine.

"May I?"

She turned. He was holding out a hand.

"Thank you, Alex."

"The same?"

She nodded.

He turned and moved down the steps. She was reminded of a dancer, or acrobat: someone more in balance than the average person. She waited for his head to disappear.

Then she ran.

She rotated a carved wooden knob, rushed inside and slowly closed the door behind her. She heard voices from below. He was on the floor: chest, carpet, jacket, all darkened with a deep red that reflected like plastic. The telephone handset hung straight down beside the black shoe on his left foot that had caught under the desk, and was now twisted outward.

She looked up for cameras.

She reached inside her dress.

His head was rotated, right cheek to the floor, arm reaching out as if begging for alms.

She flipped open the kit, dipped the first swab in his blood, placed it back in the kit.

His mouth was partially open. The upper row of teeth even and straight, the bottom overlapped.

She placed the second swab in his mouth, counted to three for it to absorb. Placed it into the kit.

The eyes were open. Brown, dry, not shiny.

She held the kit to the outstretched hand, pressed the thumb, index finger, middle finger into ink that would evaporate from his hand in seconds. Billy wanted hard data to be able confirm identity.

She stood. Blood pushed up from the hole in the man's chest like a miniature oil well. Just once. She saw a second wound at the back of his head.

She closed the kit, turned it over, lifted it to her eye, snapped a picture. Two steps sideways. Snapped another. Two steps. A third.

She pushed the kit back down her dress into an elastic pocket and moved to the door. She inched it open with her eye to the crack.

Empty.

She stepped into the hall, easing the knob counterclockwise so there would be no latch click.

The back of Alex's head was just visible on the staircase. She took two long strides toward the forest-mist painting. The tiny screw-on heel of her sandal snapped and her body weight crushed the outside of her right ankle.

She fell hard on her hip and elbow, directly in front of the painting.

She saw his shoe a foot from her face: black loafer. A small chrome ornament in the center reminded her of a headlight.

"Would you like your wine down there, Kara?"

"I'm fine, thank you for asking."

He squatted and placed the glasses on the floor.

She pulled her feet under her, removed the broken sandal, and took his hand. It was solid yet smooth, like a man who wore gloves to work. Standing on her bare foot, she felt smaller, and vulnerable. Her right ankle throbbed. She held up the sandal with her index finger.

"Broken shoe and twisted ankle. I'm in no shape to party."

"We could sit in the den," he gestured toward the closed door behind her, "make sure you're all right."

The dead man's open eyes flashed in her head.

"Thanks, but I had better go. It was nice to meet you, Alex."

"Enjoy our roads with that fine carriage."

She smiled and limped away on one shoe, retracing her path to the coat check. Kim Su's face showed confusion as she handed over the numbered bundle with her right hand.

Claire didn't try to explain. In the restroom she repacked the dress and zipped into the suit. She made certain the broken heel went with her. Once outside, she saw that the valet had simply walked her bike ten yards and left it with the helmet on the seat. Her gloves were in the helmet.

She flicked the bike alive and looked over her shoulder. The corner of her eye caught Alex standing in the double doorway of the main entrance, sipping wine. She felt a strange shiver as she realized thirty people were socializing six feet under a dead man.

Alex lifted his glass in a mini-salute.

She nodded her head and twisted the throttle.

Her display showed 18:21 beside a timer counting down from 6:39:14.4.

Chapter 33

THE OLIVE DRAB SEDAN PULLED away and left Mrs. Norton standing at the curb holding Billy's hand in her left, and his suitcase in her right. The boy flew a small black plane about with his free hand, but made no sound.

Which is why she was all the way to Anchorage standing in front of a special school. He hadn't uttered a word since two men sat in her living room and explained about that silver machine while sampling her secret-recipe cinnamon cakes. As they were leaving they handed over more money than she thought she would ever see as long as she lived.

They had been clear about one thing: the machine was a secret. A real secret, like spies and super-weapons. So she and Billy were never to speak of it. Which was easy for her. She minded the office at the town newspaper and would happily trade one secret for the briefcase, let alone the monthly checks they promised. She could send Billy to a real college and stop worrying about heat.

But Billy hadn't spoken since.

She thought of how his exuberant play with those cartoon characters had driven her batty, and the day she sent him to his room for pushing his sister. That night he found the machine that started this. For just an hour of yelling right now, they could have all the money back.

She faced a tall gray medical center that made her afraid. This wasn't right. The men told her it wouldn't be like a hospital at all, just a boarding school like any other with private rooms, a nice cafeteria and special teachers to help her Billy.

She released his hand and placed the suitcase on the sidewalk so she could dig into her purse for the address. She had written the details out carefully, but wished the driver had pointed to the door she should use.

Billy ran down the sidewalk with his plane over his head, turned and flew back past her. He seemed happy, just silent.

144 Suite-E. She looked up at the huge prison-like building and prayed it wasn't the school as she searched for numbers. She found them painted on the glass over a door. Wrong by twenty. She waved to Billy, picked up the suitcase and went left. He flew back and forth behind her until she found a

long low building made of orange brick.

She heard children playing, relaxed and managed a small smile.

As she passed through a wood-framed door the world of gray clouds and concrete changed instantly. A young woman in a green uniform sat behind a narrow counter in the middle of a hallway with a shiny floor. She led Billy past walls covered with huge pictures of hot air balloons in vibrant colors to the desk.

"Hello, I'm Mrs. Norton."

The girl smiled and turned to a computer. She nodded and slid a clipboard across the counter.

"Please sign in, Billy's room is ready. I have a note here from our Dr. Kimmer. Have you met him?"

"Yes, he came to the house," she turned, "didn't he Billy?"

The boy lowered the plane and nodded.

"He'll come by after you get settled." The girl put both elbows on the counter, causing her blond hair to fall forward to her chin.

"Hi Billy, my name's Samantha, but you can call me Sam. I help out here at the school."

Billy waved to her.

"I've got something for you."

Billy's eyes widened, his face turned towards his mom and then back to Sam. He inched closer to his mother.

She put a white box the size of a book on the counter, and tilted it up. "See, it's addressed to you, it was here this morning when I came in." She smiled. "Maybe it's a welcome to Providence School gift."

Billy didn't move.

Sam inched the package across the counter. Billy watched his mom. She nodded. Billy took it.

"What do you say, Billy?" Mrs. Norton said, knowing he wouldn't talk.

Billy pushed the box under his left arm, reached up with his right hand, smiled and shook Sam's hand.

"Would you like to see your room?" Sam said.

Billy held the plane and the package to his chest, moved still closer to his mother, and nodded yes.

"This way." Sam led them down a carpeted hall past classrooms with small groups of children, mostly sitting on the floor. They went outside into the gray to a second, taller building. There were no hot air balloon pictures.

"This is where our young men live," Sam said.

Billy smiled as his head twisted right and left taking in the rows of doors, each personalized with posters, hand-painted pictures, and plastic toys.

"I'll bet twenty-three is your lucky number," Sam said, pressing the up button on the elevator. Billy's face turned to the lighted numerals. Soon Sam was pressing buttons to open a combination lock on a plain wood door.

"We can change the combination, Billy. Think of four numbers that will be easy for you to remember, okay?"

Billy nodded.

When Sam opened the door he raced into the room and began exploring.

Mrs. Norton hung back.

"How long will he have to be here?"

"Depends on how he progresses. It's really up to you and Dr. Kimmer. Some kids are here a couple of weeks, others for years. So long as we're helping them," she hesitated, "and they qualify for government assistance, we're happy to have them here."

"Are you full?"

Sam shrugged. "We're busy, but we keep class sizes small. Our focus, as Dr. Kimmer probably mentioned, is a great deal of individual attention. We need to find the activities that help the child respond. Each case is special, here for a different reason. We never know what's going to create a breakthrough."

Sam paused, poked her head in the room to check on Billy, and returned. "I glanced at his file, but it didn't say much."

Mrs. Norton knew why it didn't say much. And also knew she wasn't supposed to say anything to *anyone, ever.* The big man had made it clear.

"He stopped talking, all of a sudden."

Sam nodded, as if all young boys ceased speaking with no apparent reason.

Mrs. Norton turned. A red-haired girl was racing toward them wearing blue jeans and sneakers. Her light green T-shirt had a sketch of a schoolhouse with kids running out of the front door. It read, "Summer."

"Hi, Sam," the girl called out when she arrived. She poked her head around the doorframe to peek inside. "Who's moving in?"

"Hello, Grace. This is Mrs. Norton. Her son Billy will be staying in room twenty-three."

"Neat." She turned. "Hi, Mrs. Norton. It's nice to meet you."

"Hello, Grace. Billy's inside, but he doesn't say much."

"That's okay, I talk a lot." The girl slipped past Sam and into the room.

"The girls are on odd-numbered floors," Sam said. "We want them to interact, but not too much." She smiled.

"Why did Grace come here?"

"She probably went to the front desk, couldn't find me, peeked at my computer and saw the room number." She looked into the room. "Whatever she wanted from me couldn't compete with a new arrival."

Grace's voice called out from inside the room, "Well open it."

Tearing paper sounds followed.

"Wow," Grace said.

Footfalls preceded Billy, Grace close on his heels. He held up his gift with both hands for his mom. It looked like a little flat television.

"Isn't it cool, Mrs. Norton. Someone sent Billy an iPad," Grace said.

"Well, that is very nice," Sam added. "Those can really help with your lessons."

"They play great games too," Grace said.

Mrs. Norton smiled. "That's wonderful, Billy. Who sent it to you?"

He handed her a folded greeting card. She opened it and a rectangle floated to the floor. Billy retrieved it. She read the typewritten message.

Hello Billy: Here's a tool to help you be a good soldier. Keep it by your side and protect it. —Uncle Sam

Mrs. Norton looked up. "Do all the students get one of these?"

Samantha shook her head. "No. They can bring their own, but we don't provide personal computers."

Mrs. Norton showed the note to Samantha.

"Well, Billy, your Uncle Sam must like you," Samantha said. "That sure is a nice back-to-school gift. And a prepaid card so you can buy apps for your new computer."

Billy hugged the flat machine to his chest with both arms.

Mrs. Norton pressed her lips together, and gazed silently at her son.

Chapter 34

CLAIRE DOVE THE BIKE INTO the gulley and west through a dry creek bed. Rocks, and grass a foot high, limited travel to 40 mph. She tapped with her left hand to wake the GPS and select the rendezvous point: 111.6 miles. She checked fuel, her third biggest worry after a bullet and a flat tire: 131 miles remaining.

She doused the headlight and switched to night vision, turning the trees to otherworldly shadows. Her body felt good—100 miles would be easy. She froze. Escaping from a communist country after killing a man had nothing easy about it.

A flash washed her vision to green-white.

Lightning meant rain. She had hills to climb. If rain hit on the way down—she stopped those thoughts, knowing an image of her lying against a tree with a broken leg slowly starving to death was coming. She checked the sky. Dark blobs scudded toward her.

Four hours later the GPS showed Claire at the top of Fu Nye Pass with 02:43:31 remaining when fat raindrops popped against her shield. Four hours of darkness, dust and dodging ruts. She stopped. Her body buzzed with vibration as she stood over the bike to suck fluid from a tube. The throb in her ankle attracted her attention.

Climbing this pass had been slow, jagged rocks making it difficult to carry speed uphill. Now, no more passes, only a last long hill between her and rendezvous. But rainwater made for mud-slicked rock—and gravity complicated braking. She set her jaw and started downhill, speeding up to blow water off her face shield.

She was watching raindrops explode into puffs of dust on a trail just wide enough for donkeys when a small tree branch she figured would bend touched her right hand. The guard protected her fingers, the branch bent, but the one hidden behind it didn't. The bars turned. She fought back.

She was airborne.

She landed with one hand holding a grip. She and the bike slid through jungle brush and slammed against a trunk the size of her thigh. She was on her left side, the bike burbling on top of her. She heard insects chirping, and water pinging her helmet.

She swore aloud and freed herself. The exhaust was dented but quiet. Dirt and grass covered the engine. She sighed. The rain was getting worse so she would have to slow down, which would make it difficult to see, so she would have to slow down more.

Which meant she might be late.

She swung her leg over the bike and a sharp pain shot along the iliotibial band of her right leg. She gritted her teeth, revved the engine and eased back onto the trail. She looked down to check location. The GPS was black. She tapped it with her index finger. Wiggled the cable going into its base. She pulled plants and soil from behind it, and shook the cable again. She smacked the side with her palm.

Still black.

She squinted through the raindrops gliding down her face shield and tried to think. She had maps and a compass, but would have to stop to use them. She peeled back the cuff of her glove. 10:38 PM. Pickup was at 01:00.

She checked the fuel gauge and saw another black screen. A blur on the side of the tank indicated gas. Cracked? That would change the pressure and reduce mileage. Or seep gasoline onto the engine and kill her in an explosion. She looked up the trail and forced herself to calculate how fast she needed to ride.

Without the computer, she wasn't sure. But rolling downhill in the rain, her rear tire sliding and the front dancing on mossy rocks she couldn't see, her answer was *faster*. She eased the throttle open, making the droplets stream horizontally, and tried to visualize the satellite image of her location. Visibility improved. She stood on the pegs, moved her weight toward the rear. The outside of her right leg ached. The trail approached a stream with water oozing through cracks in the mud banks.

The water slowed the bike as it split the stream like the bow of a ship. The front wheel dove so she shifted her hips back and increased power. The front wheel lifted, hydroplaned across the water and drove into muck on the opposite bank. And sank. And sank. She was nearly up to the hub and spinning the rear wheel to keep the machine moving before realizing what was happening.

The bike pivoted around its front axle, somersaulting her up the bank. She landed with her spine flat to the ground.

Breathing heavily, she stared at the water collected over her eyes wondering if she had blacked out. She wiggled her toes and fingers before rolling carefully to her right side. Her left shoulder shot pain toward her elbow. She moved her arm, which ignited new pain in her neck.

She sat up very slowly.

The bike wasn't running.

Something undefined disturbed her, like someone had moved her furniture. She held her breath, and heard the sound of an engine on the wind. She yanked at the buckle and lifted off her helmet. The hills could be playing tricks, but it seemed to be coming from the trail she had just ridden. Could she have gotten out faster than Cam or Wu even with the verification?

The rumble was behind her, and close. Would anyone else be out here? She took her mind back to the party. Other bikes? Tread marks? No, but she hadn't been looking. She slammed her fist into the earth and examined the resulting mud on her glove as if it were blood.

Stupid. Be calm.

Black muck sucked at her clothing as she crawled to the bike. The front wheel was free but pointed in the wrong direction. She lifted with her right arm and pressed the starter, then sighed with relief, gave it power and pushed as pain sizzled from her shoulder.

The bike reared up. She stepped back to let it spin then fell on her stomach on the seat and squirmed up the bank onto the trail. She needed to think about her fuel situation, location, map, compass and the time ticking. But the only thing in her mind was that sound. If it were Cam or Wu, she would happily follow their GPS. But if not? And they had seen her. And were trying to catch her.

Holding tight and riding faster than was smart, she test rotated her left arm. It hurt, but didn't make her pass out. She came to the first of two forks and took the left that hugged the stream. It had been big enough to see from the satellite images.

She counted fifteen slow even breaths, placing her about a minute beyond the fork, made a left, rode slowly across a narrow section of the stream and up the opposite bank. She turned left again through broadleaf evergreens three feet high and stopped under a banyan tree. She flicked the bike off, looked up, and remembered that banyans were called "strangler figs" because they could encircle a host tree.

She scrubbed mud off her watch. 12:11 AM. Less than an hour—she must have passed out—and no measure of distance remaining. She peeled off both gloves. In less than a minute her R-21 was pointed at the fork.

She could hear the soft brrr of an engine and tried to decide if it was like hers. If it took the same fork she had, following her tracks, what would she do? Take the shot, or let the rider pass and follow.

She waited.

The sound became a growl, a beast fighting its way through the forest. She saw it ride to the fork and stop. The rider, six foot, medium build, looked down at his tank bag. She could see a map through her scope. His head lifted to face down one trail, then the other. His engine grew silent. He stood over his bike with a finger on the map. The bike was bigger than hers, with pistons sticking out of the sides.

An easy shot.

She waited. Water dripped from the barrel. Her breathing was even, like at a match. She had killed one man today. Why not two if it would protect the mission?

The exhaust puffed smoke and the bike moved up the right fork. She eased her trigger finger, wondering if she was making a huge mistake. Seventy-five seconds passed, she stowed the rifle, pulled on wet gloves, and rode.

Chapter 35

CAM PUTNAM STOOD BESIDE the wide overhead door of a rotting plank shack once used to store munitions, worrying. The area 200 yards west where the chopper was supposed to land was filled with trees eight feet high. He wished they could blow it open with an explosive charge. But that would leave a scar, so cables would be needed to lift the bikes out one by one. Not fast.

He checked his watch for the twentieth time in three minutes.

"Where's Ferreti?"

Wu stood to his right, both men scanning the hills Claire had to cross to reach them.

"She'll be here. It's only rain."

"She doesn't have your experience. And we don't know she got out." He lifted his arm to flick a cigarette into the forest, stopped. He swung his heel back to dig a hole in the wet earth, dropped the cigarette and pushed mud over it with his toe. "One of us should have gone in."

"We all agreed. A woman had a better chance of being considered harmless, a Chinese guy's toy, safe to ignore. If you had gone in, someone would call a tank to stop you."

They looked through black rain.

"Do you hear anything?" said Cam.

They stood in silence.

"Drizzle on Jack Fruit trees. Our mufflers are good though, she could be close."

Cam looked at his wrist again. "Eighteen fucking minutes." He walked through the open door and picked up his rifle, leaned against the side of the building and scanned the forest through the scope's night vision. He could see the trail he and Wu had both taken. It was now a stream of brown liquid becoming a waterfall.

"Thoughts?" Cam said.

"Bike failed, she's walking," Wu said. "GPS failed, she's lost. A crash and she's hurt. Someone grabbed her at the house and she's screwing a Chinese kingpin to protect her cover."

"Thanks for the reality check. What can we do?"

"In eighteen minutes?" Wu asked.

"Seventeen."

"We each do a fifteen minute loop, two minute margin. Or we go straight out and back and see if we can find fresh tracks."

Cam walked to his bike, mounted, spun a 180 in the slurpy mud.

"I'll take the south trail to the river. There were three crossings." His bike revved.

"Insanity," Wu said to exhaust fumes.

Cam didn't ride up the trail so much as swim as water rushing downhill filled grooves that tried to trap his front tire. He climbed for most of five minutes, swept left along a ridge, and almost missed the first crossing. He slid to a stop. No tread patterns. He shut off his engine and listened to a drizzle that reminded him of the crap foofoo massage parlors played to go with their incense. He thumbed his starter and climbed.

The second crossing was easier to find at the bottom of a mini-valley, slick mud in both directions. He had used six of his seven and a half minutes. But he figured he could stretch that. He had a two-minute buffer and he wouldn't have to stop on the way back to listen.

He climbed out of the valley with a rooster tail of black water behind him. His GPS showed four minutes to the waypoint for the next intersection. He accelerated.

When he arrived he could see cross tracks from thirty yards away. He stopped above them, looked back. They matched his. He was out of time, but they had to be Claire's. If they missed the pickup, at least there would be two of them trying to get out with no support. He guessed and turned right. In fifteen seconds the tracks grew dim.

He planted his left foot, spun the bike and raced back through the intersection. He rode hard, watching the tracks in front grow fresher. A rise in the trail sent the bike into the air. While airborne his goggles filled with blinding white. Without vision, his timing was off when the bike landed, twisting left while his body continued straight.

He rolled and popped to his feet to see a silhouette against a headlight. He raised his right arm to protect his eyes and switched off night vision. The world turned dark except for a small strip of sewer-like mud running toward his boots and a person holding a rifle. The image moved toward him. He looked left, dropped to one knee and grabbed for the automatic inside his boot. As he rolled for cover he heard, "Cam, is that you?"

"Claire!" He stood. "What the hell?"

"There was a bike following me."

"Are you okay?"

"I can ride."

He scrambled to his machine, "We have six minutes to make rendezvous."

"My GPS failed."

"We're close, follow me."

He dug his bike out of the weeds. Moments later they were at the crossroad. His GPS estimated 07:17 to target, his clock showed 00:55:02. Four minutes and fifty-eight seconds to contact.

He accelerated.

With less than a minute remaining the shack appeared through gray sheets of blowing rain.

Chapter 36

"GOVERNOR TYNE DUE IN two minutes, Mr. President," Spin said.

Across the room, seated behind a low dark desk, the President nodded but continued reading. Beside his elbow lay a folder labeled "Secret." Bert hadn't seen inside. Bert only saw projects that needed sugar coating for the public—usually later than he preferred.

Like this pipeline. It was all about public, and how the future would be presented. And delicate. The Governor of Alaska had his PR people spinning stories, and his own reelection to think about.

Bert rotated his chair, keeping one eye on the clock in front of him, and the other on the President. He loved this room. Loved that it had telephone feeds and big monitors and video and Internet and 3D virtual imagery and satellite connections to everywhere in the world, and even a couple to outer space. It could feed data to the big man like no other room in Washington. It was sound proof, and as secure as any room the President visited.

That was the good part.

He glanced sidelong at a wall of fancy electronics. It was supposed to record the actual conversation between the President and the Governor. But how could Bert know, really know, that it wasn't secretly recording everything he said and did? And someday a video of him giving advice to the President would suddenly appear on the Internet?

He couldn't.

But he also couldn't be careful. His job was to tell the President how to spin information to the public. Or to Tyne. Or to anyone else the President wanted to influence.

That's why he hated this room. It looked like a room that wanted to listen…and remember.

He touched the insert in his ear where he would hear the conversation, and repositioned the microphone in front of him to be used to speak privately to the President.

The phone rang: a plain jingling bell. The screen showed a mapped location and address in Juneau, and identified the caller with his picture and name.

The ringing stopped. Screening was underway. Bert waited.

The President slipped the papers he had been reading inside and pushed the folder away. He nodded toward Bert.

They waited.

A red light glowed on a black handset. President Mallor picked it up.

"Hello, Governor. Are you satisfied with the progress we're making against this pipeline issue?"

Bert nodded slowly. The President had opened exactly how Bert had suggested. Make this about how Tyne was feeling, not about what was or was not being provided to his state.

Tyne's voice filled Bert's ear. "Yes and no, Mr. President. As you know, the owners have agreed to cover the full repair. I quote, 'The Trans-Alaska Pipeline System is critical to our present and future operations north of the Arctic Circle. It will be repaired and fully operational before the coming winter.'"

Tyne cleared his throat.

Bert watched the President's face for hints.

"Excuse me," Tyne continued. "However, they want to deflect responsibility for damage to the manufacturer of the pump, who claims there is insufficient evidence to make them responsible. In addition, the insurance company insists that the entire collapse was a single incident, and therefore will only pay the maximum once, rather than for each successive pump that was overwhelmed."

"That tremendously limits their liability," Mallor said, following Bert's advice to shine light on the bad guys.

"Yes. And it will limit Exxon Mobil's contribution to clean up, and to the infrastructure required to support the thousands of workers who are about to descend on Alaska looking for a piece of the repair gold."

"So you need to invest in infrastructure?" Mallor asked.

Bert tried to relax his jaw.

"That will be difficult without the pipeline pumping, because the state shares in revenue generated by the pipe. No pumping, no revenue. A direct road to a local recession, just as we need to be investing in infrastructure."

"I see," Mallor said.

Bert smiled. Mallor was making Tyne do the suggesting.

"In addition," Tyne said, "Exxon is lowballing me on the future revenues estimates. They would be more comfortable if they knew they could drill offshore to the north. Global warming is opening up shipping lanes, they're anxious to get started."

"They're looking for concessions?" Mallor asked.

"They want to reduce the state's share to help cover the environmental cleanup and to pay for insurance premiums for the new wells, which of course just went up drastically. They're also whispering about a cap."

So far so good, Bert thought. Except for the cap. He wondered if Exxon was serious.

"So Governor, if I may, you would like me to allocate federal funds for cleanup, matching funds for infrastructure development, and put federal tax pressure on Exxon to encourage them to leave the state allotments alone, including no cap on payments to Alaska."

The phone was quiet. Mallor had tossed a hairball. Tyne was probably going down a checklist with a pencil.

"Yes, Mr. President, that would be very helpful. We need to prevent a cap because no one can predict how much oil might be found to the north. Which brings us to the larger issue."

Mallor said nothing. The line was briefly silent.

"Oil companies are nervous about federal drilling approval over the next four years. Is there anything I can say at our next meeting to convince them to move forward with their investment?"

"That depends," Mallor said, "on who they vote for." He laughed, even though, in Bert's opinion, he had spoken the truth. "Seriously, Thomas, I can't help if I'm not reelected. There is intense media attention on Alaska. What you as the Governor say to the nation matters a great deal."

"Yes, Mr. President, I understand. Which is why I wanted to talk with you about my concerns before going public."

"Just so I'm clear, Thomas. We're not concerned here with the three electoral votes of Alaska, though every one helps. There is the larger issue of how voters across the nation perceive the way Washington is handling the pipeline crisis on all the fronts I mentioned: environmental, infrastructure, the price of gas, and, of course, national security. So Exxon and their friends need to cooperate." Mallor lifted his eyes to meet Bert's. Bert nodded. The issue was on the table. Tyne's move.

"I'm most worried about that cap, Mr. President. Estimates for the northern fields are quite large. If they turn out to be even bigger than we think, well, I'd hate for the people of Alaska not to benefit."

Bert smiled. Tyne would hate to see Tyne not benefit—financially and by being reelected.

"I understand you have people at the University of Alaska interested in aeronautics," Mallor said.

The line was quiet. Bert could almost hear Tyne shift gears.

"Why yes. We have a growing effort."

"As you know, drone development for our military is a top priority of my administration. I think we're behind." He paused. "Alaska is uniquely situated geographically. Hell, you can see Russia and almost touch China, plus you have the extreme weather conditions required for operational testing. It strikes me that research monies for a next generation robotics effort would be well placed in Alaska. We prefer to start investing at the graduate student level, so we develop not only technology, but the researchers of the future who will lead American technology forward." He paused again, reached over and pushed the folder with the secrets. "Naturally, pilots to fly these robot drones should be nearby, perhaps a facility in the islands, but you would know better than I where best to locate a training facility." Mallor leaned back in his chair. Bert saw his eyes drift to the large red numerals of the wall clock.

Tyne was silent for less than three seconds.

"I'll work with Exxon and BP to get the word out on the freak mechanical failure. We'll highlight how State and Federal government are working seamlessly with private industry to bring the pipe back online as soon as possible, and jointly moving forward with the new fields to help meet the growing energy needs of the U.S. in the future."

"Thank you, Thomas," Mallor said. "I appreciate your help. You can let the oil men know that permits to drill will be difficult to obtain if they insist on revenue caps to government. After all, if things go well, we should all benefit."

Mallor hung up, but didn't take his hand off the receiver for a full five seconds.

Bert smiled.

Mallor stood. "What's that asshole Petry saying about me now?"

Bert stopped smiling. He spun in his chair and swiped his fingers across a pad. A hi-def video frame of Petry's face filled both monitors.

"He's spending, Mr. President. Network, cable, and regular YouTube posts that are clearly professionally produced, but made to look candid. We also have a cell phone recording from a private fund-raiser."

"Let's see the fund-raiser," Mallor said as he began to pace.

Bert tapped the pad until he found the file sent by their spy on the street.

He started the movie. The quality was good and the shooter had somehow stabilized the camera. Petry was standing at a podium between stacks of bright yellow flowers waiting for applause to fade away. There couldn't have been more than a couple hundred people in the room.

"My opponent worships at the alter of Deus." He waved his arms. "No, not more of the Christian God, but the D, E, U, S gods of technology. Today I would like to talk in detail..."

"How much a plate?" Mallor asked.

Bert looked on the computer for the details that came with the file. "Ten thousand. In Southern California."

"Aerospace," Mallor mumbled, and continued pacing.

"'D' means drones," Petry said from between the flowers. "Our military loves drone attacks. A young man who grew up playing video games sits in a cubicle in New Jersey or Nevada while a Predator under his control kills people anywhere in the world. Thousands of such attacks have taken place, killing thousands of people. Some we didn't bother to identify before ending their lives. Some were our own soldiers. Hundreds were children. We are on track to spend almost $100 billion..."

"First point," Mallor said. "Mistakes are made in war, not just with drones."

Bert pulled a ballpoint out of his pocket and scribbled notes on a legal pad.

"Latest polls?" Mallor asked.

Bert knew to have the numbers in his head. "This morning, forty-eight percent. Petry's up to forty-one. Historically, still a winning position for an incumbent."

Mallor nodded.

"As we invest," Petry droned on, "the manufacturers go to a "Fly In" in Singapore, or Paris and what happens? They sell to anyone with the money to pay. Who then clone our work. There are fifty countries actively building war robots, that accounts for..."

Bert watched the President pace. His eyes were drifting around the room like he was thinking about what color to repaint it.

"'E,' yes, Education. Robotics contracts awarded to our excellent institutions of higher learning where American enrollment continues to drop and American professors are becoming an endangered species. These institutions educate foreign students who return to their own countries, taking the knowledge we pay to develop with them. At the same time, our K through 12 system graduates barely ten percent of its students into science. That number in China is fifty percent. And the Chinese greatly outnumber..."

Mallor stopped moving, but didn't speak. That was Bert's cue.

"He doesn't like the research labs you're funding to keep us competitive."

"He thinks a bunch of high school kids are going to win the next war? Point. All those bright foreign minds are over here working on technology for us, which we then own. So who's being exploited?"

Bert scribbled notes.

"...we are expected to believe that building unmanned machines to fight wars is wise economics. The President points to lives saved by robots removing landmines and doing surveillance. I agree. But then...*then*...he makes a great leap forward to a world where swarms of autonomous robots flock into battle, make decisions of their own, reconfigure themselves. I can't seem to find a robot vacuum that doesn't hang up on the furniture, so I'm certainly not prepared to put a rifle in the hands of an autonomous robot. Why would we endeavor to create..."

"How do we educate people about this problem, Bert? Asymmetric warfare, emerging superpowers, unforeseen technology. Petry doesn't understand that we don't get to pick the time and place and nature of the next war. We have to prepare for them all."

Bert scribbled and nodded. He knew it was his job to create a compelling story, and that the story had to be about defense and economic growth, just like always.

"Which brings us to the 'S' in Deus, this imagined techno-god that is usurping the financial resources of our great nation. Space. Yes, the President wants to invest in systems that will allow us to, and I quote, 'Control the new International Commons of space and cyberspace, and pave the way for a new military service — U.S. Space Forces — with the mission of space control.'" Petry paused.

Bert looked to the President, who was now staring at the image on the screen.

Petry studied his audience, appearing to make eye contact. He slowly took a drink of water from a bottle with a large green leaf logo.

"The man quotes our documents, but has no understanding," Mallor said.

Petry continued. "Ladies and gentlemen, the United States cannot afford another space race. We have spent billions upon billions to build nuclear weapons that we are now, under treaty negotiations, spending billions to dismantle into zombies. At the same time, we have successfully limited the use of biological weapons by treaty because we don't want them on our planet. I implore you, do not place the future of our country on the altar of this false robo-god. Begin negotiations now, begin strategic robot limitation talks now, and severely curtail the sale of our war technology so as not to provide every angry young man with superpowers of destruction. We must focus our technology efforts toward the abundance robot socialism could provide. A world where robots are producing, not destroying, our way of life. Let us pave the way to universal prosperity and world peace where slums and anger need no longer exist. We must do better than squander our opportunity to lead this great planet by chasing after the shadows of Deus." Petry paused, looked down, then up. "Thank you. I very much appreciate your support."

Applause erupted, and the image shook as the spy slipped the phone toward a jacket pocket.

Bert waited.

The President stared at the blank screen, turned and left the room.

Chapter 37

THE MAN STANDING ON A RIDGE holding recording binoculars to his eyes leaned against a 300 year-old banyan tree. There had been three riders two kilometers away: one waiting, two racing uphill beyond safe limits. Then the hovering Osprey, a thirty billion dollar military extravagance, had fired. His guess was anti-tank missiles, detonation by GPS, no chance of a miss. A pair of them.

The melted roof glowed with heat; the man inside vaporized. The Osprey was lifting away to the north. Two twisted bodies lying on the hill were not moving. Someday he would like to know what had just happened.

He switched off the safety on his QSZ-92 Chinese Ruger clone, chambered a round, opened a zipper on his thigh and slipped it into the pocket. He mounted his motorcycle and rode slowly toward the inferno.

He dismounted fifty meters from what was left of the building, pulled out the Ruger with his right hand, pointed its rail mounted laser at the bodies, and approached on foot. Neither moved as the red dot danced on their clothing. He could hear the sizzle of raindrops superheated by the chemical fire.

The rider further uphill had the solid athletic build of an Olympic rower. The explosion had seared off the front of his riding suit and charred the flesh. His head faced downhill. The man pointed his revolver at the head and touched the rider's throat. No pulse. He removed a glove to check again. He flipped open the face shield and listened. He moved on. Later he would bury the man, and salvage the bikes.

The last of the three was the furthest from the blast lying face up with a motorcycle covering the top half of the body. The blue and white roundel of BMW was visible above the single cylinder engine. He worked his way around the machine, pointed his firearm at the face and pulled the right glove off. The slender wrist confirmed a woman with a faint pulse was trapped beneath the machine. He stood. Her clothing was intact; he didn't see burns. The man must have been between her and the blast.

He examined the bike. It had a torn side panel that held pieces of a sniper rifle. He pocketed his gun and lifted the bike away from her body. As it moved her head twisted. Leaning the half-lifted bike against his hip, he bent over. A metal foot peg had pierced the front of her helmet and was stuck in the shell. Liquid had pooled behind the face shield. Still holding the bike, he flipped the shield up. Blood flowed over the chin bar and dripped onto her chest. He pressed the helmet with one knee so her head and neck wouldn't move as he lifted with both arms. The ratcheting sound of steel scraping fiberglass filled the jungle. Blood filled the hole. He was running the risk of injuring her neck, but if he didn't do something, she would bleed to death. Or drown in her own blood.

He twisted the front wheel and overturned the bike onto its seat, away from her legs. He worked the double-D rings of the helmet strap, pulled the safety pads and eased the helmet from her head. The left side of her face was a mass of matted blood. Fresh red liquid flowed from a gash above her left eye. The socket was caked over. Driving rain diluted the ooze to a watery stream that looked like ink slipping beneath her collar. Bubbles of dampness dotted her forehead.

He elevated the head, trotted back to his machine, and rode up beside her. He popped the seat off and fumbled for tools and a first aid kit. He gently pressed a pad over the gash. He wrapped a gauze strip around her head over the pad, then once around with duct tape. He broke bits of fiberglass off the inside of her helmet where it had been penetrated, then pulled it over the bandage and wet hair.

He knew the jungle was a dangerous place to be injured; infection hid everywhere. He wished for the luxury of an evacuation chopper. But who would fly here in the middle of a storm? He glanced toward the burning hut, remembering rockets.

He dismissed the waiting option.

He flicked his flashlight at her face. The pupils in her green eyes responded but she was clearly unconscious, with a weak pulse, and losing blood. He looked at his bike and thought about the trails he had ridden to get here, and where he needed to take her. None of it was his first choice.

He lifted her onto the bike and duct-taped her boots to the passenger pegs. Then he mounted in front and ran big loops of tape just below her armpits and around his chest. Her arms dangled at her sides and her head tilted back. He pulled her head forward and put tape around his helmet and hers to hold her in place above his right shoulder. He then brought her arms under his and taped her wrists together, like she was hugging him from behind. He rocked the bike. Her body remained in place.

He stomped into gear with his toe and rolled away slowly, letting the big knobs of the rear tire chew into the muck. Rain dripped from a duckbill visor onto his night-vision goggles.

Chapter 38

BILLY WILLIAMS WALKED BESIDE the shallow pond west of the 555-foot obelisk dedicated to George Washington wondering how many secret meetings had been held out here in the open. He stopped to study the reflections, wishing he were sitting inside breathing air-conditioned oxygen. A woman passed in the wavy water wearing a pink dress, holding a black umbrella open against the sun. He was reminded of a fairy-tale witch: the good one, who made nice things happen.

He smiled.

Big Bird had visited the little house on the prairie, all that remained was to assure the President things were under control. He sat on a low wall and watched the huge gray monument wiggle in the water. He imagined it was the pipeline, a valuable asset on U.S. soil, attacked by roving machines the experts had never seen. Troubling. But a terrorist taken down by snipers? That was his kind of war. He had known Ferreti had skills the first time he met her. He also knew they would one day be useful. He hadn't thought it would be so soon...or temporary.

He clenched his teeth. Mallor's obsession with secrecy was forcing unusual actions.

And the Chinese. They spent a smaller percentage of GDP on arms, but with over a billion people...this country needed Mallor. He thought about what would happen to the U.S. if it ever needed a highly trained, technical Army, unmanned drones and all—and it wasn't there.

He noticed Spin on the other side of the pond carrying a gray umbrella between his balding head and the sun. Billy stood and waited.

Spin didn't smile, but he did extend his hand.

"Hello Bert, Alaska is under control," Billy said.

"Do you mean the billions of dollars it's going to cost to clean up that mess, the panic that's forcing gas prices up just because a lousy four percent of American crude can't reach market, or the drop in the President's rating in the polls? Exactly which part do you have under control?"

Anger crawled up Billy's spine before he realized that Spin, a man who shaded shades of meaning for a living, was asking a serious question.

"The part about it not happening again."

Spin's eyebrows were the only indication of surprise.

"You've taken care of that?"

"Yes." Billy wanted to elaborate, but fewer words carried more power with Spin.

"Side effects?"

Billy shook his head. "None. No leaks. No loose ends. Nothing to find when the records are declassified by some bleeding-heart judge on the take."

"No attitude there," Spin said. Then he smiled. "Someday, when I'm lying on my death bed, I'd like to hear how you did it. But for now..." his voice trailed away. "I'll inform the President, assuming that's what you want me to do?"

"That's your department. It's unclear to me if it's better for him to be informed, in case this is relevant to other activities, or not know, so he has deniability." Billy returned Spin's smile. "He probably won't sleep much until November either way."

"I'll consider the options, General. Thanks." Spin turned and looked down at the pond as if considering the pleasure of a dip in cool water on a hot day. Then his smile evaporated and he walked away.

Billy strolled the length of the pond, wishing Typhoon would make contact, and the satellites would get the sun angle they needed to give him a better look at the little house.

Chapter 39

RICHARD TONVER HAD RIDDEN a thousand miles after leaping from the Russian train. Now he stood beside Dr. Ming in a narrow hallway. The Doctor scribbled ferociously on a clipboard and spoke at the same time. "She remains in a coma. It has only been twenty hours, so we are not yet overly concerned. Her right leg is heavily bruised. Left collarbone is broken. I have adjusted and immobilized it with a quick cast. It is properly aligned."

He paused and continued to write.

Richard waited. Ming often saved the worst for last.

"Head," Ming began. "Yes, the head. Our patient was struck hard. Above left eye." Ming touched his index finger to his face to indicate the exact location. "The injury is deep. I have cleaned and sutured it, but the skull." He stopped writing and looked up to meet Richard's eyes. "Without proper scanning equipment, it is difficult to know."

"Do I find a scanner and move her to it?" Richard asked.

Ming didn't look away. "We wait. Respiration is fine. Pulse is low at 56, as is her blood pressure, 105 over 65." He signed his name to the document. "We wait." He gave a closed lip smile before walking away.

Richard stood outside her door and debated what he could accomplish by going in. It was doubtful he could learn more than Ming had just told him. And there was work to do. But he turned the knob quietly and stepped inside. The afternoon sun sneaking through a bamboo shade cast golden stripes into the room. The wall behind him was solid, but the other three were thick nylon, borrowed from surplus military tents. They were durable, showing no sign of having been in place for almost six months. Fortunately, the wind had departed with the rain, leaving the room in a cave-like quiet. He listened to her slow breathing, wondering what she might be thinking, or dreaming—if her brain was doing anything at all.

He moved to her bedside. Her left shoulder was in a cast from elbow to earlobe. Her face was bandaged so only her nose and part of her right eye and cheek were visible. He tried to imagine what a motorcycle in the face would feel like. Enough force to puncture a helmet. She had been beyond lucky the peg had missed her eye.

Richard circled around the foot of the twin bed and looked into her closed right eye, willing it to open. No matter how he thought about it, he couldn't make sense of the missiles, even though he had recorded their firing and watched it replay a dozen times. The mere presence of a vertical take-off plane made no sense. She could shed light on the situation, if she didn't die.

Her right hand was palm down outside the single gray blanket that covered her body, exposing smooth white skin and short nails painted crystal blue. He put his thumb and index finger around her four fingers, the way one might take a child's hand. She was warm, but not feverish.

She didn't return his touch.

"Why do you travel with a weapon made in China, and illegal to export?" he said softly.

She was silent.

"And ride a German motorcycle?"

He watched clear liquid drip into a tube, and followed it with his eyes to the needle in her forearm.

Chapter 40

THE FIRST THING SHE SENSED was the distant sound of giggling. She saw only darkness. A roiling ball of fire silhouetting the shape of Cam on his bike grew in her vision. She reflexively lifted her left arm to protect her eyes. Pain enveloped her shoulder, the side of her neck, down her spine. Blackness. She lay still and waited for her breathing to slow.

She heard the giggle again.

She concentrated on opening her left eye only—still black. Panic rushed through her heart as she realized she might have been blinded by the blast. She thought about living the next fifty years in darkness.

Her breathing accelerated.

She forced her right eye open and saw a curved shadow. She moved her eyeball and the shadow danced. She could see something. Relief rose in her chest like morning vapor from a lake. She tried to focus, made out the shape of a window. Color emerged. The yellow-tan of bamboo undulated against a green sea. She let her eye drift closed.

The giggle, then a whisper of a voice, not speaking English.

She turned her head toward the window. Stiffness caressed her neck below the right ear. She reopened her right eye. Her left arm was covered in white. Her toes—she could see them under a blanket. She was in bed, in a room. The door beyond her feet was open ten inches and a small boy's face peeked through.

She could see. She sighed with her entire body as it relaxed into the caress of the mattress.

She tried to say "Hello," but only moaned.

The door closed. Slowly the knob turned and the door inched back into the room. The face peeked in again, no giggles.

She whispered a hoarse, "Come in" with unused muscles. She hoped the face wasn't an angel.

The door swung open and she heard pawomp pawomp. The giggling face arrived at her right side. A caramel skinned boy of perhaps ten or twelve stood beside her, his face not much higher than hers. He was smiling under a matte of straight black hair. And he was on crutches.

"What's your name?" she asked in a whisper, her throat dust-storm dry.

"Me Quan," he said, pointing a finger at his nose. "Who you?" The finger turned and touched her face.

A good question. Who was she? Oh, she knew who she really was. But who should she be to this boy and this room and whoever had brought her here and saved her life.

The little boy stared at her right eye, not flipping back and forth between both eyes like most people do when meeting a gaze. She panicked again; what was wrong with her left eye? She suddenly lost all motivation to lie.

"Claire."

"Hello Cu-a-lair," he said, pronouncing her name carefully.

"Hi," she said, and smiled. Her lips worked, but the left side of her face flared with heat. She stopped smiling.

"You wake up," he said.

"Was I asleep?"

"You sleep since first day."

First? "How long since first day?" she heard herself ask.

The boy named Quan counted silently on his fingers. She saw him switch to his other hand.

"Eight."

Over a week since the hit—what was going on in Washington? What about Cam and Wu?

"Did my friends come with me?"

His little brow creased. He shook his head. "You come with Bike Man." He said the name with the reverence reserved for Super Man, or Spider Man. Balancing on his crutches, he put both hands in front of him in the universal motorcycle riding gesture and twisted his right wrist.

She hadn't seen anyone except the guy she almost shot at the fork. But he had turned north. A memory of a hovering aircraft invaded. There was supposed to be a chopper. That plane had fired at them. A streak re-crossed her eyes in night-vision green, the last thing she had seen before the explosion. Yes, she was certain the plane had fired.

The boy stared at her, his eyes round and friendly. She tried to smile a very small smile with just the right side of her mouth. It partially worked—her head hurt but didn't spasm.

"Where is Bike Man?" she asked.

"He busy but say you wake up he come want me go get?"

She held her little smile. "Yes, please. I would like to thank him."

150

Quan spun and pawomped across the room. She turned to watch him with her one good eye. As his back disappeared through the doorway she noticed his right leg didn't reach the floor.

She sank into the pillow. Her body ached everywhere. She tried to float into sleep as the extraction events replayed. She had been lost, the trails confusing in the rain. She almost shot Cam. They raced back together. That plane. Why was there a plane?

* * *

The fog of sleep burned slowly away and revealed a man sitting beneath the window. The bamboo shade was closed. Sunlight through the slits painted zebra skin on her blanket, the stranger, and a large paper he held that looked like a map. She watched. He could be American. Solid, maybe six foot. Dark hair cut military short over a square face. He needed a shave two or three days ago. He was wearing a black T-shirt with a sketch over the left breast and black jeans held up by a drilled black leather belt. She couldn't see the buckle. He had his left ankle crossed over his right knee and he was barefoot. He studied the large paper intensely, like he could win the Super Lotto if he solved its puzzle.

"Good morning," he said, without taking his eyes from the document. "Did you have a nice nap?"

She blinked in slow motion. "Is it morning?"

"Actually, no. It's dusk. This room faces west." He began folding the map-thing. "I just said that since your day is beginning." Still sitting with his legs crossed he looked at her for the first time. "It's good to have you with us, Claire."

She stared. He knew her name? She didn't know him, though he looked familiar in a *maybe he went to my high school* sort of way.

"Quan told me," he said.

"Who is Quan?"

"My friend. Little guy about so high," he held his left hand out a foot above the bed. "Black hair, big smile. Calls me Bike Man. He came to get me."

She remembered, though her dreams and experience were not totally separate in her head. He hadn't mentioned Quan's crutches.

"He said you brought me here," she managed.

"What was left of you," he said, finishing his folding and slipped the paper into a back pocket. He stood and walked to her bedside. "My name's

Mike," Richard Tonver told her.

"Mike and the Bike," she said, striving to smile. "They wrote a book about you."

"Mine have motors, like Mike "The Bike" Hailwood: famous racer. How are you feeling?"

"Glad to be anywhere." She paused, took a breath. "Quan told me I've been out for a long time." Her voice was soft, barely controlled.

"Coma for nearly a week. Awake for only a few seconds at a time since then. Dr. Ming was worried." He paused. "He's not a man to worry."

"So how am I?" She looked him in the eye as best she could, "Really?"

He hooked his thumbs into jean pockets and met her eye. "Are you feeling up to a status report?"

She shivered. Maybe she was, maybe she wasn't, but she had to find out sometime. And start making a plan.

"I'll do my best. If I pass out, stop, okay?"

He grinned. "Sense of humor, intact," he made a little checkmark with his right index finger in his left palm. He walked to the end of her bed and returned with a clipboard. "Right leg, severe contusion, left collarbone broken, puncture wound above the left eye. Is that about how it feels?"

"Yeah, hurts like hell." Her eye. Just the thought of...she fought for courage. "My uh, that puncture. How's my..."

"Your left eye should be fine, the wound is above it. Doc wants to do some tests now that you're awake." He lowered the clipboard. "Thank your helmet manufacturer."

Her whole body floated like she had just had a good massage. She was left-handed. She aimed with her left eye.

"Thanks. I mean, shit, my eye. I..."

He touched her hand. "Anyone would be. I'll let Doc Ming know you're awake." He turned to go but stopped at the foot of the bed. "Are you hungry?"

She forgot about her eye, and thought about her stomach. "I'm starving."

"I'll see what I can do," he said, opening the door. "Nice to meet you, Claire."

"Um..."

He stopped and turned.

"Thanks," she said.

"Sure. You would have done the same for me."

"And Mike." She licked her lips and formed a question. It sounded foolish even as she said it. "Where am I?"

"A good question. Technically, you're on South Vietnamese soil. Practically, you're in the middle of nowhere. A philosophically better question might be: Who am I?" He waved with two fingers and stepped out.

She felt heavy wet concrete being poured on her body. She had larger problems than a broken collarbone. How was she going to explain three riders in China for a rendezvous at an abandoned hut?

Three riders. Coma. Her eye. Wu. Riding lessons. Cam. Chocolate bullets. She drifted toward sleep. Isolation. Billy's voice...*if you don't get out.*

A tiny drop streamed across her right cheek.

Chapter 41

A MOUNTAIN OF BRAISED rice noodles, four kinds of fish, colorful vegetables flavored with Thai basil that reminded her of sweet licorice, and three days later she heard a commotion in the hallway. Mike bumped into the room pushing an empty wheel chair. "Doc Ming says you're ready to walk. The exercises you've been doing with Quan are about to pay off."

"If I'm going to walk, what's the chair for?"

"When you crash."

"Your confidence overwhelms me," she said.

He helped her swing both legs to the floor. She looked down. A deep black bruise reached from mid-thigh to below her right knee. It hurt just to flex the leg; she doubted it could support weight.

"Oh boy, we going to dance?" Quan asked as he swung into the room on his crutches.

She laughed.

Mike lifted under her right arm. The room remained stable. Her legs felt like wooden stilts. She shuffled forward.

"Wanna race?" asked Quan.

She laughed again. "Not yet. But watch out, I'm coming after you."

She made it to the hall leaning hard on Mike's arm. Quan threw his crutches across the wheel chair and pushed it along behind her with a ride and hop motion. It was comforting knowing she had a place to sit down.

They inched down a corridor six feet wide, passing small rooms like hers occupied by Asian men, women and children. Most had casts or bandages on extremities: a leg, an arm, the side of a face.

A little girl rolled herself toward them in a pint-sized wheelchair, dark curls bouncing with each push forward. She greeted them with, "Hi Bike, Hi Quan," and a big round stare at Claire.

Quan hopped over to the little girl. "Suong, Suong, this is my friend Claire."

"Hello, Suong," Claire said gently, struggling to stay upright.

The big eyes didn't get smaller, but her mouth curved into a tiny smile.

It was then Claire realized the little girl ended at the chair; no legs protruded forward from the seat. She felt pain and nausea, and put more weight on Mike's arm.

"It is very nice to meet you, Suong," she said softly.

She was rewarded with a tiny squeak of, "Hi."

"Suong, get out of the way, we're exercising," Quan said.

The girl spun her wheels and moved to one side. Claire put on the brightest smile she could muster and walked past her in slow motion.

"What kind of a hospital is this?" she whispered to Mike.

"The kind that's needed out here."

"But the children."

"Victims of war."

She stopped to look at his face.

"War, what war?" she asked.

"In Suong's case, the war with the United States for Vietnamese self-determination."

"But—"

"Yes, it's been over since '75, ever since the Domino Theory of one country after another falling to the evils of Communism went the way of the dodo."

She shuffled forward. "I don't under—"

"BLU-44," he said.

"Agent Orange I've heard about. But blue?"

He laughed. She could feel his chest tense against her arm.

"Dioxin poisoning. Leukemia rates four times other countries. Twelve million gallons poured over millions of acres along with the Rainbow herbicides: Agent Pink, Agent Green, Purple, Blue, White. Half a million dioxin-related birth defects. So you know about it, huh?"

"I've heard of it."

"Because it affected returning U.S. veterans. Otherwise, the word wouldn't be in your dictionary."

She glared at him with her exposed eye, but realized that was how she had heard of it. But leukemia in children? She decided to keep her mouth shut. "What's this 44 stuff?"

"Military casualties in Vietnam." He helped her inch forward. "And civilian."

She was quiet, wondering what could be so powerful.

They walked in silence to a corner. He guided her to the right. "Are you strong enough to go outside for fresh air?"

"Sure," she said, feeling anything but. Then asked, "What is it?" thinking of some sort of chemical weapon that had been used against the U.S. Army.

"Scatterables," he said.

"Scatterables? What the hell are—?" Then it clicked, "Landmines?"

"The Dragontooth. Seeded from aircraft. Used for the first time in Vietnam. Troops trapped by their own mines. Injured some fine soldiers."

He grew silent in the way people do when they turn inside to a memory. She stopped shuffling and watched. His eyes blinked but didn't focus. "Including my father."

She pulled back and teetered. "Your father was killed by a landmine?"

He blinked again and met her eyes. "Not exactly. He was injured by a mine repurposed by the Vietcong, but died of an infection on the evacuation path back to the U.S."

Mike was a walking statistic of a decades-old war. Now she knew why. Not knowing what else to say she said, "I'm sorry."

"Yeah, me too."

"Don't they clear mines?" she asked.

"They?" He paused. "Tough job. And no German POWs like after World War II."

Quan hopped past pushing her chair and used it as a battering ram to open a bare wood screen door. He held the door with one hand and the chair with the other; his wide grin made him seem the happiest person in the world.

She and Mike squeezed through the door together. Their bodies touched. The jolt made her realize she was taking comfort from of a man she hardly knew.

"Your poor mother must have been devastated," she said.

He led her around to the front of the wheelchair so she could sit down. Quan grabbed his crutches and disappeared.

"What brings you to our wonderful country?" he asked.

An icy sense of isolation trickled down her back. She needed to contact Billy so he could extract her, but she had nothing resembling a secure channel. He would extract her, wouldn't he? His voice echoed from the briefing: *We officially know nothing about you.*

She shivered. "Just traveling through."

"Business or pleasure?" he asked, like a customs official.

She smiled at the absurdity of his comment. Not many people rode jungle for fun.

"It's a long story."

"Take your time, you'll be here until that shoulder heals." He crossed dusty grass and leaned against a pole supporting the canopy over the doorway. His back was to her so she couldn't read his expression.

She forced a laugh. "Am I a prisoner?"

"If you want to be."

She owed him. She felt safe, inexplicably. But she lacked a plan. She lacked a method for developing a plan. She shouldn't even tell him her name, rank and serial number.

"Were you there?" she asked, the question popping in from nowhere.

He lowered himself to a cross-legged position on the grass to face her, pulled up a long blade, and chewed on it like a farm boy from Kentucky.

"Yes," he said flatly, "I was there."

She wanted to ask how. How had he happened on them in the jungle? Why was he there at all? But she said, "What do you ride?"

His eyes flickered. "Lots of things. For long distance trail work, a GS. The one with the old boxer motor." He moved his fists back and forth like he was stretching a huge rubber band. "Where the pistons stick out."

She swallowed, remembering a man in her gun sight.

"What did you see?"

He pulled a cell phone off his belt and massaged it with his thumbs. "This."

She reached for the proffered phone. The picture was dark, but she could see jungle, and the building, and Wu inside. She and Cam rushing up the hill. The only sound was the hiss of heavy rain.

She watched mesmerized, like seeing a playback in her mind's eye. The plane. Fireball. Her body hit by Cam's bike, slammed backward down the hill, tumbling with the machine, cage fighters locked in combat. She closed her eyes. Sweat formed on her skin. She felt a hand take the phone away.

"There's something I don't understand," he said, clipping it to his belt.

"What were you doing out there?" she whispered.

"Trying to understand why you were in China."

"I wasn't in China. I was in Vietnam."

"Only after you were in China."

She opened her eyes, gazed at his face.

"What something don't you understand?"

"Why your bike was carrying a Chinese long-range rifle? Not the kind of thing a pretty girl uses for self-defense." He smiled and added, "I've read

Chinese assassins favor them."

She wondered what he knew and how much he was fishing, reminding herself that she wouldn't be breathing if he hadn't dragged her body out of the jungle.

He spoke into her silence.

"It had been fired recently. Your friend's had been fired too. I think I know where to find the bullets. But you know what strikes me. No uniform, no ID, a German motorcycle without identification numbers. An attractive woman in a mini-dress," he paused, "or riding leathers. People like you do not come to visit often."

"You, uh...what happened to my friends?" she asked softly.

"I buried one of them, a big guy. His body protected you from the blast. The other was killed in the fire. I couldn't find his body or bike. Whatever burned that shack was not meant to leave traces. The other bikes I retrieved. I think I can make one good one for you."

She tried not to cry for her colleagues. She tried to hide her shock that he had gone back to bury them. And had stolen the bikes. That meant there was nothing out there to find.

"There's nothing left," she mumbled. Her right eye was growing wet and she couldn't stop it.

"Whoever ordered the Osprey surely double-checked the site as soon as the weather gave the satellites access. If they saw bikes on that hill, they might visit to count bodies."

And they wouldn't have found her and would have come to save her. No. Billy said he couldn't risk another team. Not to China. But he could activate his clandestine network and help her get out. Now, he would think she was dead.

"They think I'm dead," she said, her voice wavering.

"Lucky for you."

He let her cry for half-a-minute.

"Do you know the V-22? A vertical takeoff and landing aircraft developed by the U.S. military. Has seen duty in Iraq. Even made the cover of *Time* magazine. Rolls-Royce engines. There's not much like it." He leaned toward her. "Now why would an Osprey show up when you expected an extraction by helicopter?"

She turned and stared with her uncovered eye. "Did I mention a helicopter?"

He smiled. "Didn't have to, your reaction tells me I guessed right. I've been through dozens of simulations, and found only one plausible explanation."

"A chopper wasn't available? A mechanical maybe."

"Your government has boatloads of choppers," he said. "Literally."

"I don't have a government."

He stood up in one motion without using his arms, like a yoga instructor at the end of class. "No? You're out in the jungle with your Chinese popgun all by yourself. No orders, just a Sunday ride to do a little wilderness camping. Want another guess?" He turned to her, suppressing a smile.

"The Osprey was closer. Or bigger, to make extraction easier." She was giving away information, but it was just hypothetical. "Hypothetically."

"Three people and lightweight bikes. You don't need much to extract that."

She didn't know why the Osprey had been sent, who sent it, or why it fired. Perhaps the Chinese had found out about Demon Drop and moved to block it. She struggled to think clearly.

"Someone didn't want us to get out."

He looked at her with a pleased smile. "Precisely. Notice anything special about that plane?"

"I was sort of busy. It hovered; I saw that. And maybe fired. Something left a bright trail in my night-vision goggles."

"All good points. But its key feature is what it lacked. No markings. Not one." He pointed. "Just like you." He stopped smiling. "My friend Maxx has analyzed the video."

"So? Whoever tried to get us out didn't want to be recognized."

"True," he agreed. "But you know what kind of planes don't have markings? Prototypes. The official V-22 has an air speed of 240 knots. There are rumors that new versions are twice that fast. And can be flown unmanned. Now why would someone want to use a very fast VTOL drone?"

She closed her eyes. "I'm getting tired."

He unlocked the brakes on her wheelchair and started pushing. About half way to her room he said, "Anyone who analyzes the required flight path won't believe a VTOL could be fast enough. And nothing but a chopper could get into that valley, and they're not fast enough either. Therefore, no aircraft could have been there."

She wanted to ask how he knew about the flight path, VTOLs, Chinese rifles. Was he an American operative? But since he was talking, she decided interrupting was a bad idea.

He continued, "I think that plane was meant to be invisible by virtue of a super-tight timeline and superior speed. It hit the building at precisely oh-one-hundred. What were your orders?"

She answered before thinking about the word orders. "Be inside the building at 01:00. Wait for the bay to open. Ride the bikes directly into the chopper."

"Which meant the bikes would be inside with you."

She was quiet as they rolled into her room.

"But we were late."

"Just enough to keep you alive. The Osprey hit from the front, which faces north. And exited to the north. It never even saw you."

He said it as if she should be reassured.

Chapter 42

MOONLIGHT STREAKED THE FLOOR through the shade-covered window. Claire heard jungle insects arguing. She touched her cheek with the fingertips of her right hand—she was sweating or crying, or both. The image of little Suong in the tiny wheelchair joined the insects.

A thought formed. She tried to contain it but the thing seeped out like air escaping through a puncture: *Billy sent the Osprey.*

No. It couldn't be...he would never...must be a different explanation...he *loved* her.

She stared at the dark ceiling. Billy: intense ambition, dedication to the President, need for validation at the highest level. And the way he had made love to her before she left. Would he sacrifice soldiers?

The answer was immediate: The moment the mission required it.

But this?

She had been in Alaska. She had been in China. Was *she* the connection between the roving bomb and the Osprey?

She thought about Mike saying it was a good thing no one had seen her. Which meant no one knew she was alive. Which meant they wouldn't come to silence her.

Her heart raced. Her mind chased it.

How had Mike known...

Doc Ming came in as morning sunlight began to brighten the room carrying a pair of kinked silver scissors. "Let us look at your head today," he said, as he began cutting through the bandage. She closed her eyes and felt pressure ease as he unwrapped gauze. Her closed left eye saw deep orange. Not bright, but no longer black. She was afraid to open it.

"Eyes closed," he said. She saw the light beyond her eyelids get brighter then darker, like he was waving a flashlight. She heard footsteps move around the bed.

"Open slowly, together. I'll block the light from the window."

She crept her eyes open like a coffin being exhumed, afraid of what she might see—or not see.

The dim light hurt her left eye. She closed it. Reopened it slowly. Doc

Ming leaned over and stared at her eyes. "Good, good, it is working."

The face she saw in front of her left eye was blurry. But the fact that it *was* a face brought a smile to her lips.

"Be careful not to overwork it. If your vision becomes blurry, cover with this pillow for thirty minutes." He handed her an elongated pad the size of two small pincushions made of soft silk. He was quiet for a moment. "You are still beautiful...you might have a scar."

A scar on her face seemed a small problem compared to being blind. Or staying alive. Yet, it bothered her as she thought about it for the first time.

"How bad is it?"

"Hmm. I have something. I will send with Nu Mai."

After the door closed she played with her new eye. Up down, left right, like she was taking an eye exam. She focused on the ceiling, the door, the window, her toes. Then she remembered the doctor's warning, and put the eye pillow over both eyes to rest.

She heard a scuffle and removed the pillow to see a Vietnamese woman backing through the doorway carrying a tray. "Hello, I have breakfast for you." She wore a loose tan shirt that hung to mid-thigh over blue jeans and a pair of white Nike running shoes. She had a small red scarf around her neck and a big wristwatch that looked like it could contact Mars.

Claire remembered a flowing red dress. This woman had answered the phone at the party. She elbowed herself up in bed.

"Good morning," Claire said, "You must be Nu Mai."

She bowed and smiled. Her teeth were jumbled together like they were playing musical chairs. "I have something special for you," she said, nodding quickly. Nu Mai picked up what looked like a tea bag and taped it carefully over the stitches. "Good herb for head."

Claire touched the little pack and heard a crinkle while hoping the doctor knew what he was doing. Her head hurt less each day, but she longed for an MRI scan or something equally high tech that would let her know she was okay.

Nu Mai lifted metal covers to reveal a soft-boiled egg, toast and a bowl of pho noodles that steamed and smelled of spices Claire didn't recognize.

"Thank you for breakfast and the herbs," she pointed to her head.

"You rest, be well soon. My boy take care of everything."

Claire raised an eyebrow.

"Have I met him?"

The woman put her hand over her mouth and giggled like she had heard an embarrassing joke. Then she did the same biker imitation that Quan had done. Only she added, "Brrrrooom, brrrooom," to the twist of her wrist.

Mike was her—what had she said, *boy*? Couldn't be. Why not? her head asked, there was more than one child born to a U.S. soldier and a Vietnamese woman. But Mike didn't have a trace of Asian features.

"Is he your son?" she asked, defaulting to the direct approach.

Nu Mai frowned and stepped back. She shook her head like she was trying to shake a bug out of her hair. "I raise him since," she said, and held her hand palm down about waist high.

Something in Claire's gut told her not to ask about Mike's mother.

"He saved my life."

Nu Mai became very solemn. She placed her hands together and bowed toward Claire. "We all happy you with us. We not have American Princess here for long long time."

Chapter 43

THEY WERE TALKING UNDER the back canopy again, watching the sun drop over hills covered with a variety of double-needle pine tree Claire had never seen. An empty trail wound to the northwest, Quan chased a soccer ball in the dust, and she sat in the wheelchair that followed her everywhere.

"You're beyond crazy," Mike said.

Her face felt better and her head hardly hurt anymore, just sometimes at night. The bruise on her leg was mostly shades of brown and tan like a muddy puddle. Doc Ming still wouldn't let her move her left arm though.

"Why not?" she asked.

He paced perpendicular to her line of sight so his body moved in and out of her field of vision. He was wearing his T-shirt and blue jeans uniform, but no shoes.

"Why not? That's easy, you'll never get out alive."

"You sound like a Hollywood Western."

He stopped and crossed his arms over his chest. His forearms looked powerful: that supple, fast kind of power she had seen martial artists possess.

"If you're recognized, you're dead."

"Okay, so I won't be recognized." She shrugged. "Seems simple enough to me."

"And you only have one arm. Not to mention a scar."

"But the scar is new. It's part of my disguise." She forced a smile despite the fact that she knew the size of the bet she was placing. "And I promise to wait until the arm is, oh, eighty percent."

"Eighty percent of what? You have the physique of a bamboo shoot."

She grinned.

"Part of your disguise, right?" he said, clearly exasperated. Then he laughed.

She grew serious. "I know you think that Osprey was following orders. But we don't know that for sure. There could have been a communication problem. Or a mistake. Or maybe it was following Chinese orders, or Communist orders. Hell, maybe the plane was stolen."

"Your glass sure is half full today. How would someone who stole a prototype aircraft know when and where you were supposed to extract?"

She thought hard. "They planted a bug on one of the bikes. Or inside a rifle that was supplied to us. Or intercepted the orders. There are a hundred ways."

"All of them with the probability profile of a tsetse fly."

"But we don't know *for sure*, Mike."

"And you think it's worth risking your life to find out?"

"I don't know that I would be risking my life."

"But you might be risking your life. For what?"

"To find out if I can go back to the U.S. and lead a normal, happy, consumer-driven existence. Or if I'm a fugitive of some sort."

He bit his upper lip with his lower teeth. She could see his frustration mounting.

"Damn it, Mike, I want to know what the hell happened to my mission."

He held up both hands palms out. "OK, OK. If you're going to visit the dragon, I'll build you a sword."

Chapter 44

GENERAL WILLIAM "CALL ME BILLY" Williams leaned against the bed's headboard with his legs stretched out on the mattress, listening to the quiet absence of Claire. Once again, his instincts had proved correct—she had achieved the mission. The same traits that made her a fantastic woman— depth, persistence, obsession with performance, perfectionism—also made her a superb weapon. He hated giving her up so soon, but it would have ended eventually. She had been great when not pestering him about being a workaholic. He sighed. There would be others. After the election he'd do another campus tour, maybe the west coast this time, find a natural blonde.

He flipped forward through the pages of his journal. Only a portion of the verification data had been transmitted from Claire's onboard. This troubled him, but electronics could fail in the field. And there had been a storm. The weeks since with no contact from the team he considered a good sign. But Typhoon had a six-figure incentive to provide his own verification. A guy like him not collecting money could mean one of two things: he was dead, or someone had bought him. Billy didn't like either option. There could be a third choice: both. That would be acceptable. If Typhoon had double-crossed him, he hoped the guy was dead.

He continued to worry the team had missed the target. But, someone would have signaled him—unless they couldn't. Possibly they hadn't even reached the house. Or maybe they were captives. All three? That struck him as unlikely. There hadn't been time to capture one soldier, torture him or her long enough to obtain details, then find the other two. And even if the first one talked, he wouldn't know exactly where the others were located.

The house in the hills.

They all knew where that was. Even their GPS units knew where it was. Yes, it was possible the entire team had been neutralized at the target.

He hated missions that required blacked-out communication. He smiled, thinking that he also *liked* them because he had latitude in the details of execution. Everything in life was a compromise. He stared at the journal. The President was now operating as if the threat had been neutralized. If that turned out not to be the case...

Billy closed his journal, locked it, and flipped it onto the nightstand. He flicked the switch at the base of the bedside lamp, hoping sleep would come more easily tonight.

Ten minutes later he was sitting up with the television on, surfing channels for news. He saw Petry sitting on a couch. An interviewer facing him leaned forward on his elbows.

Billy turned up the sound.

"...you say the war of the future will involve these science fiction robots you talk about?"

"No," Petry said. "I am not talking about a war of the future, this isn't the Sci-Fi channel. I'm talking about machines that exist right now, ordered and paid for by the Department of Defense, by the thousands, in some cases, tens of thousands. Killing people."

"Surely you exaggerate their capability."

"Robots in the Middle East can hit a target seventy out of seventy times, in a dust storm, at night, using radar and lasers. Machines that no man could hope to emulate, capable of running a four-minute mile for hours on end. We are building, with billions upon billions of dollars in investment, an army of electronic storm troopers that can be controlled from thousands of miles away, at great detriment to our economy and relationships with other nations."

"But we have invested in defense since the days of the steel-clad USS Monitor. Why stop now?" the interviewer asked.

"Where does it end? We have megatons of nuclear weapons we can't use without destroying our planet. Now we're building intelligent machines that can achieve mission objectives *all by themselves* without a man in the loop, a landmine with wheels and a brain. Who programs them? Who controls them? Is this the best we can do for America?"

"Yes," Billy said, and switched off the TV.

Chapter 45

"I HAVE TO," CLAIRE SAID.

They had traveled to a cabin located miles from the makeshift hospital, her first trip since the Osprey's visit. The place wasn't much: a large room with sink, stove, table, bed and the remains of two motorcycles stacked against the back wall. More of a garage with beds than a house.

"Understood. You want the truth about the explosion. But you'll be walking into grand central jeopardy. You're in danger before you even clear customs if they recognize you, or have a security computer trying to find your picture. They could pick up a fingerprint or a voice: biometrics you can't change."

She slurped a wide flat noodle from chopsticks using her left hand. It was working better, but not at the 80% she had promised.

"The solution is obvious. *I* can't walk in."

His eyes didn't look convinced. "That's what I've been trying to tell you. You can't go, it's suicide."

She chewed her lip. Each day she became more dependent on Mike. Yet he refused to talk about why he was in Vietnam. But first things first, she had to find out about Billy.

"Let's send my sister."

He stopped eating.

"You have a sister? Is it safe?"

She sipped warm tea.

"No and no."

He dropped his chopsticks on the table and let them rattle to a stop. Then he laughed.

"Some suggestion," he said.

"No, I mean, yes. I'll go as my sister. It's safer than going as me."

"Has this Billy person ever met your sister?"

"Uh, no."

"Has he ever talked to her?"

She shook her head.

He frowned. "Does he know she exists?"

"Well, no, not exactly."

"Not exactly?"

"I mean, we never talked about her, but we didn't talk about my family much."

He paused to drink. Stared at her.

"Does he think you're an only child?"

"Well, uh, yeah, he might think that."

"But you're going to show up as your sister. Great plan. Love it. Can't possibly fail." He picked up his chopsticks.

She studied her noodles for a long time, like they were trying to send her a secret message.

"Why are they called *pho* noodles?" she asked, deflecting attention from her plan.

"Because the Vietnamese appropriated the French *feu*, as in *pot au feu*, pot on the fire."

She was silent.

"Do you have a specific hospital where you would like me to have you committed?" he asked.

She spit noodles across the table before she could cover her mouth. Pain seared through her shoulder as laughter turned to choking. It took her the better part of a minute to recover. He watched calmly the entire time.

"Good," she said, "that was good."

"Timing is everything in comedy," he said. "There must be more to your plan."

"Promise not to laugh and I'll tell you what I'm thinking."

"Laugh? Would I laugh at your obvious strategic brilliance?"

She ignored him.

"So, I've lost a lot of weight during rehab here. I was 130 pounds of athlete, now I could qualify as an anorexic runway model. Except for the scar."

He waited.

"I mean I'm skinny. So what if I stay skinny, dye my hair, change my clothing style, work on different speech patterns. And—"

He raised his eyebrows in feigned excitement.

"Go as the black sheep gay sister the family doesn't like to talk about. Billy hates gay men. His motto is more like, 'Don't ask, just shoot.' A lesbian might make him uncomfortable, distract him, make my job easier."

"Unless he sees her as a personal challenge to his manhood. But you're thinking out of the box. Two questions: What's the job, and why would your sister go see Billy?"

"I've thought about that a lot."

She picked up her bowl and poured the dregs down her throat. She licked both lips in one motion.

"Money."

"The great motivator," he said.

"Yeah." She sat back and crossed her legs, miming she was wearing a miniskirt instead of black jeans that needed washing. She flipped her hair over the right side of her face to expose the healing scar tissue and spoke fast, as if she were trying to talk her way out of a speeding ticket.

"Like, Claire, she was such a sweetheart." She fumbled in an imaginary purse, removed a pack of cigarettes and lit one. "She would always, well not always, but you know, like often, send me money. Not lots. Well, I guess that depends on how much you make, it didn't seem like lots. But it was really helping me out, you know. And she was so great; she would send cash so I didn't have to hassle with the silly bank accepting a check. Banks don't like me." She drew a long breath on a cigarette that wasn't there; blew smoke puffs like a movie star. "So, well, when no money came for, how long now? almost three months, I thought maybe Claire, like, is pissed at me and I don't know why. So I called, but she never called back." She pursed her lips into a pout. "So I thought, well, maybe I should go visit big Sis and see if I can, uhm like, patch things up. I have to be careful, you know, she never, um, approved of my, you know, preference… especially after that one time in her bed." She waved her cigarette. "Never mind that." She flicked her right wrist like she was chasing mosquitoes away. "So I came to DC and tried her place, but she's not in. So I like, talked my way in and looked around a little. I found your address in that little address book thingy on her computer. And, surely, you know, her boyfriend, you're her boyfriend aren't you? Or something, she mentioned you in her letters. Well, I figured *surely* you would know how to find her. I really need the money, I got, you know, sort of a need for it."

Mike leaned back on his chair.

"Holy crap. Who was that?"

"Drama class. I've been practicing when you hang with Maxx," she said, flipping her hair back across her head with her right hand.

"You can't touch anything. No fingerprints, nothing that can be DNA tested. He could try for a voice print if he has a recording of Claire and can get one of, uh, what's your sister's name?"

"Donna. You know, like The Donnas all-girl rock band from California. I think this Donna would like them."

His eyes defocused for a split second. He recovered.

"Uh, nice to meet you Donna. Does Billy have a recording device handy?"

"I think he has cameras all over the condo, like those reality shows where you can see the people in every room. Uses them for security. Don't know if they have audio."

"We'll find out." He sat very still. Sipped tea. Stared.

"What's the job?" he asked.

"He has something we need to see."

Chapter 46

MIKE STOOD ON A LOW STEP that had been carefully constructed of hand-shaped stones. He knocked three times on the vertical wood slats of a door nailed together before the invention of the transistor. The wood had a smooth deep yellow finish showing someone cared about it. He knocked twice, waited. He knocked four times.

The screech of a sliding lock welcomed him. The door inched inward only far enough to reveal a black iris under a gray eyebrow.

"Ah, it is you. Please, come in. Your package, it is almost ready."

Mike closed the door behind him and screeched the lock closed. He was in a room half the size of a one-car garage, lit only by a cluster of white LEDs hanging from a black wire over a desk placed precisely in the center. The desk held tools: knives, cutters, pens, ink, stacks of paper. To one side a laptop with a glowing Apple was connected to a long printer that occupied the end of the desk like a roll of colorful paper at a gift-wrapping center.

Mike bowed. "Wan Tong, it is good to see you again."

"And you, my young friend." Wan Tong returned the bow, looked up. "Today, who are we?"

"Mike."

Wan Tong nodded. "Mike, you have woman of great beauty." He walked slowly to a cracked leather chair behind the desk. His wrinkled figure resembled a porcelain statue surrounded on four sides by bookshelves holding hundreds of disheveled volumes.

"A friend. I haven't known her long."

"You do great service for your new friend," Wan Tong said as he stroked camel hair lightly against stiff paper, sounding like a miniature jazz drummer using brushes.

Mike watched the man bind paper and cloth with a needle and synthetic thread creating a perfect imitation of what a machine did for most governments.

"She has a problem."

Wan Tong pulled hard on the thread. "Problems swirl like the coming typhoons. Find peace in the eye."

Mike hoped the eye was in Washington.

Tong dusted the documents with a light powder that made them shine ever so slightly.

"Come, see what I have for you."

Mike worked his way around piles of books and a foot high wood sculpture of the Buddha until he stood by Tong's left side.

"They are quite beautiful," Tong said. "Look closely." Tong held a six-inch magnifying glass out. "This is a passport issued last year by the U.S. government. Notice the paper. Very difficult."

Mike studied the intricate detail of the paper.

"And compare to this." Tong floated the glass across the desk, making the image twirl like a bad drug trip, until it came to rest on a document bearing the name and picture of one Donna Ferreti.

Mike looked carefully, could discern no difference.

"And," Tong held up the passport book. "See here." He pointed to the corners. They were bent slightly, forming dim white creases, a passport that had been used. "Your friend will have no trouble." He paused. "The chip you provided is in place, of course." He lowered the big glass and picked up an envelope that had bubble wrap integrated into it. He poured its content out on the wood desk.

"I have for you: driver's license from Iceland, birth certificate from Baltimore, Maryland and—" he moved a curved finger through the small stack of documents, "here. Credit card bill, AAA motor club membership, and a receipt from the Crown Princess Bar in Reykjavik." He smiled, his teeth yellowing, but remarkably straight.

"You have chosen wisely," Mike said.

Tong bowed. "You have brought an old man interesting work. Thank you."

Each time Mike was newly amazed how Asian craftsmen thanked him for bringing his work to them. He paid well, but it wasn't the money. It was something about their understanding of how all things were connected, and the opportunity to serve with their skills. He reached inside his leather jacket and removed a thin block wrapped in the cover of a European motorcycle magazine and secured with a band of silver duct tape. He placed it on the desk beside a framed photograph, put his hands together under his chin and bowed to Wan Tong.

"Thank you, my friend," he said softly.

Wan Tong bowed and smiled without parting his lips.

Mike studied a photograph of two small children, perhaps five or six years old.

"How is Trinh?"

The old man's eyes turned to the picture. "Trinh is stubborn."

Mike waited.

Wan Tong carefully inserted the documents back into the bubble envelope.

"She stays in your Boston. Likes your graduate school."

Mike took the envelope, and remained still, watching Tong gaze at the picture.

"When I hired Professor Gregory to teach you two English the American way, I thought." Tong looked up, blinked. "Mike will go back to America and find his way. Trinh will stay with me, and together we will handle the Americans."

"Swirling typhoons bring many winds," Mike said.

Wan Tong laughed. Not loud, and in slow motion. "You were listening."

Mike nodded. "Always."

"Trinh has sent gift from America. Do you have time?"

Mike bowed. "For you Wan Tong, always."

The old man stood and shuffled to the back wall. From the chest pocket of his blue shirt he removed a key, and opened a low door. It screeched like the lock.

"Come."

They entered a second room identical in size to the first, but instead of a workbench in the center there sat a shiny silver motorcycle lift. Strapped to the lift was a dirty frame. No wheels, no engine, no seat. Just bent black pipe and grease.

"A new project bike?" Mike asked.

The right wall held rows and rows of shimmering hand tools above a narrow workbench. Mike smiled, remembering that they were arranged so he could only reach the ones he was qualified to use. None had been moved. One day, he had grown tall enough to reach the welding torch, and Wan Tong had given him a key to the garage to celebrate. To the left of the torch four wooden crates covered with shipping stickers were stacked into a tower.

"*The* project bike," Wan Tang said. "Trinh found it on your eBay. Much trouble to pass through Vietnamese customs."

"She found the Triumph for you?"

Wan Tong smiled and nodded. "1973 Bonneville T140."

Mike walked around the frame, studying it as closely as he had ever studied a sculpture in the fine art museum in Saigon.

"Not crashed," he announced.

"I agree," Wan Tong said. "Make good foundation."

"How may I help?" Mike asked.

Wan Tong held up both hands making a big round circle. "You come, explain British electrical circuits. I provide beer."

Chapter 47

CLAIRE SAT IN THE ISOLATED garage-cabin shortly after Mike's return, the personal documents for Donna Ferreti spread across the table in front of her. She studied them to the aroma of fuel and rubber emerging from the crashed bikes in the corner.

"These are amazing," she said, her eyes wide. "Where did you get th—" She looked at him and shook her head. "Never mind, I don't need to know." Her eyes danced from the documents to Mike's face. "I'm not sure I want to know."

"The passport indicates you arrived in South Vietnam two weeks from now. So you should be leaving in four weeks, placing a two-week visit on your passport. Donna's vacation in Vietnam will allow you to leave on a standard commercial flight." He paused, smiled. "Rather than say, sneaking across the border on a motorcycle."

She stared at the documents. "Can anyone do this?"

"You mean provide high quality documents for your every need? No, almost no one can do that. I just happen to know this guy..." Mike's voice trailed off.

"How do you find these people?"

"I've lived here all my life. One makes friends."

She held up a card. "A triple-A membership? What's that for?"

"In case your rental car breaks down."

"And the Crown Princess?"

"Want to guess what kind of bar that is?" he said.

"Donna would like it, huh?"

"Yeah, probably has frequent-flyer points for the place."

"One question. Why is Donna living in Iceland?" she asked.

"Two reasons. My reason is so your friend Billy can't use U.S. government connections to access information we haven't fabricated. He has much less power in Iceland."

She scratched her left index finger on the table like she was trying to remove the lacquer. "What's the other reason?"

"You'll have to ask Donna," he said with a grin. "Maybe she has a girlfriend who likes ice, or she's into those magic elves that live up there."

"Magic elves? Oh yes," she cooed. "If that's real, she would be so into elves."

"If that's real? Do you hear yourself? Your brain is shrinking."

"You know what I mean. If the people in Iceland really think they have elves, well, Donna would go look."

"They move roads for elves in Iceland." He sat down and said softly, "I'm not much worried about the travel."

She watched his eyes. "But you're worried about something."

"Cameras. If he records you visiting the bookcase, you're toast. Donna would have no reason to snoop."

"He usually only has them on when he's away. They're connected to the computer in the den. I've seen him review what they record." Her face flushed bright red.

He looked up. "Something unusual?"

"Not if you work in the porn industry."

"While you were, uh, visiting?"

"Yep."

"How's the color reproduction?" he asked, and broke out laughing.

"The lily white was balanced perfectly," she said like an engineer discussing product specifications. She tried to look stern, but a big smile worked its way onto her face.

Once the laughing settled he asked, "Do you know how many cameras, and where they're located?"

"No, they're hidden in books and lights and stuff."

"We'll have to jam them all. Are they wireless?"

"Oh yeah. He showed me how to install one. Definitely wireless."

"And they're all the same?"

"I think so, he ordered a whole box to get a discount." She turned her eyes to meet his. "The Army doesn't know about them."

"Okay, I'll work on jamming. He'll be suspicious, but at least he won't have pictures."

He stood and walked to the cabinets, banged a few open and closed until he found a big bag of corn chips. "Small lunch. Care for a chip?"

"No thanks, but do you have a coke hiding in there?"

An open fizzing can appeared by her left elbow. She studied the escaping carbonation.

"What worries you the most?" she asked.

"Do you mean the highest probability failure point? The weakest link?"

"Yeah, I guess."

"Getting it back before he knows it's missing, because the timing depends on his actions. If he comes back early there will be an ugly scene with a horrible ending. That's the weakest link." He crunched for a moment. "But what worries me most is you getting killed on my watch."

"It's not your watch," she scoffed. "I'm the one who wants to do this."

"But I failed to talk you out of it."

"That doesn't make me your responsibility." She crossed her arms and scowled. Then added softly, "Thanks for saving me in the jungle."

"I had to earn my merit badge." He shoved more chips in his mouth, but she thought he blushed.

She drained her coke, returning the can to the table with a clink.

"What worries you the most?" he asked.

She inhaled deeply, and blew like she was extinguishing birthday candles. "What we'll find."

Chapter 48

BILLY NORTON SAT CROSS-LEGGED on the floor of his room staring at the download icon, waiting for his new app. He scratched his left ear and tugged at the back of the yellow T-shirt Grace had given him because it was just like hers. Two boys had called them "Twinkies," but he didn't care. He liked it when Grace was around, because she talked so much he didn't have to.

He had been at his new school for weeks, and it was okay, but the adults kept asking him to talk. And he didn't want to. And when he started to think he might want to he saw that big guy in his mom's house with crumbs on his chin saying he could never talk about the secret, or bad things would happen to his mom and the whole country. Once he started to say his lunch was cold, but the ground shook and the air turned to yellow smoke like it did that day the shiny thing he found under the oil pipe blew up.

He watched the icon move.

Today Dr. Kimmer had talked about creativity and making new things and what did Billy want to make? He didn't have to think for even a second. He wanted to make a Batman comic book. Only he couldn't use Batman, because someone else had already done that. So he wanted to make his own "sort of like Batman but not really" comic book.

He knew how to draw a little, but he liked having an eraser.

This was his fifth try. The other apps all wanted to make stuff from pictures. He didn't have pictures. He just wanted to make stuff with his fingers.

Still downloading.

Someone knocked on his door. He turned and moved his mouth, but "come in," didn't come out. He placed his computer gently on the table and ran to the door and swung it open.

"Hi, Billy," Grace said. "What are you doing? I want to go see the movie tonight. It's the new zombie one. Are you going?"

He shook his head.

"Hey, I like your shirt."

He smiled. She wasn't wearing hers. She was wearing a black one with a head drawn on it that probably wasn't meant to be alive.

She raced past him into his room and saw the iPad on the table.

"Hey, are you working on something?" She stared at the screen.

He went to his backpack, pulled out the assignment that Dr. Kimmer had given the class on creativity, and handed it to her.

She read with her lips moving, mumbling softly.

"Something creative, huh? Sounds fun." She pulled the front of her shirt flat to show him the picture of the dead head. "Hey, let's make our own T-shirts?"

Billy pursed his lips, wondering if he could make a T-shirt and still do his own book.

"Yeah," Grace said. "I'll go to the movie and get some ideas. I bet Sam can help us get empty shirts to draw on. This'll be fun!"

Five seconds later his door clicked shut behind a running Grace. He wondered if she ever walked anyplace.

He checked the table. The download icon wasn't moving. He found the picture of KapowDraw, and tapped it with his finger.

The screen went black, then put up a one-word question.

Title?

He sucked on his lower lip. Batman was a cool title. What kind of title could he use?

He carried the computer to his bed, crawled up, fluffed the pillow and sat cross-legged against it. He closed his eyes and tried to see the title that would appear at the beginning of his comic book.

Captain. Captain somebody. Or Leute...no, that was too hard to spell. Captain would mean Army. No, he could be a cop. Sometimes the cops were bad guys. He'd be Army. But not an adult. Hmm.

This was hard.

He put the computer aside and got a pencil and paper. Like a hundred times before he sketched the silver machine he had found under the big pipeline. The sketch suddenly looked like a little dog to him, so he put eyes on the end opposite the handle.

A robot dog. Yes! What would he name it? He stared at his sketch, the hard tail, the round head. Spike? Rover? Then he thought of it racing across the grass with the treads spinning like a little tank. Tank! He would name the robo-dog Tank.

The assignment sheet was lying on the table so he went and got it. He saw his name at the top and started playing with the letters. Captain Billy.

He frowned. Cap Norton. He put a finger over parts of his name. Squinted. Read them backwards.

Notron!

Notron and Tank.

He crawled up on his bed and typed. The program drew four empty comic book frames on the screen, except in the very first one was the title *Captain Notron and Tank* all written out in really cool letters.

Billy grinned.

Chapter 49

DONNA'S FIRST IMPRESSION was colorful rooftops. Why in the world did the people of Reykjavik care about the color above them? But it made for a beautiful storybook city from the air, and contributed to the feeling she had been living a fantasy since rolling out of a plane on a motorcycle.

The flight led to two days of anonymity at the National Library studying the location and behavior of Iceland's local elf population: the "hidden people" living in another dimension and invisible to most humans. She was thrilled to read in a brochure published by the Icelandic Elf School that some elves are lesbian.

But her primary purpose was to put days between her arrival and departure flights, in case Billy tried to trace her. She finally flew to London, and on to Paris, arriving at Dulles International airport twenty-six miles west of Washington D.C. on Air France flight #1571, 4:53 pm Eastern Daylight Time.

She stepped into the jetway in four-inch black heels and the shortest skirt she had worn since high school—and almost suffocated from the October sun beating on the makeshift tunnel. Vietnam had been moist and hot, but the air was clean, begging to be inhaled. This heat felt like it contained particles of human breath and sweat that were attaching to her exposed skin. She put wiggle in her walk and moved fast.

Her hair, dyed light blonde with a dark pink stripe, was cut short on the left, revealing the scar over her temple like a piece of jewelry, and long on the right. Men's eyes looked and then flicked away like they had touched something hot. She carried a big pink shoulder bag containing a water bottle, Larabar munchy, cell phone with scrambler channels that Mike had given her, remote control he claimed could jam wireless cameras, and a little black box called a Magic Smithy that was made of carbon fiber and ceramic. Mike had insisted she carry the tools so the timetable couldn't be destroyed by lost luggage. So far, the only thing airport security had examined closely was her legs.

As she exited the jetway the cool recycled air of the terminal slapped her. She slowed to look for a sign to customs. As she searched, Mike strolled past wearing the uniform of a rock-and-roll roadie: black engineer boots, blue jeans, black T-shirt and a jacket that combined thick leather and space age synthetics. He ignored her. She followed him. Her own jacket was shiny pale blue silk with a map of Iceland on the back and an elf over the left breast, cut short at the waist so people behind had a good view of her skirt.

She was about to pass under a row of monitors, each silently showing a different channel, when Mallor's face appeared. She slowed and sidestepped until close enough to read the closed-caption text. He was at a fund-raiser in Boston speaking to a thousand awfully well-dressed people. Behind him the projected image of a tank-like vehicle raced across open desert launching rockets.

"We are engaged in fighting a new kind of war. A war based on machines in the battlefield providing aerial surveillance to our troops so they are safer as they attack. A war where machines crawl into caves, search for improvised explosives, and demine waterways while our soldiers remain at a safe distance. These machines have better eyes than a human, and can attack autonomously when necessary. We need this technology for national security, to attack or defend on whatever scale necessary, and I am committed to invest in companies like yours that provide our great nation with these marvelous robotic..."

Donna ducked below the monitor, wondering if she could find a transcript of that speech on the Internet. Roving war machines made her think of a little boy, and a large explosion.

She waited in a long line, fidgeted with her hair, and tried not to think about her documents. Eventually, she was next.

"How long will you be staying in the U.S.?" a pepper-haired official asked from inside his protective booth.

"About, like, a week."

"Business or pleasure?"

"Pleasure," she said. "Well, you know, sort of. I'm visiting family."

He looked at her face before his eyes landed on her enhanced by Miracle Bra breasts pushing up through the half-open zipper of the jacket.

"Where will you be staying?"

"The Marriott. The ugly one on F Street, not the super one downtown."

He looked closely at her passport picture, then at her face, then at her passport, then her face. His eyes danced back and forth like the pendulum on a cuckoo clock long enough for frantic thoughts to race through her head. He thought the papers weren't real. But the picture was her, it had just been taken. Maybe that was the problem; it was too recent. But she appeared tired and in need of make-up just like any other government photo. She looked at the guy's creased face and smiled, shifting her weight from one foot to the other, crossing her ankles, trying to appear sweet and innocent in an experienced kind of way.

"Hmm," he said.

She started to panic.

"What flight did you arrive on?" he asked.

"Uh, gee," she dug into her big pink bag. "The ticket is here somewhere. The one from London, but I started in Iceland. I think the plane said, like, France or something on the side."

"Iceland?" he said, as if he had never heard of it.

The man standing at the waiting line behind her cleared his throat.

"Big cold place," she smiled. "I live there."

His eyes narrowed. His fingers flipped the pages of her passport. He leaned toward her.

"Miss, how long have you lived there?"

"A couple of years. I like snow, it's so pretty."

"Have you—" he stopped.

She waited. Then inched closer to the counter when he didn't speak.

He whispered, "Have you seen any elves?"

She tightened her throat so she wouldn't laugh. He must have read the tension in her face as excitement.

"I've read all about them. I really want to visit," he said.

She leaned closer and whispered, "I haven't seen any. But I traveled past some of their rocks and seen how they can make machinery stop working. It's amaaaaaazzzzing."

"Ah, that would be something." He picked up a big metal stamp, stomped it onto her passport, and scribbled something over it.

"I hope you get to see one," he whispered.

"Me too," she said with a big smile. "If you visit, come in springtime, they're much more lively."

He beamed. "Thank you, I'll remember. Enjoy your visit..." he glanced at her passport, "Miss Ferreti." Then in a big boom of a voice he shouted, "Next."

She rolled out of baggage claim towing pink luggage that matched her shoulder bag, its two huge wheels bumping across the tile joints. She wished for a weapon; not having one felt like someone had stolen her comfort blanket. As she waited at the curb, hot concrete pushing through the thin soles of her shoes, a guy in a limo whistled. She looked the other way. A small dark-skinned man with a toothpaste-commercial smile approached, saying, "Need cab? Have good cab. You ride with me," and grabbed the handle of her roller bag. She poked his hand with a fingernail. He backed away.

A noise like a snake's rattle emerging from the shoulder bag reminded her of the scrambler phone. She dug around for the unfamiliar object and stuck it into her ear like a foam earplug.

"Hi, this is Donna," she said, trying to sound cheerful after ten hours in the air.

"White van arriving from your left. Next step, we confirm our equipment is operational. If Williams keeps to his schedule, we call tomorrow, mid-morning and get in before lunch. Don't want him to have time to poke around Donna's background before you walk in."

She rode in the van with one hand placed flat against the door glass, staring at concrete. Had Billy really done it? She was here to know. Needed to know. But seeing her lover would be beyond traumatic. Her gut vibrated. "Beyond traumatic," she whispered. "I'm starting to hear Donna in my head."

* * *

The following morning Claire found herself wearing a tight powder blue shirt unbuttoned too low, a black bra that pushed up too high, a white miniskirt, and pumps with straps whose heels again tested her ankles with every step. Fortunately, she was sitting in the back of the van, sipping Chinatown coffee from over on H Street. A nude thong touched places she wasn't used to having touched, and a graphite men's tie with silver stripes occasionally covered her cleavage.

Canvas folding chairs and a card table with collapsible legs comprised their headquarters. To her left, Mike tapped on a laptop computer hooked to a stack of black boxes the size of cigarette packs. The packs blinked occasionally. They were connected to an antenna on the top of the van made to look like old TV rabbit ears. The side of the white van now displayed an ad for M & D Antenna Repair with a picture of a guy inserting a screwdriver into the back of a TV set. The slogan *No TV too large or too small* and a phone number were printed below the picture.

Donna said, "You know Sweetie Pie, there like haven't been rabbit ears on TVs since the Russians sent that Sputnik thingie into outer space and made us go to the moon."

Without interrupting his tapping he replied, "Retro is in. If it's not, it will be."

They were parked in a two-hour zone on North Darville Street, south of 10th, two corners and three blocks from the tower that held Billy's condo. It was 10:48 am.

"Are you ready?" Mike asked.

She looked at the scrambler phone in her hand, down at her bare legs below the tiny skirt, up at his eyes.

"Wish I like had, you know, my trusty little rifle with me."

"Where would you hide it?"

Chapter 50

BILLY WILLIAMS LEANED FORWARD on both elbows trying to make sense of the statistics in the report Spin had given him. Mallor was slipping in the South, Petry was holding. The desk phone rang. Who was calling him at home? He let it ring a second time.

"Williams here."

The voice was young and spewing words rapid-fire like a teenager trying to convince Dad to loan her the car. Something about it disturbed the hair on his neck.

"Uh, hello, Donna."

He listened, deciphering meaning from the unneeded verbal punctuation with difficulty.

"Corporal Ferreti is on our sharpshooting team." He pushed the report aside. "Yes, I know her." As he said it, he realized he had just confessed real information to a stranger.

"Not recently. Why do you ask?"

He pressed a button on his desk phone to record the call.

"I could take a message." He slid open the center drawer and withdrew a sleek black mechanical pencil. He pressed it twice to extend the fine lead.

"Sister?" He dropped the pencil. It missed the desk, landed point down on his thigh and bounced to the floor. "Damn," he hissed, rubbing the thigh.

"I'll let her know you're in town, but the match isn't for weeks, I doubt I'll see her before then."

The woman continued speaking in staccato punches.

"She told you that?"

He turned toward the computer, considering a phone trace.

"I see...reading between the lines."

He made a big decision with little data—something he felt was the true test of reasoning power.

"I'm free until noon."

He bent over and picked up the pencil, put it back in the drawer. He pressed his lips together and tapped them with the knuckle of his right thumb.

"Number 421. Do you need directions?"

"Yes, smartphone, I see. Fine, call if you have trouble."

He hung up. Claire never talked about a sister, certainly not one in Iceland.

He played the conversation back. His voice was calm. She sounded perky, hyped, nervous. Probably drugs. He opened the middle drawer of his desk and peered at the handgun. He didn't expect anything from a kid sister, but her tossing Claire's name around Washington wasn't something he could let happen.

With an open palm, he rubbed the hair on the back of his neck.

Chapter 51

"HE'S GOOGLING DONNA," MIKE SAID.

She watched a list of hits for Donna Ferreti appear while slipping on pink leather driving gloves that matched the streak in her hair. They stopped halfway up her forearm.

"You're looking at his computer?"

"Cloning the screen." Mike pointed, "He's visiting our dummy sites. He'll know more about Donna by the time you get there."

She watched Williams navigate the pages of her fictitious past. He enlarged a photo, and Donna's dark blue contacts stared at her. She felt fear, anger, and resolve sizzle together inside her body. She wiggled her way forward to the passenger seat. Through the window she saw a tall man in a tan sport coat rush past. She took item one out of her bag and inserted it deep into her right ear canal, fluffing her hair down over it. Two girls strolled by arm in arm, both in heels as high as hers. With a quick crooked smile and a blown kiss she pulled the door handle, and fell in behind them.

"He's searching for your passport number, which should be confidential. I'll help him find your last flight."

Her comm module was working.

"Break a leg," he said.

She slipped the module from her ear to her bag.

For a moment she thought about Billy recognizing her, making her disappear. What would happen to Mike? And Quan and Suong? She could stop now, fly to Iceland, become invisible, get on with her life. She walked. No...she wanted to see Billy's cool blue eyes as he lied to her. Only then.

She strolled past the condo on the wrong side of the street like a tourist trying to find a street number. On her second pass she stopped in front of concrete steps, looked at the Grandeur name over the archway, glanced down at a piece of paper in her hand, and walked up carefully, doing her best to appear as if she always wore hose and heels. She ran her finger down a list of buttons, carefully reading each name as a newcomer would. She rocked her head side to side like her neck was loose, and shuffled her feet, assuming he was watching on a surveillance camera. She pressed a button and waited.

The door buzz made her jump. She reached for the handle, but the buzzer stopped. She waited. It buzzed again. She lunged for the latch, pressed with her thumb, and pulled the steel and glass door open with two hands by shuffling backward on her high heels.

She looked down a long hallway leading to four apartments, pretended to be confused while her eyes adjusted to the dimness of the interior, then strutted toward the elevator at the end of the hall. If anyone who knew Claire saw Donna, she wanted her body to be speaking a foreign language.

She stared at the closed metal doors remembering a red dress the night Billy carried her from the street like a knight saving a damsel. She had fought the hem down with both hands, and pushed the up button with the pointy toe of her shoe. She couldn't remember what they had been laughing about.

The door opened. The car was empty.

She stepped in, consulted her slip of paper, and touched the button with a recessed number four.

How many times had she ridden this elevator? Half-dozen a week for months. Including that midnight ride when she slipped her hand through unzipped trousers as soon as the doors closed on the first floor. But the elevator had stopped at the second floor, and while she stood in front and leaned against him, Mrs. Prowser wobbled on and rode to the third floor, because her friend Mrs. Tamp couldn't sleep and they were going to have tea, and what are you young people doing up so late? Then, without removing her hand, she had led him like a puppy on a leash to the bedroom.

The elevator dinged. The number four lit.

She stepped straight out and consciously didn't turn right where she knew Billy waited. She located numbers on a placard with an arrow, touched the sign with her finger, and ran down until she found the 420s. Only then did she turn right.

As she approached 421 she remembered their second first kiss. The first first kiss had been in front of her tiny studio apartment on the base, an area he carefully avoided except on that second date. The second first kiss was the first time she visited his condo. She was leaving to return to her quarters, and he had stopped her at the door and explained how he wanted the memory of a first kiss at his door, too.

She reached out and touched the door with her fingertips, the memory warm on her lips. Had that been real? Or was she the biggest sniper patsy of all time?

She took a deep breath, pushed the red dress, zipper and first kisses back in her mind, down under a pile of black dirt and stomped on them with both feet. She pictured a lesbian elf stopping machinery beside a big rock, smiled, checked her fingernails, and knocked a little dance rhythm on Williams' door.

Chapter 52

BILLY SAT BEHIND HIS DESK watching a security camera image of a thin, possibly anorexic, young woman wearing the shortest skirt he had seen in a long while. He whistled; nude fishnets were rare in Washington. She was almost sexy in a starving waif sort of way. But her hair was a weird blonde with a stripe of pink in it that looked like a chemical spill—buzzed on the left and swept over her ear on the right.

He heard a knock and watched as she fidgeted. She stood on one foot and tugged at a shoe heel, flipped her hair to the left then back to the right, scratched a pushed-up breast. A shiny white line split her forehead above the left eye. He wished he knew why Claire never mentioned her.

He walked to the living room and opened the door.

"Hello, Donna"

"Uh, hi. Are you, um, like Billy?" she said softly.

Her face was narrow with dark blue eyes instead of Claire's bright green. But there was resemblance, especially around the mouth. Claire had always been fit. Maybe she would have looked like this if she had a desk job.

"Yes, I'm General Williams. Would you like to come in?"

"Uh, sure. Thanks."

She slunk past, ducking her head like he had a disease. She stopped in his living room and looked around. Her twiggy legs fought to keep her on tall heels.

"This place is yummy. I love your furniture. Ecru is so me. You have lots."

"Thanks. I was preparing for a noon meeting." He gestured to his left. "Let's talk in the den."

He led her through a wide doorway she had seen a hundred times. Nothing had changed.

"Please sit down." He motioned to a wing back chair upholstered in dark blue facing his desk.

"Thank you. This is nice. Very, um, manly in a GQ kind of way."

She lowered herself onto the blue leather and crossed her legs. His computer sat behind the desk at a 90-degree angle. She could see the security video cam showing the hallway. Mike had been right about that.

Billy walked behind his desk. He moved the computer mouse until the screen was empty, then sat down and smiled.

"So, Donna, how can I help you?"

"Well..." she looked down at the carpet as her voice faded. "I, uh, need to find Claire right away." She raised her eyes without lifting her face.

He examined her very blue eyes. They looked lopsided under the weird haircut. Why would anyone shave half their head and expose a scar like that?

"That shouldn't be hard. Have you tried her apartment?"

The girl wiggled in the chair and uncrossed her legs.

"Oh yeah. I tried there first for sure. Then—" she paused and dug around in the big pink bag she had carried in on her shoulder.

He wondered what girls carried that required something so large. It made her look even smaller than she was.

"Then I remembered she mentioned a guy in her letters, and I thought she might..."

"You thought she might be here?"

"I thought that maybe she, uh, had moved here or something." She smiled a timid little grin and tilted her head.

Billy watched her carefully, still wondering what she wanted.

"How did you locate me?" he asked with the warm smile of a preacher accepting a donation.

"Well, I was at her apartment building and I sort of talked to this old cleaning woman who—" She frowned, causing her scar to crease. "Maybe I shouldn't tell you, aren't you like a cop or something?"

"No, not a cop," he smiled. "Just curious."

"Well, she let me in and I sort of peeked at Claire's computer."

Her eyes danced above a gremlin's grin.

"I see. It was nice of her to help you. Why would you think your sister might be here?"

"The letters. She wrote about Mr. Macho. She was hot hot. I figured a big crush or you know a Daddy complex thing."

The General shifted in his chair.

"Sorry. I didn't mean, I just, well, I'm sure you two make a fantastical couple. Claire is so like happy happy dreamy thrilled to her pink panties."

She pulled a small canister from her bag that at first he thought was mace. He moved his hand across his lap, instinctively headed for the Colt

1911 and its 45 caliber rounds he preferred. She uncapped the small gold tube and smeared frosty redness onto her already red lips.

"I'm glad to hear that," he said. "Claire never mentioned she had a sister."

She shook her head vigorously. "Oh no, she wouldn't." She waved her hand like she was drying her nails. "The family never talks to me. Only Claire. She's so nice."

What he knew of Claire's family he had found during the security check. She rarely talked about them.

"They won't talk to you?"

He didn't care; lots of families didn't talk to each other. But he wanted this girl to go back to Iceland and not stomp around Washington.

"They're old-fashioned. It's fine for Claire to be all rah-rah patriotic soldier tomboy and shoot people. But what I do disgusts them."

He could ask, or he could wait.

She examined fingernails that matched her lips.

"You military guys don't like us, either."

Skinny wannabe supermodels in miniskirts? He knew guys that would chop through bamboo with a butter knife for that.

She re-crossed her legs right over left and tightened her lips as if she were concentrating on a hard test question.

"Don't ask and I won't tell," she said.

He relaxed. A gay kid. Some parents would have a hard time with that. He flashed to a naked Donna with Spin's secretary. Suppressed a grin.

"How can I help?"

"Claire's a totally great sister."

"Yes, I imagine she is. Hell with a rifle, too."

"Yeah, she likes to shoot first and ask questions later, like the old west." She made a finger gun with her right hand and laughed a little huffing sound like she couldn't get enough air.

The room was quiet. Why was this girl here? Someone rapped on the front door. He twisted his head toward the computer to see who it was, but the screen was blank. Of course, he had shut it down so she wouldn't see the security cam.

"If you'll excuse me, my apartment is a busy place today. Please make yourself comfortable."

She felt a slight breeze on her legs as he moved past her chair. She turned to watch his back disappear through the double doors between the den and the living room.

She reached calmly into her bag and pressed a green button on an object shaped like a tin of Altoids. Mike assured her everything would be fine if the button glowed. It did, a deep indigo. She slipped the thin cylinder that housed the cell communication to the truck back into her right ear. Ninety-seconds she reminded herself: Mike's estimate of how much time she had. She wrapped her fingers around the Magic Smithy in the bottom of her bag, stood, and moved left toward the wall of books.

Floor-to-ceiling shelves sat behind three pairs of wooden doors with etched glass. All locked. She ran with short steps, grabbed the lock of the furthest pair in her left hand and rammed the Smithy into it, like pushing a tiny cock into—she shook the image from her mind. She waited, counting breaths.

"I have image," she heard Mike say in her ear.

She felt something inside the device move.

"I'll have it in...."

The lock popped open.

She heard Billy's voice from the outer room. "I didn't order pizza."

She opened the left door, dropped to one knee and ran her gloved finger along the titles. *War and Peace.* She yanked the heavy book out of the case.

A boy's voice insisted, "Oh yes, Sir, extra large mushroom, double cheese, and green peppers. See here Sir, on the order. Right there, is this your phone number?"

The book had a leather flap and a small padlock. She inserted the Smithy.

"I have image," Mike said.

"Will you get out of here? I don't want any pizza," Billy shouted.

"But, Sir."

The little lock clicked.

She opened the cover over her knee and flipped pages. About a third of the way through it flopped to the middle and she was staring at a red leather notebook. She reached in and grabbed it. It wouldn't budge.

"Yes, yes that's this address," she heard Billy say.

She turned the big book over and the red notebook slipped from the silk lined hollow carved out of Tolstoy's words and dropped into her right hand.

"Okay, yes, I'll take it. I think I know who ordered it. Here let me pay you—"

She re-latched *War and Peace.* Pushed it in. Aligned it. Stood. Closed the door silently.

She tried to close the padlock with one hand. Her gloved fingers slipped.

"Thank you, Sir. I really appreciate the tip. You know it's not often—"

She pushed the notebook up under her right arm and squeezed the lock. It snapped, sounding like a crash of thunder in the empty room. A whispered, "Shit," slipped out.

"Eighty-three," Mike's voice insisted in her ear.

She spun on her toes.

"That's okay, that's okay. Thanks," Billy said.

She heard the front door latch. Two steps, she dropped her bottom into the chair, grabbed the book with her left hand and shoved it deep into her bag.

Billy's voice came around the corner and through the open doorway just before he did.

"Some guy delivering a pizza."

She rummaged around in her bag, tried to reproduce her earlier position, pressed the Altoids can, came out with the lipstick. Her pounding heart threatened to drown out all sound.

"Your earphone is still active," she heard Mike whisper.

She turned her left side toward Billy.

"The pizza's here. Oh super," she said.

She applied lipstick with her left hand and flipped her hair to puff it up with her right. On the second pass of lipgloss she grabbed the earphone with the fingertips of her right hand. When she opened the bag to push the lipstick back in she leaned over, peered into the bag, and dropped the phone in too.

"I want to go like picnic after we talk. I'm starving."

Women could still surprise him. He placed the box on the corner of the desk and checked the time on a digital strip that synchronized to Colorado. "I only have fifteen minutes. Where were we?"

"Claire was shooting up the wild west," Donna said, making a pistol of her right hand again.

"You were saying what a great sister she is."

"She sure is..." She lowered her eyes as her voice trailed off.

Shy and wears fishnets at noon. He decided only the direct approach would make progress. "Is there anything I can do?"

"Well. See. Claire is so wonderful, she sends me money every month and I sort of got used to it, you know. And, uh, well." She looked down at the carpet. "It like stopped."

An alarm dinged inside Billy. How deeply would this girl dig?

"I see. Perhaps she's out of town. How long has she been helping you?"

"Ever since I moved north, almost," she tapped a finger against her lips, "two years ago. Gee, it doesn't seem that long, you know?"

"You mentioned Iceland on the phone. What took you so far away?"

Her eyes brightened. "The elves of course. They have so many of them."

Half a deck, Billy thought, finally seeing the problem in sharp focus.

"Well, since Claire isn't available, maybe I could help you. She and I can work it out later."

She sat quietly for a moment, her eyes vacant. Maybe she was figuring how much to tap him for, or seeing elves dance in her head. Then she popped to life like her named had been called in a lottery.

"Wow, that would be totally great. Claire's right, you are so super."

He opened a side drawer on the desk and removed five one hundred dollar bills. He thought about how many weeks since Demon Drop and decided to make it ten. He pushed his chair back as he stood and walked around the desk directly toward her.

She squeezed her bag closed and swung it onto her left shoulder. She stood up fast.

"Here you are, I hope it helps get you through."

She held the bag closed with her left elbow and took the money with her right. She fanned through the bills.

"Thank you so so much, I really, really *really* appreciate this," she said, hopping up and down slightly. "When you see Claire, ask her to, like, write, okay?"

"I sure will."

She flicked her head sideways to throw her hair over her right ear.

"Uh," she mumbled.

"Is there something else?"

She pointed at the desk.

"Could I please take the fabo pizza?"

Chapter 53

ON THE STREET SHE FLAGGED a cab stopped in traffic by wagging first her pizza box then the back of her skirt. She ran between cars and slipped into the back seat, feeling like she was carrying a bomb.

"Lincoln's monument, please."

She twisted and stared out the rear window, wondering if Billy had put a tail on her. A herd of automobiles inched forward.

"We are in the top five cities in United States for traffic congestion," the driver offered.

She checked the sidewalk. Thinking of Mike, she looked for a motorbike or bicycle slicing through traffic.

Nothing. And everything. She wished for a scope so she could see eyeballs.

She stepped out of the cab and fumbled for one of Billy's hundreds with the pink gloves. Gloves she didn't plan to take off until she was back at the Marriott in the room registered to Maria Mancotti. He started to complain until she tipped him two twenties. She slipped square white-framed sunglasses over her contacts and thought about being a movie star to help her walk better.

She ascended wide stairs, watching the statue of a seated Lincoln come into view. She thought about security cameras that covered this area twenty-four seven. Could Billy access them?

She sat down in the shadow of a huge torch sculpture, opened the box and took a bite. She rummaged in her oversized purse, found the plastic bag, inserted the book, and sealed it. She thought of being caught with Billy's journal and tortured, and choked on a fat mushroom.

She watched a plump woman in a pale blue dress fight her way up the steps on the arm of a man in khaki trousers wearing a T-shirt that read "Ducks Unlimited" who was watching Donna. She smiled at him until he looked away.

She slid her pink bag across the cement until it rested between her ankles. Her gaze wandered up the stairs, searching for eyes watching. She leaned forward, slipped the book from her bag into the pizza box, and let the cover drift shut.

Donna's yellow puppy wristwatch with the pendulum tongue told her it was 12:12.

She stood brushed off her skirt, picked up the box with her right hand, and slung the bag over her left shoulder. She raced down the steps and turned toward a white trashcan with four rusty feet. It took every bit of her belief in Mike to stuff the pizza box in.

She walked fast past a homeless man wearing an olive drab overcoat in the warm October weather who walked with a hunched left shoulder and wore plastic tortoise-shell sunglasses with a cracked left lens. She turned and hailed a cab.

* * *

Claire stood with one foot on the counter of the steamy bathroom running a fat hotel towel down her leg. She could still feel where the thong bottoms had been hugging her when she glanced in the mirror and was shocked by the girl with blue eyes staring back. She finished the leg, dropped the towel and worked Donna's contact out of her left eye. She was just starting on the right when a loud knock made her jump and drop the blue lens in the sink. She grabbed jeans and a pink T-shirt, wiggled them on and rubbed water out of her hair. She slow jogged to the door and put an eye to the peephole. Only the patterned carpet of the hallway looked back.

Another knock, to her left. Of course. She walked to the door connecting her suite to the next and opened her side.

Mike stood in the doorway in a dirty brown hat and gray whiskers wearing baggy pants.

"You're pretty convincing. I mean if you ever need a new career," she said.

Mike smiled with sparkling eyes, "Always thought it would be fun to be an actor. Come on over."

She followed him to the corner of his room where he had a small camera duct taped to the hotel's desk lamp.

"Bond would not be impressed. Don't real spies have slick gadgets?"

"I wouldn't know. You're the one with professional training."

He was guessing, but it made her wonder about his background. He was good at a lot of things.

He opened the bent pizza box and placed it on a chair. Wearing thin black gloves of the sort used for summer driving he withdrew a tomato sauce coated plastic bag. With great care, he opened the bag and extracted a red leather notebook.

She felt a chill. "What if he misses it?"

"Then our plan isn't working."

He placed the leather book on the desk and touched the camera to shoot the front cover, then went to work on the lock with a thin rod-shaped tool a dentist might use.

She watched, wondering where the man who saved her life had learned about locks. Maybe from a guy who could make passports.

The latch popped and he opened the journal to the first page.

It was blank.

He turned and looked up.

Her eyes dashed back and forth between the blank page and face.

"Have you ever read this?" he asked.

"No. But I've seen him write in it. I know, well...I'm pretty sure that's his journal."

Mike turned the page. Blank. Another. Still blank. With his right hand he fanned through blank page after blank page.

Her heart sank closer to the carpet with each flash of whiteness.

Without warning the pages became scribbled with handwriting, diagrams, timetables in careful columns.

"Jackpot," he said. He found the first page of writing, adjusted the book until it was flat. "Reverse chrono. Writing starts in the back so the newer dates are closer to the front. Your Billy is a strange cat."

Her Billy?

He tapped the camera, turned the page, tapped the camera.

She watched him shoot a page a second like a human Rube Goldberg copy machine. In less than two minutes he was shooting the back cover. It was 12:28 pm.

She realized she had been breathing faster with every picture.

"We're halfway," he said. "Donna needs to leave the country. You pack, I have a delivery to make before one o'clock."

She stood behind him and placed her hand softly on his shoulder.

He turned slowly in the chair.

"You worry too much," he said. "The Smithy already knows how to open the locks. I'll be there for less than thirty seconds. Everything will be fine so long as he doesn't come back early."

She released her hand. "He gave me a thousand dollars when I told him

Claire had been sending Donna money."

Mike frowned. "Probably can be traced. Maybe hold onto it until we have a plan."

"I already paid the cabbie."

He didn't stop frowning.

"Maybe not a problem. You did what you said, went and had a picnic with Abe. Protect the rest, we can use it."

She felt stupid. Of course it was traceable. Billy would have stacks of the stuff for just that purpose.

* * *

Donna moved a high heel carefully from the plane to the portable stairway, remembering another stairway in Alaska a few months before. Iceland was pretty in autumn. Pretty cold. She wobbled down the steps wearing capri jeans and a big cream-colored faux deerskin jacket with fur around her neck and thighs. She turned up the collar, worried someone was following her, and thought about Mike twelve rows back.

The first thing she did was find a Starbucks inside the airport and break another of Billy's hundreds, leaving a trail of dollars like Hansel dropping breadcrumbs. Then she wandered outside. She paid a taxi driver with her own cash to drive loops around the airport while she peeled off the heels and capris, slid into black jeans, tucked the deerskin in her luggage and yanked on black leather. The makeup came off with Handi-Wipes. She tied her hair into a lopsided bun and became a shoulder-length redhead from a wig. The elderly gentleman under the Greek sailor's cap even averted his eyes during the fun parts. For another hundred, he agreed to deliver a package to a shop downtown three blocks from the Eagle Street address Billy had seen in his Google search. The shop would say Donna had been in and dropped off a dress for alteration—if anyone happened to ask.

The driver stopped at the curb in departures and waved goodbye from his dusty green van. She stood tall and walked toward the gates, making no eye contact. She patted the breast pocket of the leather jacket, assuring herself again that the passport for the redheaded woman was there.

Chapter 54

TWENTY-SIX HOURS, A PALE yellow taxi, a pedicab ride, and a long walk to the garage followed by many miles on a motorbike put Claire in a hut in the vicinity of Hanoi, wishing she could go to sleep.

"How did we do?" she asked, finally feeling she could talk freely.

"I haven't read everything." He met her eyes, looked away. "There's some of what you're looking for."

Her heart didn't know if it should fly or sink. What she was looking for was an answer. Billy's eyes had contained only intense calculation, not a trace of sadness.

"It's late," she said. "But I've got to know."

He rotated the device toward her.

"I'll leave you to it. Happy reading."

He stood, crossed to a folding cot, dropped onto it fully clothed, and flipped a gray wool blanket over his chest.

She tapped the screen. There were rows of numbers that meant nothing to her along with phrases like, "President insists," and "Spinmeister worried." No indication of what was being insisted upon or worried over. The numbers might be cross-references to another book or a computer file, or a code. But she had no idea how to decipher such things. She grew sleepy but struggled to keep reading, the words floating in liquid as her eyelids lowered to half-mast.

She awoke frightened, her eyes darting around the shack until she realized where she was. She heard Mike's slow breathing. She blinked hard. In the middle of the page she saw, "Demon Drop." Billy had met with the President and written: "*This meeting never happened and you didn't get this from me,*" next to Spinmeister.

She wanted to know what he hadn't gotten. Words streamed past *trio...airdrop...high risk...absolute security...beyond classification.* She fought to continue, needing something definitive. She pushed herself until three words shocked her awake.

Terminated as intended.

Her heart fell like a stone toward the ocean floor. She blinked herself awake, pressed fingertips into her temples, and reviewed the words twice. Then read the next sentence.

Notify families at the appropriate time: MIA.

* * *

As the blackness of unconsciousness faded she heard rain whoosh against the thatch above her. She felt dried tears on her cheek. Then she remembered the journal and started shaking with rage: at Billy, the Army, a world that needed snipers. Her left shoulder reminded her that it wasn't completely healed by shooting pain up her neck. She rolled onto her back.

Her eyes felt glued down. She squeezed both shut and tried to open them twice before the lids lifted. Governments had been sacrificing people since before waves of soldiers ran into machine-gun fire in World War I, and the U.S. destroyed two cities with nuclear bombs. She frowned. Hadn't Mike talked about casualties from a flying land mine?

She rolled to her right. His cot was empty. She lifted her head. He wasn't in the hut. She smelled coffee. Through the window swirling clouds darkened the sky. 11:08 am. She pushed herself up from the cot and stretched tall, taking care with her shoulder, wiping her eyes against the baggy sleeves of the size XL T-shirt she wore.

"Damn you, Billy," she said aloud.

She wandered to the cabinet that served as a kitchen and found a coffee maker burbling. What kind of guy would save her from a jungle fire? A really good Samaritan who just happened to be riding by in a typhoon? Not a chance. So who was he? And why would he fly to the U.S. to visit a man who had tried to kill her? Maybe tried to kill her, she didn't claim to understand what had happened or why. Not yet.

She poured coffee into a cream-colored ceramic mug that had a red circle with a wing inside painted on it. Below the circle was the inscription: ChunFeng Holding Group Co., Ltd. Nothing made sense. Which she had come to learn meant the real agenda was carefully hiding somewhere.

She stood in the doorway of the hut watching the rain, feeling like an orphaned child: nowhere safe to go, no one to trust. That bastard and his glorious President and precious armed forces that needed so damn much money—she pounded her fist against the doorframe, knowing it was stupid. She did it again.

She argued herself into thinking about the future. Assuming Donna had been convincing, Billy wasn't looking for Claire. She tried to remember the look in his eyes. Did he believe Claire was dead? She thought yes. And if he thought she was dead, she'd have to figure a way to stay dead.

She dug around in the luggage from the bike and found a half-eaten Mojo bar. Peanut butter. She checked her scrambler phone and thought about calling Mike; he might want to know she was awake. She dipped the bar in her coffee, shoved it into her mouth, and crossed to the bed for the blanket. She wrapped it around her, thought of a squaw with a buffalo robe before the Europeans arrived.

She placed her coffee next to the computer and sat down on the woven seat of the chair. She touched the screen and it lit up with Billy's journal. In her haze of fatigue the night before most detail had been lost. She started reading. There were comments about trouble at a manufacturing plant, and a failed electronics company. She paused when she reached the pipeline, remembering riding in a chopper, and a little boy running as fast as his legs would carry him, just before his new toy blew a mini-van sized hole in the ground.

She thought about Master Norton, wondered if he was back to normal yet. Trauma had a strange way with people, especially kids.

"Related?" she said. Billy thought these events were connected to the Daemon person. Seemed like a lot of activity for one guy.

As she read, a ball of fear grew in her chest. She whistled—organized destruction of military suppliers. Wow. What a clever way to attack the U.S.

"So that's why you wanted him," she murmured. "Hit too close to where you live, huh, General?"

She sipped, but the coffee was cold and starting to taste like gasoline from the odor of the bikes.

Chapter 55

BILLY WILLIAMS SAT UPRIGHT in a cloth office chair and rolled backward in the small dark room. He looked between Jojo, his imaging specialist, and the static on the left monitor.

"We have no signal for eighty-seven seconds?" he asked, even though that's precisely what she had just told him.

"There's a signal. But that snow you see is it. The level is so hot the auto adjusters couldn't record the cameras. It happens three times on this file. I checked the other files. It happens a couple of times later in the day too. Was there something important there?"

Billy screwed his lips like tasting a lemon. "Don't know. I was hoping you could tell me."

"Sorry, General. There's nothing for us to extract. The recording path experienced an intermittent failure. It's been hot out, you could have an amplifier overheating."

Billy thought about the probability that an amplifier had failed while he stepped out of the room to pay for a pizza he hadn't ordered. But he had scoured the apartment that afternoon after reviewing the video. Everything was locked and in place, including his journal and guns. The failure had repeated half a dozen times. He would have his security system checked.

"What do the biometrics say?"

Two side-by-side monitors lit the small viewing room with a picture of Claire's face above the collar of a camo shirt.

"Exhibit A, taken six months ago," Jojo said.

Graphics overlaid the picture, an orange line connecting the eyes, a triangle from the eyes to the tip of the nose, a line measuring the width of the mouth, curvature of the face and relative location of ears and eyebrows.

"These are the primary bio-measurements. While not unique, like a fingerprint, they are rarely duplicated exactly. Naturally, they're genetic, and the source of the, 'He looks just like his Daddy,' comments women make about babies." Jojo smiled.

The right monitor changed to a pixilated blow-up of Donna's face from the security cam. The same lines appeared.

"The resolution isn't as good as Exhibit A, so take my comments with a grain of statistical salt. But we see similar eye-to-eye distance, a more elliptical shape and higher, well-defined cheek bones on Exhibit B."

"She claims they're sisters. Seems reasonable to me."

A column of words popped up over Exhibit B.

"Comparing measurements we get the following ordering," she pointed to the screen with a fingernail painted pale green. "Siblings, twins, second cousins, unrelated. The computer likes that order. We're building this to track families, since they often work together. If you call terrorism working."

"So she's her sister."

"Maybe," Jojo said. She frowned under blonde bangs and tapped a keyboard.

The General glanced at her.

"Maybe?" He laughed. "That's your carefully considered scientific judgment?"

"I added a few of the less proven metrics. Jaw shape, tips of the ears, estimated on Exhibit B because her right ear is completely obscured, cheek to cheek to tip of the philtrum." She glanced at him. "That's the little cleft over your upper lip. Stuff like that. But more important, because I was experimenting, I used prototype software that checks to see if the pictures are of the same person, just so we know we haven't introduced errors in the code."

The entries shifted.

"Now we get original after siblings, but before twins."

The General's jaw tightened, but he willed himself still.

"How good is this prototype?"

"It's crap. But it can usually pick out the original, since we've been matching faces for decades. Your pictures aren't very good though. Just thought you should know in case it meant something."

"Thanks, Jojo. Good work."

Chapter 56

THE 250 CC POWERED CHINESE dirt bike flung mud straight up the back of Mike's waterproof suit. He enjoyed rain and the wet-concrete muck it created. But he was worried about Claire, wanted to be watching her instead of chasing for groceries for their little army of two. The impact of seeing Williams, learning the truth, would hit her. He just didn't know when. Or how.

He leaned the bike against a tree-trunk post that helped hold the hut a meter above puddled water, and carried two plastic bags in each hand up a tilted ladder to the only door. He slipped in quietly. Her back faced him. The computer was in front of her as if she had been reading, but its screen was black.

She didn't turn. He placed the groceries on the shelf next to the coffee maker and studied her. She was hunched forward, wrapped in a blanket like a human burrito, her shoulders bobbing. He leaned closer. She was sobbing, tears dripping onto the hand that held the blanket gathered beneath her chin.

He unbuckled boots that had been cleaned by the driving rain and stepped onto the bare wood floor in polypropylene socks, guaranteed warm even when wet according to their packaging. He quietly removed his damp jacket and lowered it to the floor next to the boots. He moved toward Claire and knelt down beside her on one knee.

She didn't move.

He put his arm around her and placed his right hand on her shoulder, pulling her gently toward him. She didn't resist, or even seem to notice, but her head fell sideways until her face rested on his shoulder. She rocked slowly. He listened to the rain.

"Mom thinks I'm dead," she mumbled into his shirt.

"Missing In Action isn't dead." He admired precision, and if Williams had told her family Claire was MIA, her mother would certainly assume she was alive somewhere.

She pressed her face against his chest. "That…fucking…bastard."

Executing a man without even the shadow of a trial. Sacrificing the team.

"Bastard" was being kind.

She sat up and wiped her eyes with both hands.

"Sorry." She sniffled loudly. "Some soldier I turned out to be."

"You were just doing your job."

She met his eyes. He admired the shiny wet greenness of hers, like stones polished smooth by surf.

"Do you think so?"

"Yes. Don't you?"

She rotated her head back to the dark computer screen and pulled the blanket tighter around her shoulders. "I don't know. I'm too confused."

He backed away and stood slowly. Confused was a reasonable reaction. But he wasn't confused at all, and was rarely accused of being reasonable.

"You're not the first person to be fucked over by her boss."

She turned her face up to look at him.

"And you're far from the first soldier to be sent on a suicide mission. That's been going on for thousands of years." He paused. "Remember the Japanese kamikaze pilots in World War II?"

She gave a one-huff grunt. "The little guy gets it, huh?"

"War is hell, haven't you heard?" He couldn't make light of a severe situation. But he could help her see it wasn't about her.

"We're not at war...exactly." She sniffed slightly. "It's hard not to let it get personal."

He waited for her to relax. The tears were mostly dry.

"Did Williams assign you to the mission?"

She frowned.

"No. He tried to stop me. Wanted other, better people. Said I couldn't ride well enough." She rubbed an eye. "We all volunteered."

He waited for more. It was a short wait.

"But you know, he had me pegged. Knew I would insist on going." She was quiet, chewing her lower lip on the right. "I feel so fucking manipulated."

It looked to him like the tears were coming back.

"Consider the silver lining," he said.

She leaned back in the chair and met his eyes, but said nothing.

"You're alive," he said.

She erupted in strained laughter.

"Yeah, great. The world thinks I'm dead. Oh, excuse me, Missing In Action. I can't show my face or I *will* be dead, and I'm in the middle of nowhere in a thatched hut in the rain." She stopped. "And now I don't even have a job."

He marveled at the way she processed stress. He'd be halfway to America to take Williams out. She was looking for a job.

"Did you read the part about the conspiracy against military suppliers?" she asked.

He straightened. The girl could shift gears.

"Yeah. Seems tenuous to me."

"Well, there's the destruction MO."

"Only three events. The fact that they were all military suppliers could be happenstance."

"I doubt it." She tossed the blanket across the back of her chair. "No matter, there won't be a fourth."

He watched her stand and go for the coffee. She poured a cup from a pot that had been brewing during her cry. Her eyes scanned the groceries. He knew there were only a couple of choices, although she probably hadn't thought about them yet. And now they had something in common: General William Williams wanted them dead.

"Why do you say that?" he asked.

She turned around slowly with both hands on the coffee cup and leaned against the counter, crinkling grocery bags. She brought the cup to her lips and met his eyes. He saw the green sparkle.

"I say that because I saw the target lying with a bullet hole in him on the carpet of a very fine house in China."

"Would that have been a Chinese bullet?"

He sat down at the table and lowered the pad computer that had been propped up for reading.

She sipped and watched his face over the edge of the cup.

"I didn't see a bullet."

He moved his hand out from under the table and flicked his wrist. An object flew through the air. She caught it in her left hand without spilling a drop. She looked down at a chunk of steel-jacketed lead in her hand.

"This isn't..."

"The best of three."

She rolled the metal cylinder between her fingertips.

"Why do you have this?" she said softly.

"So you wouldn't leave evidence at the scene." He paused and tapped a finger against the computer. "No evidence means you were never in China.

Just like Williams wanted."

She crossed the floor and placed the bullet on the computer.

"Who are you?"

"Let's work this together." Williams wanted them both. Better a coordinated defense.

She stared down at him.

"You saved my life. You took me to see a dangerous man. You're crazy to keep helping me."

"You're trapped in Indochina with no money. You can't speak the language. And a terrorism specialist will kill you if he finds out you're alive."

She held up both hands, but looked at her feet. "Okay."

He stared at her downturned face, watched her take a deep breath and become slightly taller, saw her searching for strength.

"I promise. You can help me," she said, barely above a whisper.

He pointed at the bullet standing erect like a tiny monument.

"Wrong man."

Her eyes flashed from the bullet to his face, to the bullet, to his face. Her mouth opened, but made no sound. She dropped into the chair, and stared across the bullet at him, her green eyes distant.

"All that," she whispered. "All that work...and Cam..." She seemed to melt into the chair as she pulled the blanket around her. "My team. And we got the wrong man? How can you know this?"

She fell silent, her eyes fluttered shut. Perhaps she was visualizing the mission.

They remained closed for a long time before he realized she had fallen asleep.

Chapter 57

MIKE'S CELL PHONE EMITTED the rising bellow of a thousand yogis chanting om. Claire stirred on the cot where he had placed her after she had fallen asleep sitting up: the strangest reaction to bad news he had ever seen. The hut was filled with the aroma of sizzling vegetables.

"Hello, Maxx," he said softly into the phone.

"Action on the computer in Washington."

"Go ahead."

"It has tracked $100 to a cabbie in Washington, and another $100 to a bank in Iceland. No backtrack beyond the bank as yet."

"Jam the Iceland backtrack," Mike said.

"False tracking info provided. Crosscheck time estimate: one point seven weeks."

"Good."

"Additional," Maxx said.

Mike noticed that Claire's eyes were wide open. He guessed her ears were too.

"What's that, Maxx?"

"A missing persons bulletin was filed on Donna Ferreti six hours ago. A picture is being circulated."

Mike took the phone away from his ear and watched an image load to its screen. It was Donna all right, a frame taken from the security cameras in Williams' condo. Not great, but not terrible either. Donna was holding a gold cylinder.

"Where are they looking?"

"This picture has been posted to four missing-persons websites. Reprints have been made. Shipping records show them en route to Iceland. Operating assumption: they are to be circulated by hand in Reykjavik. A Facebook page has been created with this picture as the profile."

"Thanks, Maxx. Any reports yet?"

"Affirmative. Sixteen sightings: two in Washington, one in San Francisco, one in Chicago and twelve spread over three cities in Iceland. All sixteen are being investigated by the nearest Army MPs. No one has been given the reward."

Billy suddenly wanted to find Donna.

"How big?"

"Fifty thousand U.S. dollars."

"Thanks Maxx. Keep me posted."

He hung up and stared at the picture. Cute, but she looks better without the blue contacts.

"What's going on?" Claire asked, sitting on the edge of her cot.

"You fell asleep."

"Thank you for stating the obvious. I meant the phone call."

"It's been a tough week. Are you taking the herbal medication Dr. Ming gave us?"

She nodded. "The phone call?"

"It's about your sister."

Color faded from her face, "Billy's trying to find Donna."

"You'd make a good game show contestant."

"Funny. Why?"

"That we do not know. But we know how."

She stood slowly, one hand pressed to the wall for balance. She walked toward the table. "You know how? How the hell can you know how?"

"I've got the right brain on the problem."

"Anyone I know?" she said, dropping heavily into a chair.

He shook his head. "Billy has filed Donna as a missing person. Your sister's picture is on the Internet and wanted posters will soon be floating around Iceland. Fifty-thousand dollar reward."

"Wow. He *really* wants her."

"He'll find her." He paused and folded the omelet in the pan. "When we're ready."

She watched him work over the electric hot plate.

"You have a plan?"

"I had a plan," he said. "But you weren't in it. Your *persona non grata* status requires a new plan."

She pointed to the hot plate.

"How do you power that thing out here?"

"Chinese clone of a Honda generator under the hut. Runs on bike gas."

He folded a smooth omelet onto a handmade ceramic plate colored in orange and placed it before her.

"Mike." She stared at her food. "Why are you helping me?"

212

"We have a common enemy."

"You mean Billy?"

"And I saved your life so the Buddha says I now share responsibility for it."

"He really taught that?"

He met her eyes and grinned. "It's open to interpretation." He sat across from her with his own omelet and opened a box of orange juice that claimed to be Tropicana but looked like river water colored with Tang left over from a moon mission. He saw her staring at the liquid. "The sidewalk markets in Vietnam are not entirely truthful about their advertising." He took a long drink and smiled with an orange mustache.

"Billy is the present incarnation of the enemy, " he said.

She forked into her omelet. He watched the muscles in her arms tighten as she chewed.

"I have so many questions. And feel..." she began.

"Let me guess. Betrayed. Angry. Afraid. A bit lost. And given your training, eager to go shoot someone."

"Thank you, Doctor. Maybe you should buy a couch."

"Not much demand for expensive shrinks around here. We have religion. Lots of it. Catholic, Hindu, Buddhist, Protestant. Take your pick. And if those don't work, there's a thriving opium trade."

"Since you're giving free advice. What do I do next?"

He held up his index finger, "Step one, stay alive," added his thumb, "Two, examine your options." He lowered his hand and met her gaze, "Three, execute."

Her face froze mid-chew.

He waited.

She placed her fork down on the table and swallowed. Her skin turned ashen.

"Who was he?"

Her green eyes were vacant, staring into a place fifty meters behind him.

"Who was who?"

"That bullet...you said 'wrong man.'"

He sat up and leaned forward on his elbows, looked deep into her eyes.

"You were supposed to leave and convince your friends back home that you had been successful." He paused. "Instead you hang around half-dead with bodies and motorbikes scattered in the mud. Such things trigger investigations, and in Vietnam—or worse, China—they have a way of finding things out. These are communist countries who don't like strangers."

She lowered her fork and her breath caught. "You're manipulating Billy."

He said nothing.

She started eating again slowly, her cheeks beginning to glow pink.

"I have pictures."

"And fingerprints." He waited. "Dominic Kalstin, aka Typhoon: world traveler, man about town, spy, mercenary. Sells whatever he has to the highest bidder. He had Caucasian parents so you accepted him as the target when he picked up the correct phone at the appointed time."

Her eyes widened in surprise. Or awe. He couldn't be sure.

"We didn't know," she said. "Demon's ethnicity was undefined."

He nodded, but didn't comment.

"That party. You fed info through this Kalstin, knowing we would come."

"Me? Never met him. I'm just an innocent biker riding through the jungle."

"So I shot Kalstin," she said flatly, her face a blank stare of distant thought.

"You shot the man your information told you was the operative—the entire reason for your mission. You did your job...sorry, I'm repeating myself. If you had gone home, everything would be fine." He chewed slowly. "Now there are complications."

"I have enough angst over this mission to last the rest of my life." She perked up, surprising him. "How about explaining something?"

He hesitated. "Maybe."

"Now that you've enlightened me, I'm a security risk to the awfully well-informed people you work for."

He shook his head. "You can't prove anything. Except that you screwed up and shot your own informant."

She flinched.

He continued, "Everything else is hearsay. Once I ride away from this muddy haven, I'll be impossible to find. Especially if you're dead."

She went pale. "Billy wants me dead. Now you want me dead?"

He looked straight at her. "Would we be having this conversation?"

She stopped eating. Her frown morphed to a twisted question.

"You're one confusing human being." She looked up. "You are human, aren't you?"

He laughed, and choked on a mushroom.

She fought it, but her body shook, wanting to laugh with him.

"Seriously. What are you doing out here? Why the hell did you save me? Didn't your mother teach you not to laugh with your mouth full?"

He became very still.

"Too many questions, huh?"

He sighed. "No, you're fine. You mentioned my mother."

She said nothing. Slowly she continued eating.

He leaned back and stretched his arms over his head. "You know about my father." He lowered them and pressed his hands together. "My mother was six weeks pregnant when he was evacuated. She never got a chance to tell him." He finished the Vietnamese orange juice, looked at Claire but saw a rice field, felt the touch of his mother's hand, heard a child's memory of her laughter.

"I—" She stopped. Waited. "He never knew," she said flatly, echoing the obvious.

"No. Mines explode here a thousand times a year. You saw our portable hospital." His eyes focused on her. "We take care of farmers...children...poor people collecting mines to sell for scrap. Mines are hard to find; it's difficult to know when they're all gone." He slowly licked orange from his lips. "Did you know there are millions of mines lying on our planet?"

"I wondered why the walls were canvas," she said softly.

"We go where it's needed. Sometimes it's needed in more than one place."

"I'm so sorry," she said.

He was quiet. His eyes roamed the room as if checking the roof for a leak.

"Me too. It's why I chose this profession."

Chapter 58

"THE QUESTION IS, DO YOU HAVE CONFIRMATION?"

"Mr. President. In my line of work, confirmation is a relative concept—"

The President lifted his hand, palm out.

"Hold it, Billy. The polls have me below fifty percent and dropping faster than Galileo's rocks. That's relative. Either you're confident there won't be a repeat of Alaska—a disaster I hear about daily from voters who probably couldn't find it on a map—or you're not."

"I'm confident we have the situation contained, Mr. President."

The President leaned away from the table.

"Thanks, General. I have a thousand other things to worry about. Can I really forget about this?"

"I have confirmation from eyes in space that the mission concluded as planned. The intelligence channels are quiet, not even a hint of a rumor of another event. There is only a minor loose end."

The President's eyes tightened like he was about to growl.

"There are no minor loose ends, Billy."

Billy hesitated, then said, "We have been unable to contact one of our informants. An inconvenience, really."

The usually silent Bert Spin interjected, "How much does he know?"

"He helped identify the manufacturing location of a component. And he arranged for invitations to a business gathering. He knows nothing of mission objective, team size, timing. Nothing."

The President clasped his hands behind his head. He worked his mouth like he was chewing tobacco.

"Where is he located, Billy?"

"China, Mr. President."

The President mouthed the word "fuck" but didn't say it aloud.

"I told you to stay away from the Communists." The President wagged his head, "Christ, Billy."

"We have operatives in every country of the world, Mr. President—most in communist regimes. He's only one of many who operate in China."

"And that's supposed to make me feel better?"

Spin jumped in, "Mr. President, China is a non-issue in this election. Your constituents have accepted globalization; half of what voters buy is made in China. A communication problem with an operative really is a minor issue."

The President's brown eyes, the color of wet sand, shifted from one man to the other.

"All right, gentleman, if you say it's under control. But Alaska has everyone on my ass. The big companies don't like their stock price, the oil lobby is going crazy, Alaska wants Federal aid, and the media won't let the terror angle rest even after five oil giants detailed how a pump exploded and created a domino failure down the line. I don't have wiggle room." He began to stand but dropped back into his chair. "And don't get me started on the tree-huggers. Now they want to stop drilling I've already approved."

Spin's eyes flashed to Billy and back to the President. "We're watching this carefully. If there's anything even slightly unusual, I'll call another briefing."

"Fine Bert, but call it before the next pipeline explodes." President Mallor stood. "I've got to get some coffee." The President headed toward the door and his guards.

Bert and Billy were silent. Billy could almost hear brains gathering thoughts.

Bert said, "How about a walk?"

* * *

Beside the reflection pool minutes later Bert said, "I don't like the way your eyes were moving, General. What can you tell me without informing me of something I wouldn't want to say on Congressional reality television?"

Billy held his left wrist with his right hand behind his back, swaying gently as he strolled.

"All evidence points to a successful mission."

"Then why the worried look?"

"Because, despite what I told the President, I personally like unequivocal confirmation: pictures of dead bodies, DNA reports, that sort of thing. And I don't have it."

They both smiled as they passed between a chubby lady wearing a bold green and blue print dress having her picture taken and a skinny guy in a Hawaiian shirt trying to take it.

Bert said, "Do you expect it?"

"Yes. There are two outstanding sources of pictures...plus a fingerprint scan. If I find even one of them I'll feel better."

The burning afternoon sun added to the sweat on Billy's forehead. He felt he had a successful mission. But Typhoon's silence and that girl Donna...how the hell could he not know about a sister? His gut hurt worrying about how to keep everything quiet until the election. Six weeks, he needed six weeks.

"Bert, how about an opinion? I know Mallor would be angry, but what kind of hit would he take in the polls if another Alaska happened?"

They walked and Billy waited. A child's electric motorboat buzzed past them in the pond. Billy wondered if that was even legal. Imagined a pond with hundreds of such boats.

"The man will be righteously pissed off. The hit really depends on the details, though. People give a damn about oil, especially the price of gasoline. It's not rational, but there's something about filling up at the pump that feels like crap compared to a nice dinner for two with wine and candlelight, even though gas is a bargain in this country. Voters could switch to smaller cars or hybrids rather than bitch at the President. But they think there's an article in the Constitution that guarantees the right to drive an SUV suitable for the Baja 1000. So, it depends on what you mean by *another Alaska*."

"It could be anything," Billy said. "I would have never guessed the pipeline, it only supplies a few percent of our oil. And we still don't know why. No one is taking credit. A huge hit like that, and no one takes credit? Almost makes you lose faith in democracy."

"Funny, Billy, real funny," Bert said making a U-turn back toward his office.

Chapter 59

JONNY PACED WITH LONG strides on the sidewalk in front of a low brick building. The afternoon sun was warm enough that perspiration had started to form along his spine under the leather jacket he wore. He figured the kid would dig a leather jacket, maybe relate to him better, become a chatterbox and tell what really happened.

He stopped and studied the sign again. Providence School.

Jonny had followed the pool-shooting chopper pilot's info to Nolan. And yes, there was a big hole in a field that looked like a World War II artillery shell had landed. But no one knew anything about it, or where it had come from. Even the woman, Mrs. Norton, who could see the hole from her porch claimed to have no idea how it got there.

But he had checked her out. Divorced with two kids, not just the little girl that had been hiding behind her skirt when she answered the door, but also a little boy everyone in town seemed to know, who hadn't been seen since the pipeline explosion. Jonny followed the name Billy Norton until a young freckled friend told him Billy left in a big car with his mother.

So he had watched the mother. She mostly went back and forth to work at a tiny office that printed the Nolan News. Then he got lucky again. Knowing she was at work, he opened her mailbox and just happened to glance at her mail. He didn't open it or try to read it with a candle or anything—mail tampering was a Federal offense and would surely trash his chance for the Pulitzer. But he could see who was sending her stuff, and when he saw the return address for this school he knew right away it was pay dirt.

So now Jonny was here. But how was he going to get in to see a little kid? Improvise.

He took a deep breath and headed for the door. Inside bright colors hurt his eyes, but the slender blonde girl behind the counter soothed them.

"Hello, I'm Jonny Munch."

"Hello, Mr. Munch, how may I help you?" Samantha said.

"I'd like to talk to one of your students, Billy Norton."

"I'm afraid that won't be possible."

"I need to—"

"What I mean is. You could talk to him, but he won't talk to you. Billy doesn't talk to anyone."

Jonny wanted to pull out his notebook and write that down, but he restrained himself.

"I see. Well," and it came to him in a flash. "I'm a friend of his father, Peter Norton. As you probably know, Peter doesn't live in Alaska anymore." Jonny was suddenly glad he had followed up on the deadbeat dad. "He heard that Billy moved to your school." Samantha looked at him with soft blue eyes, making it difficult to concentrate. "So, he asked if I might stop by and just see how Billy's doing."

"Well, I can tell you Billy is a fine student and seems happy here. He's made a new friend named Grace and they do all kinds of extracurricular projects together. Let me check with Dr. Kimmer, and see what we can do. Would you like to take a seat?" Samantha gestured to a row of eight chairs that together made up the colors of the rainbow.

Jonny thought of Roy G. Biv, picked the green one, sat down, and wondered what he was going to do if they tried to call Peter. The father's name and contact info were probably on file for emergencies, but it was 10 pm on the east coast. Maybe they'd send the girl with the Samantha nametag in with him. He smiled.

"Mr. Munch. The doctor says you can see him in our community room for a few minutes. But the kids have dinner soon. Please don't make Billy late."

Jonny grinned. "Thank you, Samantha." He pointed to her nametag.

She gestured with a curved finger. "This way, Jonny."

She led him to a room even brighter than the hallway that could hold twenty kids in little undersize chairs and left. He sat down to wait in a chair at the end of the first row with his knees almost to his chin. From the pocket of his jacket he withdrew sunglasses and slipped them on. His eyes felt better. He was flipping through the pages of his notebook, making sure he had written down everything Samantha had said, when the door opened and a whirlwind spun into the room and danced across the floor.

"Hi."

"Hello. My name's Jonny."

"I'm Grace. Billy will be here in a sec." She reached out her hand and stroked his shoulder. "Nice jacket."

He smiled.

"Why do you want to talk to Billy? He never says anything."

"Just wanted to say hello, see if he's okay. Does he like it here?"

"Oh, yeah. We like it a lot."

The door opened and a little boy strolled through looking down at the iPad he was carrying. Grace ran to his side.

"Hey, Billy. Jonny wants to say hi."

Billy walked right up to Jonny and looked him in the eye. Jonny was glad he was sitting low.

"Hi, Billy. Your Mom and Hattie say hello."

Billy nodded. Grace moved from Billy's right over to his left.

Jonny noticed Samantha's blonde hair at the small window in the door. He wondered if he was being videotaped.

"How do you like the school here?"

Billy looked at him and shrugged. That's how Jonny felt about school too when he was young. Jonny took off his glasses and squinted in the fluorescent lights. He held them out to Billy.

"You should have sunglasses living here," Jonny said. "How about you take mine?"

Billy looked at the glasses, then turned to Grace.

Jonny glanced at Samantha in the window. She was smiling.

"Go ahead, Billy," Grace said. "Take them."

Billy released one hand from his iPad and took the glasses. Grace helped him get them onto his face straight. He smiled a big wide smile that made Jonny want to hug him.

Billy reached out his right hand and Jonny shook it.

"You look cool," Grace said.

Jonny struggled with how he was going to extract information from a mute kid who may or may not know anything. He sure couldn't start talking about the pipeline and craters with Grace standing there and Samantha watching him. He had pictures of the hole in his pocket, but he couldn't pull those out either. His Pulitzer hopes began to backslide.

Billy sat down next to him and pointed to the iPad. Jonny's first reaction was to resist. He was the journalist; he'd guide this interview. Then he read the first frame of a pencil-sketched graphic novel.

The Adventures of Notron and his Robo-dog Tank

There were characters and text bubbles and sound words. The kid was clearly having fun. But this was a waste of what little…then the name hit him. If Billy was Notron, who was Tank the robot dog? Was that Grace?

Jonny showed keen interest in the comic and Grace ran around to look over his shoulder. In the first six frames the heroes ran out to save, he double-checked, yes, they were standing on TAPS. What a coincidence.

"Nice work, Billy," Jonny said. "Is there more?"

Billy swiped the page to reveal six more frames. Jonny read them. Someone was trying to blow up the pipeline with black robo-dogs that were just like Tank, only they were bad dogs, hell-bent on doing evil. The kid must have been working like crazy, because there was a helicopter, and an explosion, and a girl in uniform who saved Tank.

A girl in uniform? Club Rotor.

Jonny had read perhaps ten pages when he heard the door open. He turned to see Samantha walking in.

"Time to go to dinner."

"Sorry," Jonny said. "Billy was just showing me his graphic novel. He's doing a good job, don't you think?"

"He's doing a great job," Grace interjected.

Samantha smiled. "Yes, Billy is becoming quite skilled with that drawing program. Aren't you, Billy?"

Billy nodded with his eyes down, back to being shy now that people wanted him to answer questions.

"Samantha, do the kids have email?"

"Sure, though we monitor what they do closely."

"Would it be okay for Billy to send me his novel, so I can see how it ends?" He winked at Samantha. "I mean, if it's all right with Billy."

Samantha dropped to a crouch to be at kid height. "What do you think Billy? Would you like to send Mr. Sunglass Jonny your novel so he can read it?"

Billy nodded and smiled from behind his new glasses. Then tapped the screen.

"He'll need your email address," Samantha said.

"Just tell me," Grace said. "I can remember that stuff easy."

Jonny thought about his blog, and decided maybe he didn't want Samantha checking that out just yet. "You can send it to me at jonnymunch at iCloud dot com." Then he spelled Jonny for her.

"Got it," Grace said. "Let's go eat, Billy."

Billy held out his hand and Jonny shook it before the two kids ran off.

"Thanks for stopping by," Samantha said, "the children don't get many visitors. They come in here, and people get busy and forget about them."

Jonny could feel her studying his face.

"They get even fewer gifts," she said. "He'll cherish those for a long time."

Jonny blinked, and felt uneasy. But he managed a smile and a shrug. "I hope he likes them. I won't forget about him."

Back on the sidewalk he walked fast for a couple of blocks and found a bus stop. He sat down, pulled out his pad and wrote down everything he could remember and how he thought it related to the pipeline—a pipeline that he was now thinking had been sabotaged, even though he didn't have much in the way of evidence.

He thought for a long time and tried out a whole page of ideas before heading back to his car. On the way a title for the article popped into his head: *Do Robot Dogs Eat Oil?*

Chapter 60

"TWO DAYS, NO RAIN," MIKE SAID.

Claire stared out a boxy window, the image of the hillside distorted by wavy glass. Vegetation in brilliant greens, most of it taller than a man, hovered over tan clay so smooth it glistened. The hut had been their shared home while he pieced together one good motorcycle from the two in the corner. The smell of damp foliage, rubber and gas created an aroma that inexplicably was making her thirsty.

"Is it always so wet here?"

Lying flat on a cot staring up at the slanted roof he said, "Only when we have visitors."

She turned. "No really, I feel like I'm trying to breathe underwater. I knew Vietnam was humid, but this is worse than Washington in August."

"Are we in Vietnam?"

She frowned with her right eye. "Didn't you say—" No, he hadn't said. She assumed they were in Vietnam because that's where she had ridden after...she saw Cam and Wu and fire and felt searing heat.

"If you don't know where we are, you won't need to lie during interrogation. Want to take a ride?"

She lifted her face. "Anything to get out of this hot house. I'm nearing stage three of hut fever: start a fight to create excitement. Do you have transportation?"

His hand moved just far enough to lift two fingers.

"How many wheels?" she asked.

"Two for you, two for me."

"Can't you just steal, uh borrow, a Jeep? Maybe one with air conditioning?"

A slow smile crawled across his lips. "It wouldn't take us where we need to go."

She waited for an explanation. She hadn't been able to figure the first thing about what she should do while Billy searched for Donna. Mike told her to examine options. Near as she could tell, she didn't have any.

"Let's ride," he said, twisting his feet to the floor.

Thirty minutes later she was standing outside the hut in 90 degree heat covered head to toe in riding gear he assured her would breathe once they got moving. She felt like it was raining inside her clothes, and her shoulder pain was back.

"Stay on the trail," he said. "I'll go slow."

She glared at him and examined the dirt-bike helmet of a decade-old design in her hand.

"Don't you ever get anything new around here?"

"That is new. I measured your head while you were asleep. We don't have the latest materials so we copy older designs. It's good, works well in fiberglass." He slipped his own lid into place, which looked just like hers only with a thousand scratches. He tapped the outside, "Hope it fits."

She lowered the shiny black helmet. Peering through the goggle hole, she realized it fit better than her helmet ruined in the explosion. In fact, it felt soft inside, like a ski cap. She wondered how many measurements he had given the builder, and if it had been made by hand just for her.

His bike sizzled to life and puffed gray smoke out a tailpipe mounted high and to the left.

She studied his machine. It was the same bike she had seen that night in the jungle: a beast that looked too bulky to be agile. She pulled on gloves and mounted the Franken-bike he had created from the crashed machines. It felt solid, like a newer version of the one she had ridden into China: except for a funky front fender curved like a dolphin's nose.

He twisted to face her. "Stay on the trail."

"What's the big deal?"

She kicked and her bike remained silent. She yanked again on the choke. Another kick, more silence. As if to taunt her, he revved his bike. She "Grrrr'ed" at him from inside her shiny new helmet, and kicked harder.

She was rewarded with vibration in her hands and a bup bup bup beneath her butt. She smiled and rolled her left shoulder in small circles to loosen the muscles.

"Land mines," he shouted, before disappearing into the underbrush.

She caught him a hundred yards later, his bike ramming through shiny green bush like there really was a trail. Dirt revealed itself every ten seconds or so. She thought about mines.

"How are you doing?"

His voice through the helmet radio startled her. She swerved. Nothing exploded. She realized she was holding her breath.

"Is there really a trail in this garden?"

Her earphone crackled. "Yeah. I use it all the time."

She twisted to miss a fallen branch. "No one has used this for weeks."

"Nine," he said. "You know that the U.S. deployed landmines in Vietnam from aircraft. No one kept count. Maybe a million, maybe two."

Hadn't he just said—? "But we're not in Nam," she protested.

She looked back and could barely make out where their two bikes had cut through the jungle.

"Neither are the mines."

She realized this wasn't a trail—it was a maze. And she was trusting him.

But he had manipulated Billy. He could manipulate her.

Chapter 61

HYPNOTIZED BY AN HOUR of following a slithering tread pattern, Claire thought she saw a large animal with black, shiny skin. She braked hard and skidded to a stop.

"How are you feeling?" he asked.

"Tired, sore, thirsty, hungry."

"Almost to the restaurant. Have to wait for dark."

She flipped up her clear face shield. "It is dark."

"Watch."

To her amazement the world plunged into a black silky stillness. The greens of the forest faded, replaced by a photographic exercise in subdued monochrome. She swiveled her head, but saw only trees that looked like every other tree she had just passed.

"What's happening?"

"We're being covered by the shadow of a mountain. In a few minutes, we can move without lights."

She blinked to help her eyes adjust. "I can't see the ground, how are we going to ride?"

"Guardian angel."

"GPS?"

"A friend."

A friend. Only Mike knew she was alive. She wasn't sure anyone else should find out.

"Am I going to meet this friend?"

"That's where we're headed."

"Your friend lives in this wilderness?" She could barely see his eyes behind the shield.

"It's where we meet. Don't worry, you're as safe there as with me."

How safe is that? "You sure I shouldn't stay invisible?"

"You'll be more invisible."

Before she could think of how she could become *more* invisible his bike blasted past. No lights, no moon, no night vision goggles. She chased the sound of his machine, like a bat following an echo.

They stopped at a creek, tiny points of silver sparkles suggested it was moving rapidly.

"Don't tell me we have to cross that," she said, whining more than intended. Tired and thirsty, getting wet didn't sound fun.

"Nope."

She had breathed the first half of a sigh of relief when he added, "We ride up it."

"Bet your friend doesn't get many visitors." Why would he live in such a strange place? Or did *she* live in a strange place. Claire felt oddly annoyed and gassed it into the water.

Later, soaking wet and with the easy vibration of the engine massaging her legs, she saw a small crescent like a new moon above her. She watched it grow larger. With this new light she could make out reflections from rock in a cave the size of a hangar for a jumbo jet. She saw a natural shelf a meter wide jutting out on the right. He was riding on the shelf, in the dark, on wet rock.

Then he disappeared into the light.

She took deep breaths.

Thirty seconds later she shot into the light-emitting hole. Mike was parked in the middle.

She slammed her foot down and watched in amazement as a flat disk the size of a truck rotated over the opening she had just ridden through.

"Welcome," he said.

She looked around. Light glowed from above. All around her she saw only cave wall.

"A bit Spartan."

He was smiling as he pulled off his helmet and killed the motorbike, now gleaming like it had been through a car wash.

"Funny girl. Let me show you around."

He dismounted and walked away. She followed. The overhead light flickered and went out. She could see nothing, but heard his breathing, slightly louder than the pounding of her heart. The black sightlessness made her unsteady. To distract herself, she unbuckled her helmet and pulled it off. She felt less safe.

"This way."

She reached out and touched his shoulder. He led; she shuffled through the darkest black she had ever not seen.

"Close your eyes," he said.

She saw her inner eyelids begin to shade red.

"Okay."

She opened her eyes to a natural cavern bathed in low artificial light. It was the size of a small house. A group of canvas-walled rooms had been erected within the irregular shape and interconnected with tubes as tall as a man.

"Welcome to the Double-D ranch. This way."

She followed him down a ladder and into the first cabin.

"Kitchen, vented to the outside through a chimney that lowers the exhaust to ambient temperature before it leaves the cave." He smiled. "Wouldn't want Uncle Sam to see the heat from my pizza."

The room had a counter with folding legs, a microwave in the corner, a tiny refrigerator, and a table with two chairs.

"Not a lot of people around," she said.

He was still smiling. "Just Maxx and me. You're our first visitor."

Being first didn't make her feel safer. "What's this place for?"

"Maxx lives here. I come up to work."

"You set up tents inside a cave to work?"

He nodded, crossed the kitchen to a narrow door and disappeared. She followed him into a round pipe that smelled like the motorcycles tires she had been living with in the hut. The air was warm.

"It's nice in here."

"Maxx is particular about his environment. It was a challenge to figure out what to do with the heat so it wouldn't be detected, but the obvious finally struck me." His hands made a wavy motion and she realized he was pumping heat into the stream she had just ridden.

"What heat?"

They reached the end of the pipe and stood in front of a narrow door. Remembering her first view of the cave, she guessed this door opened to the big room in the center.

"Claire, I'd like you to meet my good friend, Maxx."

He opened the door and let her step through first. She stopped. The room was black: walls, floor, ceiling, and filled with a hum. She saw rows and rows of what looked like silver pizza boxes stacked one on top of the other. A quick assessment of perhaps twenty stacks of twenty meant she was looking at 400 machines.

"Maxx?" she asked.

He nodded.

"Maxx is a computer?"

He laughed. "Lots of them. Say hello, Maxx."

A male voice said, "Hello."

"I'd like you to meet Claire. She has a problem I'm helping her sort out."

The not quite low enough to be a baritone voice said, "Hello, Claire. It is a pleasure to meet you. I have heard much about you."

"Uh, hello Maxx," stumbled out. What to say to a huge machine? "How are you today?" She looked at Mike.

"I'm fine, thank you for asking," Maxx said. "Many humans become anxious around a talking computer. There have been psychological studies undertaken to ascertain why."

She knew why, it felt damn weird. Her eyes searched for Mike's.

He grinned. "He doesn't bite. It's just like giving your cell phone voice instructions."

She chewed on the inside of her right cheek thinking this was an awfully huge cell phone. "Maxx, how does Mike ride in the dark?"

Mike's face went blank with surprise.

"I help him," Maxx said.

She watched Mike, but spoke toward the stack of machines, "How, Maxx?"

A projector lit up the right wall with an aerial photo of a river, surrounded by bramble and foliage. A squiggly yellow line cut through the green. It was surrounded by hundreds of orange dots.

"I have terrestrial coordinates for each safe path up the mountain. I track the motorbike by homing signal, then provide aural and visual guidance."

"His bike sends out a homing signal?"

"Directional and encrypted. Used only when necessary. Difficult to detect."

"Sounds fun," she said, wondering if her bike could do that. It occurred to her that the direct approach might work with a computer, even if it sounded like a man. "Maxx, what do you know about the Daemon?"

"A code name used by U.S. intelligence for an operat—"

"Thanks, Maxx" Mike interrupted. "Firesnake status?"

The projector sprayed new data onto the wall. With the additional light she could see a black desk in the corner and a pair of keyboards. The wall became a mesh of graphs and colors that meant nothing to her, but two long numbers caught her attention. A rising one with a dollar sign in front reminded her of Vegas where an electronic display above slot machines counted up and up until someone won the jackpot. The other had no dollar sign, and was slowly becoming smaller.

Mike examined the numbers and said "hmm" a couple of times.

"Are we on track?"

"Affirmative. Ninety percent complete. All prices holding."

"Excellent," Mike said. "What interval?"

"The past week," Maxx said. "This is the total."

The dollar number was over a billion, and grew in fits and starts. The second number was at 300 million and drifting downward.

"Must be a big project with numbers like that," she said.

"Lots of little projects. Have a seat."

There were two chairs: one in front of the desk, and a La-Z-Boy lounger with a hassock. She took the La-Z-Boy and swung her wet boots up onto the stool.

He glanced at the water pooling under her leg. "Want to change, or get to work?"

Her lips twisted to one side. "Well, I don't know what we're working on, I'm wet and tired and my shoulder aches. I'm also hungry, but by all means, let's work. Where should we start?"

"Review what we know…change into something more comfortable…"

She noticed he was forcing himself not to smile.

"…then contemplate options over dinner."

She nodded.

He sat in the desk chair and swiveled toward the projected data.

"Maxx, where is General Williams?"

A satellite image of the Earth flashed and grew large as if she were falling from the space station: planet, ocean, Eastern U.S., Washington DC, Darville Street, roof of a condominium complex.

"He's at home?" she asked.

Maxx said, "Internet usage pattern indicates Williams has been using IP address 192.166.2.28 for the past six hours."

Talking to Maxx seemed perfectly natural. But her skin felt odd, like it was moving.

"What else would you like to know?"

"Has he found Donna?"

"Maxx, Donna search." Mike pulled a keyboard toward him and began typing.

A map of Iceland replaced Billy's condo. Claire counted eighteen red diamonds.

"These are sightings reported to www dot finddonna dot com," Maxx said.

A picture was added to each diamond.

"These were submitted by those attempting to claim the reward. It has not been paid."

Claire studied eighteen people who made her feel like a mouseketeer popped out of a mold at Disney.

"Has Billy brought them in for questioning?" Mike asked.

"All eighteen."

Mike mumbled, "What does he want?"

"To find Claire," she said.

"Why not find you directly? He knows where you were last located." He frowned.

Fan noise filled the quiet.

"Why try to find Claire at all?" he said softly. "He should believe she's dead."

Claire switched to chewing the right side of her lower lip. "He does. But it's not easy to search Vietnam without raising suspicion. He'll use satellites."

"He hasn't seen much. I pulled you out in a typhoon. By the time it cleared there was only the heat of the burned building, which he would expect."

Her mind returned to Wu's silhouette. A flash.

"You mentioned options?" she said.

He rolled his chair over to face her, propped his feet up beside hers and tapped the toe of her boot with his.

"Like something to drink before we solve our mutual problem?"

The hair on the back of her neck stood up at the word *mutual*.

"I'd love a hot shower. And food."

"Suits me. An Army General is trying to make sure you're dead. He can wait." Mike jumped up and started walking. "This way."

She followed him back through the round walkway. It made her think of the miles of tunnels the Vietcong dug during her Dad's war. The idea of fighting underground made a submarine seem attractive. They passed through the kitchen into another tube. He stopped at a door that came up to her chin.

"I only have one bedroom; it's yours. I'll stay with Maxx."

He opened the door to a 12-by-12 foot room with a single bed covered by a taut blanket. Above it a red climbing rope stretched across the room held a half dozen T-shirts and two pairs of Levi's. Two rectangular aluminum boxes sat at the foot of the bed. Along the left side of the far wall was another small door, also made of dark plastic.

He pointed. "That's the shower, hot and cold running water, the backbone of modern civilization. Towels. Wear anything you like. Come find me when you're comfortable, we'll rustle up dinner."

"Thanks. I'll be quick, I'm famished."

"Ride to eat, eat to ride, the biker's motto," he said with a smile. "See you in a few minutes."

The door closed softly behind him.

She started to sink down on the bed from fatigue and confusion but stopped herself at half-squat realizing her riding gear was wet and full of river parasites. Pushing herself back to standing she took three steps, opened the door and found a tiny room with a shower on the right and a toilet in the corner. There was no stall, just a shower handle at the end of a flex hose hanging over a drain. To her left was a stack of six road cases like the ones by the bed. She opened the top one and found towels, soap, shampoo, and an Army kit with sanitary supplies for females. She didn't need it just yet. She froze, realizing she had no idea how long she would be in this mountain cave—or if he would let her leave.

She twisted the shower handle. Hot water rained over her fingers. She was suddenly cold. She stripped fast and let the heat work through her shoulder and neck. Toweling dry, she felt a warm glow down to her toes. She dragged a green plastic comb through her hair, not quite to her shoulder on the right with dark roots above Donna's blonde and pink, and barely an inch on the left. She should do something with it.

But what? She didn't know who she would need to be next.

Working naked she found a T-shirt with some stretch to the material. She slipped into the light blue cloth and it drooped to mid-thigh. She hung her riding jacket and pants at the far end of the rope, then unlaced the boots and inverted them against the canvas wall.

She went through the cases in the shower room and dragged out black sweat pants with a drawstring. She slipped them on, overlapping the material, and sat on the edge of the bed to roll them up to her ankles. In the two boxes near the bed she found a pair of gray hiking socks that became her shoes.

She stepped into the shower room to examine herself in the small mirror, being careful not to get her socks wet on the damp floor. She looked like a young woman who had stayed over at her boyfriend's place spontaneously and didn't have a thing to wear. She smiled.

Back in the bedroom her eyes scanned for something to cover the T-shirt and found a small picture taped to the wall beside the bed. She dropped to her left knee to look closely. A smiling woman held the hand of the young boy next to her, who was standing on a small boulder to make him appear taller.

A sense of uneasiness toyed with her spine. She waited while a buried thought moved about her consciousness. She closed her eyes and saw a similar picture through the scope of her rifle on a desk in an empty room.

Chapter 62

BILLY WILLIAMS STARED AT a matrix of faces. After seventeen hours, they all looked like Claire, then none looked like her, and a few minutes later they all did. At the same time, they didn't look like his recollection of the impish Donna either.

"Jojo, I'm getting bleary-eyed."

The technician pushed her black-framed eyeglasses up her slender nose for the hundredth time and sighed. "We have a whole lot of nothing. The system doesn't think any of these people are related. Not to your image of Donna, and not to each other. Eighteen separate people. The Faces production system agrees with the HOMER prototype in all cases."

"So, a bunch of losers are trying to collect my reward? Are you confident enough that I can reject the claims?"

Jojo said, "The best match we have is between Donna and sighting number twelve. It's above random, but not enough to convince me twelve is your girl. Yes, I'd reject them all."

It was Billy's turn to sigh. He was getting nowhere. Not that he actually had a problem. There were no rumblings about terrorist activity, he hadn't heard from Donna since giving her the cash, and there was no indication that Demon Drop hadn't gone exactly as planned. Still, he couldn't sleep. Donna kept showing up in dreams offering him a huge pizza.

"So Jojo, we wait?"

"Unless you want me to obtain more photos of girl number twelve, see if I can raise the matching statistics with different lighting or skin textures."

The General chewed the thumbnail of his right hand. "I hate waiting."

"You want me to run these against camo-girl? The resolution is better."

Billy thought about what it would mean if one of the pictures matched Claire. The significance of such a result eluded him. "How much time do you need?"

"I already have the analysis of all eighteen samples. Just need to run them against the new picture. Have a coffee, I'll see what I can do."

Billy pushed his chair back. "Do you want anything, Jojo?"

"Bottled water, thank you."

Billy headed for the narrow room where they stored minimal refreshments for long nights in the lab. He grabbed the glass container from the drip machine and poured coffee into a cardboard cup. He added a dull powder and two white sugars and pulled a bottle claiming to be Fresh Spring Water from behind the cooler's glass door. As he started back toward Jojo's workstation his cell phone vibrated against his left thigh. He looked around for somewhere to set the coffee, but there was nothing in the yellow hallway, so he turned back for the kitchen. His phone was on its fifth buzz before he pressed the answer button and lifted it to his ear.

"Williams."

"Hey Billy, Edward. I've got those pictures you asked about."

"Thanks, Ed, what did you find?"

"A lot of godless communist rocks and trees. Want me to transmit?"

"Sure. I'll take a look soon as I can."

Billy watched his phone perform a secure download of satellite pictures along the China-Vietnam border. He had told Ed in Surveillance he was working on war game exercises and was interested in new terrain ideas, thought he might find something in the area. Ed had come through quickly.

Billy looked at the first image, taken fourteen hours after the Osprey strike. Demon Drop had been carefully scheduled to avoid radar-capable satellites over the area. The storm had blocked the orbiting geo-stationary cameras. Originally he had been pleased with his luck, now he wished he had pictures.

Fourteen hours was a long time for a site to change—or be modified. *C'mon Billy, who the hell would be out in the middle of nowhere?* The building was warm according to the sensors, but vacant. Good. Body parts identifiable by the Chinese government would be a problem. He stroked the phone to zoom, looking for anything relevant: chunks of metal, piece of a motorcycle wheel. He found nothing.

He slipped the phone into his pocket and lifted the drinks from the counter. He sipped the still warm coffee in his right hand. He turned to head for the workstation to see what Jojo had found and his phone vibrated again. He thought about ignoring it, but it might be Ed calling about a problem with the transfer.

He put the drinks back on the counter.

"Williams here," he answered.

"Hello, General Williams, this is Detective Qigiq. We met in Alaska. Would you have a moment to talk?"

Billy didn't give an endangered spotted owl hoot about Alaska. Yes it was a mess, but he just wanted to know that the perpetrator was permanently out of the picture.

"Uh, sure Qigiq, but only for a minute. I'm headed to a meeting."

"We've been tracking the components from the pictures you took of the LTB."

The only pictures he took were of that mobile bomb before it ran away.

"LTB?"

"We named it Little Tractor Bomb. There is something unusual about the parts."

Billy already knew that cylindrical cell module had a source in China.

"Unusual?"

"Would it be possible to open a secure channel, or better, might I visit Washington and see you in person?"

This wouldn't be over until he had confirmation from Typhoon. Why his ground team hadn't transmitted data he still didn't know—not a single verification picture, let alone the fingerprints specified in the mission plan. All he had were sporadic partial attempts. Probably weather interfering with their low power transmitters. He made a snap judgment.

"Be happy to meet with you, but that's a long flight."

"It will be nice to escape the midnight sun," Qigiq said. "I'll be down as soon as possible."

As he closed the call Billy wondered if Qigiq had found something that might point to a different perpetrator. That would be very bad. Not only had he hit the wrong man, but the right one was at large and likely planning an act that would stop Mallor from being re-elected, putting large question marks in his own career path.

He picked up the bottle and his coffee. The tan liquid was cool, but he drank it anyway.

"Did you get lost in the dense jungle foliage between here and the coffee machine?" Jojo said as he entered the lab. "I'll give you GPS coordinates next time."

"Couple of phone calls. What've we got?"

"Nothing to hurry back over. None of the eighteen match camo-girl either," Jojo said. She watched the General's eyes scan the twenty pictures. "Donna still matches camo-girl best. Mind telling me what we're looking for? Might give me some new ideas."

The General continued to study the pictures as he replied. "We're working on disguise technology. We want to know if you can see through it."

Jojo leaned back and pushed reddish-brown hair behind her left ear. "Wouldn't it be easier if you told me who was who?"

Billy turned toward her with a smile. "It wouldn't be a blind study then, would it?"

She shook her head. "But we'd be able to find the strengths and weaknesses of your technology, and ours for that matter, a whole lot faster."

"Let's do it my way for now. If the results aren't promising, I'll reveal what's behind the pictures."

"If that's what you want," Jojo said. "We're only burning trillions of computing cycles looking for matches that might not even be there."

And I sure hope aren't, he thought. Claire had special skills, but she better not be alive. For some reason, he felt sure Donna could help him find out.

His phone buzzed again. He glanced at the time on Jojo's computer, almost 17:00. People must be squeezing in their calls, trying to get home for supper.

"Williams," he said, watching Jojo's eyes.

"Hello, General, Billings with the Agency. You asked me to check out the Ferreti's. They were at the address you gave us. Like you said, if they have a daughter named Donna, they won't admit it, even after we showed them the birth certificate from the online resource."

"Thanks."

"You'll like this. The old lady accused me of being a terrorist."

"Funny. Do you have time to extend the search?"

"A quick pass, see what comes up besides this Facebook page. The lady has almost a thousand good-looking friends," Billings replied. "But after that we'll have to log a project."

"Do what you can. This isn't important enough to make official."

"Got it. I'll get back to you."

Chapter 63

BERT SPIN SAT IN WHAT he thought of as the "invisible" conference room a few hundreds yards from the oval office. In this room the President could meet with anyone he wanted, and the press wouldn't see entrances or exits. The room had become Spin's second home since Alaska. He sipped rich black coffee and listened to the President finish a phone conversation with the First Lady that apparently wasn't private enough for him to chase Bert out of the room.

"I know you told her she could go, but Secret Service has to be with her," Mallor said into the gray phone.

"Yes, all the time. I don't care if she's fifteen years old."

"No, she can't go alone. She can't go anywhere alone."

"Yes, that's final," he shouted.

"I know she hates me, it comes with this job. She should be used to the Service by now."

"I agree. It's tough to be the President's kid. Ask her if she would like to trade places with a starving teenager in Malawi, I'll have my staff work out the arrangements."

"Of course I'm serious. If she doesn't shut up, ship her out. I'll pay for the ticket."

He slammed the phone down on the table, even though it was his personal cell.

"Sorry, Bert. Crazy kids don't understand my job. They'd love it if I lost the election. More freedom for them."

The President didn't say anything for a moment. Bert remained frozen in place.

"This isn't news, but Alaska is hurting me. We've agreed to federal aid to help clean up, which is all I should really do. But the environmental lobby wants an investigation. They seem to think Exxon Mobil is getting sloppy."

Spin lowered his coffee. "Oil companies have a record of sloppy. They give us an annual pipeline leak or well explosion. Let the tree-people have an investigation. Assign a committee leader to do a preliminary, announce results after the election. So long as he says nice things about how you're supporting him until then, it should only help."

"But I don't know what they'll find." Mallor dragged a chair out and sat down. "And I'm not getting good vibes from Williams." He stared into the corner. "Remember those Firestone tires that caused Ford SUV's to roll over and kill people? The company should have made a statement and moved on instead of talking about it for years. You know 'Look at the changes we made. Look our cars are safe.' But they kept bringing attention back to the original issue, made people nervous. The Exxon guys are doing it right. Stop talking about it so it can be buried under a stream of new media bullshit."

Bert put his elbow on the arm of the chair and placed a closed fist against his cheek. "We could distract them with bigger excitement: a missile gone awry, or an attack on one of our ships—like the *USS Turner Joy* back in '64. Get their minds off the pipeline."

The President screwed up his mouth like he was trying to get spinach out of his teeth. "I don't think that works this time. The oil companies are using Alaska as an excuse to pump up prices."

Bert grimaced inside, didn't react to the pun, said, "Force prices down. Subsidize them, tax them, do something to push the price back in line. We know taxpayers never vote for the guy who gave them high fuel prices."

The President stood. Bert thought he was leaving, but he started pacing the long side of the table like a big cat in a small cage.

"Do both," the President said. "We find a military disaster. We pressure the oil companies. And let's PR the hell out of the aid we're giving Alaska to protect the land and rebuild the local economy. All three moves should be worth a couple of points in the polls."

"Mr. President, I agree we should continue the PR about the aid you're providing. But voters worry about two things: their safety, and their wallets. If you can convince the oil companies to drop prices, even a tiny bit, that would be best. Then find out what happened, or convince voters it really was a pump failure with weird domino consequences."

Bert hesitated. He hated to disagree with the President because the man didn't like it. But advising on public perception was his job. "I think another disaster, even if it was military and on the other side of the globe, is going to make people scream incompetence. It might take the polls even lower."

The President stopped and frowned. Finally he turned to Bert, "And you suggest?"

Bert pushed his chair back and stood up, it made him feel weird to be sitting while the President was standing.

"Focus hard on Alaska, show people we're paying attention and that the country is in good hands. Let's get a story out about faulty maintenance, or a manufacturing defect. Some company might have to take it in the shorts, but so what? Hire independent consultants to establish that the pump was a critical link in the original design. Make sure it was made in China, that will help, voters love to blame the Chinese. Show the design for a new pump that doesn't share the flaw and release a schedule for when the replacements will be installed. Put heat on the oil companies, they can take it."

"And?"

"And get those jerks to bring the price of gasoline down. Find any excuse. Promise them something after the election if we have to."

"Okay, Bert, sounds simple."

"But..." Bert said.

The President sat down. Bert poured him more coffee. Bert took silence to mean approval to continue. "But it wasn't a pump and we know it. That machine Williams found, and thankfully destroyed and classified, was a bomb. And a whole bunch just like it took out that pipeline. Weirdest attack I've ever heard about."

"And no one claiming responsibility,"

"Not a whisper. General Williams believes he has neutralized the guy that did it. But how could anything that big be one man? I think the Chinese are messing with our finances and this was a shot across our economic bow. They don't like our military presence in Asia."

The President remained quiet, thoughtful. "If you're right, they can replace the one man a billion times over." He tapped the tip of the ring finger of his right hand on the desktop like he was playing a note on the piano. "And if they do that, the next disaster will be larger, and no doubt within days of the election."

"They want you out. It could happen."

"And what about Williams? Has he really found this guy?"

"He says yes, but the look in his eye...I'm not sure. Personally, I think something went wrong, but I have no data to support that view." Bert swallowed. "And your office shouldn't really know details, it's too dangerous."

The President stood again; fortunately Bert hadn't sat down.

"You know, Bert, sometimes I wish we had a fucking window in here so we could enjoy the sunshine."

"Wouldn't be safe, Mr. President."

"I feel like my daughter, caged by the Secret Service." The President sighed. "So we follow Billy, that's your suggestion?"

"Yes, Mr. President. Have the FBI watch him so we can better evaluate the situation. If something else is coming, I wouldn't want to miss it just because Billy was...distracted."

"It's not that I don't trust him," the President said. "He's been an unwavering supporter of my administration for years. And his future is tied to my policy. If Petry gets in—hell, he'll downsize the military to a couple of gay guys with slingshots."

"Maybe Billy could use some help," Bert offered.

"Couldn't we all. I sure would like to know what happened to that pipe." The President stopped pacing. "Okay, Bert. Call Zaluski at the Bureau, but keep it quiet."

Bert nodded.

The President didn't move.

Which meant Bert didn't move.

"Petry," Mallor said.

Bert was trying to figure out if the President wanted a summary when he continued.

"What do we do about him? I mean, look. A terrorist just hit a pipeline on U.S. soil, though the voters don't know it. We're going to keep fighting wars because people won't stop attacking us. In the Middle East robots have proven beyond doubt that they can help."

The President sat down and stared as if there were a window in the wall.

"Bert, it's a no-brainer. Robots find IEDs. We can fly, drive and swim them unmanned from New Jersey. The Navy keeps drones aloft for what, months? They save the lives of our soldiers. What's to argue about? Reason says there will be a next war. History proves, and Petry even admits, we're lousy at predicting where it will be or how it will be fought."

Mallor jumped up and started pacing again.

Bert knew he was planning, so he waited. Time passed. He listened to the second hand of the wall clock.

"Petry believes that because we can't predict how to fight it," Bert offered, "we shouldn't allocate funds."

"His thinking is overly narrow. DARPA invests in graduate students, research, basic capability. The 'D' means *defense*. We have to be ready to protect this country from anything, no matter how bizarre," he paused, "like this pipeline."

"Spending is never attractive in an election, Mr. President," Bert said. "We have to find a different way to hit him."

The President stopped moving. "Bert, we need a knife fight." He glanced at the wall where he had suggested a window. "And a handgun."

Chapter 64

MIKE STIRRED PASTA WITH HIS left hand and pulled a flat cell phone out of his right pocket. He popped the Bluetooth adapter off and stuck it in his ear, pressed a speed dial number and dropped the phone back into his pants.

"She's here."

He listened for five seconds.

"No good options, connects directly to Williams," he said. "He can't identify me. She doesn't know who I am." He waited, stirred. "Tell her?" He lifted the pasta and watched it fall back into the pot. "Depends on how she handles Williams."

He heard the door to the kitchen rattle, and shifted the earpiece to his pocket.

"Smells good," Claire said. "Were you talking to someone?"

"Checking details."

She looked around. "You have phones in a cave?"

He turned the heat off. "Cell."

Her brow crinkled. "Your cell phone works here and mine won't work in Washington? You have a great provider." She laughed.

He placed the empty pan in the sink. "Micro-cell."

"Connected to what, Iridium?" She waved her hands in an arc. "Don't they have sixty-six satellites circling the planet?"

He splashed white wine into the pasta. "Too much energy. I like fiber."

She picked up a slice of bread and tore a corner. "Who in their right mind would run fiber up here?" She laughed and popped the chunk into her mouth.

"Me."

Silence filled the space between them.

Ten minutes later they were seated in the computer room. Maxx was improvising an electronic flute solo over a simple arrangement of *Three to Get Ready* by Dave Brubek. They had moved the desk and covered it with a white sheet. A peach colored candle glowed in the center.

"How did you bake fresh bread in the time it took me to shower?"

"You take long showers."

She tilted her face and met his eyes.

"Okay, it was frozen. Eight minutes in the oven. Not the best, but better than trying to store bread up here and eating stale rock hard crust."

She watched him.

"Yes, speaking from experience."

She tasted the wine. "Your own supercomputer, freezer, hot water, oven. You must use a load of power in your vacation hideaway."

"A bit."

"Where does it come from?"

"China Power. They beam it to me from Three Gorges Dam." He chewed, smiling.

She placed her glass on the desk. "We're hundreds of miles from a well with a hand pump. And not even the Chinese can beam power." Her eyebrows drew together.

"Big batteries?"

She shook her head. "Hidden solar cells?"

"Good try, but no. Last guess."

"Wind?"

"You noticed the windmill farm, did you?" He picked up the bottle and poured the last of the wine into her glass. She seemed too relaxed for someone being hunted.

"There's a lot of water around here. Could hydro work?"

"Half a bingo. Turbines in the streams, batteries, geo-thermal installation."

She whistled softly. "You're self-contained."

She meant the facility, but he was self-contained in more important ways. He worked alone, trusting only those who had proven themselves. Her he would watch closely.

"I make a food run now and then. Other than that, I'm free to work." He finished his wine.

She leaned back in the big La-Z-Boy, holding the wine glass in one hand and pulling the big T-shirt around her with the other. She sipped, letting it linger in her mouth.

"Work?"

A red flag waved in his head. He said nothing.

"You work here?"

"I work lots of places."

"But Maxx. He's huge. Someone went to a lot of trouble to program him."

"Not so hard with engineering degrees available over the Internet," he said, wondering where she was going.

She sipped. "You programmed Maxx? Seems like a big project to me. But I'm a sharpshooter, not a programmer."

"I had help. Maxx runs a lot of open source software. You know, freely available over the Internet. I modify pieces to do special things."

"Does it, uh he, um…"

For a moment he questioned his decision to use her to eliminate the dual threat facing him: little B's Rat, big B's hunt for the Daemon.

"Be right back." He pushed the rolling office chair out from under him. In a minute, he returned with two bowls of gelato with caramel and fudge twirled on top.

"Only had vanilla."

"How did you get a big freezer up here?"

"I didn't," he said, scooping in.

She cocked her head.

"It's like Maxx. I start with one component, bring more and more until I have a matrix. Redundancy. If one fails, the others keep going."

"How'd you get them here?"

"Same as everything else."

She sucked on the spoon and frowned. "I've only seen you on a motorcycle." Her head swiveled. "Impossible."

He leaned away from his empty bowl. "Really?"

She examined the room. He knew she was mentally dismantling each piece of equipment.

"It would take hundred of trips," she said.

He crossed his arms, watching her think. "True."

"And months."

"Years," he said.

"But why?"

"Obscurity is the best form of security."

"Why do you care about security?" she asked.

Maxx's flute solo ended mid-note. "Excuse me."

"Go ahead, Maxx," Mike said.

"You wished to be informed on data access."

A digital pickpocket was always of interest. He watched her eyes but spoke to Maxx. "What do you have?"

"The data caches on Donna Ferreti have been tapped. Three times in the past sixty-seven seconds."

She frowned and said softly, "What data caches?"

"Remember the web information I set up before we went to see Williams? He accessed it as soon as Donna walked out of the condo. I added more treasure in case he came back."

"Speaking of treasure." She held up her empty bowl.

"Sure." He stood. "Wine?"

She hesitated, smiled. "Iced?"

He grinned.

"Fantastic."

He headed for the door, stopped. "Maxx, fill us in."

She twisted in her big chair. "Don't you want him to wait?"

He pointed up. "Speakers."

Maxx said, "Donna's personal profile on Facebook has been accessed six times via a Google search for Donna Ferreti. The link from it to the home page of her personal website, donnaferreti.com, has been followed twice."

While Maxx talked, Mike walked the tube to the kitchen to locate his oldest port. It wasn't iced wine, but it'd do.

"All pages on her home site have been accessed and the pictures copied to the accessing client. Tracking client activity reveals searches for the following: "high school, birthday, age, parents, military service," attached to the name Donna Ferreti, D. Ferreti, and all spelling variants of Ferreti, combinations of double r, single r, double t, single t."

"Someone wants to find you, Donna," Mike said to himself.

"Tracking the IP addresses of the accessing machines yields an ISP in Washington DC and a government facility on Alexander Ave. Best estimate, the Federal Bureau of Investigation."

The door opened with a light squeak. Mike carried another bowl of gelato and two small, stemmed glasses containing dark purple liquid. He handed a glass to Claire as he passed her chair.

"Why FBI, Maxx?" he asked.

"Key indicators, dot gov name on ISP e-mail, physical location of access point, form of e-mail address enumerating agents—"

"Thanks, Maxx."

He sat down.

"Know anyone in the Bureau?" he asked.

Her lower lip rose to cover her upper. "Not offhand. I shoot against them now and then, but don't really have friends there."

"Enemies?"

She frowned. "No, of course not."

"Does Williams?"

She sucked the right side of her lip. "Billy knows everyone. I'm sure he has contacts inside the FBI."

She spooned the gelato, then sipped the dark liquid. "It's so sweet. Another Chinese clone?"

"Pit'n Bull. From Portugal." He drank. "So Billy has the FBI searching for Donna. Maybe even searching for Claire. Maxx, Claire search?"

"No access to the sites. No searches for Claire or C. Ferreti from the identified IP addresses."

"What do you think?"

"Billy thinks I'm dead. But Donna makes him nervous."

Mike crossed the room to the leftmost stack of computers.

"I agree." He slid a black tray out from the stack. It held a keyboard and touchpad. He typed. The projector lit up with a map of the world. Blue lights popped on.

"The geographic location of IP addresses that have accessed two or more caches. One might be accidental, but I figure two indicates a real search."

She studied the map. "D.C. isn't surprising. But why three in Iceland?"

"He sent someone to find Donna. Nothing official, probably private investigators."

Her face lost color. "He's trying awfully hard."

"Something bothers him." He was quiet. "Maxx, causality on access."

"Clients are professional. Single residential address belongs to Williams. Style indicates tracking."

"Does he mean they're trying to find her?" Claire asked, frowning slightly that she had just called a machine he.

"Yes," Maxx answered.

"How can he, uh, Maxx, know that?"

"He mines content. Like Google analyzing your e-mail and browsing habits so they can better sell you to advertisers."

"But why, what can Donna tell them?"

"Good question." Mike returned and sat across the desk from her. "Williams might think she was fake, not really your sister. In that case, he wants to know what her game is."

"Does he know we saw the diary?" she asked, her voice shaky.

He squinted. "I would say no. If he thought she saw that diary, I think he would personally go to the extraction site to verify."

She was silent.

"Not good," he said.

"What? What?" she spilled her port, caught the drops in her left hand and licked them off her palm.

"He's checking the site. And something else."

"Maxx, satellite images. GPS from primary bike: Big Bang."

"What?"

"As soon as the weather cleared."

"Day and time?" Maxx asked.

"Honey Pot timing. Scan weather. Visible and infrared."

"It was raining like hell when you—" she chugged the rest of her port, "when you saved me."

Pictures of the charred remains of the shack glowed on the big monitor. Mike walked up to examine them.

"Time lapse."

Images played in slow motion. Mike stared.

"There," Claire called out. " One of the bikes moved."

"When I went back to bury the body it was still raining. Later I brought the bikes out, but the weather hadn't cleared."

"Something shifted in that picture. Is that before you went back?"

"One bike was on fire when I pulled you out. Had to be scorched."

"Will Billy notice this?" she asked.

"Only if he looks carefully. It's within twelve hours of the incident. The weather was overcast, and these images are reconstructions from infrared."

She squirmed in her chair. "If you were Billy, what would you conclude?"

He studied the screen. "I would want to know if anything moved that couldn't have been caused by high winds or water erosion. Maxx, subtraction."

The image dropped to black except for a skeletal outline of a front wheel and the edge of a seat.

"Looks random to me, maybe shifted as the bike burned, like a dying campfire.

"Maybe," she said. "But if he figures a bike was there, and now it's gone..."

"Locals could have stolen it. If he checks after the weather cleared, the scene is clean. He doesn't have the topology of the site to do reconstructions like this; they came from my bike. It's important he doesn't see a disappearing body. He won't care about the equipment, none of it is U.S. issue." He met her eyes. "I assume that was on purpose."

She looked away. "Where's Cam?" she asked softly.

"A few clicks up the trail. Williams has no reason to look for a gravesite."

They fell silent.

Mike broke it. "You gave me an idea. Maxx, Donna submissions."

Mike raised both hands toward Claire. The room flashed. She jumped. "What the—?"

"Need a pic," he said, smiling.

To her horror a picture of her in the oversize shirt and sweat pants, no make-up, and stringy two-tone hair showed up life size on the big monitor next to the pictures of Donna.

"What do you think, Claire, sisters?"

She looked at the images. "A slight resemblance."

"How about you, Maxx? How are the images related?"

They watched as two-digit numbers spun over each picture.

"Relation to Donna image from website," Maxx said.

The highest was the new picture of Claire, at seventy-eight percent.

"Sisters or first cousins," Maxx said.

She sat straight up, her mouth agape. "You think Billy is doing an analysis like this?"

"Almost certainly."

"With what pictures?"

"Donna from his condo security cameras. And he must have pictures of Claire."

She swallowed hard. "He has lots of pictures. What do you think he'll conclude?"

"Hopefully, the same as Maxx." His eyes held her. "We knew it was dangerous to see him."

"I had to," she said. She leaned back into her big chair and licked the rim of her empty glass.

He put both forearms on the desk and interlaced his fingers. With motionless eyes, he stared at her for a long moment. "What would you like to do next?"

She slouched into the soft warmth of the chair. "Billy..."

"Will kill you to keep the mission secret. We know that. We don't know if he's aware you're alive. Either you stay invisible, or you eliminate him."

Her eyes widened, "Billy?"

"Kill him...or put him in prison." He leaned away. "The former is a longer term solution."

They watched each other for many seconds.

"The former is also safer," he said. "But it's not my specialty."

He watched her face carefully, but couldn't read her thoughts.

"It's yours."

Chapter 65

QIGIQ'S ECONOMY SEAT JOSTLED his backbone as the fat tires of the 737 screeched against concrete. Being trapped inside a metal tube with hundreds of people violated his sense of order, but he needed to see General Williams. The man had classified all information about the roving machine. Legally, there was no one else he could talk to.

He shouldered his nylon bag and stepped from the plane into the sunlight and heat of an October afternoon in DC. Perspiration began to form where his tan shirt touched his spine even though it was designed to wick moisture and contained silver strands to kill bacteria. A jacket was out of the question.

He walked down portable plastic stairs and followed lines painted on concrete into a building where a blast of conditioned air chilled the wetness on his back. Overhead flight monitors showed 4:00 pm. A woman bumped him hard. He turned to see her dragging a roller cart in one hand and a six-year old in the other. She scowled at him.

"Excuse me," he said, though she was already too far away to hear.

Riding the shuttle with a dozen other people he thought about the LTB. It was very fast across the ground. Could it have traveled a great distance? The hole it left matched a dozen others. Why was Exxon Mobil insisting that a pump caused a reaction fracture?

After dinner, alone in the Embassy Inn, he reread his report. It raised many questions.

* * *

The following morning Qigiq tried to relax in an air-conditioned taxi darting from his hotel toward Georgetown. He imagined a dozen conversations with Williams before stepping out on Marshall, ducking to miss an umbrella being used as a shield against the sunshine, and crossing the street.

He turned toward the Pentagon, walking briskly with a single folded copy of his report in his breast pocket. An automatic rested in a shoulder holster he rarely wore because he didn't much like guns, but he wanted to appear professional by Washington standards. He ascended stone steps and stopped at a guard station immediately inside the door.

"General Williams, please. I have a nine o'clock appointment." He handed his business card to a uniformed guard.

The guard's eyes flicked between Qigiq's face and the card as if he were comparing a picture.

"ID, please," the man said.

Qigiq offered his passport and Fairbanks detective shield.

The guard's eyebrows lifted and he started to smile but caught himself. "Cold up there, huh?"

Most people had no idea of the real temperature variation in Alaska. "Anything would be cold compared to here," Qigiq offered.

"You got that right," the guard said, picking up a telephone receiver and punching numbers. "Guy here from Alaska to see Williams. Yeah, that's the name. Yes, I've seen his badge."

"You'll have to leave firearms here."

Qigiq slipped off his tan blazer, unbuckled the holster and handed the bundle to the guard. He lifted his left pant leg and withdrew a knife with a carved handle. The clerk's eyes followed the knife handle as he slipped the weapons into a drawer. He passed Qigiq a slip of thermal-printed paper that listed time, name, visitor and a code for the drawer.

Qigiq pulled his jacket on and passed through scanners and a turnstile to elevators. On the third floor he turned right and walked down a wide hallway. After making an obtuse-angle turn required by the five-sided building, he found a closed door that matched the number Williams had given him. He knocked.

A young woman in a green uniform with caramel colored hair opened the door. Her chest badge said her name was Latell.

"Mr. Qigiq," she said, almost correctly, "welcome. The General will be with you in a moment."

He stepped into a small outer office with two guest chairs. He sat in the furthest chair and smiled at Latell while she faced sideways towards a black computer supported by an L-shaped beige desk. The walls were pale green under fluorescent tubes looking down on dark green carpet. He was reminded of money.

"Excuse me, Ms. Latell." He pulled a Lucky's pack from inside his jacket and held it up.

She smiled. "The surgeon general has determined thou shalt not smoke on government property."

An inner door opened and Williams stepped into the small room. He handed a folder to Latell. "Has to be there by noon."

"Yes, General. Your nine o'clock is here." Her eyes motioned behind him.

Williams turned but didn't smile. "Qigiq. How was your trip? Come in."

Qigiq followed him into a much larger room with windows, a long desk in dark cherry and gray carpet instead of green. The desk supported two frames whose pictures faced away from him, a large calendar blotter, and a round black ashtray that was perfectly clean. Another L-shaped piece held a computer like Latell's.

Williams walked around the desk and spun into a high-back black chair. He dropped both elbows onto his desk and gestured for Qigiq to sit in one of the pair of four-legged cushioned chairs facing him. Qigiq saw his eyes flash to the left to a round white-faced wall clock whose hands were just touching 9:00 am.

"How're things in the sunshine state?"

Qigiq wondered if the General was making a joke about Alaskan summers. He resisted the urge to say "Smokin'," and said, "Cooler than here."

"Most places are," the General replied. "What can I do for you? You seemed uneasy on the phone."

Qigiq grinned to project a comfort level he didn't feel, and got to work. "I've been examining the data you collected on the machine found by the boy."

"What you called a tractor? We've been analyzing those pictures ourselves. Never seen anything like it."

"Nor have I," Qigiq replied. "But the parts are familiar."

The General frowned.

Qigiq wondered if the General had already made the parts connection, because he looked like a suspect stifling a reaction.

"Notice anything unusual about them?" Qigiq said, watching Williams' eyes shift. His instincts vibrated.

Williams didn't speak. He pulled open a drawer and extracted a file. He flipped through loose papers. "We found something about a cell phone module. Yes, here. There are two manufacturers, both in China."

Qigiq was surprised, but he didn't show it. There was only one manufacturer. If the General had found a second, the first had lied.

"Tried to trace the unit back to the manufacturer, but they build a gazillion of them every year," Williams said.

"So you weren't able to find the factory that constructed the cell module?" Qigiq asked.

"Not even close. We don't have a serial number, just pictures showing the design." Williams flipped to a page of numbers in the report. "There sure are a lot of cell phones in the world."

Not small, round, low-power ones, Qigiq thought. But he said, "These were somewhat specialized."

"This says they were low-power yet satellite capable. Not your everyday cell phone."

"Could we talk about the manufacturer?" Qigiq asked.

"Two outfits in China. Han Chao Exports and Ming Foo Electronics. Neither answer phone calls or e-mail. I'm thinking about sending a Chinese-speaking soldier in, but the Communists hate that kind of thing. We've asked our Ambassador to intervene. With the red tape, it'll take months."

"I see." He had found Ming Foo, but nothing related to Han Chao.

"Plus, I don't have the data to be able to ask the right questions. I have no idea when this was manufactured, or who ordered it, or what it was used for." Williams looked up. "Well, we know what it was used for, but it's doubtful the guy who made the—what did you call it, LTB? —revealed what he was doing with the modules."

"Makes backtracking difficult," Qigiq said.

"Sure does."

"Have you examined other parts?" Qigiq asked.

"Generic stuff made by dozens of companies. If we had a metallurgy sample we might be able to narrow it down. But we don't, unless you found one."

"We searched for trace elements in the boy's room, but only found gravel from the treads. Analysis showed it consistent with the permafrost where Billy found the machine. Nothing unusual."

"Unfortunate."

"There is one thing though," Qigiq said.

Williams raised his eyes from the folder without lifting his head. Qigiq thought he looked unhappy that there might be new information.

"Our forensics team reverse engineered the parts from your pictures. Fortunately you took orthogonal close-ups." He held up his hand. "This requires many assumptions because we don't have access to internals."

Williams closed the folder. "We weren't aware your team was even working on the device. I thought you were leaving that to the Army."

Qigiq watched the General's eyes: blue and alert. "We don't usually have resources to follow a hunch, especially after Exxon's statement. But the more I looked at the LTB, the more it resembled a commercial device. I began to wonder how many of these might have been made."

"So you pursued it?"

"Investigated. What motivated me was the tread pattern. One of our techs said it resembled drive belts for an overhead-cam engine. So we looked at the size, groove shape, tooth spacing, and texture. Most flexible material like that is a composite, and that's precisely what we found."

"A drive belt? You're not serious," Williams said, crossing his arms on his chest.

"Ducati motorcycle overhead cam, Product Code MW:81910171A. The similarity is uncanny. You had enough pictures that we feel confident of the match."

"A match based on pictures? Isn't that questionable procedure, Detective?"

"The results are quite convincing, an exact match in every detail we could measure."

General Williams wasn't smiling. "Exact?"

"Within fractions of a millimeter."

"And that proves?"

"Nothing. But do you remember when the device fled through the open door of the shed?"

The General picked a pen from his pocket and reopened the folder. He scribbled.

"Yes, I remember very clearly. It was quite fast."

"So fast that the torque from what we believe is an electric motor from a Piaggio scooter starter exceeded the available traction."

The General's eyebrows knitted together, but he remained silent.

"I was able to take samples of the skid marks on the wood floor of the shack and compare them to the compound used to manufacture the cam belts."

"And?"

"A chemical match. There is no doubt those treads were Ducati belts that drive their patented desmodromic valve system."

"Well, I'll be," said the General. "Clever work."

Qigiq shifted in his chair, watching the General's face. He thought Williams could be playing poker. "Not much help though. Ducati builds thousands of them every year in a factory in Thailand."

"All with the same material?"

"Yes. Often from one batch that is sent to multiple sites."

"Not interesting," Williams said with a slight twist in his grin.

"Key, actually. It pointed us in a direction we hadn't considered."

Williams tapped a pen against the closed folder. Qigiq read him as anxious for the meeting to be over. "What direction?"

"The reason I came here. We analyzed the drive gear, tail section, housing, everything we could see in your photographs."

Williams waited.

"They share a highly uncommon characteristic."

"Something our military analysts missed, apparently. We couldn't even identify the parts."

Qigiq said as agreeably as he could, "Everything we saw could be tracked to a part number in a catalog."

The General's eyes opened wider.

Qigiq was confident his news came as a surprise. The military people hadn't figured it out. But he had.

"What kind of catalog sells parts for a mobile bomb?"

"Motorcycles. Every part can be ordered for a machine made in the past five years. A variety of brands: Honda, Kawasaki, Ducati."

Williams was quiet.

Qigiq watched him think.

"You mean the LTB was assembled from old motorcycle parts?"

"Not old, General. Brand new. Any of the parts can be ordered today. And they share another characteristic."

Williams turned his office chair sideways and stared out the window. "What the heck could a bunch of junk from a parts bin have in common?"

"Suppliers in China."

Williams spoke to the window, "And what could that possibly mean?"

"Are you asking me to speculate, General?"

Williams turned to face him, his features creased with worry. "Yes, please."

"My initial reaction was that our builder is Chinese, and therefore had access to parts manufactured in China. I tried to trace the parts to establish that they had come from Chinese suppliers, but I don't have enough information."

"And now?"

Qigiq leaned back slightly. "Now I think the Chinese manufacture is coincidental. Our builder could have easily procured parts from any country, though perhaps the Chinese don't create quite the audit trail that others might, or share it so readily with U.S. authorities. What might be more important is that these are all *motorcycle* parts. Our builder is somehow related to two-wheel machines."

There was a light knock on the door. Latell poked her head in. "Your 9:30 appointment is here."

"Thanks, get them coffee. We'll be finished shortly."

The door closed with barely a click.

The General closed his eyes and began rubbing his temples with both hands. "You think motorcycles have something to do with this?" He looked up and met Qigiq's gaze.

"I think the builder has intimate knowledge of motorcycles and knows we can't trace parts that are made by the thousands. Very few people could assemble an LTB from parts built for other purposes. And the fact that each part has multiple sources," except for that cell phone, he thought, "was not an accident."

The General glanced at his wrist. "Sorry I don't have time to delve into this. Intriguing information, not sure what to do with it though." The General stood. "Any suggestions?"

Qigiq wondered if he knew what to do next, would he share it with this man. "I hoped to discuss how we might pursue the builder."

"Of course, the builder is not necessarily the terrorist," the General said from behind his desk.

Qigiq nodded. "But he might lead us to him...or her."

The General looked at his watch again, so Qigiq stood. "Could you tell me how to find Corporal Ferreti? I'd like to say hello."

The General's eyes moved slowly to Qigiq's face. "Corporal Ferreti is on assignment."

Seven minutes later Qigiq exited the five-sided building and thought about what he had accomplished with his trek to Washington. How many people could build a remotely guided, mobile bomb from a catalog, tediously searching for exactly the right size and material and weight?

He stared across the Potomac River at the spire of the Washington Monument as the sun heated his jacket, even though it wasn't yet ten o'clock. Hundreds of tires on pavement created a buzz that was making him nervous. He thought of a giant treadmill.

The Chinese parts seemed significant, though he couldn't demonstrate why. He was after a person who could create from a parts bin, but couldn't fathom where to look for him.

He crossed a parking lot large enough to hold an Alaskan village and shifted perspective: Why build the tractor? *Cui bono?* Who could benefit from damaging the pipeline?

He looked down the street, searching for the bus, wishing for more clues, hoping they were hiding in the offices of Exxon Mobil. The General had been surprised, there was no doubt, but he hadn't seemed eager. Qigiq was eager.

Chapter 66

"YOU'RE INSANE," MIKE SAID.

"Always so agreeable in the morning?"

"Only when I hear crazy talk. You can't meet Williams, he'll snuff you."

Frowning, she shoveled scrambled eggs with cream cheese into her mouth. "Of courth I can."

"Not if you want to stay alive."

She swallowed. "I have a plan."

"Tell me you have a brother." He laughed.

She shook her head. "No really. I have to know if Billy set us up. If so, he has to be stopped. There are lives at stake."

"Yours, for one."

"Others too. Cam, Wu."

"You can't bring them back."

She placed her fork on the table, studied her orange juice glass. "I know, but I can prevent more from joining them."

He frowned.

"Okay, I can try."

He placed his glass on the shaky table and said quietly, "His journal hasn't convinced you?"

Was she simply refusing to believe she could have been so completely deceived by a man she thought loved her? She wouldn't be the first.

Mike's voice broke into her thoughts. "What do you have in mind?"

"We devise a plan that brings Bil...Williams to us on our terms. We have a foolproof escape strategy. And we pray for luck."

Mike laughed softly. "I've heard of praying for many things...but luck? Does your God give good odds?"

"I take what I can get."

"You're praying for two inside straights, you know."

"Bad, huh?" She frowned. "Why two?"

"First, you have to find the truth, Williams isn't going to tell you. You'll have to force it out of him, or trick him."

"And seconth," she said through toast covered with apricot jam.

"And seconth, you have to stop a General in the U.S. Army who can easily marshal more strike force than Vietnam and China combined."

"So we have to think hard."

"And."

"And?" Claire repeated slowly.

"You have to stay alive. Long term, not just for the next few weeks."

She pursed her lips, holding her fork in midair. "No loose ends?"

"No loose ends."

She swallowed the last of her coffee and held out the porcelain mug for a refill. "When can we start?"

He pushed his chair back; the feet screeched. He reached out and took her cup, overlapping his fingers on hers. Her eyes flicked upward before she released her grip.

"This morning, unless you want to go riding in the mud again."

"Had enough mud. Let's start now."

He poured her coffee and took it back to the table. He crossed the kitchen, pulled open a drawer and removed a roll of white butcher paper.

"Do you prefer to work in the kitchen, bedroom, or in the office with Maxx?" he asked.

"Well, I've been told I do my best work in the bedroom and the rifle range," she smiled. "But this is cozy, let's stay here."

He shook his head. "Army girls." He taped one end of the paper to the wall beside the door to the walkway and started unrolling. He bumped past the table, nudging her sideways, and continued all the way to the wall behind her. He tore the paper off the roll and taped the end into the corner.

She laughed. "Awfully small, isn't it?"

"It'll get us started."

"Do you always work in miniature?"

He faced her. "I like to see relationships."

"So what's the giant scratch pad for?"

"Our time line," he gestured left to right along the bottom of the ten-foot section of paper. "And this," his left hand indicated the vertical, "are events we have to make happen to achieve your objective," his eyes met hers, "and mine."

She gazed back and forth along the white expanse. "What's your objective?"

"Keep us alive, and out of jail."

She nodded. "I like those."

"Step one. We need some equipment..."

Chapter 67

BERTRAND SPIN SAT IN A LEATHER chair the color of ox blood in his downtown office reading the FBI's report on project Warner Brothers. The office was long enough for a little putting green when he was in the mood, and smelled of polished wood that made him feel successful, rather than like a gopher for the President. He *was* a gopher for the President, but he still liked to feel important, and this private corner office helped.

The document provided background information on Williams' activities over the past three months, and detail for the two-week period starting on the day Spin had asked the FBI for assistance. Bert scanned a list noting that Billy made a lot of phone calls, even by Bert's standards. He slid his index finger down the column: number, city, state, country. Billy had contacts all over the world. He wondered absently how many of these calls were to spies—people who didn't officially exist and whose phone records would disappear if they were ever investigated.

His finger stopped.

Two calls to China. Bert flipped forward a few pages. Two more calls to China. Two short calls to China virtually every day over a two-week period. Always the same number. China and Alaska. Bert closed his eyes and thought back to the meeting where Billy presented his findings to the President. A part. A part for the bombs that had nixed the pipeline had been made in China.

And something else.

Billy had a contact, the guy who told them about the manufacturing facility. Bert kept reading. He was just getting to a section covering the meetings Billy had attended when his phone rang.

"Bert Spin."

"Hello, Mr. Spin. We would like to provide you with some information. Please visit the website at www.misterspin.is, it will be available for the next five minutes."

Spin jerked forward. "Why? Who are you? How did you get—" But the phone was dead. The voice had been calm, like a professor who had given a lecture too many times. He tried to attach a name or face or an accent to the man's voice without success as he replaced the receiver. Five minutes. What country's top-level domain was "dot-is?" He thought about all the nations that mattered in the world. He didn't know a "dot-is."

He turned to his laptop and typed the URL into FireFox, the browser his security people made him use. He started his computer's screen recorder.

A plain white window opened, then a picture the size of a good cookie at Starbucks faded up. Under it a caption: *You know this man.* "Yes, I do," he said aloud. The picture was a headshot of Billy in a green polo shirt. Whoever had been on that phone now had his full attention.

He kept his eyes glued to the screen and reached his left hand out for the handset. His assistant answered.

"Hi, Stacey. Get me someone in the tech group with security clearance who can track down the location of a website. The geographic location…in less than five minutes…I wish I were joking, do the best you can. Thanks." He placed the handset into its cradle, eyes still on the screen.

The display changed to a one-page newsletter like the ones on kiosks in the neighborhoods where yuppie singles hung out. It had a waist-up picture of a woman and a $50,000 reward for information leading to her whereabouts. He studied the face and thought about the dollar amount. Her name was Donna Ferreti and she looked like those scrawny models Spain was banning from fashion runways.

The caption below the picture said: *Why is your man looking for this woman?* Bert had no idea. But he hoped it had to do with some sort of sexual fantasy and not something that really mattered.

He drummed his fingers on the table and watched the website, hoping the tech would arrive before it disappeared into the ether. He picked up the phone again. "Hi, Stacey. Can you reach General Williams?" He stopped. Maybe not. "Thanks, just e-mail me the number. I'll call when I've finished with this report. You're an angel."

The screen went white. A FireFox error message complained it couldn't locate a server for www.misterspin.is. He hated that they had used his name. He wanted to be far far away from whatever was happening here.

He made a pyramid with his fingers and blew through them. What the hell was this about? The delivery method alone gave him the heebie-jeebies. He tried to reload the page. Nothing. He told his machine to stop recording.

Tapping rattled the door.

"Come in."

"Hello, I'm Mark from IT. Stacey said you needed a guy ASAP. What's up?"

"Hi, Mark. Can you tell where a website is located?"

"Sometimes we can trace back to the owner and see what ISP it's attached to. Takes a little while."

"That might be a problem. When I try to access this site, it's no longer there. But it was five minutes ago."

Mark scrunched his mouth sideways and put his hands on his hips. "They probably took it offline. We might be able to find something cached in the big search engines, or at the ISP. How long was it up?"

"Oh, I'd guess about three or four minutes."

Mark looked at Spin like he was intoxicated and asking to drive his new Corvette. "Minutes you said? Nothing happens that fast. I'd be surprised if there's any trace at all. Be happy to look, Mr. Spin. I haven't had anything weird to study for weeks."

Spin considered. He didn't know jack about how the Internet actually worked. Maybe Mark could find something. "You have clearance?"

Mark replied, "Oh yes. For anything that isn't nuclear."

"Can you keep this quiet? I mean, you," Spin pointed at the man's chest, "me," he pointed at his own, "and Stacy," he pointed at the closed door. "Or do you folks have protocols?"

Mark relaxed his arms to his sides. "We have protocols for everything. We can use *feasibility study* and spend a few hours. If I can't find anything, then maybe we never met."

"Mark, you're a mind reader. Take a look at this."

Spin showed Mark the legal pad where he had scribbled *www.misterspin.is*. "I went to this URL and found a couple of pictures with captions. But one of the pictures was military so I'd like to know who's behind the site."

"Iceland?" Mark said. "Not much goes on there."

Spin thought about Iceland. "Maybe those gnomes they have, my wife has a statue of one in our garden."

Mark laughed. "I hear they're really into the Internet. I'll let you know what I find."

"Thanks, Mark, the sooner the better."

Mark shut the door on his way out while Bert pulled at his pursed lips like he was trying to remove a stain. He struggled to imagine what Billy had been thinking when he posted a reward for a woman in Iceland. What could be more visible? He imagined a number of things Billy could be doing with that girl, and making any of them public would be a net loss for the reelection campaign.

He stared at the error message on the white screen. Billy was normally meticulously clandestine, which meant something was in play making him careless. Or stupid.

Should he or should he not inform the President? He'd never be able to withstand the barrage of questions Mallor would hit him with, because he didn't know what was really happening. That would frustrate Mallor, and make Bert look incompetent. He was confident Billy was the source of the problem, so maybe he should talk to the man directly. But then Billy would know that Bert knew, which could scare Billy even more. That might lead to something awful Bert couldn't predict because, back to square one, he didn't know what was really happening.

If Mark found anything, the FBI could follow up. They were good at keeping themselves out of the news. And when they found the girl, Bert could ask her why she was on that website.

He picked up the handset and pressed Intercom. "Stacy? Would you please find a way to contact," he looked down at the report, "Agents Giller and Hemper, the guys that provided this report on Warner Brothers?"

Bert returned to the report. Those repeated calls to China and a woman in Iceland floated in his head. He sighed. How the hell was he supposed to control public opinion when he didn't know what was going on?

Chapter 68

MIKE STOOD IN THE KITCHEN close to Claire. She was holding a Dr. Pepper and staring at a huge sheet of butcher paper with Project Goat written above a series of circles and squares connected by labeled arrows.

He pulled a cell phone from his pocket and read a text message that began: *Donna has been kissed.*

"Mister Spin has accessed our bait," he said. "He watched for three and a half minutes and was still connected when Maxx took the site down."

The muscles in Claire's neck visibly tightened. She sipped her soda.

"We're underway then, huh?"

"A journey of a thousand miles begins with a single step," he said with a big grin.

She didn't move. "Okay, Buddha man, now what?"

"We wait. He won't ignore an opportunity like this. I'd better check in with Maxx."

Her face was blank, stiff.

"What?"

"Nothing."

He knew that wasn't an answer; it was an invitation. "Are you worried about what we've set in motion?"

"No."

He frowned. He was losing what little ability he had to predict her. "I know it's complicated and dangerous, but it's what you want, isn't it?"

"I said I am not worried about Goat."

He watched her stare at the butcher paper, her eyes tracing each step as she sidestepped her body slowly along the wall.

"Claire, what's bothering you?"

"Nothing. Are your ears going bad?" she said, facing the wall.

He walked up behind her and held her upper arms in his hands.

She said, "Go play with Maxx, he's waiting for you."

Ah, jealousy. "Sorry I need to leave, but I have work to do."

She spun to face him. "Yeah. Work I know nothing about. Maybe I could help."

"I told you. I work alone. It has to be that way."

"You're not working alone on Goat," she said.

"It's not my project. I'm helping you."

"So it's okay for you to help me, but it's not okay for me to help you?" she said, crossing her arms over a maroon, oversized T-shirt.

He shook his head. "I've been at this since a borrowed computer on a library dail-up line. I don't know what it would be like working with someone else."

"Only one way to find out."

He paused, considering. "Would you like to see what I do? It's mostly for charity."

"Yeah, show me, I don't see much charity going on."

He grinned slowly with one side of his face, knowing in advance he might get punched. "I took you in?" he said, and laughed.

"You bastard."

She turned away but he grabbed her arms and spun her body to face him. He pulled her with both hands and kissed her hard on the mouth. She didn't let her lips yield, so it felt like kissing a mannequin. Even so, cosmic energy entered his body. He eased the pressure, but didn't release her.

She resisted for five seconds...ten. All at once, her mouth opened, her lips softened, her hands reached out to pull him closer.

He felt a black hole open. He pushed away.

"You swear you won't divulge anything you find out."

"Top Secret," she replied, crossing her heart and holding up her right hand with two fingers vertical.

"What if I'm a hired assassin who does special projects around the world? Or a jewel thief? Won't you turn me in? And if you try to, I'll..." He froze. A woman's voice in his head said, *Maybe it's time.* He blinked twice, "I don't want to have to stop you."

She reached her arms up around his neck and pulled his face down.

He closed his eyes.

She kissed him hard, and soft, and hard again.

The black hole spun and curved arms of light disappeared.

She pushed away. "Show me."

They walked hand in hand through the tube to Maxx's big office. Mike led her to the La-Z-Boy. He sat down behind the desk and faced her.

She licked her lips, smiled, leaned back and crossed her legs. She flicked a big borrowed sandal off her top foot and wriggled her bare toes.

"Ready for the show. Let's see you work."

He spun in his chair. He typed and the big screen beyond him glowed. The first graph was of the S&P 500 for the past five months. It was down about eighty points. The second graph was the Dow Jones, also down, by more than 250 points.

"You're a stock trader?" she said.

"Partly."

"Don't seem the type. No tie, no suit, no shoes with little simulated holes." She shifted in the chair. Re-crossed her legs.

"Behind the scenes. Visibility is bad."

"That obscurity thing you talk about."

He bent over the keyboard. "As a baseline, you recognize the two major indices of market value."

"Sure, the Dow and the 500. Everyone knows about them."

"Correct. They're each a composite index of how the overall market is doing, meaning their value is based on the price of hundreds of individual stocks. But I don't care about the overall market, what I care about are very specific industries."

He looked up. "Maxx, Firesnake portfolio for today."

A new line joined the other two on the big display, beginning near the Dow and remaining level through July, after which it dropped by twelve percent over eight weeks.

"Hmm," she said. "Not good. Looks like you're losing fast."

"The key is to predict the future. Up or down doesn't matter. I play the downs."

"Isn't that backwards?"

"Only for the uninitiated. If you know that a stock is going down, what do you do?"

"I sell it and get the hell out," she replied.

He shook his head. "That's step one. If you're confident it's going to crash, you also sell it short."

"Short?"

"Yeah. You borrow shares at the current price and promise to give the shares back. Then you sell them and wait. When the price drops, you buy shares at the new lower price and give those back. The difference between the two prices you put in your pocket."

She shifted slightly in the big chair. "You can do that?"

"Sure. There are many ways to buy and sell stock. That's only one of them. But it's the one I like."

"Sounds risky. What if the stock goes up?"

"Then I have to find the extra money to buy the shares back, and I lose." She frowned in confusion. "I need a drink."

"The key," he spun to face her, "is to be really sure the stock is going to go down. Sell it short, then cover at the right time."

She stood and walked over to the big screen, one foot bare, the other wearing his oversized rubber sandal. "So if you knew right here," she pointed to the Firesnake portfolio, "that these stocks were going to go down, you would sell short and cover for them, as you said, over here." She pointed to the line as it dropped off to the right.

"Correct. And the lower it goes before you cover, the more money you make."

"Amazing," she said turning to face him. "You're betting the stock will drop."

His lips shifted in a strange way. "It's not exactly a bet."

"Okay, an educated guess. Your careful analysis of the financial state of the companies predicts they will go down."

"Something like that," he agreed, leaning back in the swivel chair. It squeaked.

"So you're a trader." She looked at the graphs. "Is this Firesnake thing real?"

"Very. I've been working on it since before we met."

She gazed at the graph. "What happened here?" She pointed at the kink where the graph turned down.

"The companies had a setback. Shareholder reaction was to sell, which drove the price down."

"Looks like they're still selling."

"It takes time for a company to recover once the investment herd starts migrating."

She rubbed her chin. "Can this really work?"

"Yep."

"How much is Firesnake worth?"

"You only want my money?" He grinned.

"Not your money, just this one example. What are you dealing with here?"

"Maxx, current gain on Firesnake."

"Gain," she blurted. "But that line has dropped ten, maybe fifteen percent?"

"Have you been listening, Claire?"

"Yes, but—"

"Two hundred and fifty eight—" Maxx said.

Her forehead scrunched. "You made 258 bucks? Wow, you can get new tires for your bike."

"You cut him off. Maxx, units please."

"Million."

Claire choked, and coughed. Coughed again. Continued coughing. Her eyes started to water. She ran through the door into the kitchen.

Mike waited, wondering where the conversation would go. Wondering what she would do when she understood. Wondering if he could make her understand...*hoping he didn't have to stop her.*

He heard a knock on the door.

"Come in, Claire. Are you okay?"

She stepped into the room wearing an embarrassed smile and walking with one bare foot carrying two glasses of red wine. She handed one to him and dropped herself into the lounge chair. She smiled.

"Sorry, I don't always understand Maxx. He couldn't possibly have meant that the gain on the Firesnake portfolio was two hundred and fifty-eight million US dollars. That's impossible, right?"

"Why's that?"

She squinted. Her normally green eyes glowed like wet pebbles in moonbeams from the dim light of the display. "Well, it's just so much. You must have borrowed a huge number of shares. What if they had gone up?"

"I would have a very large bill."

"Then you must have been terribly confident those shares were going to drop."

"More than confident," he said. "A sure thing."

She examined his face. "There are no sure things in the stock market." She frowned. "What's in that portfolio anyway?"

"Sure you want to know? There's still time, you can choose to remain ignorant."

She sipped the wine, and freed her other foot. Wiggled all ten toes.

"Yes," she said.

He gave her time to change her mind.

"Oil stocks."

Her face pinched like the wine contained lemon. "Oil. You mean wells and gasoline and stuff like that."

"Stuff like that. Supertankers. Offshore stations." He watched her cheeks, blushed slightly from the wine, the smooth curve of her ears, the soft blur of hair with pink highlights. Then he added, clearly so she couldn't miss it, "And pipelines."

She choked once and stopped. She stared. She coughed again, a single dry hack. She poured wine down her throat.

"Pipelines? Not like—" She pattered over to the screen in bare feet and squinted at the dates on the graph. She pointed at the downturn. "When was this?"

"Did you hear about that big fire in Alaska?"

"Oh my god," she said, spinning to face him, her glassless hand lifting to cover her mouth.

"It was shortly after that," he said.

She turned slowly back to the graph and moved closer to study the details like it was a painting in a museum.

"You *knew?*" she breathed.

He admired her slender body, and her bare feet, straight toes, delicate ankles. "Knew what?"

"Oh my god," she said to the big room. "You and Maxx sat here knowing that fire was going to happen? And you bet big on oil stock."

"Not that big, really," he said.

"Not big? Over a quarter of a *billion* dollars is not that big?"

She dropped crossed legged to the floor and poured the rest of the wine down her throat. She leaned against the wall and stared up at the ceiling.

"How could you have known? How? It's not possible."

He moved to the lounge chair and stretched out. "Maxx, is it possible?"

"All things are possible," Maxx said. "To the man who prepares."

"You programmed him to say that," she accused.

"Of course. I program everything he does."

"But the fire. You couldn't possibly have known. Was there a leak through your network of friends? You knew that pump was going to fail soon."

"No. No leak." He chuckled.

She lowered her face to watch him. "The pump manufacturer. You had inside information about the pumps. Oh shit. What you're doing is insider trading. That's illegal!"

His face broke into a broad smile. "You said I had inside information, not me."

"How else could you have known when that pump was going to fry? Even the owners didn't know or they would have fixed it."

"Claire, you know it wasn't a pump failure."

She pushed her lower lip out to a half pout. "Maybe. But how do *you* know it wasn't?"

"You're going to keep your promise?" Mike asked.

"Of course."

"Even if I'm insider trading?"

She stared at the empty glass in her hand. Frowning she said, "Yes, of course. I promise."

"Maxx, what's the best way to predict the future?"

"'The best way to predict the future is to invent it.' Alan Kay, Computer Scientist, Xerox Palo Alto Research Center, 1971."

"That was back when mice were something you caught with cheese," Mike said.

"Invent?" she muttered. She placed her glass on the floor and spoke softly, "You knew someone was going to bomb the pipeline." It came out as a statement, not a question.

"Bomb the pipeline? Where did you get a crazy idea like that?"

"And you knew when. So you sold short, like you said. And cashed in on the disaster." She sat frozen in place.

He sipped his wine and relaxed in the lounger so there could be distance between them.

"You're working with terrorists," she said.

"I told you, I work alone. Just Maxx and me, isn't that right, Maxx?"

"Yes. Alone," Maxx said.

"Why, Maxx? Why do I work alone?"

"The only certain way to maintain a secret is to not tell anyone."

Claire still hadn't moved. "Could I ask a question?"

"Sure." He drained his glass, wondering if he'd need another before she was through with her questions.

"Am I on the right track, you made all that money by trading stock?"

"Yes."

"And you knew the stock was going to drop?"

"Knew is not quite right. 99.2% confident."

"How?"

"How what?"

"How could you possibly know?"

"Logic and precedent. The explosion of the BP platform in the Gulf of Mexico caused significant stock price fluctuation. I was therefore confident a large environmental disaster would cause public sentiment to turn against the oil companies that owned the facility. Six in this case: BP, Phillips, ExxonMobil, Williams LLC, Amerada Hess and Unocal. The right-of-way land is mostly owned by the Feds and the State of Alaska."

"But how? It's like knowing the drunk captain was going to run the Valdez aground."

"I didn't know about that one. But I hear they should have blamed the bean counter who didn't approve the budget for radar maintenance."

"How did you know about this one? The only way you could know for sure—"

He grinned with only the left corner of his mouth.

"You work alone?" she asked.

He nodded.

"The pipeline was bombed?" She watched him with eyes growing rounder by the second.

He nodded.

"Invent the future?"

He nodded.

"The Demon," she whispered. She jumped up from the floor in one smooth athletic motion and raced toward him with clenched fists. She stopped. She spun on her left foot toward the tube.

He leapt from the chair. By the time he got there her body had fallen and lay like a rag doll. He worked both arms under her, and lifted gently.

Chapter 69

BERT CLOSED HIS LAPTOP AND was thinking about a nice lunch at the Sports Machine, and maybe shooting the breeze about gold prices with Dino behind the bar when the intercom buzzed.

He took a slow breath and pressed the button. "Hi, Stacy."

"Mark is here to see you. Sorry, he didn't call ahead."

"That's okay. I asked him to get back to me fast. Send him in."

Lunch would wait. He thought again of his surname embedded in a domain on the international Internet, and continued to hate it.

Mark came through the door in a hurry, out of breath and looking like he hadn't slept in the past twenty-four hours.

"Mark, you okay?"

Mark placed both palms flat on Bert's desk, panting a little too close for Bert's comfort. He held up a palm like a traffic cop and continued breathing hard. It was a full thirty seconds before he spoke.

"Sorry," he gasped. "I've got to get in better shape." His chest heaved up and down three times before he continued. "I followed your IP address."

Bert looked at his laptop. He hadn't given Mark an IP address. They must have grabbed it while he was here working. He felt a little violated. Not a new feeling, being in politics.

"Uh, okay. Did that help?" Bert asked.

"A little. The site is definitely gone. Sort of."

Bert furled his brow involuntarily. "How can it be sort of gone?"

"We can attach to the IP address. So the machine is still there, but the domain name registration is gone."

"I only speak English, Mark."

"Sorry, Mr. Spin. I pulled some info from your computer to help me find the machine you connected to. That machine is still connected to the internet, but not accessible with a standard browser just by typing the URL."

"So you were able to access it?"

"Sort of." Mark smiled. "I mean, yes, but we didn't get very far. The machine responded to us so we knew it was there, but blocked anything we tried to do. We have a hypotheses on why that would be, but no proof."

"Like what?"

"Like the owner wants you to know it's there."

Bert knew it was there. "Why should I care?"

"Got me. Something weird happened while I was trying to look at the machine."

Bert motioned Mark into a chair. The guy was still mouth breathing.

"My department got another request to look for a website that had only been active for five minutes. The access times indicate it might have been the same five minutes, though perhaps not the same website."

Bert pulled the legal pad he used for notes out of his desk drawer. "Where did this request come from?"

Mark looked stricken. "I can't tell you, it's classified." He held up his hand again. "I'm sorry, I know it's stupid. If the sites are the same, or the IP addresses are the same, or maybe it's two sites being served from the same machine, well, then they're surely somehow related."

Bert was sure they were somehow related. And without thinking very hard he could guess where the other request originated.

"I know about the other request. I'm not asking you to reveal anything."

"You do? But—" he hesitated. "I guess you know a lot of things working for the President. Still this was mil—" he stopped.

"Mark, it's okay. I work with General Williams all the time. Don't worry about it."

Bert saw the man visibly relax, like a Kenworth had been lifted from his shoulders. He had guessed right. Whoever wanted him to see that site, had wanted Billy to see it too.

"Thanks. I'm glad you two are working together. It makes things a lot easier."

Bert put his pencil down to help Mark relax; most people didn't like having their words recorded in a notebook. "You raced over here for a reason, Mark. I'm sure it wasn't to tell me that you couldn't tell me anything."

Mark sat up. "I wanted to tell you what we found. I can't be certain it's right, but I have an address where the machine you accessed might be located."

"An address?" Bert said. "Do you mean a 123 Pennsylvania Avenue kind of address, or one of those computer things?"

Mark smiled, more relaxed than ever, "A real street address. I tracked through registration records and purchase records and tried to find the connection through the ISP. I got lucky and found receipts on the machine itself, including one for the registration for the website you visited."

"Where is it?"

"Iceland. Like we thought. 54 Skipholt, in Reykjavik."

"It's incredible you can do that," Bert said, truly admiring what some men can do in less than an hour.

"I have no way to verify this location actually exists," Mark said "But it gives you a place to start. There's definitely a computer that responds to my pings."

Spin wondered what a ping might be, but said, "Thanks, Mark, I'll see what we can find out. Will you be providing the same information to General Williams?"

Mark's eyes dashed to the windows. "No, not me. I'm not officially on that project. The General talked to a different tech, unofficially, but I ran into her during my search, so we *unofficially* pooled our information. I assume she'll report her findings to the General."

An unofficial request. What was Billy up to? "Any reason I should know who this tech is?"

Mark wouldn't meet Bert's eyes. "Uh, not sure. She's been around for years. She, uh—" He looked like he was grinding his teeth together. "Well, she seems fond of the General."

Bert gave Billy credit for knowing how to get information. But what happened to the sharpshooter? He grinned at the idea of dating a sharpshooter, perhaps not the wisest choice for a guy who liked changing horses.

"Forget it, Mark. I'll talk to the General directly. I appreciate your finding this information for me."

Bert watched Mark's face relax into a small smile. "Thanks, Mr. Spin. Let me know if you need anything else. This one is kind of unusual, it'll be interesting to see how it turns out."

"Yes, it sure wi—"

The intercom buzzed. "Hi, Stacy." He watched Mark stare out the window. "Yes. Could you keep him on the shelf for a minute? Almost done here. Thanks."

Bert stood and shook hands. "Thank you, Mark. I really appreciate you getting back to me so quickly. I'm sure you have bigger projects to fry."

Mark grinned. "Yeah, there's always something going on with the net that requires hunting. Glad I could help."

Bert stood behind his desk and watched Mark close the door behind him. He thought about a computer sitting in Iceland feeding him a website about Billy and a young woman. It made no sense, which made it important. He should tell the President, but had no idea what he would say.

He sighed, but didn't sit down. Mallor needed a response to Petry's robot-paranoia that was succinct and man-on-the-moon simple. But he hadn't been able to think of a way to reduce armies of smart robots carrying deadly weapons to a sound bite that would play well on Fox News. He needed more time.

And now there was a detective in his waiting room.

He buzzed and glanced at the clock in the little window on the phone. After one. He was hungry, and a little bummed he wouldn't see Dino today. "Hi, Stacy, send in our friend. What was his name?"

Bert remained standing to greet his unannounced visitor. Normally he would be out, but this guy was a detective who claimed he had just been to Billy's office. And Billy's name was coming up uncomfortably often today.

Long-legged Stacy led in a man of modest height with very dark straight hair that was a shade long for a businessman. He wore a tan jacket that looked too heavy for Washington in summer.

"Mr. Spin, this is Qigiq," Stacy said. A slight shrug of her slender shoulders indicated she didn't know why he only had one name.

Bert extended his hand. The man shook it with a solid, no-nonsense grip and bowed his head slightly.

"Thank you for seeing me."

"My pleasure. Stacy tells me you're from Alaska."

Stacy smiled from behind Qigiq and stepped out of the room, closing the door softly, leaving the soft scent of lilacs in her wake.

"Yes. A native." He smiled, revealing full square teeth that reminded Bert of Chiclets gum commercials.

"What brings you to the Capitol?"

The man frowned, creasing his brow in dark lines. "An investigation. I was with General Williams the day the pipeline..." he glanced around the room, "caught fire. There have been unusual findings and I came here to discuss them with him."

"The pipeline is quite a disaster. A high-pressure pump failure if I recall," Spin said, watching the man's dark eyes carefully.

They didn't blink, or turn away, but met Bert's with firmness. "So the oil companies claim. But I think there is another, more reasonable explanation."

"Really? I haven't read anything of it."

"You won't," Qigiq said. "The information has been classified by General Williams and the federal investigators. If I hadn't been there that day, I wouldn't have access to it myself."

"You think this information is relevant?"

"Most certainly. But there are many unanswered questions. And some answers are…" Qigiq hesitated before saying, "not being discussed."

Spin scratched his nose. "How can I help you?"

Qigiq shifted in his chair and crossed his left ankle over his right knee. "I am not sure you can, Mr. Spin. I only know that you are close to the President and perhaps could share information with him. I also know you have been on General Williams calendar five times in the past six weeks."

Bert tried not to look surprised, but he was. A civilian shouldn't have that information.

"We meet often. General Williams acts as an advisor to the President on terrorism. There is much to be aware of in our world."

"I suspect so." Qigiq straightened his jacket and removed a small notebook from an inner pocket. "May I assume you have sufficient clearance that we may discuss the findings in Alaska?"

Bert leaned back and took a deep breath. He knew about the crawling bomb Billy had found. And that Billy had wanted to go after the guy he thought made it. But what did this Detective know?

"Certainly, I have discussed the Alaska situation with General Williams on several occasions."

"Then you are aware of the bomb?"

Bert's stomach growled for two reasons. He leaned forward and buzzed Stacy, who opened the door behind Qigiq. "Sorry to bother you with this, Stacy, but could you have lunch delivered? Would you care to join me, Mr. Qigiq?"

The dark eyes turned to face the young woman. "If Mr. Spin can spare the time to talk with me, I would certainly appreciate joining him for lunch. Thank you."

Spin nodded her away and waited for the door to close. "A bomb? I remember there was something found by a boy. I didn't realize there had been a conclusion it was a bomb."

"It exploded trying to escape," Qigiq said. "That seems like conclusive evidence. More important, the crater it left was similar to a dozen others found along the pipeline. Yes, I believe it was a bomb. One of many."

Spin stood, walked to his window and watched a sea of pedestrians move in lines like crawling ants. He envied them their time to dine leisurely, wondered if the Sports Machine was full yet.

"So you hypothesize that the pipeline was destroyed by a series of bombs? Whatever for?"

"We have no idea. But we had one bomb in our possession, and evidence of others. Someone wanted the pipeline to fail."

"How can we know that?" Spin asked.

"Why else place dozens of bombs to explode simultaneously and spill oil over our land?"

"Many reasons. Perhaps a diversion." He hoped it wasn't a diversion because he had no idea what it would be diverting them from, except perhaps a successful election bid this year.

"I too considered the possibility of a diversion, Mr. Spin. Perhaps you should be in law enforcement."

Spin turned and half-sat on the windowsill. "What kind of evidence do we have that would bring you all the way here?"

"It's not exactly evidence—more of an analysis. The General felt it bordered on speculation."

A knock interrupted them.

"Yes."

Stacy swung the door open and an Asian boy with an armload of sandwiches, salads and cans entered. "Please, right here on the desk." Bert looked up. "Thanks so much, Stacy."

She smiled and took the boy with her.

"Speculation?" Spin said as he opened the bags, releasing the aroma of warm meat.

"Yes. General Williams wasn't entirely in agreement with my interpretation of the data."

"Ham, chicken or veggie, Qigiq?" Bert was growing used to the single name, like Sting or Beyoncé.

"Chicken, if you don't mind."

Bert placed a wrapped chicken sandwich and a cup of macaroni salad on the front of his desk. He shoved the ham, his first choice, potato chips and a cookie to the back. He chose a Coke. "Please help yourself," he said. "Sorry for the lousy accommodations."

Qigiq dragged his chair to the front of Spin's oak desk, smiled and began to unwrap the sandwich. "Plush by igloo standards."

After Spin had swallowed his first bite of warm ham and thick Swiss cheese, he resumed the conversation. "What didn't Billy like about your interpretation?"

Qigiq drank from a can. "The General didn't think my findings were particularly relevant."

"Were they related to the bomb?"

"Yes. Specifically to its origin."

"You mean how it got into Alaska?"

"No, I mean how it was manufactured."

"Where it was made?" Spin asked, munching chips.

"Yes. In particular, where the parts suppliers are located. In this case, there are known suppliers for all parts in China."

Spin stopped chewing. Billy had focused on China. Something about the cell phone led him there. "China's a big place."

Qigiq drank and met Bert's eyes.

"Yes, quite large, with many companies who build machines for the West."

"So what about this bomb?"

Qigiq placed his sandwich on the wrapper, careful not to drop anything on Spin's desk.

"There are two characteristics of note. First, all of the parts that we were able to view from the outside of the device could have been manufactured in any one of several factories located in China."

"You think we have a Chinese terrorist?"

Qigiq shrugged. "Unknown. I do believe the bomb maker resides in or near China. Cost certainly wasn't an issue. So the next concern is one of access. But this alone is not so important."

Bert waited. Everything was made in China? Billy hadn't revealed that. He wondered if the President might have felt differently if he knew all the parts were Chinese.

"The parts all have a common purpose. This I believe is the more relevant observation," Qigiq said.

"Common purpose? Like they're all military or something?"

"Or something," Qigiq said. "General Williams has not communicated this?"

"I haven't met with Williams for over a week," officially, he added in his head. "How long has he known?"

"Just this morning," Qigiq said, scribbling briefly in the little notebook with a yellow pencil like Spin used on a golf course.

"He will no doubt inform me shortly," Spin said, not at all confident Williams would ever tell him. "But it might be better if we could proceed now."

"There isn't much to tell. Only that not only could all of the parts have been manufactured in China, they can all be found in catalogs for motorcycle parts. Many are Honda, though several are Jincheng, a Chinese company, and the grooved treads are Ducati."

Spin felt a headache form in the middle of his forehead. He buzzed Stacy for coffee to chase his Coke, hoping more caffeine would help.

"Motorcycle parts. All of them?"

"Except for the cylindrical cell phone. But the rest, yes, they are standard parts for motorcycles."

Spin thought about what that could possibly mean. Motorcycles? What could they have to do with anything? No one would blow up a pipeline to make a statement about motorcycles. The only people who cared got tattoos and wore black leather. More important was China.

"An intriguing find. How did you ever do it?"

"Residue analysis."

Bert didn't remember Billy saying the word residue. "I'm not a professional investigator, so please excuse my ignorance. What can we conclude from this?"

Qigiq returned to his sandwich—Bert thought he was buying time. Or maybe he was just hungry.

After a bite and another shot of Squirt, Qigiq said, "If you allow me to speculate, I would say that the bomb maker has an intimate knowledge of motorcycles. And I would also make the somewhat outrageous claim that the bombs were delivered by one or more motorcycles. And from these two insights, I would suggest that the delivery boy and the maker are one and the same person."

Spin wasn't chewing or swallowing but he choked anyway. "A single person?"

"Yes," Qigiq said. "I believe we're dealing with one man who designed, constructed and delivered upwards of thirty LTB's. We call them Little Tractor Bombs."

"But why?" Spin said. "What possible motivation?"

Qigiq used a white plastic fork to chase a slippery macaroni and replied without looking up. "There are many: environmental statement, big business haters, poor locals who resent the pipeline because they don't make money from it, general terrorists who like to destroy things. A single person could have many motivations. Perhaps there are even religious reasons to resent the pipeline."

"Enough to destroy it?"

"It's impossible to know until we find him…or her. But I believe we are looking for a motorcyclist with ties to Asia, specifically China."

What worried Spin most was the C-word. The President had benefactors in China who secretly supported his campaign. An ugly scene with a Chinese national…

"That's quite a theory. But there are millions of motorcyclists in the world." Bert paused and drained the last of his soda, wondering where Stacy was with the coffee. "I don't understand how I can help."

"Now that Exxon has made a public statement, Governor Plake feels there is no longer a need for an investigation. It would be helpful if someone at the federal level, ideally the President, asked him to verify the explanation provided by the oil companies."

Qigiq paused and stared into his Squirt can.

"And if it's not too much to ask, perhaps provide a bit of funding for the investigation to continue."

It seemed like this guy had done a good job, why didn't Plake want him tracking this down? Bert answered his own question. Plake was Governor, his primary job was to milk the Feds. Hell, it couldn't cost much. And Bert sort of liked Qigiq's style: intellectually aggressive but not outwardly obnoxious.

So long as it was kept quiet.

"You have a unique theory, it deserves to be pursued. I'll see what I can do."

Qigiq smiled. "Thank you. And thank you for lunch, Mr. Spin."

"Sorry we were rushed. I appreciate your coming by." Bert felt sort of warm inside. He hadn't said that in a long time and meant it.

"There is one other small item," Qigiq added.

Bert's warning meter fluttered.

"I'm looking for Corporal Ferreti. Do you think your assistant might be able to help me locate her?"

Ferreti? He had just seen…that poster. What the hell?

"Sure, ask Stacy, I don't know her myself," Bert said.

Chapter 70

MIKE SAT ON A STOOL BY the side of the bed watching Claire breathe. A pink stripe of hair bent like an elbow above her forehead, revealing the white scar. Head trauma. *Difficult to predict the extent of damage*, Dr. Ming had said. Watch her, he had added.

Mike saw a hip rotate an inch under the light blanket, her body a twig, atrophied from disuse. Now it was part of the Donna disguise that was keeping her alive.

Claire's eyes opened with a flutter of lashes, tiny green searchlights moved, turned up to the roof of the bedroom, rolled to the night table where a pistol lay, its barrel pointing toward the wall.

He worried she would collapse again. Maybe somewhere he couldn't help her.

She blinked hard and rolled back on the pillow to face the ceiling.

"I can't believe they sent me to China to shoot a fucking stockbroker."

He tried hard not to, but burst out laughing.

She was quiet for a time, her eyelids half-open.

He sipped at now cold tea. "Would you like something to drink?"

Her head moved slowly side to side. "What's in the pain killers Dr. Ming gave me?"

"Ancient Chinese secrets. Are you still taking them?"

"Doubled the dose this morning. My shoulder felt like it was being torn off by an angry tiger." Her eyes closed slowly, then re-opened. They were shiny, like spun glass.

"Not a good idea with alcohol," he said.

The corners of her mouth flickered a smile. "The man shot that night?" she said, her eyes still closed.

He leaned forward and placed two mangled bullets on the night table next to the pistol. "The third one missed, probably because the shooter fired late, passed through the wall. We found it two rooms over."

She rolled to her left side and stared at the lumps of metal. "We don't even know which of us shot him."

"A firing squad, the way your team did it."

She remained quiet.

The room held the sound of rushing air, distant moving water, rhythmic breathing. She reached for the pistol, touched it gently with her fingertips, stroked the cool dark metal, dragged it to her chest like a favorite teddy bear.

"Tell me about him."

"Dominic Kalstin, code name Typhoon, spy for the U.S. military. Has been known to sell information to the Chinese, the Vietnamese, the Russians and occasionally the Japanese. More of a mercenary than anything."

"Did you know him?"

Mike placed his teacup on the table. "Knew of his activity. Had a channel to reach him. Never met him."

A tiny tear streamed sideways from the corner of her right eye, over the bridge of her nose. She blinked it away.

"Why? No wait," she said. "How did we miss?"

"You executed to plan."

Her eyes darted toward him. She slowly cradled the pistol with two hands.

"You knew about us?"

"Not you precisely, but I assumed they would send someone. A colleague told me Typhoon was making inquiries about a cell phone part, so I knew the Rat found by the boy had been analyzed." He saw her brow tense. "Rats record their environment. I can play your conversations for you." He leaned his back against the wall. "So I took preemptive action."

"You acted?" she said, staring at the pistol, holding the fat barrel in her right hand.

"Created computer records, allowed Typhoon to find them, along with invitations to the party. Let him forge invitations through my supplier. He did two. One for himself, and a second for you."

"But the—"

"Phone call? Would have been an easy guess. The caller asked to speak to the host's name from the invitation. A name I leaked through the manufacturing records for a person who doesn't exist."

"Would have?" Her eyes were distant, like she was dreaming, perhaps seeing that evening happen all over again. Her fingers tightened around the barrel.

"Wasn't necessary to guess. Typhoon kept his computer in a hut in southwestern China. He was easy to follow after he broke into our facility. Once I knew where he was, I watched, listened, put the pieces together."

"Clever," she said.

"Dangerous. But Rat 31 didn't go off."

She was quiet, her eyes resting on the pistol.

"Strange gun."

"Chinese. Has a special feature."

She turned toward him.

"The two barrels rotate, one is blocked," he said.

"So if I pulled the trigger?"

"You'd want to know which barrel was up."

She drifted away for a few seconds. "You're testing me."

He watched her fingers caress the steel. "Letting you know you have options."

She was silent for half a minute. Then said, "Why not?"

"Because unit 31 sensed a biped, deactivated and informed Maxx. Asimov's First Law—a robot may not injure a human."

"The little boy had it in bed with him."

Mike took a long breath. "I'm glad the detection circuit worked."

"It put you to a lot of trouble."

"More than I ever imagined." He watched her face: thin, creased with worry. "Because of you."

She rolled away onto her right side. "Me? I'm just a hired shooter."

"True. And if you had disappeared as planned, it would be over. Unless the General got lucky with another little boy, he'd never find me. And until my next project, he wouldn't even know to look." He paused. "But you got in the way."

"How's that?" she said to the opposite wall.

"I met you at the party, we drank wine. I think you insulted me."

She rolled over and looked at him across the barrel of the pistol. He didn't flinch. "The mustache man in the light suit?" She squinted. "He was darker, and had greasy hair." She lowered the pistol. "And black eyes."

"Simple disguise, not effective except in a fast moving situation. Or a party where no one is looking."

She rolled back to gaze at the ceiling, lowering the pistol to the bed.

"Now what?" she said.

"Same as before."

She popped up to one elbow. "You mean we stop Billy?"

"If that's what you want to do."

"But you're a—" her eyes danced over his body, "what...a thief?"

"Beats being a lawyer." He smiled.

"All that money. Why?"

"Because of machines that kill, like the BLU-44. No man in the control loop; they can't be turned off."

"That land mine you talked about. From airplanes."

He was quiet.

"Who's that woman?" she asked, pointing to the frame on the nightstand with the barrel of the gun. "She's beautiful."

He remained silent, his face taut.

"Don't tell me, that's okay. I already owe my life to a thief, I don't want things to get weirder."

"My mother," he said. "Six months before she died."

Claire studied the picture. "She's so young, what happened?"

"You're going to think I'm making it up."

He watched Claire's eyes move around the room. Beyond them he saw a flash, felt his mother's soft upper arm press against the left side of his face as she was blown towards him. Saw her not move as he called out over and over.

"I'll believe you," Claire said. She placed the gun back on the nightstand. Spun the barrel to the wall.

He rubbed the heel of his hand into his left eye, then his right. He blinked. He sighed a deep exhale.

"A BLU-44 along the edge of a rice paddy hadn't deactivated properly. We were going to help plant a new crop. I was five and a half. It killed her instantly, and would have killed me if her body hadn't protected me."

Chapter 71

CLAIRE'S EYES GAZED AT the picture of the woman and imagined her slender body protecting a five-year-old boy. Reflected in the glass she saw Cam between her and a fireball, his crazy candy gun and the muddy rear fender of a motorcycle. She closed her eyes.

"My God, I'm so sorry."

She stepped out of bed to face him; her head began spinning. Before she could fall his hands gripped her biceps. She saw pain in his eyes and fell against him, burying her face in his dark shirt, thinking of the woman, maybe only as old as Claire was now, her life ended by a stupid chunk of leftover ordnance—a young boy with no mother or father. She heard a rifle shot, saw Typhoon fall. Screw Billy and his political anonymity. She cried softly.

He held her.

"I don't understand," she finally said, still leaning against him, his arms tight around her.

"The money?"

"Why do you need so much?"

"To solve big problems," he answered instantly.

She moved away and sat on the edge of the bed facing him. She wiped her eyes with the back of her hand. "Like what?"

He half-grinned. "Landmines, for starters."

"Huh?"

"Elevated leukemia rates, Dioxin levels a hundred times accepted standards. Oh, and birth defects."

"You can't save the world."

"Not trying. Only helping the people who cared for me."

She coughed, her throat thick from crying. "Vietnam? Why?"

"I know I'm a broken record: BLU-44s, Agent Orange."

"Weapons of war," she said.

"Yeah. The ones left behind that hurt innocent people who hadn't even been born when the war was fought." He grew quiet. "Not to mention my father and mother."

"How?"

"How do they hurt people?"

"No. How can you help?"

His grin came back. "I raise money for charities. They do the real work."

"All that money? For charity?" She lifted her eyes to find his.

"More than that. What you saw was only Firesnake."

She dropped her body flat on the bed and put her forearm to her head. "But you're stealing it."

"You called me a stockbroker." He moved closer to the bed. "Think of it as economic warfare."

"With inside information. That you create."

He nodded.

She looked straight up at the fabric ceiling of the bedroom. "How can you move that much money? They'll catch you eventually. Transactions can be traced."

"I have a little trick."

She twisted her feet to the floor and sat on the side of the bed. Something spun once behind her eyes. "Hundreds of millions of dollars and you have a little trick?"

"Well, billions actually."

She inhaled. "That makes it easier, huh?"

"No. It's quite difficult to hide that much money."

"I bet. Hide some in my bank account." She lowered her eyes to the floor and felt herself blush, her face probably matching the Donna streak in her hair. "Sorry, didn't mean that."

"It's like computing. You saw Maxx, lots of machines. He's distributed across them."

She held up both hands. "I'm officially confused."

"I don't give billions of dollars, I help other people do it."

"Other people?" She frowned deeply and shook her head, which hurt a little. "This is too complicated."

He sat down facing her. "Let's say a hundred thousand people each make a hundred dollars on a short-sell stock play. Then they donate the hundred to charity. That's ten million dollars Adopt-a-Minefield or some other organization has to work with."

"But where did the money come from?"

"The move in the stock price. I have to be right about that. So I help it a little." He made a fist with his right hand, and splayed his fingers outward.

"Boom."

"You call blowing up a pipeline helping a little?" She had raised her voice. She tried to relax, whatever had happened, she couldn't change it now.

"In the long run, Exxon won't blink, it'll be good for the local economy, and the investors who don't panic will make their money back."

She squinted at him, furling her forehead. "You're punishing them."

"Who?"

"Big companies, the ones who make mines and those agents named after colors. They make gazillions of dollars on war, paid for by Uncle Sam. You're out to get them."

"That's a side effect of helping the charities." He paused, stiffened. "And the people I see every day: Quan, Suong." He stared past her. "Quan's an orphan you know. Like me." He found her eyes. "You've looked into their young eyes, seen them try to make sense of why their bodies have been mutilated by secrets in the ground."

"Like Robin Hood."

He rolled his lips together. "He was fighting oppressive political structure. I'm just, um...encouraging people to take responsibility for their past actions. As you said, these companies and the people who run them profit handsomely from war." He grinned. "But if you'll be Clorinda..."

She frowned, trying to place the unusual name.

"Robin's first sweetheart," he said.

She blushed, smiled and shook her head, slowly so it wouldn't hurt. "Where did you ever get an idea like this?"

"From Clinton."

"Bill Clinton, former President of the United States? Monica with the blue dress? That Clinton?"

Mike nodded. "Clinton purportedly received campaign funds from China, something like $450,000 at one point. But there are limits to what a politician is allowed to accept. So the funds arrived as hundreds of money orders for $1,000 each, sequentially numbered, different names, but the same handwriting. I'm not sure if the story's true, but that gave me the idea for many small transactions."

"But hundreds of thousands of people, how can you possibly get them to do what you want? And the timing is critical. Sounds impossible."

"Maxx takes care of that end."

"A computer," she said flatly.

Mike stood and paced three steps toward the shower room, turned and strolled back. "He works twenty-four hours a day, and he's very fast. All he has to do is pretend to be someone else, open an account, make the investment, peel off the gain, and send it to a charity in the original name. Everyone is happy."

She held up her thumb. "You're stealing identities." Raised her index finger. "So you can inside trade based on industrial accidents you know about because you cause them." Her middle finger went up. "And you give the money to charities trying to fix the problems that killed..." She dropped her hand and was silent for a moment. "Am I close?"

He smiled. "Close enough for government work, Clori."

She reached under the domed shade of the bedside lamp and flicked off the light. The room plunged into the black of a cloudy night. Space around her seemed to expand, as if they were alone on a desert plain. She stood slowly and peeled the borrowed T-shirt up over her head, felt it slide softly down her arms and drop away. A tiny square of nightlight flickered on, bathing her skin in dim lunar shadows. She waited while he did the same. Saw the flash of a symbol on his biceps, a pair of intertwined rings. Wondered what they might mean.

With two steps forward she was able to press her breasts against him and squeeze his body hard, her scarred forehead buried under his chin. She lifted her face and pulled his lips down to her parted ones. She moved her hands and felt his solid body under her fingers, electrifying them, heating their tips. She leaned her whole body into him and pressed her nails into his back, holding tight, feeling that click-click anticipation of the first hill on the highest rollercoaster in the world. Her insides bubbled a blast furnace of hot metal: gold and silver, lead and steel...pressure. Pressure. She dragged her right hand around his waist and found the belt buckle. She felt him against her thigh. Her hand drifted down, pressed tight by their bodies.

He pulled his lips away, but remained very close.

"A lot has happened. Maybe this isn't the best time."

She squeezed him harder, flattening her breasts against muscle.

"But it's a good time," she whispered.

She took a breath, smelling his closeness.

"Just tell me one thing. Is Mike your real name?"

"No," he said, before she kissed him again.

They were still kissing when the clattering of wooden wind chimes filled the small bedroom. Claire pulled away.

292

"What's that?"

"Maxx telling me something important has happened."

She let out a long sigh, and held him close.

"I should check," he said.

She nodded, but didn't pull away.

She felt him dig in his pocket.

"Damon," he said.

She erased the name Mike inside her brain and replaced it with Damon. She imagined his face and repeated the name silently. Then she felt the word Daemon appear and shuddered. She frowned against his chest.

"Remember Billy Norton?" he asked.

She pushed away. "What's happened?"

"A story about him appeared on a blog thirty seconds ago under the headline: *Do Robot Dogs Eat Oil?*"

"Is he okay?"

"Let's go read it and find out."

She saw him glance at her body in the combined glow of the nightlight and the tiny screen of his phone.

Neither moved.

She heard a heartbeat.

She saw little Billy running and orange flames reach into the sky.

"I'll get dressed," she said, dropping to one knee to find her shirt.

Chapter 72

BILLY WILLIAMS HAD BEEN WATCHING the apartment building for two hours. No one had entered, and only an old woman had exited. The place was a low-income stack of gray units dropped onto a street of small houses that had been there for a good long time. The weather was clear and warm, not what he expected from a place called Iceland. And finally the sun was fading and the street had become dark enough for an approach.

He lowered the 10-power binoculars and slipped them under the seat of the gold Chrysler SUV from the rental agency. He turned the overhead light to always-off and opened the driver's door. Nothing moved on the cracked-asphalt street. Billy closed the door softly and walked along the shoulder opposite the building, watching the numbers without appearing to. He continued around the block, imitating a tired father out for an after-dinner stroll. As he approached the building displaying 54 on his second lap, he turned up concrete steps.

A row of square black buttons beside names handwritten on white tabs protruded from a metal plate. His eyes tracked down the list. Ferreti was penciled on a slip of paper with brown curled edges. Billy wondered how long she had been here. The paper was old, but maybe it had a different name on the back and she had just flipped it over. He pushed and held the button for three seconds with the gloved finger of his left hand.

Nothing.

He tried again. Turned to check the street. Waited.

Nothing.

He tried the main door. It moved half an inch and stopped against a lock. He removed his right hand from his pocket and slipped a slender black tool into the keyhole until he felt the movement of metal on metal. There was no lock that could stop the U.S. Army.

The door opened.

He stepped through the opening and let it click quietly behind him.

* * *

Damon lowered the SK-145 marksmen scope. "The Goat is in corral," he whispered into the headset connected by wire to a miniature satellite cell phone at his waist.

He heard Maxx through his earphone, "Confirmed."

He repositioned the scope. "I've got two guys, dark suits, opposite ends of the street. The one in the abandoned gas station is using binoculars. Neither is moving."

"Got it," said Donna.

"The other guy looks like he's reading, having coffee. Maybe backup."

"Confirmed," said Maxx.

"Anything else?" Donna asked.

"No one else visible. There are a hundred places to hide though. As designed."

The comm link fell silent.

Chapter 73

BILLY WALKED SLOW AND STEADY up three flights of stairs to the top floor. He followed the U-turn at the landing to pass apartment 34. The last of the evening light turned the yellow walls gray and the thin gray carpet charcoal. He stopped at the door for 36. Did the intercom button work? he wondered. Or was Donna sitting behind this door without a clue he had buzzed her. The building was quiet, no voices or televisions oozing sound into the hall. He voted for no one home.

He removed his right hand from his pocket and worked the tool's slight curve into the door. He felt a scrape, heard a click. The knob wouldn't turn. Footfalls on the stairs below froze him in place. They stopped, a latch snicked, a hinge creaked, a door slammed. He returned to work. Another few seconds and the door to 54 Skipholt, Apt 36 opened.

Billy eased the door closed behind him and stood in the near darkness. He rated the room *Early College*: faded orange shag carpet and a futon in front of a small flat-screen TV on a long bookshelf assembled with the metal latches that IKEA was fond of. The occupant hadn't spent much money. A print hanging over the futon was full of colorful shapes and no detail. The TV remote lay on an end table with dark wicker legs. Beneath an iron lamp on the same table were two pieces of mail.

He moved in the shadows along the wall, pulled a thin tube from his pocket and pointed it at the mail. A single LED glowed bluish white. The top enveloped was an electric bill, addressed to D. Ferreti. He couldn't see the addressee on the one below it. He moved the light to check the return address. Blank. The postmark was Washingon D.C. Perhaps money from Claire. He squinted, couldn't make out the month, but it had been sent this year.

He backtracked toward the front door, then forward down a hallway. He passed a small bathroom on his right and headed for what he thought must be the bedroom.

"Hello, General."

His heart rate doubled. He pressed himself against the wall of the hall and doused his flashlight. It was a woman's voice, but it had been too sudden for him to identify.

He rotated his head to scan the apartment behind him: dark, nothing moving. He stared into the bedroom. Shadows shifted on the floor, like a cloud was passing over the moon. He crept toward the door, his eyes watching those shadows stroke worn green carpet and a pastel pink quilt. At the door he reached inside his jacket and withdrew a 38-revolver: not military, not traceable. Holding firepower made him feel more comfortable.

"General?" Donna's voice chimed. "Are you coming?"

He lowered the gun behind his back. The door swung to the right and was standing open against the wall. The room was to the left. He eased himself in with his back against the door; saw no one. The room contained a bed of pewter colored metal, a floor lamp in the far corner and a desk with chipped edges pressed against the wall just to the right of the sliding door for the closet. That door was closed; he needed to exercise caution.

His eyes followed the edge of the closet door. It didn't move. He traced a line to the desk. It held a small lamp with a flex neck, a plastic box of brushes and make-up, and a small computer monitor. He dropped his eyes. An old tower computer stood under the desk. A green light glowed in the upper right hand corner. The damn thing was on, but the monitor was dark.

"Yoo-hoo, General? In here."

His eyes darted to the closet, back to the desk, and to the far corner beyond the bed. He settled on the computer, stepping toward it carefully. As he reached the closet he brought the 38 forward and pushed the left sliding door open.

Clothing. Jammed to bursting. He dropped to one knee. Dozens of shoes. He reached into his pocket and brought out a gray box smaller than a cell phone. He pushed a switch with his thumb. A red light blinked three times and went dark. With one hand, he reached into the closet and back around the wall to place the box far out of sight.

He moved along the floor behind the cover of the bed. With the barrel of the pistol he pressed the space bar on the keyboard.

Chapter 74

FOUR HUNDRED METERS AWAY Damon stared through a scope. He had seen Williams go in the front door and was able to observe a shadow moving through the living room of unit 36 in the back corner of the building. The shadow had gone toward the bedroom as expected, but had dropped out of sight.

"No longer have visual," he said to his microphone.

"Understood," Donna said. "He touched the keyboard; should have a display now."

Damon saw a faint glow behind the brown tweed curtains covering the bedroom window. "The room is lit. Shadow by the desk. He's low and close."

"Attaching video."

"Affirmative," he said. "Watchers have not moved. Friend reading the paper is paying attention."

"Engaging now."

"Affirmative," he replied, and listened carefully.

* * *

The little screen glowed blue in Billy's face and he ducked lower to prevent a silhouette against the curtains. His eyes barely above the keyboard, he studied the screen: logo in the corner, no files on the desktop. He grabbed the mouse and opened the Documents folder. There were 114 files, and folders named Receipts and ToDo. He had assumed he would find a computer, though he wasn't sure if this one hosted the website. He reached into his trouser pocket for a USB thumb drive and pushed it into a port. He thought about copying the Documents only, but opted for the entire user environment. It was named DFerr. Seemed right. He watched the progress bar begin to move. There were over a thousand files.

A flash blinded him. The dark room had turned bright white like a photo booth on Atlantic City's boardwalk. He dropped his face to the carpet. It smelled of cat urine. He looked up from the floor, searching for the built-in camera on the monitor. He found it top dead center. Had he been high enough for it to capture his face? He didn't think so.

He thought about trying to find the photo to delete it, but whatever had triggered the camera, possibly even a timer based on his touching the machine, was probably sending data out of the room already. He considered finding the wireless hub to terminate the transfer.

"Hi, General."

He was close enough to tell the voice was coming from the computer tower. He looked up at the monitor. A video chat window had opened and there was Donna in her miniskirt, though this one was blue, and a white top held up by narrow straps over skinny shoulders. He opened his mouth to answer, and froze his throat just in time. Of course it would be recorded, how stupid could he get?

He tapped the top of the desk with the barrel.

"Don't you want to chat, General? After coming all this way to see me?"

He watched her image. She was leaning back in a small chair with her legs crossed. He pulled a drawer open on the desk: make-up brushes. He opened the next one: nail polish. He looked for a dark color, found Asian Blue that looked almost black in the bottle. He twisted the cap off.

He crawled to the side of the desk and stood. Holding the bottle and the 38 in his left hand, he used his right to paint a thick coat of polish over the lens of the camera.

"You don't want me to see you?" she said.

Good, she was live. He thought it might be a timed trick, like a delayed landmine trigger.

He pulled the chair out and sat in front of the keyboard. No way was he going to allow anyone to obtain a picture or a voice recording. But he could type; anyone could pretend to be him on a keyboard. He placed the 38 on the desk, close to his right hand.

"Hello, Donna."

Her voice and image replied, "Hi, General, is that you? I thought you might come to see me. Did you get my little message?"

He typed, "I received a message. Wasn't sure it was from you."

"Oh good. You see, I like heard you had been looking for me and then I saw your announcement for a $50,000 dollar reward and, wow, that's a lot of money."

He should have known. The little bitch could smell a dollar sign.

"Yes, I am looking for you," he tapped out with gloved fingers.

"You found me," she said, "thanks to my little web note. Does that mean

I get the reward?"

"You'll have to come to Washington to claim it."

He saw her frown and fidget on the screen. "I can't. I don't have enough money to buy another ticket."

"I'll arrange transportation," he typed.

"Oh, that's super, General. Thanks. Why did you want to find me so much? I mean, a reward and everything. You make me feel special."

How could this pink-haired ditz be related to Claire? Genes were such a crapshoot.

"I'm looking for Claire. Thought she might have contacted you by now," he entered.

"Claire? Oh. No, I haven't heard a thing, that's why I came to see you, remember?"

He typed, "It's been weeks. I thought you might have received another letter."

"Gee, General, no. I'm so sorry. I sure wish I could help you, I mean, wow, for fifty large I want to do something really nice for you."

The copy to the thumb drive finished.

He told Chat to save the session to the drive, including video and audio. Maybe Jojo could find something. He dismounted the device and put it back in his pocket, hoping it contained a clue.

"Did Claire say anything about where she might be going? She had leave coming up," he typed to Donna.

"She doesn't tell me much. Only asks how I'm doing and like sends money. She's so sweet. This last time, she said she might be gone awhile so not to worry. And she sent a double check." She looked embarrassed, her cheeks pink on the screen. "But I spent it all, that's why I came to you."

He stared at Donna and wondered about HOMER's rating. Could he imagine, even by a long stretch, that this skinny creature was Claire? And if it was, what the hell was going on? His eyes drifted to a plastic case on the table. The hairbrush. He picked it up. The hair was pink and blonde and several other shades. He pulled strands loose, wrapped them in a ball and stuck them in with the thumb drive.

"Nice talking with you, Donna."

"Oh yes totally, General, so fun. When can I come get my reward?"

He wondered who she knew that had rigged the website—awfully extravagant.

"Where are you, Donna?"

"I'm out of town, um, with a friend. We're sort of on vacation for a little while. I've been watching my home machine in case you stopped by." She smiled and tossed her hair with two fingers.

"Should I send the tickets here?" he typed.

"That would be grand. I'll pick them up soonly."

"Come by my condo when you arrive in Washington, I'll have a check for you."

"Oooh. Thank you General-ee, you can't believe how much this means to me," she sing-songed. "I'll try to think of a way to find Claire. And if she sends me the slightest little thing, I'll make sure you know right away."

"You do that, Donna. You do that."

He shut down the machine and thought about Demon Drop. If it had worked, this was all a distracting sideshow. Donna was a flake, but everything made sense if he just assumed she was chasing the almighty buck. He touched the pocket containing her hair.

Chapter 75

"*THE GOAT IS EXITING*," Damon said. "Left, circling toward his vehicle."

Claire said, "Black Box confirms Goat copied DFerr account and a partial of the chat session."

"We are on plan," Damon replied. "Heads-up, gas station man pulling onto street. Rolling west. Newspaper reader still in place."

Damon tried not to relax. He was still at the target. He looked up at the emerging stars peeking from behind a partial cloud cover to rest his eyes. Then he returned to the scope. The Goat turned the corner and was walking toward his gold SUV with both hands deep in his trouser pockets. The newspaper reader watched him.

The Goat entered his vehicle, but the interior remained dark. Damon saw a puff of smoke from the exhaust, and a moment later the SUV pulled away. The newspaper reader talked on a cell phone, started his car and drove in the same direction. Damon watched the street, lying cool and gray under the evening sky. Nothing else moved.

He waited to see if the first watcher would return. He guessed no—that was probably the purpose of the cell phone call. He rolled onto his back away from the hole in the bricks he had been using for sighting and began to pack the sensitive scope into a long thin box, careful to align it properly. He slid the box into his black backpack and moved the zipper closed slowly and quietly.

"The Good Shepherd is heading home," he said softly.

"Confirmed," Maxx said.

"Confirmed," Claire said.

Damon crawled across the roof toward the iron fire escape he had used to ascend. A scratching sound froze him in place. His eyes scanned the roof and found a Butterfinger wrapper spinning in the breeze to his right. He moved his right foot to begin to crawl but stopped, feeling something in the air. He listened to the night. The sound of an engine was on the breeze. He remained still in the center of the roof and tried to place its direction.

He rolled onto his back so his ears faced up. Small bore, getting closer. Without sitting up, he turned 180 degrees and retraced his path to the gutter.

"Good Shepherd hears a lost sheep. Remaining in place to investigate," he whispered.

"Affirmative," Maxx said.

"Virgin Mary staying online," Claire said.

Back at the low wall he carefully unpacked the scope. The sound grew closer. He guessed a 650cc thumper, one big piston, most likely Japanese. He reviewed his three exit strategies in case this person got too close: down the fire escape, inside and down the elevator, or rappel over the south side.

He watched the street. Smiled. A muddy Honda trundled down the two-lane. A tall bike, legal on the street, but built for off-road use in places like Baja, California. The rider was wearing dress pants with loafers showing light-colored socks, a black leather jacket with a fur collar like moto cops wore, and a white helmet that covered his face. His gloves had a white stripe on the back of each hand.

The bike purred past without slowing. Could be anyone. This section of town wasn't popular, which is why he had chosen it, but it wasn't entirely deserted.

The rider slowed as he approached the corner, even though the cross street had the stop sign, made a wide left turn and disappeared. He wondered why the sound had attracted him—it was just traffic.

Since he had the scope out, he checked the front door of Donna's apartment building. It was closed. No movement. The three parking spots were now empty: the Goat's and the two watchers that appeared to be following him, guys he thought of as Shepherds, like himself.

He rolled onto his right shoulder away from the gutter and lowered the scope. On his back under the starlight he listened. The bike was moving away, the sound fading like the crowd at a concert becoming quiet for the encore.

It turned.

Why was this bike so interesting? Bikes were interesting. But a lone rider out here? Why not? This was as good a place as any to get around by motorbike, especially one as capable as that Honda.

The sound grew louder; the rider had backtracked.

"Good Shepherd remaining in place. Lost sheep is running in circles."

"Black Box confirms," said Maxx.

"Virgin Mary confirms," said Claire, her voice tense.

The sound was west of him and growing louder. He rolled back into position and placed his eye to the scope. The same bike came into view, again moving slowly, a second-gear idle. The rider rolled past Donna's apartment and slowed for the corner.

This time he didn't turn.

The bike swung a wide arc in the middle of the intersection to U-turn. He idled back past the apartment, past The Goat's parking place, past the newspaper reader's parking place and U-turned again, swinging wide, much wider than the bike needed.

At the end of the turn the engine revved as the rider downshifted, barely crawling along. As Damon watched, he pulled into The Goat's spot, parking parallel to the curb like a car. He slid off the seat, hopping with his left foot while the machine was still rolling, managing to stop the bike and lean it onto its stand before it fell on his leg.

"The lost sheep is short for the donkey," Damon said. "Has stopped to graze."

"Confirmed," Claire said.

Damon watched the rider remove the key and step back to look at the bike.

"Five foot nine, a hundred and sixty pounds. Wearing helmet."

The rider removed thick riding gloves with high cuffs and placed them on the seat of the bike. He pulled thin black gloves from his pocket.

"Possibly Asian based on hoof coloring," Damon said. "Sending visual."

He held the scope steady and pressed a recessed button to capture an image and send it via his cell phone to Maxx. The rider still had one glove off.

"Black Box receiving," Maxx said.

The rider rotated and faced Donna's apartment complex. He reached up with both hands to remove the helmet. As it came off, Damon sent another picture.

"Black Box receiving two of two," Maxx said.

"Dark hair. Gender unconfirmed," Damon said.

He tracked the rider through the scope, hoping for a full-face view if he turned to check the bike. But the rider crossed the street without looking either way and headed directly for the door to Donna's building. He walked up the steps, and ignored the row of intercom buttons. His gloved hand touched the knob and twisted. His free hand slipped into and out of a jacket pocket. The door inched open.

"C'mon Lost Sheep, give me something," Damon whispered.

The rider didn't look back at the street, but walked straight in like a resident returning home. The door began to close and Damon still saw nothing. He pointed the scope at the back of the rider's head and poised his finger over the shutter release.

As the door was about to slam, the rider turned to hold it. Damon snapped three pictures.

"Black Box receiving three of three," Maxx said.

Damon watched the rider move along the path The Goat had followed, his feet disappearing as he climbed the stairway. He moved the scope to Donna's living room and watched for shadows. He had waited less than two minutes when Claire said, "We have identified the black sheep."

His surprise shook the scope. What were the odds a guy riding out here would be in a database?

"Go ahead, Virgin," he said, and couldn't stop a smile.

"The Virgin met him in Al—" she paused, "in the land of Firesnake."

Claire knew him? His neck itched. A shadow drifted across Donna's window. Someone had entered her apartment. Bets were on the rider.

"Entry into Virgin's living room," Damon said, realizing he sounded like an erotic audio book. "ID?"

"Qigiq."

Damon strained his memory. Kah-jeek didn't mean anything he had ever heard.

"What's a Qigiq?"

"Detective," Claire replied.

Damon watched more carefully—a detective from Alaska entering an apartment in Iceland. How had this guy known about Donna?

Or had he? The timing was incredibly close.

"Can Lost Sheep be trusted?"

"Unclear," Claire replied. "Competent. But no known motivation."

"Shred the files," Damon said.

"The Goat shut down the machine," Claire said.

"Remote silent boot underway," Maxx said.

Damon wondered why the Goat hadn't left things the way he found them. A reboot didn't hide much.

But it did take time...time for this detective to reach the computer...to copy files before Maxx could shred them remotely.

Damon watched the shadows. Qigiq, if that's who it was, moved slowly across the living room and held a dim light over the two pieces of mail on the end table.

Chapter 76

BILLY CAREFULLY UNPACKED the prescription bottle. He pressed and twisted the safety top, counted two pink, two blonde and three brown hairs, and replaced the cap. He placed it on the bathroom counter. He began opening drawers, believing she must have left one someplace.

In the third drawer down on the right of the sink he scored a comb and two brushes, both able to provide the sample he needed. He opened a second prescription bottle and began removing individual dark hairs from the stiff bristles. He wondered how long it would take the lab to do an analysis. And exactly what he would tell them it was for. He slipped the bottles into the thigh pocket of his pants and zipped it shut.

He went to the kitchen and found a Sapporo in the door of the fridge. He held it to the light and stared at the golden liquid, remembering it had been Claire's favorite. College kid. She had been a good choice, turned into the killer he thought she could be when they met. He had good instincts when it came to killers. He popped the top and gazed out the fourth floor window at the top of a lone tree.

He thought about the thumb drive. He had the entire DFerr account on it, but no real idea what he was looking for. Donna wanted the reward money, and to get it, had to prove she knew where Donna was. He hadn't considered the lady herself answering the ad.

Would he pay her? Hard not to. If she made noise about not collecting, people might ask questions about why he had been looking. And it wouldn't help Mallor's campaign if she decided to flaunt her lesbo status, or worse, make a fuss about her missing sister, who happened to be his former mistress.

He swallowed the beer and dug in his pocket for the device. He should probably store it someplace, but having it with him felt safe, like he could guard it. He carried the bottle to the den and sat down in front of his computer. He flipped the drive around between the fingers of his left hand wondering what it could tell him.

He plugged it into his computer and waited. It had come from a Mac so he wasn't sure he could even read it.

It mounted as dferr.

Thousands of files—where to start? He drank.

He started McAfee and scanned the device. The last thing he needed was his home machine infected by some weird virus from Iceland.

He continued drinking. Nothing, nothing...it was finding nothing. Maybe Donna had a virus scanner on her machine too.

He held up the beer, half gone. Pace yourself, Billy, this might take a while. He noticed it had put a "suspect" icon on a couple of files it didn't recognize. He would avoid those for now.

Finished. He opened Donna's Documents. Many programs defaulted to this folder and most people ignored where things were stored. It was a good initial bet.

Two hundred and six items: Word files, pdf's, something with dot pages. He opened one at random.

The letter started "Dear Mom." The address matched the people he had sent the FBI to interview. He scanned. It appeared she wrote regularly, they just didn't write back.

Next.

An online shopping receipt. Amazon. Shoes. Address of the apartment. Name of Donna Ferreti. Red pumps. He imagined her in red pumps and a miniskirt. Too skinny.

He swallowed more beer.

A rent receipt for the apartment at 54 Skipholt, electronically paid and electronically acknowledged. Claire's sister was a child of the Internet.

Another receipt. Overhead cam gear. He leaned closer to the display. Cam gear? Yes, there was a Honda Motor Company part number. He scrolled down. Shipped to her apartment in Iceland.

He read the document. Origin: Xining, China.

His jaw tensed. How could Donna be connected to China? His arm froze mid-swig like a 300-pound bouncer had grabbed it. The customer name on the invoice was Mr. Williams. He panicked for half-a-second, then relaxed. It was a common name; she likely made it up.

He worked his way through the files. He found two articles containing advice for lesbians living in straight communities, and tips on how to please a woman that had been copied from the Web. More letters to Mom and an application for employment at a place called The iNotel Boutique.

Then he found another parts order, this one for an extended-life battery for a Piaggio scooter, ordered by Mr. W. Williams. He took a deep breath.

Felt his hand shaking. He pushed his chair back and headed to the kitchen for another bottle.

When he returned, he told the machine to search the entire content of the Documents folder for any reference to "Williams." It found eight files. He checked them one by one. All were invoices or orders for motorcycle parts from companies in China.

He thought of Qigiq's visit and the odd hypothesis that a motorcyclist was key.

All orders had been shipped to Iceland, ordered by Mr. Williams, or Mr. W. Williams or William Williams. Two were ordered by Billy Williams and gave a Washington DC bill-to address on Montmarte Blvd.

He opened his browser and entered the address into Google maps. Fong Weng LLC, Chinese motorcycle importers. *More bike for less.*

He noticed a drop of sweat slide down his armpit. The desk thermometer showed 71 degrees.

He asked the machine to search for Williams on the entire DFerr volume. It put up a progress bar.

First it found the receipts.

Then a few pictures.

And ten files in a row with a Mail icon.

Three more documents he hadn't seen.

He stopped the search.

With one eye on the list he took a long pull on his Sapporo. What the hell was this Donna woman up to?

He opened the e-mails. The first was a mention of him in a message from Claire to her sister. Maybe that was where Donna picked up his name. He relaxed a little.

Four e-mails later he choked and spit beer. He was staring at a message from Donna to his personal e-mail: billyboy@gxardent.com. She had written gibberish about having obtained the "ingredients" he requested.

He felt for a brief moment that he was losing his mind.

He launched his Mail client and waited for it to update. This had to be faked. But who? Why?

He searched his e-mails for a message from Donna's address: shiver44@comcast3.is. He grinned, must be cold up there in those miniskirts.

Messages found: 6

Impossible. They showed as having been read and received between May and July of this year. He studied them one by one. They matched those on the DFerr copy exactly, all referring to ingredients ordered or arrived. One talked about Chinese spices.

He dropped back against the chair to think. He sat up and opened the JPEGs, drinking at the same time. The first showed his face from the bridge of the nose up, hiding behind a keyboard. "Camera in her bedroom," he said softly.

The next one showed him sliding the closet door open with his back against the wall and his revolver in plain sight. *She was taking pictures before I ever touched that computer.*

He blew a stream of air between his teeth. He'd bet this was going to cost more than fifty thousand. The bitch was planning to blackmail him. *That* would make sense of this mess.

He opened the next picture.

He squinted. The shot was a black and white blow up, grainy like an old photograph.

"Shit."

He recognized Spin standing near water, the Washington Monument reflected behind him. And next to him, Billy Williams, clear enough to identify. Who could have taken that? A fluke from a tourist and Donna got her hands on it? Had Spin taken it for some kind of weirdo insurance?

Billy upended the beer and drank long.

Or had someone been following him?

He slammed the bottled on the desk. Who cares? He talked to Spin all the time, what was the difference if they said hello on the sidewalk?

Unless, of course, the photographer also recorded audio—that would up the ante.

Billy dismounted the thumb drive and placed it in the zipper pocket of his pants with the vials of hair. He jumped up and banged his thigh rounding the desk.

Chapter 77

SPIN WATCHED A MAN'S WAVY reflection move along the edge of the pond toward him. He would arrive momentarily.

"It's nice to see you again Detective, though I am surprised you wished to meet again so soon."

"As am I," said Qigiq. "I came to see if you found Ms. Ferreti." He paused. "She was quite kind when visiting us; I wanted to thank her personally."

Spin's eyes narrowed. He thought the chick was in Iceland. Had she been in Alaska too?

"Sorry, I can't help you. I've never met her." Which was true. Spin stayed far away from working stiffs. It saved him all manner of complications.

Qigiq watched Spin's face. "If you do see Corporal Ferreti, please extend our thanks. It was nice of her to take our problem in Alaska seriously."

Corporal? He made a mental note to do research. He thought it hugely unlikely that he would ever see either of the Ferreti sisters, but he said, "I most certainly will."

Spin looked out over the golden pond. He loved dusk, the tone of the soft light making the world look like it was made of colored marshmallows, cooler temperatures allowing him to breathe outdoors, and no more meetings in front of him.

"How else can I help you, Qigiq?" Spin struggled with dropping the Mr. every time.

"I'm not sure you can, Mr. Spin. But I might be able to help you." He sat down on the wall of stone surrounding the water and reached inside his jacket.

"I've taken a short trip with some interesting people." He raised an eyebrow. "People you know."

Spin knew a lot of people. He waited.

"I found something. I'm not sure what it means, but its existence is cause for concern."

Spin watched Qigiq's hands unfold a manila envelope and undo the metal clasp.

"Could you describe what you have and I'll look later? Assuming you can leave a copy."

"The documents are difficult to explain. And a recording of our conversation may reveal more than they do."

Spin wanted to become invisible like some sort of superhero. He couldn't meet in his office; he couldn't meet on the street. Maybe he would move to Mars.

"Good point. Let's see what you have."

Qigiq handed him pictures. Two were of General Williams. The third was of Williams and him. Right there by the pond where he was now standing.

"Where were these two taken?"

"A woman's apartment in a cold country," Qigiq said.

Spin sighed. "Name of Ferreti?"

Qigiq studied Spin. "Yes."

Spin studied the pictures. What the hell was Billy doing in Iceland? The election was only weeks away; Billy should be lying low, not tracking pink-haired bimbos. He tried to think. Heard shuffling paper. Looked up.

"There's more?"

Qigiq handed him four documents. They looked like invoices.

"There's a name you might not expect."

Spin's eyes settled on "Williams." Billy wouldn't use his real name. No one would do that. He remembered the picture of the girl on the ephemeral website. Yes, maybe.

"Interesting parts," Qigiq said.

"Sorry, I don't recognize them."

"Remember our LTB friend? And its components?"

Spin remembered. He had been worrying about it since the Detective had mentioned motorcycles. Why couldn't the world ever be simple? Why not a silly pump failure—a typical disaster, instead of a complicated, sinister one?

Spin nodded. "Yes. Wheels. Two of them."

"Correct. And one other thing."

Spin saw it on the invoice before Qigiq spoke. It fit with those phone records the Feds had provided.

"Everything sourced from the same country," Spin said.

"Right again, Mr. Spin."

"Do I want to know where these documents came from?" Spin asked.

"I retrieved them from the lovely young woman's apartment, as her computer was shredding its own files."

"I see." He smiled. "Actually, I don't see much."

Qigiq took the documents and slipped them back inside the envelope. He pressed the metal clasp closed and handed it to Spin. "For you."

"Thank you, Detective. Suggestions?"

Qigiq's dark face smiled, the first time Spin could remember. He looked almost happy.

"Standard detective stuff: keep one eye on the guy, find the girl. That is, if the boss approves the expenditure."

Chapter 78

"MAXX CONFIRMS OUR VIRUS LOADED," Claire said. "I bet Billy's already cross-checked the files.

Damon watched the big screen. Maxx was buying Mobil and British Petroleum as their share price continued down.

"Maxx, has Billy accessed the decoys?"

"Four of six," Maxx said.

"And the pictures?" Claire asked.

"Ask Maxx," Damon said.

"Maxx, did Billy open the JPEG files?" she said, growing more comfortable talking to a stack of blinking boxes.

"Three of three JPEGs opened," Maxx said.

"I see why you like working with him," Claire said. "He's quick."

"Yeah, and never wrong. If you ask the right question."

She walked up from behind and wrapped her arms around his chest. She bent over and kissed him. "How about me? Am I ever wrong?"

"If you are, I'll let Maxx tell you," he said with a grin.

She popped him on the shoulder with her left fist.

"So we should be expecting him," she said, more thinking aloud than a question.

Damon turned away from his work and watched her pace slowly along the row of machines. "Not sure. We need to anticipate every action he might take...and be ready to counter." He waited, took a deep breath, and added, "It'd be more efficient to shoot him."

"Quit teasing me about being a sniper. You know we're not going to shoot him, Mister *sensors in your bombs so they won't go off around humans.*" She stared at Maxx. "But we have to find a way to prevent him from doing this again."

"Expose him?"

"Confront him."

"Confront a manic General in the armed forces? Do you own a tank?"

"Once he knows how much information is stacked against him, maybe we can negotiate his resignation," she said.

"Your glass is half full," he laughed, turning back to the stock market display.

She flopped into the La-Z-Boy. "I hope negotiating works. It'd be easier for me than shooting him."

"What about your idea of forcing his resignation from above?" he asked, without facing her.

"It'll stall in red tape and we'll lose our leverage from the upcoming election."

"Remind me not to vote against you."

"Maxx, the flights?" she asked.

"Negative," Maxx said.

"Maxx, please show me what you have?" she said.

The financials on the big screen faded to a map of the world centered on China. She popped out of the chair and walked to the screen. Tracing with her finger she said, "Here's where we flew in, from the north via Israel. We jumped, or rather drove, out of the plane here on the border. Billy was paranoid about touching Chinese air space so we shadowed the path of a commercial flight, after arranging to have it cancelled."

"Using motorcycles to penetrate China?" he said.

She nodded.

"I hear you," he added. "But the records show that flight went to Beijing, It was never even near Vietnam."

"I don't understand. You can't fake flight records, tower communications, departure and arrival times. That stuff tracks reality."

"Ah, you do believe in the tooth fairy. Any digital record can be faked. One just needs access."

Her body sagged. "What about Qigiq?"

"Your detective buddy? Ask—"

"I know, I know, ask Maxx."

"I'm sorry, I do not understand the question."

Claire glared at the monolith of thin machines. "Maxx, what do we know about Qigiq in Reykjavik?"

"Detective Qigiq was inside the Virgin's apartment for forty-three minutes and twenty-one seconds. He accessed twenty-three JPEG's, fourteen e-mails, and seventeen text documents before the shredding operation completed, its onset delayed by the need to cold boot the computer because General Williams had turned it off. He did not insert any device into the computer. We have no record of his activity because of camera damage inflicted by the General."

"What do you think?" she said.

"Not sure. He could have been looking for something specific."

"I think he's trying to solve the pipeline fire. He was there when Billy took pictures of your Rat."

He smiled. "Claire, you're a genius. Of course, Qigiq was taking pictures. That's why there's no digital trail. He only took photons. With film maybe. Old school."

Her eyes widened.

"Clever man," he said.

"Do you mean he has photographs of all those files Maxx ticked off?"

"That would be a good bet."

She leaned her bottom against the top of the desk to rest her legs and rotated her left shoulder, wondering if it would hurt for the rest of her life. "But why was he even there?"

"You're good at questions," Damon said.

"Thanks, comes naturally when I'm confused. Speaking of which. That article by Munch implied that a traumatized kid might be projecting real experience into his comic book creations. And if so, there's a cover-up on the pipeline disaster."

"What about it?"

She studied him. "You didn't seem surprised."

He stopped working and turned. "We know there's a cover-up." He laughed.

She rolled her lip. "Little Billy finds your bomb then makes up stories about Captain Notron and his robo-dog Tank that looks a hell of lot like a Rat and how they protect the pipeline from bad guys. A journalist puts it on the Internet, and you're not surprised?"

He shook his head.

"I don't get it," she said.

"Did you see how Billy makes his comic book?"

"He was holding an iPad in the picture with the story. So?"

"Where did he get an iPad?"

She shrugged. "Probably the school."

He smiled, gestured to the monitor. "Maxx, live stream for Batboy."

As Claire watched the screen flashed, sparkled and a huge image of Billy Norton's face stared down at them. His little brow was furled in concentration as his hand shifted back and forth across the bottom of the display. He was mumbling softly, "Got you now, Poco. Buff! Bam! You stay away from that oil, my country needs it..."

"Is he talking?" Claire asked.

"He mumbles to himself when creating comics."

"I thought he was mute." Her eyes flashed from the screen to Damon and back. "Hey wait. Did you say this was live?"

He nodded.

"You sent an iPad so you could spy on a little boy?"

"No way."

She shifted her eyes. "No...you didn't send the iPad?"

He smiled. "I didn't send it so I could spy on him."

Billy lifted the tablet computer to arms length, apparently examining his latest masterpiece.

"He doesn't talk to anyone," Damon said. He leaned back in his chair. "I sent it so I could guard him."

She stood up, crossed her arms over her chest. "Why do you think he needs guarding?"

"A young boy involved in a billion dollar cover-up. Nasty military men making him promise not to tell what he knows. Doctors trying to cure his speech disorder."

She looked at the boy's smiling face on the screen and blew a stream of air through pursed lips. "I see what you mean."

"They're going to medicate him soon."

"And you know this because..."

"He keeps the pad with him all the time, even sleeps with it. Maxx records from its microphone and camera, scans the data and makes highlight reels for me."

"You hacked his iPad?"

"Of course not. I loaded the software before shipping it out." He grinned.

She shook her head, then became still. "It's nice that you're guarding him." She studied little Billy's face on the screen: so young, such single-minded concentration. "Do you think Qigiq was guarding Donna?"

He stretched back until the office chair creaked. "I think he was following Williams. I don't see how else he could have found Donna's apartment."

She crossed her arms over her dark green shirt. Her lower lip turned outward.

Maxx said, "Qigiq arrived on Alaska Air Flight number 651 on Wednesday afternoon."

"The day before Billy Williams," she observed aloud.

"Maybe Billy is following him," Damon said. "Or he found out Billy's plans and made arrangements to arrive early and pick up his trail as he came off the aircraft. A detective might work that way."

"And Billy led him right to Donna's apartment."

"Yes."

"And he watched Billy go in and out, so he went in himself to see what Billy was up to."

"Or." He ratcheted the wheeled chair up straight. "Qigiq came to Reykjavik to investigate the apartment and Billy happens to get in his way."

"Hmm," she said.

"Seems less likely. And we would have to explain how Qigiq knew where to find Donna."

She scooted up onto the desk and let her feet dangle. Green synthetic socks extended three inches beyond her toes. "So Qigiq follows Billy. Sees him go into a building and come out a few minutes later. Decides to investigate. Finds the computer. Can probably still smell nail polish. Opens everything he can and photographs it. So he just happens to be carrying a digital camera?"

"We don't know it was digital. He's a detective, maybe has a camera with him all the time, or a cell phone with a good lens. He was smart enough not to plug into the computer. No way to get a virus from taking a picture."

"Why follow Billy?"

"Qigiq saw the Rat, he won't buy the official story. He knows Billy classified the Rat pictures, wants to find out what else he's is hiding."

"Ugh, why do you call them Rats?"

"Rotating Axial Traction System. An old German hand grenade gave me the idea," he said, smiling.

She shook her head. "Acronyms...something made Qigiq suspicious."

"He was in Washington. Think we need to watch him too?"

She stood. "Hard to do from a cave in Vietnam."

"Not that hard. Maxx, search on Qigiq, past fourteen days." He turned toward Claire. "Are we in Vietnam?" He smiled.

She scowled.

Maxx said, "Initiating."

"Let's see what kind of trail he left for us," Damon said.

"In the meantime, can we talk about our next move?"

He scooted forward to the edge of his chair. "Sure. We know those documents will concern Williams. Where will he look for Donna?"

"He could go wait for her in Iceland."

"Might take weeks. Is he the kind of guy to sit tight and wait for prey to come to him?"

"No, he's a General. He tells people what to do."

Damon stood. "Then he's stuck. Can't bring anyone else in or he has the containment problem all over again."

"Has to do it himself, doesn't he?"

"An army of one. You thirsty?"

She nodded.

He walked along the curved floor of the tube with the assurance of someone who had done it many times. When he reached the kitchen, he flipped open his cell phone and hit speed dial while opening the fridge with his other hand.

"What do you think?"

He reached for the jug of water and a Coke. Brought them out with one hand.

"He'll come after her with the resources of the U.S. Army. And maybe the FBI, CIA, and Special Forces, if he's willing to get them involved."

The can phsst as he opened it. "He could show up with technology I've never seen. Hard to plan against." He poured a tall glass of water and placed the jug back in the fridge. "I'll search for training sessions."

He made his way back through the tube.

"Coke or water?"

"Hmm, Coke I need caffeine."

He placed the can on the edge of the desk because she was pacing in front of Maxx again.

"Come up with anything?" he asked.

"He'll seek out the companies behind those receipts. It'll be tough to keep a low profile in China, but he'll bet Donna won't be prepared for him to dig deep."

"A working base in China weeks before the election?" He sipped cool water from the tumbler. "Think he'll risk it?"

"No. I think he'll do exactly what we..." She turned sullen.

He waited.

She restarted. "I think his analysis will be the same as before. Set up in Vietnam, sojourn into China."

He picked up the Coke and took it to her.

"We have to find out where," he said. "Close to the extraction sight is high on my list."

She added, "And find a way to talk to him face to face."

He shook his head slowly, "You're crazy, Claire. He'll shoot you on sight."

She drank from the can and reached out with her free hand to take his. She pulled it toward her and touched it to her throat, down to her breast, moving it slowly across her belly to the big Harley-Davidson buckle of her borrowed belt.

"We'll have to find a way to prevent that," she said softly.

Maxx's voice filled the room.

"Summary of Qigiq activity. Embassy Inn reservation. Call to Checker Cab company. Call to the Office of Bertrand Spin. Call to Alaska airline reservation. Credit card receipt for La Fondue in Washington DC. Credit card receipt for The Ice Pick in Reykjavik. Credit card receipt for 'I Spy' in Washington, camera purchase. Credit card receipt for…"

Chapter 79

SPIN STARED AT A SCRATCH in the paint where someone had backed a chair into the wall. He had noticed it the last time he and Billy were here and now it occupied his attention like ketchup on a white shirt. He picked at the fingernails of his left hand with his right thumbnail. A piece tore off and the sensitive skin underneath burned. He swore silently, then thought about the cool taste of a Sweet-Ass martini from Zucca's downtown.

His vision was periodically interrupted by the President's light charcoal suit as the man moved along the room's long dimension like a human trapped in a giant pinball machine. Dozens of documents were spread across the table. These included Mark's unofficial findings about Donna's website and the Detective's much more disconcerting e-mails and manufacturing invoices. Bert had conveniently forgotten the shot of Billy and him by the reflecting pond. He didn't deem it relevant to the current problem.

The leather soles of the President's Guccis swished the carpet. He turned and swished back, one hand on his chin, scratching it with his middle finger. Bert stared at the data on the table. He had done his best to present what was known, the source, and the likelihood of it being reliable.

The President stopped walking and started talking in the direction he was facing, not bothering to turn to face Bert.

"Bert. Can this be real?"

"I can't be sure Mr. President. I'm in the business of distorting reality, not creating it. The documents appear authentic, but it wouldn't be impossible to forge them. Then there's the issue of why anyone would bother. Also unclear."

"I'd sure like to talk to Williams about this," the President said.

"That can be arranged. But it's a risk. If these are genuine, confronting Williams may scare him into doing something stupid that becomes public. With two weeks to the election, we wouldn't have time to take corrective action."

The President grunted. "So I should ignore it?"

Bert took his elbows off the table. He felt odd sitting while the President was standing. But when he had tried to rise, the President had waved him down.

"I'm not sure we can. Something is clearly going on between Billy and China, possibly involving this Donna Ferreti woman—who is a civilian. If word leaks, it could be a worse PR disaster than the pipeline explosion itself. We don't know what's actually happening or why. Our uncertainty will be read by both constituents and opponents as incompetence."

The President sighed. "Damn Billy. What is he thinking?"

"We will, of course, ask him when you feel it's appropriate. But this material indicates he uncovered a clandestine effort to destroy the pipeline, and didn't try to stop it."

"Or maybe he did try," the President said, "And couldn't. So he followed the trail to China." The President sat down directly across from Spin and put his head in his hands. "If he went after a target, there's an audit trail of airplanes and soldiers and ordnance. If someone discovers that..."

"Your opponent will be unstoppable. And the woman in Iceland. Williams was there. We don't know their relationship, but the press will find a scandal, no matter what."

"Where's Williams now?"

"The latest FBI report has him on an Army transport heading to Southeast Asia. He'll be in Hanoi later today."

"At least a transport won't leave public records."

"We have an agent at the destination, and another following on a commercial flight."

"Options?" the President said.

"Ask him to quietly resign. Provide early retirement for health reasons. That would put him in the public eye briefly, but without much intensity. Maybe cloud it with several other retirements so it appears to be part of a wider program, a general house cleaning." Spin smiled as he recognized the unintended pun, but kept quiet.

"The man will be furious. He's obsessively dedicated to the military and keeping the defense budget, um...robust."

"Perhaps too obsessive," Spin said cautiously.

"How so?"

"It's remotely possible that Williams was a party to the pipeline situation. These documents connect him to the manufacturers of the LTB components."

"I hate three letter acronyms," the President said.

"Little Tractor Bomb, Mr. President. Term used by the local law enforcement in Alaska."

The President sighed.

Spin continued, "Based on classified phone records, General Williams repeatedly communicated with someone in China code-named Typhoon. Williams was first on the scene in Alaska, and took control of the bomb. He also let it get away."

The President stared at Spin for three long breaths.

Spin continued, "Williams was adamant about eliminating the person he had identified as the bomber, a mysterious entity he referred to as the Daemon. What if this Daemon is the one person who can incriminate Williams?"

"You have a strange mind, Mr. Spin. Perhaps you've been adjusting reality for too long."

Spin tried to laugh but it came out as a grunt.

"Unfortunately, what you say is indeed possible. Billy is an action guy. But why?"

Spin took a moment. He had a hypothesis. "Allow me, Mr. President, to suggest that he could have been trying to help you by creating a timely terrorist event that you could respond to publicly, thinking it would help your position in the polls."

"He couldn't have been more wrong."

"True, but that may have simply been a miscalculation," Spin said. Then added, "Giving him the benefit of the doubt."

The President tapped the table with his knuckles, like he wanted it to open.

"There's another possibility," Spin interjected. "Williams could have a larger plan. What happens whenever there's an attack on U.S. soil?"

"Congress votes the budget up for about a decade," the President said. "You really think Billy is worried about the defense budget?"

Spin replied, "If I were Billy, listening to your opponent, I would be extremely concerned. Jonathon Petry is more of a dove than a gay tree-hugging environmentalist driving a Prius with a flower on the dash."

The President barely smiled. "Hard to imagine. But it might work."

"Or," Spin continued, "we know China is after our economy, oil would be a good place to start. Maybe Billy stumbled onto a plan, interjected himself, and now has half the world in play. He could be in over his head, but trying to do the right thing."

"I'd like to think so," Mallor said. He was quiet for a long moment. "But regardless of why this is happening, the voters don't like it." He leaned back and placed both palms on the table. "I have to do something." He stood and breathed out a deep rushing sound. "And soon. Keep me posted on Williams. I'll look into the resignation idea; the Army owes me favors. Getting him out of the picture will help, but we're exposed on Alaska." He began to turn but stopped. "I need something to distract the voters from oil. Something powerful and positive they can feel good about."

Mallor started for the door.

Spin began to stand.

The President spun and faced him. "Bertrand, see if you can think of something." He turned and walked out.

Spin lowered himself to the chair from his half-standing position. He looked at the papers strewn around him: invoices, names, part numbers, delivery dates. What had Billy done about that guy who was allegedly sabotaging the military supply chain? Was the China guy the perpetrator—or was Billy the perp? Or had Billy hired the China guy to be the perp?

He shuffled the papers together and reviewed each before slipping it into his briefcase. Phone calls to China bothered him, even encrypted ones. He snapped the case shut and patted it. The truth was in here. He had to find it—and spin it into voter confidence.

Chapter 80

GENERAL WILLIAMS' BUTT SLAMMED against the hard seat of the C-23 Sherpa as it struggled east through turbulence. He was staring at the report from the test lab, but couldn't make sense of it.

He had expected one of two outcomes. If Donna was really a scrawny Claire with fake indigo eyes, as Jojo's computer seemed to think, then the DNA in the hair samples would match and he would have a new problem. But they didn't, so Jojo's prototype was hallucinating. That meant Claire Ferreti had gone the way of Putnam and Ching as intended.

The other outcome he was ready for was a partial match that showed Donna to be what she claimed: the black-sheep sister. That wouldn't be hard to deal with; he'd just shut her up by stuffing money in her mouth.

He shook his head. The DNA didn't flag Donna as sister, distant cousin, or even the same nationality. Genetic testing showed 20% Caucasian, 70% Asian, and 10% other. That was as far from Claire as he was.

He ran his fingers down parallel columns of numbers. These samples were clearly from unrelated people, which left him with a brand new question: Who was the woman calling herself Donna Ferreti?

His fingers stopped moving.

The hairbrush was a plant. Someone set up the computer and knew he was coming, knew he would take samples of hair and knew he would access the files. He had, after all, been led there by a website.

Made sense, but who would mess with the Army? He had never seen Donna before. And there was only one other person who knew the details of LTB construction well enough to fake those documents.

The Daemon.

But he was dead. Maybe. Claire's confirmation data had never arrived. Presumably she had gone in to get it, but he had no way to know if she made it out. He wished for the hundredth time Mallor would let him fly low-level reconnaissance drones over China.

He shuffled the report together, stuffed it back into a briefcase and shoved it under the seat. The plane shook and the barely muffled Army jets roared at his earplugs. He leaned his head against the hard upholstery and thought about a first class seat on a United whisper jet, and a pretty stewardess serving him Stoli on the rocks while being impressed with his star.

He sighed, his chest heavy.

He knew he had to make an operational assumption regarding the hair. The safe bet was to assume the mission had failed, this Donna person was working with the Demon, and Billy Williams had a hell of a mess on his hands. But there had been no attacks for months. And the three shooters wouldn't have returned to the rendezvous point if they had failed. They'd still be in China tracking their guy.

Or he could assume the mission had been successful, which meant the Demon was out of the picture. Who then was working with Donna? She didn't seem smart enough to fly solo. And why use an Italian supermodel version of Claire? A plant to mess with his head? By whom?

He closed his eyes. Start over...think out of the box...find the motivation.

He relaxed back in the seat, waited for sleep.

He dreamt of a naked Donna with waist length pink hair running barefoot across black sand, a long rifle strapped across her back. His boots crunched hard as he chased, unable to gain ground. She was swift, floating, and he was gasping, weighed down by a huge backpack full of wet secret papers that slipped from the pack as he ran.

The plane jounced hard as it touched pavement. He woke, his mouth dusty and his body stiff, like he really had been carrying that backpack. He sat up and blinked at the dim light inside the aircraft. If Claire were alive, he couldn't begin to estimate the risk. She possessed details of the mission and might know how it terminated, making her the only other person who actually understood Demon Drop. Who would she go to? The press? The President? Or would she come to him?

He leaned forward to the window and saw only darkness.

Chapter 81

FRED GILLER WAS PLEASED to see the big plane approach. He had been sitting still for an hour and boredom was making him sleepy. He was never bored watching a suspect, but the dark empty runway was like staring at a photograph: no change, no stimulation.

He stood on a rise covered with trees that didn't reach to his shoulders. Through 100x Leica binoculars he watched the plane taxi toward a rust-streaked hangar. There were three exits from the building and he could clearly see the two largest. If the subject took the third, he would have to be on foot.

He sprayed insect repellent with his free hand. He hated disease-carrying insects. Hated standing still. He shifted the big glasses, focusing first on the door he could see on the near side of the building, then on the large overhead where the plane had entered, and to the far side to see if the subject had slipped away.

Insect noises replaced the fading whistle of the plane's engines. He heard a groan as the overhead door shifted from something other than wind. He lifted the glasses to the sky. No other planes in sight. He swung to the wooden tower. The radar had stopped spinning. Nothing else was coming in soon. He moved his big eyes back to the hangar doors. Waited.

He heard the unmistakable rumble of an automotive engine. When he had ventured in close more than two hours before, there had been nothing in the hangar except benches pushed against the wall. Now there was a vehicle. It must have arrived in the transporter, which meant it belonged to the General.

A Humvee came into view, driving backwards. It was a dull black that reflected little light. No markings. In the darkness it was almost invisible. He tried to ID the driver, but the windows were impenetrable black rectangles.

He moved the glasses to the inside of the hangar. Two men in Army flight suits stood drinking from mugs. Neither had the demeanor of the General. He flicked back to the Hummer. It was moving along the opposite side of the airstrip—in his direction.

He would have to make an assumption.

He stepped backward slowly through the mini-trees and jogged down the gentle slope to a narrow dirt road built by an ox cart. He slipped the glasses into a woven basket strapped to the back seat of a small Zongshen motorbike. Its frame was black, its tank was black, everything about it was black—like half a million other bikes in China.

He strapped on a conical hat plaited with palm leaves and slipped into a long canvas coat. He listened. The Hummer was closer. He flicked the key and kicked the 250 cc 4-stroke. It burbled like a baby blowing bubbles. He swung a leg over. The machine didn't feel much more substantial than an American mountain bicycle.

He watched the Hummer move parallel to him. There was only one road away from the airfield that could accommodate that big machine. If he rode slowly, it would get there before him.

The Hummer was coming down the left fork as he traveled the other on a collision course. He stopped and shut off the bike to simulate engine trouble. He dug around in the basket on the rear fender and removed night-vision goggles. Crouching behind the engine with his right hand on the grip, twisting like he was trying to diagnose a carburetion problem, he held the goggles to his eyes with the left.

The dark vehicle rolled toward the intersection without lights. The goggles provided a view into the passenger compartment: one man driving, shotgun seat empty, back loaded so full he couldn't see through to the foliage on the other side. All he could make out was a large rectangle. The vehicle followed a curve to the left revealing the General behind the wheel wearing fatigues that matched the paint. He smiled behind the goggles. This gig was finally getting interesting.

The Hummer disappeared. Fred strapped on the night vision system under his pointy hat and restarted the bike with the headlight off. He followed the Hummer's path for just over a mile before turning left up a steep hill onto a narrow walking trail. He rode hard and fast, needing to cover more distance than the Hummer. A single bike following for a long period of time would arouse suspicion, so he planned to let the General see three, each with a different jacket.

He crashed through the brush and charged over the crest of the hill, bushes slapping at his knees. The General was ahead and still on the main road.

He hoped Merk would show up soon—two men made tailing a whole lot easier.

Chapter 82

CLAIRE LOOKED UP FROM pancakes reconstituted from a box of powder.

"They're what?"

"Maxx says they're FBI," Damon said, flipping bubbling dough on the hot plate.

She reveled in the taste of warm organic maple syrup he claimed was imported from a sugar shack in Vermont.

"Now how would Maxx know that?" she muttered.

"The pictures I took of the two guys in Reykjavik. The ones who watched Williams enter the Virgin's apartment."

"And?" She forked dough into her mouth.

"Maxx and I made some simplifying assumptions. Who would follow Billy? Someone from an American agency. And who might that be? The obvious, CIA, FBI, NSA, some branch of the Army."

"That's a lot of people. I don't see how you could find a couple faces in that crowd."

"We made another assumption."

She looked at him cockeyed. "Isn't that dangerous? You know, make an ass out of u...me kind of thing?" She twisted the cap off a bottle of Vietnamese orange juice.

"Not if you're successful," he replied.

"Hmm."

"Any player at that level went to college."

She stopped drinking, the bottle stuck to her lips. She removed it, dribbling orange liquid down her chin. "And that matters because..."

"Because Facebook was invented for college kids, and they've been putting their faces on social networking sites ever since. All Maxx had to do was, uh...visit a few places and solve a pattern-matching problem: two faces to be found amid millions. It takes loads of processing power to do that much matching, that's why we didn't find out until now."

"And you program this stuff?"

"I get help from those open source projects, or leverage something from the operating system, like iPhoto face recognition. He smiled. "The rest I write myself, or borrow from University labs."

"Borrow? Funny choice of words." She resumed drinking.

"I grab code and use it. I don't go into competition with the authors, or publish results or enter the marketplace in any way. And if I learn something they might want to know, say for ROS, the Robot Operating System the Rats use, Maxx and I figure a way to give it back."

"Big of you. So Maxx found these guys?"

"Brute force works sometimes." He grinned, flipped another cake. "One guy is NYU, top of his class in Poly Sci. The other went to American University right in Washington. So now we have names."

"Hmm." She chewed.

"Fred Giller and Merk Hemper."

"Say that five times fast," she said. "I'm afraid to ask because I have this feeling that with the names in hand, Maxx has now cracked into each agency and figured out who these guys work for, and what their current assignment is."

"I don't want to give away secrets." He sat across from her and reached for the maple syrup. "Want to guess?"

"CIA. They seem to get assigned the weird shit."

"Close."

"Well then FBI. They're always at each other."

"Bingo."

"And what are our friends Fred and Merk doing?" she asked.

He chewed and mumbled, "Guess."

She scrunched her brow. "They were definitely watching Billy. So he either has them as protection, no, he'd use Army for that. So someone else is interested in Billy's meanderings."

"Hey, you're good."

She lowered her head and smiled. "Let's not talk about last night."

He laughed and coughed, sprinkling pancake crumbs onto the table.

"Sorry."

"So who's interested in Billy? And don't make me guess."

He washed his pancakes down with cool coffee. "The request to follow Billy came through a PR office. But my guess is POTUS, 1600 Pennsylvania Avenue."

She pushed her chair away from the table, wide eyes on him. "The President. Holy...how did you find that out?"

"E-mail from Merk to his wife, hinting that the Big Guy wanted someone watched."

"Billy met with the President to get clearance for Demon Drop." She cringed at the name, remembering that it was designed to assassinate the man across the table whose bed she was currently...borrowing.

He met her eyes. "The President gave the go ahead to assassinate an American citizen on communist soil? "

"I think it was more like the President required deniability, so Billy was on his own."

He pushed his plate aside and propped his elbows on the table. "That means the President doesn't know what's going on because Billy never told him. And now Mr. Prez is worried, and having Billy followed. Incredible way to run a country, huh?"

"Yeah. Makes what you do seem normal." She laughed. "How much longer?"

He looked at the Suunto x9i on his wrist. It did a lot for him: GPS-compass-altimeter-chronometer. It read 09:07. "Anytime before noon today. I'm not going to push— hurrying now solves nothing. The key is that there's an event. Only Williams will know what that really means." He paused, watched her.

"Will you call?"

"Only to talk to Maxx," he said. "You don't want any part of Nightrider." He stood and crossed to her side of the table, bending forward to kiss her sticky lips. "You have a enough trouble."

"Where's Billy now?"

He studied her. "Don't know. Maxx can't find anything for the past two days."

"I bet he's on an Army transport, like we took to Alaska. That first time."

A wind chime tinkled.

She looked down at his pocket and back to his face.

He pulled out the phone and read. "Maxx found a commercial flight record for Merk Hemper."

Claire stretched out her legs and crossed her arms on her chest.

He tapped the phone, swiped at it. "Hanoi."

"When?"

"Last night."

She swallowed hard. "What should I do while you're gone?"

"Nothing." He spun and rushed toward the tube to Maxx's office, calling over his shoulder, "I'm not going."

Chapter 83

"WHERE, MAXX?" DAMON ASKED.

A white circle pulsed on the big screen where the line connecting Lao Chi Vietnam with Nanning China intersected Vietnam's eastern border.

"Twenty klicks from our rendezvous coordinates," Claire said. "How did Maxx find it?"

"FBI text messages. They're not using radios."

"Isn't it illegal to read people's messages?"

He grinned. "Hard too. I learned from the guys who cracked the President of Greece's cell phone back at the 2004 Olympics."

She scowled. "You know these people?"

"The project was written up in *Spectrum* magazine—helped me understand what to look for."

Shaking her head she said, "They document this stuff?"

"Sure. Engineers love tech-porn." He spun to face her. She hadn't moved from the La-Z-boy in over an hour. "Now what?"

She downed the last of a soda and held the can with both hands. "I go visit Billy."

"You're sure?"

"I know. It's dangerous. But right now, breathing is dangerous. I have to do something."

He met her eyes. "How about we run away to a deserted island? We could even buy it legally." He grinned, but only a little.

"That won't stop him." She looked up at the canvas ceiling. "I have to. For Cam and Wu...soldiers..."

He waited for more, but it didn't come. "Let's go play spy."

"Wait. What you do. It's clever. And the end...Quon and Suong. Helping them. That's beautiful. But the means..." She studied his face. "You have to stop doing this."

He raised an eyebrow, but said nothing.

"Really," she said. "We can't be international fugitives for heaven's sake."

"Claire, we *are* international fugitives."

"I mean as a long term plan." She flipped the back of the chair upright.

"Let's talk about the future in the future," he said, leaning toward her. "First, you have to stay alive."

Chapter 84

CLAIRE CRAWLED SLOWLY across damp jungle floor away from her motorcycle and up a low rise. Being back in combat gear, rifle and all, felt foreign, almost as if she had dreamt the first mission. Beneath her fatigues she wore Donna's pink hair, soft skintight slacks and a loose rainbow colored blouse. She could change persona in thirteen seconds, including boots to the purple flip-flops in the thigh pocket of her pants. She arrived beside Damon, who was studying Billy's encampment on the screen of a cell phone connected to a low-light camera attached to a rod that poked up between two bushes.

Damon whispered inside her ear canal. "In the tent, behind desk, feet up."

"He'll always face the door," she said softly, not knowing what kind of surveillance Billy had set up. Trusting the electronics to carry her words to Damon's ears.

His helmeted head turned toward her.

"Iraq," she whispered. "His unit went into a house, didn't cover the entrance. Shots from behind, Billy spun, fired bursts. Killed two kids with handguns."

"Bothers him?"

"Hates the failed cover." She glanced at the screen in his hand. "Pistol visible. What's he reading?"

She heard paper shuffle in her ear via the camera's long-range microphone.

"Cover stamped Top Secret. Project Cashew," Damon said.

She wondered what it revealed, but had no doubt Donna was the subject. She waited, statue still, pink hair poking over her right ear and out from under the helmet.

"Drib and Drab haven't moved. FBI-style reconnaissance," he said.

She heard another shuffling of paper.

"Recognize the vehicle?"

She studied the little screen. "Humvee. Thick roof."

"Your friend has expensive toys."

She wished he'd stop calling Billy her friend.

Lights popped on inside the Humvee, like a car at the mall being remotely unlocked. Billy stood up.

"Want to see what's inside?" Damon asked.

She tried to meet his eyes, but saw goggles. "You're going down there?"

He reached into a big pocket on his black cargo pants with his left hand and brought out a box the size of a pack of gum. A push with his thumb slid it open.

"What the hell?" she whispered.

"It's a Flea."

"An acronym for some high-tech shit you invented?"

His helmet shook. "Looks like an oversized one to me."

He was right, though it was mostly a curved lump of carbon fiber with a hole in it.

He lifted his hand, palm up. She heard a faint buzz. The Flea flew. She looked up and tried to follow it with her eyes, but it had disappeared into the darkness.

Damon was staring at the phone, tilting it left and right. The display showed an aerial view of the General's camp. The Flea had eyes. She listened carefully, but couldn't hear it over the clicking, ticking, buzzing of the jungle.

The image of the Humvee grew closer and stabilized as the Flea hovered.

The General swung open the rear doors and put a knee on the deck. As he bent forward to move inside, the Flea passed into the vehicle. He swung a hand like he was chasing a fly, moved inside and closed both doors. The light remained on.

"The Flea is stuck to the roof liner," Damon said.

Claire studied the inside of the vehicle. Three monitors and an oversized game controller sat on a boxy desk along the left. She had never seen Billy play a computer game.

"Did you see a pilot in the Osprey?"

It took a moment to realize what he was asking. She thought back. "No."

"That's a drone control station."

"Do you think—?"

A clang made her look up. The front panel of what she thought was a storage roof opened above the windshield. She heard a fizzing firecracker sound as a slender shape emerged over the hood. She had seen drones before, but this one glistened in the moonlight like a creature that could swim in the deepest parts of the ocean. With a double belly, slender wingspan, and a propeller pushing from the tail, it flew into the night sky. She admired its sleekness and how difficult it was to see even though she knew exactly what to look for.

Something touched her arm.

"We're visible."

She looked up. Stars, about half a moon. She tried to find the plane for a moment, then spun, dropped to her elbows and made her way down the hill.

They had approached from the west and coasted the bikes into the valley in silence. Both machines were parked midst the multiple trunks of a huge banyan tree whose arms hung low.

"He'll have infrared. Maybe radar," Damon said. "The bikes are cold, but we're not. Stay in close."

She scuffed her bottom along the dirt and sat next to him, her back against the big tree like they were going to have a picnic. He handed her a phone. She tilted the light down and studied the screen. The Flea showed Billy with the controller in hand, the light from the displays filling the back of the Humvee. She zoomed until she could make out what the drone was showing Billy.

"Circling and gaining altitude."

"Want to guess where he's going?" Damon said, digging in his pocket.

"He'll be over the extraction site in minutes."

"Good. Means he's not here looking for us, just wants to convince himself nothing went wrong with his mission." He flicked on a second smartphone. "I'll put Maxx on alert."

She thought about pictures going from the drone's camera to Billy's screen to the Flea's camera and finally to her phone. Sure seemed more complicated than a rifle.

"Maxx is ready. Let's hope Williams buys it."

She chewed the inside of her cheek, thinking about their plan. "What if I had been five minutes late that night?" She turned her eyes toward him. "Contact was verboten. Not enough gas to ride out. A jungle hike with no ID would attract attention." She watched the drone image tilt. "Which left setting up a camp not visible from satellites and waiting for the election. A few months in the jungle is possible. Plenty of water, rations. I'm not big on insects, but they're protein. Fruit. Leaves. Could be done."

"Let's hope your friend agrees with you."

They sat in silence and watched video from the drone.

"It's following GPS coordinates and flying low," Damon said. "Williams knows exactly where he wants it to go."

She felt her throat tighten as the remains of a burnt building became visible on the tiny screen.

"Think he'll find it?" she asked.

Damon was typing to Maxx. "If he's using infrared. The black parachute is hard to see at night." He continued typing. "But I'll help him with that too."

She relaxed her jaw. The drone slowed; the ground crept past.

"I see it," she said, pointing to a bright area that could be a log, or a person in a sleeping bag. "But I know what to look for."

"He'll find it."

The drone made a pass over the building and a long sweeping curve to look inside. Then it returned to the hotspot. Lower this time.

"Our survivor should hear the drone, and get up to see what's going on."

A dim light glowed inside a makeshift tent, tossing a subtle silhouette onto the dark material of the parachute. It was on for four seconds, and disappeared.

She saw Billy lean toward the center monitor. The drone swung and descended. In a few seconds, the cameras zoomed on the parachute.

Nothing moved. Heat showed on infrared, but it was faint.

"Starting the Rat," Damon said as his fingers moved. In moments there was shifting movement under the chute.

The drone descended.

"He's getting awfully close," Claire said. "What's he looking for?"

"A face. To be sure." He typed. The Rat moved to the edge of the parachute tent, inched its way into the open carrying a cutout of Claire in riding gear, then rushed back inside.

"Did you get it?" he asked.

"I saw a head poke out. Hard to tell if it was me."

They waited.

"Rewinding," she said. "He's got a still. Zooming and enhancing." She grew tense. They were trying to convince Billy she was alive and waiting. Suddenly it seemed like a horrible idea.

"Back on live feed from the drone," she said.

"Things are about to happen fast. You ready?"

She rehearsed in her mind one last time. There were two paths, depending on what Billy did next. She went through her role in each, step by step. Only then did she nod.

The drone floated in a wide circle, accelerating until the ground passing below was a blur on the little screen as it descended to the treetops.

"That thing is fast," she said.

"Clear night. It's laser pulsing the target."

She watched for six seconds.

A streak across the screen made her jump. It ended in a fireball that incinerated the parachute.

"There's your final answer," Damon said.

Claire stared at the screen in her hand, the reality of what she had just seen seeping into her. She thought she had been ready after reading the diary, now she could barely draw a breath…yet wanted to scream. She gazed up into the forest, thick with blackness and night shadows, slowly becoming ever more angry.

She dropped the phone, stood, and stripped off her boots pants and jacket. She placed her helmet beside the tree, slipped on the purple flip-flops and fluffed her hair. From a pocket she pulled a mirror and her gold lipstick case. She painted her lips while Damon draped a blue cloth behind her. She fluffed her hair again, flipped it from side to side, sat cross-legged, breathed deep, and picked up the phone.

Damon shined a bike headlight into her face, held up three fingers, and counted down—three, two, one. He pointed at her.

She pressed the call button.

"He put the controller aside," Damon said. "The drone is on auto-pilot."

She saw Billy's face pop onto the screen of the cell phone in her hand. She took a deep breath and smiled Donna's smile.

"How the hell did you get access to this number?" Billy bellowed from the little speaker.

"Hello, General, it's nice to see you too. You don't remember? You told me that day you were so wonderful and gave me the pizza."

He paused. She could see his eyes trying to figure out if he could have screwed up in the confusion that day.

"Camera says Drib has a long-range mic," Damon said into her left ear. "He should be getting audio from inside the Humvee."

"What happened to Claire? I miss her."

She knew Billy was getting a feed as if Donna were in her apartment. Maxx was somehow adding her to a background of the bedroom in Iceland.

"You don't have a sister."

"What have you done with her?"

"Your DNA doesn't match Claire Feretti."

"My what? You can't test my DNA, I like, saw a TV show, and it said—"

"I can do anything I want."

"Where did you get stuff to do a nasty test like that?"

"When I visited you in Iceland."

"Ha. I bet you grabbed something from my roommate. She's a nice Chinese girl. Has baby soft skin, and dyes her hair to look like me so we can be sort of you know a couple."

She watched him think, wondering if maybe he had made a real mistake. Then his face relaxed.

"Hi, Donna, what is it you really want?"

"I want to know what happened to Claire!"

"Why do you think something has happened to her?"

"Because I just got this totally weird message on Facebook. It said that she was on a mission in China and if I got this message then something had gone wrong and I should go find you and try to help her."

Damon was holding his left thumb up. Billy grew quiet for a moment.

"That is a weird message. When did you get it?"

"Just seconds ago. I was sitting here trying to schedule my tickets to come see you in Washington, you know to collect my money that you promised. And it just popped in so I read it and freaked out beyond freakin' Mars you know like China and not coming back!"

Billy held up his hand. "Donna Donna. Don't panic. Yes, Claire is on a mission to China. She's been delayed. She'll be back in a week or two. That must be an auto-reminder set to go out if she wasn't back on schedule. Don't worry about it."

"You're lying, Mr. Williams. How can you lie if you loved her? She warns me right here," she pointed as if the message were on a screen in front of her, "that you might say that."

"What else does she say, Donna?"

"She says she's in Vietnam and a drone is circling overhead. She's worried it might attack and if I don't hear from her soon I should dig and dig and dig until I find out what happened and tell the American people about all the bad things you're doing. But I should be super careful because you're like really dangerous."

"That's ridiculous, Donna. She's making up stories because she's pissed we broke up and wants to lash out at me—wrath of a woman scorned and all that. We tried for months, it just didn't work out for us."

Donna froze. Claire hadn't been ready for that twist. She blinked hard, licked her lips, and forced herself to focus.

"Claire's message says right now you're in the back of a black Humvee flying a drone over the location where the team was to have been evacuated, but instead were killed by a missile that you launched from your flying machine. Is that true?"

"You can't know that," Williams said before catching himself. "The United States is at war, my pink-haired friend. Whether you're Claire or Donna or some crazy skinny whore trying to blackmail me, stop playing this game, it's too big for you."

"I'm just telling you what she wrote in her message." She paused, pretended to read. "Oh my God! You sent assassins to China to kill someone called the Demon and no one is supposed to know. That's so horrible. I'm going to share this right now. I have friends you know. Friends who write blogs and we'll make sure the world—."

The headlight went out and a hand pressed hard over her mouth. She struggled until she heard Damon's voice in her ear.

"He destroyed Donna's apartment. Maxx is calling the fire department in Reykjavik." He paused, eased his grip, turned her chin until they were face to face. "Convinced?"

She nodded.

"One hundred percent?"

She didn't hesitate. "Yes."

"You're the sniper," he said, and jumped up.

Chapter 85

SHE WANTED TO SCREAM while choking Billy with her bare hands. But she tossed her flip-flops off, stepped into her boots and grabbed her rifle with one hand and a grenade from her jacket on the ground with the other. She didn't even try to be quiet as she bent at the waist, ran up the rise and dropped into prone position.

"Claire," she heard on her intercom. "Get the drone. It's armed, we don't know what it can do by itself."

She heard a slight buzzing to her left but couldn't see the plane. Billy was still inside the Hummer. She positioned the scope to her left eye, flicked the safety, and let her mind relax to the zone. She licked her lips to get the lipstick off. Vietnam tasted like every rifle range she had ever been on: cinders and stale mustard.

The drone came in slow and landed, rolling to a halt just past the Hummer. She wished she knew where its fuel tank was.

She felt a tap on her shoulder and jumped out of her skin. Damon held out a bullet between his thumb and index finger.

"Violates the International Laws of Armed Conflict." He handed it to her. "But it'll do a number on that plane."

She swapped it for the first round of the armor piercing bullets he had given her earlier, replaced the magazine, repositioned the rifle.

She took a deep breath. Pulled the trigger.

The bullet hit the drone just in front of its pusher prop. And exploded. Which ignited the fuel and lit the night like a college bonfire on homecoming weekend.

The back doors of the Hummer opened.

She waited.

Billy stepped one foot out, his right hand wrapped around the rear door. He looked at the plane, he looked at the sky, he stuck his head back inside and reached with his left hand. His body started moving forward.

She saw the shot as clearly as a bull's-eye at a match, but couldn't move the rifle. A voice screamed in her head: *he's guilty, there is no reasonable doubt, you're a sniper, an assassin, a killer, just pull the fucking trigger.*

She shifted a millimeter and fired.

The bullet zinged off the rear door after ripping through the fingers of Billy's right hand. He fell to his left into the Hummer. He didn't come out.

Her entire body was sweating under the pink hair and rainbow blouse and stretch pants. She was panting. Her hands were slippery. Only her feet felt right in the heavy boots. She tried to slow her breathing. When he stepped out, she couldn't flinch again. Billy Williams needed to be made dead.

The Humvee's headlights came on. It started backing up. She could see Billy behind the wheel, driving with his left hand, the right tucked up under his left arm. Then she realized that a military vehicle that could launch an armed drone probably had other ways to kill.

Loud cracks pierced the night.

Machine gun bullets pummeled the hill in front of her. Billy knew combat, of course he had seen the muzzle flash and identified her location. And she was still lying there.

The Humvee headed straight at her.

She heard a rumble from behind, and "fifty meters" in her left ear. She turned to see Damon's headlight.

"Goodbye, Billy," she said to herself, and fired nine rounds from the high-powered sniper rifle at the Humvee's headlights, grill, windshield, tires. One light went out, a web of cracks spread like splattered paint on the windshield, and it stopped moving.

"Twenty meters."

She pulled the pin on her grenade and threw. It landed on the hood of the Humvee and rolled toward the driver's side. A flare of brilliant light and a huge boom was followed by a bolus of visibility-obliterating smoke.

Pink-haired Donna held out her right hand and hooked Damon's arm as he rode over the crown of the hill directly toward the Humvee. She leapt onto the moving bike like Jesse James mounting a running horse after robbing a bank.

They rode through thick smoke and past the driver's door. She saw Williams' furious eyes a meter away as the bike squirmed down the hill to the right of the Humvee. Damon shifted toward her in the seat and accelerated up a rutted dirt road that hammered her butt against her spine, and her spine against her kidneys.

Chapter 86

SHE SPIT SMALL STONES from her mouth, struggled to turn her body around to put her back to his, and squeezed the bags on either side of the bike with her legs, horseback style. They squirmed uphill.

"What are you doing?" he asked in a steady voice.

"I want to fire. I'm taking your gun."

The bike curved, climbing...the Humvee followed.

"Where the hell are you going?" she screamed, incredulous he would go near the target.

"We can out climb him."

Williams turned in their direction.

"Cases," Damon said.

She looked down at black boxes. She tucked the revolver inside her rainbow shirt and reached behind her to wrap her right arm around his waist. As the bike jumped through the bush, she flipped open the left case. Twenty polished handles reflected moonlight.

She stuck her left heel into the open case as the hinged lid bounced. She leaned forward until she could reach a handle, lifted it out and saw the ring pull of a grenade just above the Rat's head.

"Ready," she shouted.

Unbelievably, the bike slowed.

"To his left. It chases metal."

She watched the Humvee crawl like an alien Earth rover collecting samples of life as it climbed rocks the size of sea turtles. She estimated 100 meters, gathered her strength, yanked the pin, and tossed hard.

The bike accelerated while the Rat bounced and rolled like a popcorn kernel in a microwave, searching for traction. It spun in crazy circles, raced downhill toward the Humvee, and exploded ten feet from the passenger's door. She heard rocks clatter against armor.

She reached for a second Rat.

The bike slowed.

She wondered about the wisdom of letting the target get closer as she pulled the pin, heard the spit of a machine gun, and saw flames behind the grill of the Humvee. She was glad Billy was driving, aiming, and firing with a single hand. The shots went wild, embedding themselves in the hillside fifty meters behind the bike.

"Can I control the fuse?"

"Pull slowly."

She counted one Mississippi, two Mississippi, three Mississippi as she eased the pin out, then flung the Rat underhand, softball style.

The Humvee crept upward as the hill grew steeper, spewing bullets in every direction as it labored over terrain where no road had ever existed. The Rat exploded a meter from the driver's door, shattering the remaining glass along the side of the vehicle.

"He stopped," she yelled.

She saw the target's face pop up behind the damaged windshield, the left side red, an instant before the machine lurched forward, covering the ground between the two vehicles at remarkable speed, the machine gun silent. She was thinking that driving fast might be all the target could do when a puff of smoke emerged from the grill.

"Missile," she yelled, grabbing the bags from the instinct to hide and reaching for her gun. The back wheel spun, lifting a rooster tail of dirt up behind them. She pointed her arm at the Humvee and fired rapidly, hoping for a random hit.

The bike flew over the top of the rise, levitating her from the seat. She saw a smoke trail above them as the rocket missed the mountain and flew toward the next valley.

She sat up and leaned against Damon's back as he braked to slow the bike's descent. She wanted to speak, but couldn't make her throat work.

She re-tucked the pistol, its barrel hot against her, and reached for a Rat, pulled the pin faster and flicked it off the back. She repeated the motion, counting off Mississippi's to allow four seconds between tosses.

She was releasing the fifth Rat when the Hummer topped the rise. The first explosion occurred ten meters in front of the target. He didn't slow but he did restart the machine gun. Bullets pelted the earth twenty meters behind her toes.

The second Rat exploded and the target turned left sharply to avoid the dirt cloud it raised. The machine gun went silent. The third explosion drove him further to his right.

The ground leveled off and Damon powered into a hard right turn, sliding the back wheel. Moving backwards and sideways at the same time started to make her dizzy.

Another plume of smoke and dirt rose beside the truck, but it didn't slow. She worked like a machine: drop, count, drop, count.

The bike straightened and stopped bucking. She looked down at a narrow, smooth trail going by awfully fast. She reached for a Rat and pulled the pistol from her shirt with her left hand. As the Hummer reached the valley floor and slowed to prevent the suspension from self-destructing she emptied the remainder of the clip through the haze of explosions.

"Keep your feet up," he said, as if she were crazy enough to touch her boots to the ground at 100 mph.

The left case was empty. She put her foot into it and flipped open the right one. She stuffed the handgun and pulled a Rat from the case. It had a dial instead of a pin.

She poked him with her elbow.

"Meters."

She spun the dial to 50 and dropped it. She watched the Humvee twist back and forth with one wheel on either side of the foot trail, destroying tree branches and wildflowers blooming from the heavy rains. In less than two minutes her right side case was empty, the air was a blur of brown cloudbursts, and a destroyed tire had forced the Humvee to slow.

"No more," she yelled.

She felt something poke at her right shoulder blade. She turned, saw the butt of a rifle waving in the air, and grabbed it, wondering where it had come from.

The trail wound into open meadow. She raised the rifle, fumbled for the safety, and pointed it straight behind the bike, wishing that luck and technology would have made just one of those Rats go off right under his ass.

They swept into a wide curve as the target burst from tree cover. She fired, her bouncing aim focused on the driver's side of the windshield. The Humvee swerved, then left the trail to take a short cut across the meadow.

She fired and fired. Magnified through the scope she saw the windshield fall away in a thousand fragments, saw the shadow of eyes beneath a combat helmet, felt the brap brap of the rifle hammer her weakened left shoulder, saw the Humvee weave to evade the bullet barrage, saw the last Rat go off to the right of the truck, saw it veer left, saw an explosion under the left front wheel blow the hood into the air, another under the left rear wheel lift the back so high the momentum tipped the big Humvee onto the tires on its right side.

She didn't stop firing.

The target corrected and the left side of the machine slammed to the ground like the hammer of an angry Greek god. It twisted right. Two simultaneous explosions assisted reactive centrifugal force, lifting the right side of the Humvee until it careened along on the two left wheels.

She fired at the exposed roof.

The target lost his one-handed fight with the wheel and the machine tilted onto its side, plowing the ground with the driver's door. Something exploded under the left front fender, and another near the rear wheel, rotating the machine as it slid.

She was squeezing the trigger when an explosion under the vehicle sent a plume of rock into the passenger compartment and out through the windshield. She felt cold as the Humvee became quiet and unmoving, except for the roiling dust clouds storming inside the cabin.

She relaxed her left hand.

Damon rode along the narrow path for two kilometers until it twisted sharply over a low rise and into the jungle. She never removed her eyes from the Humvee. The bike slowed, she felt his back press against her. When it stopped she twisted off, flinging her left leg over the taillight. Damon followed. He lifted binoculars to his eyes.

"Nothing's moving," he said.

"What the hell happened?" she asked, his Chinese rifle hanging in her left hand.

"Antitank mines."

She stared at the back of his head as he scanned the area through the field glasses.

"We rode through a minefield?" She noticed the rifle in her hand shaking. "Are you insane?"

He lowered the glasses, turned and met her wide eyes.

"You missed your shot." He shrugged. "I didn't have a better idea." The corners of his mouth twitched towards a grin. "I told you to keep your feet up."

She was out of ideas too. She wanted to explain her initial miss, but couldn't think of anything that didn't sound like an amateur's excuse. Or a woman's.

He traded her the glasses for the rifle.

In the silver moonlight she watched black smoke billowing from burning rubber and upholstery inside the Humvee join the round puffy clouds of dust from the crash itself. She didn't see tongues of flame lapping out the windows like in the movies, which disappointed her in a vaguely childish way. The passenger's window was still up; it hadn't even shattered.

"Bulletproof," she muttered.

She looked for movement, but saw nothing through the black hole where the windshield had been.

"We're going to have to confirm," she said, without lowering the binoculars.

"Be careful where you step."

"Funny...oh my god."

"What?"

"The window...on the passenger's side...it's rolling down." She watched gray smoke exit through the open window. A hand reached out of the grayness like a zombie struggling to extract its body from a grave. It groped for the roof rail.

"He's crawling out. I can't believe he's alive. A mine exploded under the driver's window."

"Good truck," he said.

"Wait."

He waited.

"The arm, it's not black."

"You mean he changed clothes?"

She watched the hand grab hold and tighten its grip around the roof rail. A body followed through the gray fog flowing out the open window.

"Oh my god."

"You said that before. Not much data," he said.

"It's, it's..."

"Still not much data."

She lowered the glasses and spoke without turning. "It's not Billy."

She handed him the glasses. A man was halfway out of the window like a life-size jack-in-the-box, his legs invisible inside the smoke filled machine. As he twisted to free himself Damon saw his face.

"It's the Lost Sheep," he said.

"Who?"

"Your friend from Alaska."

"Qigiq? What's he doing here?"

"Isn't he—?"

"A detective," she said. "Yeah, but he wasn't driving. I saw Billy," she paused, "I mean the target, clearly through my scope. Qigiq wasn't in the Humvee."

Damon lowered the glasses and turned to her. "You mean, Qigiq wasn't visible in the front two seats."

"Correct."

"But he could have been in the back under the drone station. Do you think Williams knew he was there?"

Her lips curved down. "I doubt it. He wouldn't have gone after me in front of a witness."

"So this guy's a stowaway."

She stared at the burning vehicle. The figure seated on the upturned door lighting a cigarette was barely visible without magnification. "I think he was following Billy, but I have no idea why."

He frowned. "You have no idea why you think that, or why he was following Billy?"

She gave him a tilted smile. "Neither."

She twisted to face Damon. "Qigiq doesn't know he's surrounded by land mines. He'll be killed."

"Just so I've asked. Is that a good thing or a bad thing?"

She stared. "I don't know. I don't know why he's even here. But we can't let him die by accident."

Damon stepped over the seat of his bike and fired it to life. "He's met Claire, and was in Donna's apartment, so he'll recognize the skinny girl with pink hair. I'll take him back to Williams' camp. From there, he's on his own."

"He'll know you exist."

"Just a taxi." He flipped the dark face shield of his helmet down, and spun the bike on the trail.

"Be careful," she said to the wind swirling behind him.

Chapter 87

SPIN CLOSED THE FBI report from Giller and Hemper and longed to lower his face to the desk and weep. Not for Williams. Billy had been a good collaborator, but docked his boat too far to the right for Spin's taste. No, he was feeling beaten because he couldn't handle the latest developments by public relations alone—and that was his job. The voice recordings from Hemper might destroy them all: possible collaboration with the Chinese, secret mission in Communist territory, drones, missiles. Spin looked at his hand, wondered how he was going to stop the election from slipping away, and then squeezed it into a fist.

The desire to weep persisted.

Stacy's voice followed the buzz of the intercom.

"Mr. Qigiq is here to see you."

Chapter 88

SHE WAITED ON A CONCRETE bench across a four-lane boulevard from Spin's office eating mustard-covered hotdogs purchased from a pushcart operated by a man who spoke no English. She was wearing dark green cargo pants tied at the ankle and black flats with buttons along the side making them look like spats, a white silk shirt and black jacket. No leather. Big round sunglasses reflected the traffic on the street. Her pink and blonde hair had become a smooth chestnut red with just one streak of pink remaining. Mustard inhabited a tiny spot above her upper lip.

"How long now?" she asked.

Seated next to her, Damon chewed his second hot dog. He held up his wrist with the x9i in front of her face, twisting his hand so mustard wouldn't drip off the dog.

"Sixteen minutes," she said. "When should I start to worry?"

"Never, it accomplishes nothing," he said. "I doubt Qigiq knows more than the FBI guys."

She stuffed the last inch of bun and dog into her mouth with her left index finger.

"What if he doesn't go for it?"

"Then I keep doing what I do." He turned his face to meet her eyes.

"Awfully dangerous," she said.

"Nothing compared to what my parents lived through," he replied. "Or what the children face every day. Or what soldiers are asked to do." He paused. "This new robotics stuff will get better and bring more unsolved problems with it." He finished his hot dog. "Did you ever think of a land mine as an autonomous robot? It senses weight, decides if it's heavy enough, chooses to kill. Just like a robot. No man in the loop."

They sat quietly beside the whoosh of midday traffic.

"You saw what happened to the Humvee," he said.

She closed her eyes and revisited rocks and dirt bursting upward into the cab of the big vehicle, obliterating her former lover. There had barely been a body to return to the U.S. She swallowed hard.

"Yes."

"Besides, I rather enjoy the work." He smiled. "It's satisfying to be useful."

She watched the concrete steps across the street that rose to a black door. It swung outward.

"There he is."

Damon donned a black baseball cap bearing the logo of BMW motorcycles and leaned back against the bench, tilting the hat down to shield his eyes.

"Break a leg," he said.

She watched Qigiq hail a taxi and disappear into the back seat. It pulled away. She waited for the cab to fade out of sight before standing. She picked up her cup of Dr. Pepper and sucked on the straw, handed him the empty.

"Can you hear me now?" she said from behind a smile.

The baseball cap nodded.

She crossed the street mid-block, dodging a silver Mercedes and a city bus carrying the face of Jonathon Petry above the slogan: *Choose Peace, Choose Petry*. She ran a gauntlet of Korean imports: both the cars and their drivers. Only one honked. She walked slowly but steadily up the cement stairway, thinking she could feel his eyes on her backside.

Spin's office was easy to find in a corner on the second floor. Stepping inside, she was greeted by a tall blonde woman who offered coffee, and asked her to wait.

"Are you okay?" his voice asked in her ear.

"Thank you," she said, as she took the paper cup from the woman's hands. She scratched her left cheek just in front of her ear gently with her fourth and fifth fingers, and tapped the earpiece twice with her index finger to indicate that everything was fine. She blew softly across the hot dark liquid.

Before the coffee was half gone she was shown in to meet Mr. Bertrand Spin, the man who gave the President a face for the people.

"Hello, Ms. Ferreti, it's a pleasure to meet you in person. Your pictures don't do you justice."

Donna's pictures from the website. Spin had a good memory, or had been studying her file.

"Thank you, Mr. Spin, I appreciate your agreeing to see me on short notice."

She sat in an aqua chair with arms that swept up to become the back. It was firm but comfortable. She sipped her coffee.

"Your message intrigued me," he said. "I was quite sad to learn of General Williams' accident. You were there?"

She opened the wide orange purse slung over her shoulder and extracted a nine-by-eleven envelope that was folded in half and sealed. She reached out and placed it in the middle of his desk.

"Documentation. I am, of course, unaware of what you may have learned from your own sources. If you wish, we can review the events together. I'll fill in any blanks for you."

He sliced the end with an opener shaped like the Washington Monument and removed a dozen sheets of paper. The top page was a picture of a man lying on a nicely woven carpet with what appeared to be a bullet hole in his chest oozing bright red blood. Spin jerked upright when he saw it, stared at her, then lowered his eyes and picked up the picture to study it carefully.

"And who might this be?"

"His name is Dominic Kalstin, but your records will show him as code name Typhoon, operating primarily in Indochina."

Spin stared at the picture in silence.

"General Williams has been paying him for months," she said. "He was not the target of the assassination. He was an industrial spy who stole information from within a Chinese manufacturing facility."

"But?" Spin's eyes remained on the picture.

"But the man who *was* the target surmised we were coming, and maneuvered Kalstin into the line of fire." She took a slow breath. "Without our knowledge."

Spin dropped the picture and squinted. "*We* were coming?"

"The three specialists General Williams sent in on Demon Drop. I was team leader."

Spin leaned more deeply into the supple leather of his office chair. She watched him struggle to breathe slowly. They were now on fresh ground, just as Damon had predicted.

"Are you not Donna Ferreti from Iceland? The woman General Williams was searching for?"

"Yes and no." She gave him a wide smile. "I am also Claire Ferreti. Corporal Claire Ferreti, U.S. Army. Assigned to Special Projects. I'm a sniper."

"And Donna?"

"Donna is my sister who lives in Iceland. Only she doesn't exist," she held her smile, "in the traditional sense. She's really a collection of carefully fabricated computer documents, from birth certificate to Facebook profile. Although she did have a rented apartment."

Spin pushed out his lower lip and blew a stream of air at the tip of his nose. "I see. So this gets complicated."

It wasn't a question so she sipped her cooling coffee, noticing it was three quarters gone.

"Would you like more coffee?" he asked. "We might be here for some time."

"Thank you, that would be nice."

Within moments the blonde woman out front provided her with a full porcelain mug promoting Mallor for President *The Country, The Time, The Man* that matched the one sitting on Spin's desk.

"You were saying this gets complicated," Spin said.

"Actually, you were." Another smile. "I don't think it's so complex. Billy sent us on a mission to eliminate a man he believed to be a terrorist threat to the United States." She paused, but didn't move. "And perhaps a threat to Mallor's re-election, which he fully supported."

"Billy?" Spin said.

"Yes, General Williams and I were lovers, which I suspect you can verify. I always called him Billy."

The color drained from Spin's face.

"Unfortunately, the man Billy dubbed the Demon orchestrated a bait and switch. That's why Typhoon was eliminated. For the record, I don't believe Billy ever knew Typhoon was the eventual target."

"Why not?" Spin asked.

"Fair question. The short answer: because Billy sent an Osprey drone prototype to eliminate the three assassins so there would be no witnesses to the Drop. He also arranged for flight records to be permanently altered so there would be no trail of the assassination attempt, if anyone was ever motivated to look for it."

"So this Demon Drop project doesn't exist?"

"Not in the official version of reality."

"Then why should I believe you?" Spin asked.

She flicked her left index finger twice.

He turned to the next page.

"That's where what's left of the bodies are buried," she said. "If you like, I can give you GPS coordinates. You can exhume the remains and DNA demonstrate that Cam Putnam and Wu Ching died in the line of duty."

Spin looked at the picture of the hidden graves, and the shell of a burned building.

"There are many ways these men could have died," he said.

"Ever the spin doctor." She reached into her purse for her phone, tapped the screen a few times and placed the device in the middle of his desk. "This was recorded by someone who happened to be at the scene with long range recording binoculars. No, not me. I'm the rider closest to the camera. Cam was always faster than me on a bike." She flashed to a row of candy bullets. Wondered about an alternate reality where things had a beginning, but no end. "I could outshoot him any day of the week." She pressed her lips together and forced a slight smile to hold back the tears. "If you look closely, you can see Ching's silhouette against the flames as the missile explodes."

Spin watched the movie play on the small device, his face becoming a mask as a ball of flame reached out at a rider, and tossed him into the air in front of a second rider closer to the camera.

"Where was this?"

"In Vietnam, two miles from the Chinese border."

Spin slumped, dropping his head into his hands, elbows on his desk, staring at the tiny screen as it looped and replayed the deadly event.

"Where was this Typhoon person shot?" he asked.

"You don't want to know," she said. "But I'll be happy to tell you."

"Please, go ahead, it's best I know what really happened so I can explain it to the President."

"China. About 100 miles from where those bodies are buried."

He looked up, his eyes sagging.

"We went in from the air," she said.

"With motorcycles?" he asked, eyes wide.

"Yes. They're light enough to jump with, and fast enough to do the job. A brilliant strategy, really. Got us in and out without violating Chinese air space."

Spin straightened his spine and leaned back in his chair. "So why are you here, Ms. Ferreti?"

"Timing. A real typhoon arrived at exactly the wrong moment. I crashed my bike on the way out and the GPS computer failed, including the module that was supposed to upload the verification data. Without navigation I arrived late to the rendezvous, but just barely. The Osprey hit our location with the intention of leaving no witnesses. I survived." Her heart twisted as she fought off thoughts of her panic that night. "Again, just barely." She turned her head and shifted her hair to reveal the white scar above her left eye that looked mysteriously like a bullet wound.

"So your timing was off. That doesn't make the air strike a clean zone attempt to eliminate U.S. military personnel."

She wiggled her finger again.

He turned the page.

"These look like photographs." He looked closer. "Of hand writing?"

"You'll find the original journal tucked inside a thumbed copy of *War and Peace* in a locked cabinet in General William's condominium. In the den." She wiggled her finger to point. "All the way to the left."

Spin exhaled air like he was smoking a good cigarette.

"It will be easy for you to verify Billy's handwriting."

He shuffled through the remaining papers, not speaking for over a minute. Eventually he asked, "Was General Williams part of a plan to sabotage the Trans-Alaskan pipeline?"

She sipped coffee from the big mug with two hands. Lowered it. "Was the pipeline sabotaged? I heard there was a pump failure."

He met her eyes. She noticed his were a light, translucent blue with just a hint of gray—movie-star eyes that made you want to trust them. She wasn't sure, but she thought his mouth twitched toward a grin.

"Where does that leave us then, Corporal?"

She dug into her bag a second time and removed another envelope, this one white and standard business size. It was sealed. She leaned forward and handed it to Spin.

"There are many possible outcomes of the current state of affairs," she said. "I propose this as the best for all interested parties."

He picked up his Monument letter opener and slit the envelope. It contained a single sheet of paper. She watched his eyes dance back and forth as he read. Then they scanned up and down, likely revisiting the key details.

"A billion dollars is a great deal of money," he said.

"As Dr. Einstein taught us, everything is relative," she replied. "There is a great deal at stake."

Chapter 89

"BERTRAND, THIS IS OUTRAGEOUS. They cannot blackmail the President of the United States of fucking America," Mallor shouted, smacking the table with his fist. "It's unthinkable."

"Mr. President, they are simply trying to influence you as a politician on a particular issue. Try to think of them as just another lobby. It's done all the time."

"Usually with money, Bert. Not threats." The President glared at him.

Spin sighed inwardly. They had been jousting for two hours and the President was still in the denial phase. Bert had to find a way to push Mallor to acceptance, so they could move forward to strategic planning.

"It's a proposal. What they want isn't exactly bad. We've done worse things with a billion dollars. And they never claim, not once, that they will disclose the information to the public if we don't cooperate."

Mallor's face struggled to relax. "But they will."

"We don't know that, Mr. President. To protect you, General Williams provided very few details of what transpired. He had primary responsibility. He took his job seriously. But I think it would be fair to say that he was also ambitious." He paused, wanting to suggest a path, but not quite sure if Mallor was ready to hear it. He swallowed and forged ahead. "Williams' aggression led us into this convoluted mess. But I'm confident the American people would rather remain ignorant than have your administration invest time, energy and taxpayers' money trying to explain what went on and why. They just want you to fix it."

Mallor jumped up and said, "I agree."

Bert jerked, spilling coffee over his hand.

The President continued. "Given the choice, ignorance is the preferred path. The last thing voters want to hear about is the aftermath of land mines and defoliating agents from a war they've long forgotten, coupled to a brouhaha with the Chinese. And right before an election." He put both hands on the table and groaned. "I wish Williams was here so I could court martial him personally."

Spin hesitated, unsure of how far he could push Mallor with recent polls showing him trailing Petry in critical districts. But he had an idea.

"Mr. President, we could look at this as an opportunity."

The President locked eyes with him. "This had better be good, Bert. We're days from the biggest election of my life."

Chapter 90

"WE'RE IN A HOTEL IN DC, STILL WAITING."

"Only two days since she met with Spin."

He laughed. "It gets worse. His first name is Bertrand. Makes his initials B.S."

Damon moved the cell phone to his left ear. "If the President ignores us, the blogs and websites are ready." He paused. "Not entirely anonymous, but well hidden."

A female commentator's voice came softly from the hotel television. "Today, the owners of the Trans-Alaska Pipeline announced that the damaged line will be back in service earlier than expected, and will include upgrades to prepare it to carry oil from new fields where they plan to drill as soon as Congress approves access to Federal land. In other news, the Washington Capitals have…"

He crossed his blue-jeaned legs at the ankles, right over left, and wiggled the toes of his bare feet between him and the television.

"We're after resources for people still being harmed, like Quan, and that little doll Suong. She's only four. They need help throughout their entire lives, not just one time."

Shirtless, he leaned against a pair of hotel pillows propped against the headboard. The TV prattled a commercial for a new car that promised to enrich his life. The woman in the ad seemed to like the front fender.

Claire sat at a small corner desk in the suite and watched him over the upper edge of her laptop. She made clicking sounds with her tongue, then lowered her eyes to the screen where she was surfing for leaks about the President.

"War is just a word to hide behind," he said. "These kids weren't even alive when Nam was bombed."

"I've got it," Claire said. "This blog claims the President is planning a surprise press conference tonight at 6:30 Eastern Daylight Time."

He ended the call, checked his x9i. "Fifteen minutes. Guess we eat later, unless you want room service. How about dinner in and a political thriller?"

She leaned away from the screen that had been occupying her attention for the better part of forty-eight hours. "I'm tired of room-service vigil and 6:30 might be wrong." She sighed. "We had better order in and keep watching." She stared at him, her face taut, unsmiling.

"What?"

"It's not really my business..."

He rolled onto his side to face her.

"You have strange telephone conversations."

He grinned. "With you I have strange conversations without the telephone."

She threw the closest thing to her left hand, which turned out to be her wireless computer mouse. It missed, smacked the wall and dropped to the carpet.

He tossed his phone at her. She caught it with her left hand.

"Touch 1, star," he said.

Her eyes scanned his face. "You want me to call this person?"

"You want to know about these spooky," he wiggled the fingers of his left hand in the air, "conversations, do you not?"

She looked from his face to the phone and back. "Can't you just tell me?"

"This will be better," he said. "Go ahead."

She pressed the 1 button with her index finger, "You're sure?"

He nodded as he rolled onto his back and rubbed his left arm with his right hand. "Don't delay, Claire. Now is your opportunity."

She pressed the star key and lifted the device to her ear, her eyes on his face.

It didn't ring.

She heard the click an old cassette tape machine would make when starting to record, and a woman's voice. There was a terrible hiss in the background, like sizzling steak.

"Hello my little demon Damon. You're one year old today and I want to wish you a Happy Birthday in a way that you will have with you forever, so I'm recording this message. I so wish David could be here to see you grow, so much in twelve short months that seem like a day, and a lifetime..."

The voice described things that had happened in that first year, recounting fevers and fun with the same detail and passion. It ended with her singing Happy Birthday and a final, "I love you," then hiss for a few seconds before another click.

Claire's face was still as she watched Damon.

"What's your last name?" she asked.

359

"Damon."

She frowned.

"And your first?"

"Damon," he said. "My father was David Damon."

She frowned more deeply.

"Press 2 star," he said.

She followed directions.

The voice came back, "Happy Second Birthday my little Damon. You were a bundle of energy this year. I'm so happy we met Nu Mai. She's such a lovely, kind woman and I trust her to care for you while I visit the rice paddies. I love working in the open fields. This country we have adopted is so beautiful, and the people have been kind to us despite that man America supports in South Vietnam. I know many here hate Americans, but not Nu. She sees us only as people. In some ways it was a bad year. There were five deaths, all children under ten, in our village from those damn...no, such words aren't for your ears, from those land mines and bombs left over from the war. The war was terrible, but these devils hiding in the ground ready to pounce on innocent children are a horrible threat to our little community. I so wish someone would come and take them all away. But you my dear Mr. Damon Damon, have been talking up a storm, acting more like your father every day..."

The recording was mostly hiss for a few moments and Claire could hear sobbing. Then the woman continued talking about what a wonderful child her Damon was before singing Happy Birthday and signing off with, "I love you."

Small tears found their way from the corners of her eyes.

"There are five," he said. "One for each birthday we shared. They add up to a memoir of the first years of my life."

She lowered the phone. "You've been talking to your mother?" she whispered, her voice a stack of cracks.

"After she died," he said quietly, "on my birthday Nu Mai would have me tell my mother all about the year into that little tape recorder right at the tiny alter we kept for her. That engrained the habit of talking to her memory." He paused, stared at the ceiling. "She's gone, Claire. Has been for a long time." He stopped. Rolled onto his side to face her. "You ever carry a picture of someone important to you, a reminder of all they mean to you? Her words are like that photo, a sort of mantra to keep her in my thoughts when I'm making tough decisions."

He watched as she pulled a tissue from a box on the desk and covered her eyes.

"Amazing..." She thought of the picture in the bedroom in Maxx's cave. "Do you remember her?"

"A few things we did, like ride this tiny black motorbike she drove to the market, me tucked on the seat in front of her. And cooking rice, probably did it every day. And I remember her holding my hand as we walked."

He rolled onto his back, closed his eyes.

"I'm so sorry," she said. She pressed Off on the phone and placed it on the table.

"Many people have been hurt by war," he said. "Not just me...not just one side." He grew quiet. "Not just this war."

An excited voice from the TV speakers said, "This program is being interrupted to bring you a statement from the President of the United States of America. We will return to our regularly scheduled broadcast momentarily."

"The fine print," Damon said, "reads, 'Paid for by the Reelection Committee for Gerard Mallor.' A paid advertisement masked to look like a State of the Union?"

She stood and crossed to the bed.

"A State of the Union is always pre-scheduled. They're trying to make this look like an emergency. Or at least late-breaking news." She lowered herself to sit beside him on the bed.

The screen filled with the face of the President, graying hair, dark suit, tall and lean standing behind a darkly stained cherry wood podium. Just below his chest an array of microphones spread across the TV like shark's teeth.

"Welcome, my fellow Americans. I will be brief because I know we all have serious work to do. And it's serious work I am here to talk to you about. This week, we lost a patriot in the form of General William Williams, a man I knew as Billy, who worked tirelessly to keep this country safe. He worked for justice and cared deeply about how the United States could best use its strength to help the world. He was active in many areas, including helping to remove land mines that still plague regions of Vietnam, innovative land mines that were built in American factories and dropped by the thousands from American military aircraft. It was while working to protect the lives of innocent children who could come upon these devices that Billy was tragically killed by an aging antitank mine."

He was silent for a full five seconds.

"Problems remain in the region of South Vietnam, the land of our allies who fought valiantly with us against the Communist advance, and who today are open to free trade and economic growth because of our joint efforts."

"He's on a roll," she whispered.

"It is in the gracious helping spirit of General Williams that I have decided to set aside a tiny portion of our nation's defense budget, less than a tenth of a percent, but amounting to an important two hundred million dollars a year for the next five years, to assist in removing hazardous materials from former battle zones around the world. I will also seek matching donations from those companies who receive government military contracts with the objective of doubling this amount, allowing us to target two billion dollars over half a decade to help all people live happy, safe, productive lives in the new world economy led by the United States of America."

"Twice what we asked for," she said.

"He's not President for nothing. Maybe you'll get your new job."

She shook her head. "I'm not important enough for national television."

"So today, I am forming the General "Billy" Williams War Recovery Fund and asking an associate who has been close to Billy for years—"

"Hold onto your seat," he said, reaching out to hold the hand she was using to support herself.

"—and therefore, understood his philosophy and how much he cared about justice, to lead this effort. Corporal Ferreti, who you see pictured here, is a world class marksman, and will lead the non-profit organization being formed to administer this fund."

"Un-fucking-believable," she said. "He named it after Williams, instead of Quon like we asked. I won't work there. The jerk even called me a marksman."

"You'll be able to do a lot of good work with two billion dollars."

"I won't honor the bastard that tried to kill me. Us....Cam...Wu..."

The room was quiet. The TV switched to a news broadcast where two talking heads struggled to say something cogent about the announcement that had clearly taken them by surprise.

"Don't think of it as honor," Damon said.

She stared down at his face with narrow, angry eyes.

"Use him, Claire. Use his death and his name to channel two billion, that's billion with a "B", dollars to people who can make a difference."

She didn't speak.

"Quon. Suong. Thousands like them. Kids who can't walk, can't jump, can't make a living to eat," he paused, studied her. "I've done worse things...for less money."

Her face softened slightly, but her eyes remained thin, dark stripes.

"If Mallor can get it approved," she said.

"He'll get it approved once he wins. This will catch Petry off guard."

Her face remained frozen as she stared at him.

"What?" he said.

"If we get this money, you're not going to destroy anything else, right?"

"That's the plan," he said. "Have you changed your mind? Want me to whack something for you?"

She punched him.

He rolled away.

She stared.

"You're doing a lot of staring today," he said.

"I've wanted to ask you about something for a long time."

"Uh-oh. You figure now that you got the big executive job this is a good time?"

"No really. I think I might know, but I want to be sure."

"Sure about what?" he said, watching with one eye as the TV switched to traffic news.

She reached across the bed and poked his arm. "About that."

"My logo. I hear chicks dig tattoos." He laughed.

"I'm serious. It must mean something or you wouldn't have it."

"Youthful exuberance. I wouldn't be the first."

"It's awfully detailed. I swear the letters throw shadows."

"Letters?"

"Yeah." She traced with her index finger. "D interlaced with D. I almost dropped my eyeteeth the first time I saw it in the bedroom at the cave. Our mission was code-named Demon Drop—as in making you dead. But I knew it couldn't be that."

"Hope not. I like living." He smiled.

"So what's it stand for?" she insisted.

"Hmm...Death and Destruction?"

"Too obvious. Old girlfriend is my bet."

"Could be Donna and David, my parents."

She squinted at him, trying to determine if he was serious.

"Maybe," she said cautiously. "But you called Maxx's cave the Double-D ranch."

He looked straight into her. "Since you came along, I think of it as Donna and Damon."

She shook her head. "Don't think so. There's something else going on."

"Perhaps," he said dryly.

"And you're not going to tell me?" she said, pushing her lower lip into a pout.

He got up from the bed and walked to the sliding closet doors. He pushed the right one to the left so fast it slammed, and reached inside. He turned around, holding the black helmet he used when riding in Washington.

"I didn't mean to pry," she said. "If it's too personal I'll shut up. Please don't leave."

He stared at her, his face as frozen as Roosevelt's in Mount Rushmore. He crossed the brown carpet to where she sat on the bed.

"Hold out your hand."

She lifted her left palm.

Holding the helmet in one hand he flipped it over so the strap fell against her open fingers.

She looked down at two shiny chrome interlocked D-rings on the chinstrap, positioned identically to those on his arm. She lifted her gaze without tilting her head. Steel gray eyes set in a stone face peered down at her.

Her lower lipped quivered.

The corners of his eyes lifted imperceptibly.

She swung her left fist at the ink, he blocked with his left forearm, reached up and grabbed her wrist with his right hand, she jabbed him in the chest with her right hand.

They broke into laughter at precisely the same moment.

Chapter 91

BILLY "NOTRON" NORTON was sitting on the side of his bed with his feet dangling, tapping his black sneakers together. He held his iPad on his lap with one hand and was typing cartoon text with the other. His dog Tank had saved the harbor by helping to swing a barge to block the torpedoes from the bad Barracuda guy and protect all the fishing boats of the village. Barracuda ran out of ammunition trying to sink the barge and Notron had slipped the black handcuffs on him and trapped him around a pylon, then turned off all the black dog robots. Now Captain Notron was ready to go back home and start another adventure. But the people of Grist stood in a big circle on the beach wanting to thank him and Tank.

Billy needed an ending.

He frowned and tapped the side of the little flat machine with a finger.

He heard a loud fast knock on the door. Before he could get off the bed to answer it, the knob turned and Grace flew in.

"Hi Billy, it's time for dinner. Let's sit together again, okay?"

He looked up at her, but was still thinking about Grist so he didn't smile.

"What's wrong?"

He pointed to the iPad.

"Are you still working on that story?" She crossed the room at a full run and plopped down beside him on the bed, making him bounce twice. She read the six comic book frames on the screen, all but the last with text in their cartoon bubbles.

"Wow, you're at the end. That's great. What a cool project you did."

Billy pointed at Notron, and drew a bubble with his finger.

Grace put her hand to her chin and looked like she was thinking hard for about ten seconds. Then she sat up real straight.

"Her," she pointed to a young girl Billy had sketched into the crowd way over to the right. "She should run up to Notron and thank him with a big kiss. The hero always gets a kiss."

Billy turned to face her.

"Like this," Grace said. She leaned forward real quick and kissed Billy Norton fast and hard full on the lips with an audible smack.

Billy's eyes got wide and his lips felt like, felt like, they didn't feel like anything he had ever felt and his head started spinning like he had a fever and he thought he might pass out like that one time when he had been running really fast high on the mountain in the sunshine.

Grace pulled away with a big smile on her face.

Billy couldn't move.

"Do you like my idea?" Grace said, but Billy only heard the hiss of rushing water in his ears.

Grace tilted her head. She stared into his eyes.

"Wow," Billy said. The word actually came out of his mouth, doubly surprising him.

"Wow." It came out again.

He struggled to put the jumbled words in his head together before speaking.

"Do that again."

Chapter 92

JONNY MUNCH SAT ON HIS leather couch opening a new bag of Lay's potato chips: the size with the one-third more for the same price. He had gotten five on his last visit to Save Mart. He was watching two channels of news on his picture-in-a-picture TV, one from the east coast, and one from the west. Without warning the President of the United States had come on and started talking about a dead guy named General Williams. That reminded him that the chopper pilot in the Rotor had said something about a General and an Army babe being ferried up to Nolan, which he now figured was the Norton's place, to see the robot dog that blew the hole in the ground.

But no one had liked his *Do Robot Dogs Eat Oil* article. Most comments on his blog criticized him for fantasizing a conspiracy theory from a comic book when Exxon had already publicly stated what happened. Someone using the name meisterMeister called Jonny a wannabe no-talent journalist, then ranted against the Architects and Engineers for 911 Truth who were seeking a technical explanation for the failure of building #7 more than a decade after it collapsed. So the robot dogs weren't going to get him his Pulitzer, maybe there was something in this land mine killing a General story that he could dig into.

The bag popped open and he reached for the first handful of chips.

But where should he start?

About the Author

Joe Klingler is a programmer and musician whose first thoughts of writing were sparked by reading *The God Machine* by Martin Caidin as a boy. The thrills painted by words competed with dreams of the future of digital computing. Computing won out for a time and he became a computer scientist, pursued medical-imaging research, wrote papers, founded a software startup, and received patents and design awards. Eventually he landed in Silicon Valley where he was engulfed by the powers of corporate America. Throughout he continued to be fascinated with the art of storytelling, particularly the interplay of people and the technology they build their lives around. He writes techno-thrillers that intertwine digital technology and his passions for music and motion. Joe currently resides in California with an iMac and a handful of motorcycles.

Please visit www.joeklingler.com

Made in the USA
San Bernardino, CA
18 July 2016